"You *will* have a woman on board when next the *Meribah* sails,"

Mercy stated.

"And who might that be, Mrs. Wright?" Captain Starbuck asked, fast tiring of the cat-and-mouse game.

"Me."

"What?" he exploded. "What possible reason could you have for wanting to go whaling?"

"I intend to search for my husband, Captain."

"You're mad, madam. Your husband is dead."

"Perhaps. Two men from the *Abishai* lived. Is it unreasonable to suspect that others may have survived, my husband among them?"

Starbuck's entire demeanor darkened. "In this case, it is entirely unreasonable. I beg you to reconsider, Mrs. Wright. I understand the depths of your grief—"

"Do you, Captain?"

"Yes, damn it, I do. Stay home, Mercy. Tend to your sisters. Find another husband. Live in the world as it is, instead of chasing around after a ghost."

"A pretty speech, Captain," Mercy returned hotly, "but one that does not sway me. I sail with the *Meribah,* whether or not you are at the helm."

Dear Reader,

Welcome to the world of Harlequin Historicals, where April promises to be another exciting month.

In *Sun Woman,* by Lindsay McKenna, a young Apache woman becomes an army scout in a desperate attempt to save the last of her band of Geronimo's followers. On a lighter note, Kate Kingsley has written *Ransom of the Heart,* a fanciful tale of a penniless Louisiana belle and her swashbuckling rescuer.

Mari, by Donna Anders, is the first of two books set in exotic Hawaii, so be sure to look for the sequel, *Ketti,* in June. And with *Mission of Mercy,* Kathryn Belmont brings to life the whaling industry as we travel with Mercy Randall on a voyage of discovery and danger in the South Seas.

You'll have to wait until next month to read our May books, but I can at least tell you that you have stories from Lynda Trent, Patricia Potter, Marjorie Burrows and Peggy Bechko to look forward to. Don't miss them!

Yours,

Tracy Farrell
Senior Editor

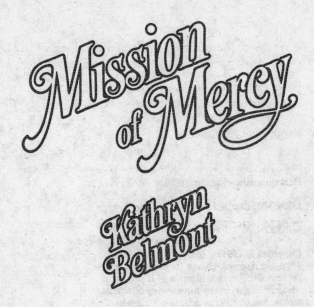

Mission of Mercy

Kathryn Belmont

Harlequin Books

TORONTO • NEW YORK • LONDON
AMSTERDAM • PARIS • SYDNEY • HAMBURG
STOCKHOLM • ATHENS • TOKYO • MILAN

Harlequin Historicals first edition April 1991

ISBN 0-373-28674-0

MISSION OF MERCY

KATHRYN BELMONT

is a former romance editor who decided to try her hand at writing and eventually began writing contemporary romances full-time. *Mission of Mercy,* her first historical, was born out of her love for the novel *Moby Dick*. While teaching a business-writing course, Kathryn came up with the idea for a romance about a woman whaler. She spent hours researching in the library in Mystic, Connecticut, where she also toured the Charles W. Morgan, a restored whaling vessel, to get the feel of being on a whaler.

Kathryn hopes to write more historicals in the future. At present, she is working at motherhood in Bronxville, New York, where she lives with her husband and daughter.

Prologue

Nantucket Town
January, 1852

Call me Dorcas.

Not my true name, dear reader, but it will serve. And though my tale may not prove as worthy or as useful as the coats and garments that the other Dorcas wove, modestly I pray it will warm you on a long and cold winter's night, such as this one on which I begin to write.

I have, you see, read a whaling saga, lately published by an author of some note, the story of a great white leviathan and the captain who gives sanity and finally life to its capture. A fine story, full of whaling lore, adventure and high-minded discourse, but sorely lacking in reference to one-half the world's people. To wit, the female of the human species. Or any species. Now that I think on it, females of the cetacean order are also notably absent from that tome.

Those of you familiar with the book—a work written by a man who lived the whaling life for men who wish they had—will remind me that a few females do people the pages of that noble tale. But they are of little consequence. Mrs. Hussey, the hostler's wife, bustles about serving chowder and protecting her property from sore-tempered seamen; her girl Betty makes a brief appearance when asked to go for the locksmith. Aunt Charity Bildad plies the *Pequod* with pickles and pen quills. But these quirky, womanly things are mere fripperies to the story.

Sundry mythical creatures and three queens—Elizabeth, Mab, and Nature—rate a mention or two. There are also such nameless, faceless female bodies as necessary to gratify the imaginations and needs of men long at sea and deprived of our comfort and company.

And, of course, the ships themselves bear names associated with subjects feminine; they are spoken of and treated as females. The *Pequod* meets the *Rachel,* the *Rose-Bud,* the *Desire,* etc., etc. I have never been able to decide whether such naming and treatment is flattery or merely the manifestation of man's inexorable but misguided tendency to wish to control and direct women.

Only once, toward the end of the tale, does Captain Ahab admit to his mate, "'I widowed that poor girl when I married her, Starbuck.'" There is no other mention of the women left at home by the whalers for years upon years. No mention of the children conceived but never welcomed into the world by their papas, children who walk and talk before their first meetings with the men who have fathered them. Such creatures are left behind in another world.

But I know two women—indeed, I am fortunate to be included in their circle of intimates—who did not allow themselves to be left behind. These brave and singular ladies went to sea in a whaling vessel, where they had adventures at least as curious and stirring as the ones recounted by my fellow author. I have spent some of my happiest hours listening to these two tell their tales. Such tales that, had I not been convinced of my friends' absolute integrity, I might have suspected them of skillful invention.

You may be thinking that in my enthusiasm for my friends and their exploits I have forgotten the many brave wives of whaling men, who have refused to endure endless separation from their mates. Indeed I have not, and I will pay my testimony to those wives here, reminding you, however, that the women whose story I am about to tell suffered as many discomforts, and all without the consoling and certain status of "skipper's lady."

Even as I write, there are whaling wives at sea, women who have left behind the succor of home and hearth to live in cramped, uncomfortable quarters; abandoned friends and relations for the society of strangers; borne children alone, unaided, in distant, sometimes hostile lands. Unless accompanied by a female child, they see no other women except on those occasions when their vessel chances to speak—meet, in whaling parlance—another ship whose captain has his lady on board. Yet they accept these hardships, and many others occasioned by a life at sea, for the sake of their families, for the sake of their husbands, for the sake of themselves and for the sake of the world.

The world? Yes, the world. At least, the civilized portions of it. For where would the rest of us be without oil to light our lamps, without spermaceti to make fine candles that burn clean of smoke or odor? And what would happen to our sex if we were left without ambergris for our perfumes or whalebone for our stays?

As to this last item, do I dare speak my mind here? Yes, I do. I fully believe that I, and my sisters like me, would experience a vast improvement in our abilities and dispositions should we but abandon these devices, thus rendering ourselves able to breathe to the full capacity of our lungs, as Our Maker no doubt intended us to do.

But a discourse on the effects of dress on health in this, the middle of the nineteenth century, A.D., is not my object. The object of this prologue is to prepare you to meet my two courageous adventurers, the likes of whom you will never meet in a whaling saga written by a man. For when these two went whaling, they went not as wives, but as women.

Unlike those two, I have neither the bravery nor the wits to attempt such feats myself. But I do delight in telling a story, and find even greater pleasure in writing stories down so that others may live them, too. With their usual generosity—and not a little pride, I might add—my friends have given me leave to record the extraordinary events of their lives.

And so, gentle reader, if you will but settle comfortably in your chair, next to a warming fire with a bracing cup of tea at hand, and transport yourself a small way back in time, less than a decade, to February of 1843....

Chapter One

Three times every day, the Portuguese bell peals in the tower of the Congregational church, calling Nantucket Town to work, to eat, to rest. Three times every day, Mercy Randall Wright counted its strokes. This cold winter morning was no different.

Fifty. Fifty-one. Fifty-two. The ringing reverberated for a moment in the icy air, then quiet settled once again over the town. It was seven o'clock. The day had officially begun.

Mercy dipped pen to ink and signed the letter she had just written. Carefully she blotted the signature, folded the pages and slipped them into an envelope, as she did each and every morning. On the envelope she wrote "Mr. Nathaniel Wright, Mate, Ship *Abishai*." Every ship that left Nantucket Harbor carried a packet of letters from Mercy to her husband. But only once, despite a solemn promise to the contrary, had a docking ship brought a missive from him in return. Nathaniel's uncharacteristic and unfathomable silence distressed her greatly, but still she kept a steady stream of letters flowing out to him.

How else could a bride keep alive the memory of a husband who had gone to sea only three months into their marriage? Endure a separation that had already lasted more than a year? Or face the uncertain years to come? A whaling voyage ends on no fixed date. When waiting has a finite end, it may be borne with some equanimity, but women who marry whaling men have no such comfort.

Mercy did not know when—or if—she would see her husband again. She could not cross off the days on a calendar, saying to herself each morning, only fifty-nine more days or two hundred seventy-five more days or three more days to endure. She had not even the comfort of a child of their union. Her hopes for such a happy occurrence had been dashed soon after the *Abishai* set sail. No, Mercy could only wait. And write. And pray that Nathaniel would return to her.

Slipping the letter inside the pocket of her morning dress, she rose from her desk, threw a warm challis shawl around her shoulders and went out into the hall. At the far end of the passage was a door that opened onto a narrow staircase. She went through it and climbed nimbly up to the walk. From that small outdoor perch she could gaze over Nantucket Harbor to the sea beyond.

No matter what the weather, Mercy came up to the walk each morning to check the flags flying in the harbor. A blue banner announced that a ship was newly docked; the ensign below it proclaimed the ship's owner. These days, a blue flag flew nearly every morning in Nantucket Harbor, so Mercy was not at all surprised to see the familiar rectangle flapping in the breeze. Her heart did hasten, however, when she identified the flag below the blue—a triangle of red, emblazoned with a yellow sun under a white crescent moon. It was her father's flag, and she rejoiced to see it. Of course, she knew the *Abishai* had not returned. Nathaniel's ship was likely to be gone another two years, if not longer. But this signal could only announce the safe return of the *Meribah*.

Racing down the stairs, Mercy called out to her sisters. "Caroline! Sarah! Papa's ship is in. Wake up! Wake up!"

The door to one of the four rooms off the corridor flew open. In the threshold stood a young woman of seventeen, her bare feet peeking out from beneath the hem of her voluminous snow-white nightgown. Wisps of chestnut hair escaped from the thick braid hanging over her left shoulder. But this early-morning dishabille did not dim the vivacity and beauty for which Caroline Randall was well known. "Papa's flag is flying? Oh, I must see it," she cried.

Another door opened and a sleepy voice asked, "See what?"

Eleven-year-old Sarah Randall was a miniature version of her two sisters, possessing the same thick chestnut hair, tawny amber eyes, broad forehead, high cheekbones, stubby nose, and lips that tended to purse when their owners were deep in thought. Unlike her womanly sisters, however, Sarah was coltishly thin, with long, unsteady limbs. She teetered over to her siblings and nudged herself between them, a young vine seeking support from its well-established neighbors.

Mercy held her small sister close. Twelve years Sarah's senior, she had assumed the role of mothering the girl when their own dear parent had died six years before. Sarah was only five then; she had now been under Mercy's care longer than she had been under their mother's, so the bond between the two sisters was stronger than is normally so.

"Put on your warmest cloaks," Mercy directed her sisters, "and we'll all go up to the walk."

When the three were lined up against the white wooden railing, Mercy pointed to the flagpole on the dock. "There's Papa's flag, the red one—"

"I know," interrupted Sarah, "with the sun and the moon. 'Because that's what I would give you, if I could.'" The elder sisters laughed gaily, hearing their fond papa's words uttered in Sarah's childish tones. "What ship is it?" Sarah continued. "Is it the *Abishai,* Mercy? Is Nathaniel home?"

It sometimes seemed to Mercy that Sarah had fallen as much in love with Nathaniel Wright as she had. "No, pet," she said gently, "it's too soon for Nathaniel to be home. It's the *Meribah.* Papa has been expecting her for weeks, ever since he had a letter from Captain Starbuck saying that he was in the Western Islands. Do you remember where they are? Across the Atlantic Ocean," she prompted.

"One thousand miles off the coast of Portugal," Sarah finished.

Before Mercy could commend Sarah on her command of geography, Caroline said impatiently, "Why are we standing here? It's freezing! Let's put on our prettiest dresses and go straight to the dock. I must learn all the news."

"An excellent idea," Mercy agreed. "I'll ask Emily to pack us a basket, and we'll breakfast in Papa's office." She shooed Sarah down the stairs with instructions to wash and dress in her green wool frock. "Oh, Caroline, I do pray there is some news of the *Abishai,* and a letter for me from Nathaniel." She spoke quietly, almost to herself, her words a mixture of anticipation and apprehension.

In all their long separation, Mercy had had but one letter from her husband. Dated Christmas Day, 1841, it had come, as most letters did, via one of the merchant clipper ships that ply the seas at the speed of lightning when compared to the pace of a whaling vessel. The short note did little more than wish her a happy Christmas. It mentioned neither other letters Nathaniel had written nor any he had received from her.

As anyone with a father, husband or brother at sea well knows, a letter is a long-awaited and much-heralded event. Small portions may be reserved for intimate communication, but writers and recipients alike understand that the greater part of the news is meant for the entertainment and edification of all. For myself, dear reader, I come by my scriveners' trade honestly. My father's letters from sea were masterly compilations, more fiction than fact I now speculate, and as rousing as anything printed on paper and bound between covers. My mother read them aloud again and again, until we knew them as well—and I even better, I must confess—than passages from the Bible.

The Randalls were no different from my own dear clan. They had clamored for Nathaniel's letter to be read aloud, but there was nothing for Mercy to read out. Mortified for her husband and herself, she explained, though could not excuse, his breach by putting the blame squarely on her own head. "I neglected to school Nathaniel in the art of letter writing from sea. I am afraid my husband thinks only of me when he writes." The humiliation was all the worse because on that same day a long and lively missive from Captain Starbuck had arrived on another merchant ship. I must caution you, friends, our dear Mercy does not revel, as some of our sex do, in culpability, wearing it like a new if unbecoming bonnet, but on that day the full weight of her, and her husband's omission bore down upon her.

Once again, on this cold, wintry day, knowing that the *Meribah* and Captain Starbuck were safely in the harbor, she shivered against the unyielding chill of Nathaniel's long, nearly unbroken silence. Her many doubts rolled in on her like the tide, impossible to stop no matter how hard she tried to push them back. For what reason, when they had been so happy a pair, could he have failed to write, he who had courted her so prettily with poetry of his own devising, and regaled her with love songs in his sweet tenor voice, accompanying himself at the pianoforte. Nathaniel must be desperately unhappy at sea, she feared. The whaling life did not suit him, could not suit him. He regretted having apprenticed himself to such a wretched business. He rued their marriage and had decided to abandon her, leaving her his spouse in name only and damning her to a life in limbo, neither widow nor wife. Or else, the unspeakable had happened and either Nathaniel or, heaven forfend, the *Abishai* was lost.

These discomfitting thoughts created a furiously whirling eddy in her mind, prompting her to cry out, "Why? Why have I heard nothing from him?" Her question fluttered in the air as if alive, as clear a signal of her unhappiness as the red triangle waving over the wharf was a sign of her father's success.

Caroline had no words of comfort for her sister, but placed one hand atop Mercy's on the railing and gave it a gentle squeeze. Mercy, tears welling in her eyes, extricated her hand from her sister's and turned away, fumbling in her pocket for a handkerchief.

Caroline remained facing the sea. "You're a cruel mistress," she called out over the water. "I'll never marry a whaling man," she declared fiercely. "I'd rather die an old maid."

Mercy dabbed at her eyes and reddened nose and looked out at the sea once again herself. "You'll marry where your heart tells you, whaling man or no," she chided gently. But she wished, even as she spoke, that her own heart had not fallen to a man who had chosen the whaling life.

After six years on shore, Benjamin Randall still missed the lulling quiet of the sea, where entire days could pass with only the creaking of timbers and the flapping of sails to be heard. On Nantucket wharf there was always a fearsome noise. The docks swarmed with men of every color of the rainbow, speaking a babel of tongues. Stevedores shouted over the rumble of barrels rolling along the piers. Wooden-wheeled drays clattered heavily on the gray cobblestone streets. There was the hammering of coopers, the squawks and squeaks of block and tackle, the raucous cries of street vendors.

Usually Captain Randall loathed the noise and longed for the end of day when he could retreat to his house on Orange Street and the soothing company of his daughters. But today, standing on the dock, watching the barrels roll off his own *Meribah,* hearing the shouts from the *Meribah*'s crew, the noise sounded more like music to his ears.

The melody in the counting house would be sweet as well. The *Meribah* had shipped home eleven hundred barrels of sperm oil via merchant clippers and arrived in port laden with eighteen hundred barrels more, as well as three full barrels of ambergris. Even after paying the crew their lays—about one-third of the profits—and allowing for repairs and outfitting the ship for her next voyage, he would make a very handsome profit.

Not that Benjamin Randall cared for money for its own sake. All he earned went to make his daughters comfortable. Since they had been deprived of their mother, money was all he had to give them. Or so he thought, however erroneously. Having spent most of his life on a whaling ship, he considered his own society poor and in no way a substitute for that of their mother, his own sweet Lucy, who had died one week before he'd arrived home from a four-year voyage.

The years at sea had sharpened Captain Randall's judgment of whales and sailors but lessened his powers of discernment where the female sex was concerned. Had he been more aware of the emotional capacities of those under his care, he would surely have known that all three loved him dearly, and for his own cherished self, more than for anything he could give them. Even Caroline, who of the three would most have missed the treats and luxuries he provided, understood the sacrifice he had made to stay close to them.

For six years he had remained on shore, spending his days in an office that seemed to him more confining than his tiny ship's cabin ever had. He often dreamed of the sea but knew he would never set sail again. He had left his Lucy too often; he could never leave his girls now that he was all they had. How could he risk returning to find one of them gone, as he had discovered Lucy's untimely death?

Even now, he had not recovered from the loss of his wife. At sea, he had imagined Lucy often, talking to her, holding her so clearly in his mind's eye that she seemed to be with him. Although he had abandoned many of his seafaring ways, this habit of private conversation with his wife was one he would never give up. She seemed alive still, so much so that he was always slightly surprised to return home at the end of the day and find her absent.

Captain Randall put aside his thoughts of his wife and looked once more at the *Meribah*. The last ship he had captained, she still commanded a great affection from him. Her specifications came as easily to his tongue as his own name: 334 tons; 104 feet from bow to stern; 26 feet wide at the beam. With her three masts and bowsprit fully rigged, she hoisted sixteen sheets of canvas. She was not fast or sleek like the merchant schooner that bobbed beside her at the pier, but she was sure and steady and could ride out even the fierce storms of the Indian Ocean or the deadly snow squalls off Cape Horn. A friend, but also a cruel mistress who had kept him from family and friends and homely comforts. One who could not, however, be denied.

Turning away from the grand old tub, Captain Randall tugged at his waistcoat and started back to his office, where he instructed his clerk, Simon Murchester, to supervise the rest of the unloading. He had another more pressing and pleasant task. Whenever one of his ships came in, he bought each of his daughters a present. Usually it was some small token, but this time the *Meribah*'s cache of ambergris would enable him to provide costly, substantial gifts. He decided quickly that a proper pianoforte to replace her spinet would suit Caroline. For Sarah, whose greatest pleasure was in drawing and sketching, her first easel and oil paints. But what about Mercy? A new telescope, to rival that of her friend, Maria Mitchell? Medical texts to aid her informal study with her uncle, Dr. Thomas Pearse?

The choice of a gift for his eldest daughter was not a simple one. Though charming and beautiful, Mercy was more serious-minded than any woman he had ever known. She delighted in discussing subjects women usually did not care for—business, politics, science, philosophy. Her independence was not only of the mind, but of the spirit, as well. She was strong and unwavering in reaching a goal once set. Captain Randall did not pretend to understand her, but he did care deeply for her.

He had known her so little as a child that in the years since he had given up the sea, they had become more like friends than father and daughter. Usually when a daughter married, her ties to her family loosened, but the opposite had happened with the two of them. Since her marriage, their friendship had ripened.

Having been so much from home, Captain Randall had never really understood the life of the women left behind. But since Nathaniel Wright had sailed on the *Abishai,* he had observed that life firsthand. Mercy never complained of loneliness, never uttered a bitter word. As she had since her mother died, she kept the house and cared for her sisters. And she returned to those pursuits she had curtailed during the three months she and Nathaniel had lived together as man and wife. Besides her other duties, she read book after book, studied astronomy with Maria Mitchell, attended her uncle's dispensary. But the bloom in her cheeks faded, the sparkle in her eyes dimmed.

Captain Randall felt a pain, a tangible physical pain, in his heart when he looked at Mercy now, especially in those rare moments when she thought she was unobserved. The loneliness escaped then, like the brazen thief it was, and stood out plainly on her face. He never spoke to her about it, though. Knowing how greatly it would displease her to learn her emotions were sometimes transparent, he pretended not to see the culprit. But pretense did not banish the swindler who had spirited away his daughter's happiness.

Would that she were as easy to please as Caroline, content with a basket of ribbons and a bolt of silk. But then she would not be the daughter he loved most dearly. Captain Randall tugged at his waistcoat again—the plentiful food and sedentary life on land had added to his girth—and took up pen and ink. As he wrote his orders for paints and a pianoforte, his mind remained on Mercy. When was she happiest, he asked himself. He could remember seeing her happy only once in the past year or so. When she was striding along the beach at Siasconset, the wind blowing the ribbons of her straw hat and whipping her wide skirts around her ankles.

Once he remembered the delight Mercy took in the wild, uninhabited side of Nantucket Island, the answer to his problem came easily. He would build her a small summer cottage there. It would give her pleasure now, and when Nathaniel returned home and there were grandchildren, it would give them pleasure, too. He would draw up the plans himself, put to use the study of architecture he had made during his spare hours at sea. Content with his choice, he brought out a fresh sheet of paper and began to sketch.

Though the distance was short, the Randall sisters' progress from Orange Street to the wharf was slow. They were stopped often by the many friends and acquaintances who had seen their father's flag flying in the harbor. And further delayed by Sarah's insistence on carrying the full basket of food all the way to her father's office by herself.

"Do let me help you, Sarah. We'll never get there," Caroline said when her sister lagged behind one more time than she could tolerate. But Sarah refused adamantly.

Mercy came to Sarah's defense. "I think it's admirable that Sarah wishes to complete the task she's set for herself. An independent will is of no small consequence to a woman."

"Independent will?" Caroline asked with a gay peal of laughter. "That's just a fancy name for stubbornness. Oh, do come along, both of you. Aren't you simply aching to know how many barrels the *Meribah* brought and if there's any ambergris?"

"Of course I want to know," Mercy replied. "But there will be the same number if we arrive in five minutes or in ten."

"Oh, Mercy!" Caroline despaired. "You're so practical."

"Someone has to be, and heaven knows it won't be you."

"For which I thank my lucky stars." But Caroline could not remain cross with her sister—or anyone—for more than a moment. Her mind, which was much like a hummingbird, flitted from place to place too quickly for her to light long in any one spot. She had hardly drawn a breath before finding a sweeter, more tantalizing topic. "I wonder what Captain Starbuck has brought us. He unearths the most unusual trinkets. Do you remember the ivory beads? And the lemon-colored silk?''

Mercy remembered all too well the presents the *Meribah*'s captain had brought from his previous voyage, his first as a captain. His long association and friendship with her father notwithstanding, she had thought his gifts presumptuous. Like the man himself. She had not seen him for over three years now and objected not one whit to being spared that necessity for another equally long period. But her father treated Captain Starbuck like a favored nephew, and he was certain to call often at the Randall home for as long as he stayed in Nantucket Town.

She had never shared her family's enthusiasm for the man. Even her mother—usually an excellent judge of character—had treated him with affection. But Mercy found him arrogant, hot tempered and irreverent. He made her uncomfortable, especially in the way he frequently seemed to be mocking her, although he did it so cleverly that she never could be sure whether her feeling came from his intention or her interpretation.

Caroline, who had only moments before chided Sarah for impeding their progress, now stopped the party as she observed the *Meribah* and exclaimed about one feature or another—how well she had weathered, how proud her masts. "And they're still unloading," she exclaimed. "Captain Starbuck must have caught only hundred-barrel whales! Papa must be so pleased."

"Indeed," Mercy agreed to this last statement. Their father had been unusually gloomy about his business affairs in recent months, and with good cause. The *Abishai* had not yet sent home any oil, nor had it been heard from in months; the *Hepsibah,* the third ship in Benjamin Randall's small fleet, had not met with good fortune, either. And like many on the island, Randall worried about the future of whaling on Nantucket. The island's sandbar was rising, making it difficult and costly for ships to anchor in Nantucket Harbor. A good catch for the *Meribah* would greatly improve his outlook, Mercy knew. But the size of the whales Sam Starbuck had taken was immaterial to her. He could have caught old Mocha Dick himself, and Mercy would not have rejoiced. She twisted her garnet wedding ring around like a talisman, visible protection that would proclaim, when she next saw Sam Starbuck, that she was a married woman.

At last the sisters arrived at the door of their father's offices. Sarah, flush faced and breathing rapidly, put down her basket one last time. Mercy bent to straighten the girl's bonnet, which had gone askew in the course of her exertions. Caroline dashed inside, calling out to their father and, without stopping to rap on its opaque glass window, flung open the door to the inner office.

At the sight of his daughter, Benjamin Randall hastily hid the gift orders and cottage plans in a desk drawer. He rose and held out his hands. Caroline took her father's hands in her own and kissed him exuberantly on both cheeks. "Are we rich, Papa? Was there ambergris? Is there news from the *Abishai* or the *Hepsibah*?"

"Slow down, my dear. You remind me of a sudden squall in the Indian Ocean. Allow me a moment's respite to greet your sisters."

At the door, Sarah declared, "We've brought a basket with all your favorite things. I carried it all the way, all by myself."

"Did you now?" Randall asked, stooping to pat his youngest daughter on the cheek and to peer into the basket. "Emily's poppy-seed cake, is it? And oranges, too. You've done well to carry such a heavy load, little Sarah." Sarah was the only one of his children he had seen grow. He had watched her change from a mischievous scamp of five to a lively, sharp-eyed young lady. But she always made him a little sad, too, for he realized how much of Mercy and Caroline's lives he had missed. "Well done," he complimented once more, looking away quickly and rising. Sarah beamed and thanked her papa.

"And Mercy. Good morning, my dear." Randall accepted the kiss his eldest daughter dropped onto his cheek, reading in her eyes the silent question: Is there a letter for me? How he hated having to tell her yet again that there was not. What was wrong with that son-in-law of his? With all his fancy Harvard education, had he forgotten how to write? Had he lost all his manners?

"You still haven't answered my questions, Papa," Caroline reminded.

"I've had a hard morning's work, Caroline. I shall need some refreshments before taking on another arduous task."

"Papa!" Caroline protested. "I shall perish if you don't tell me the news this very minute."

Randall laughed indulgently. "I doubt that very much, my dear, but since you've asked me so nicely I shall tell you."

Caroline had the grace to look abashed for a brief moment, but excitement at the *Meribah*'s good fortune soon overcame her momentary restraint. "Three barrels of ambergris?" she interrupted her father's recital. "We are rich, Papa, aren't we? And we shall have wonderful presents, won't we?"

"Caroline!" Mercy scolded.

"Now, Mercy," Randall said judiciously, "just because you don't care for ruffles and ribbons is no reason to deny Caroline her pleasures."

"Of course, Papa." Mercy accepted the reprimand graciously. She often lost patience with Caroline's love for frills and trinkets, even when she so depended on Caroline's wit and gaiety to keep her own spirits afloat. In the time since Nathaniel's departure, she had developed a keen appreciation of her sister's carefree ways. But at times, she forgot how great a comfort Caroline was to her. She was grateful for her father's reminder. "I'm sorry, Caroline. I did not mean to dampen your spirits."

Quickly Caroline linked her arm through Mercy's. "I know you didn't. And I was rude, wasn't I? I am sorry, Papa. Am I forgiven?" she asked sweetly. Given a nod

from her father, she grinned and said hungrily, "Let's un-
pack our basket. I shall perish if I don't have something to
eat this very minute."

"If you did perish every time you said you were going
to," Sarah put in tartly, "I should be very short of sisters."

The Randalls' laughter was broken by a booming voice,
in tone deep and indisputably masculine, but in volume
suitable for shouting above the surge of the sea and harsh
to the ears in a small room on land. Or so it seemed to
Mercy.

"Can this beauty be my little Sarah?" Captain Starbuck
scooped up Sarah in his strong arms, bringing her small
white face level with his sharp sun-burnished features. He
performed this gesture with the ease and authority of a
popular politician casting his line expertly for the votes he
knew he would reel in. "Not even a hello for your long-lost
Uncle Sam?"

Sarah examined his coal-black eyes closely. Her skill and
love for drawing had taught her to take her time and examine a subject closely, rushing neither her eyes nor her
mind. "You're different," she concluded.

The captain's wide, generous mouth broke into a smile
that brought out deep creases on his forehead and around
his mouth and eyes. "Of course I am, Sarah. I'm older.
And wiser. And I've fought more whales. And won! That
will change any man." He put the child down, but she was
insistent.

"No, it's something else." She considered him again. His
eyes were like others she'd seen: Mercy's since Nathaniel
had gone; her papa's for as long as she could remember.
"You're lonely."

A burble of merry laughter burst from Starbuck's lips.
"And you're impertinent, miss," he said, tugging on a
chestnut curl. "But a beauty all the same," he added with
a wink.

Then he turned his attentions to Caroline. When last he
saw her she had just crossed the threshold into woman-

hood. In three years her beauty had ripened and asserted itself most becomingly. "And how is the belle of Nantucket Town? I'll wager you've broken many a heart since last we met, Miss Caroline."

Starbuck extended a work-hardened hand, and Caroline placed her slim white fingers in his palm. "Not as many as you, I expect." She bestowed a radiant smile on him. "Welcome home, Captain Sam. We're very happy to have you and the *Meribah* safely returned."

He inclined his dark head slightly and placed his other hand over Caroline's. "Thank you. I appreciate your good wishes." Relinquishing Caroline's hand, he turned to Mercy. "And you, Miss Randall, are you also happy to have me—and the *Meribah*—home unharmed?" His eyes bore into hers, intimating that they shared some secret, that his innocent-sounding words had some meaning only they could decipher.

Mercy felt an unpleasant warmth rise in her, but answered him coolly. "I am always happy for the safe arrival of a whaling vessel. But I am no longer Miss Randall. I am Mrs. Wright."

Starbuck slowly raised a black, bushy eyebrow but otherwise showed no sign of surprise or any other emotion at the news. "May I offer my best wishes," he said formally, "and inquire about the gentleman? I take it he is not a Nantucket man."

Mercy's reply was also formal and perhaps a shade self-righteous, too. "My husband is Mr. Nathaniel Wright of Boston," Mercy replied. "He is now aboard the *Abishai,* in order to acquaint himself with the whaling industry. Upon his return, he will assist my father, here in Nantucket Town."

"So you've married a green hand, have you, Mercy?" A bout of hearty laughter ensued, as if he had just heard a very funny story. Mercy failed to see what was so amusing. "Well, well," he said, still chortling. "A green hand. I hope he is a fair match for you." There was no mistaking the inference that Nathaniel was not.

With some difficulty, she held her temper. "On the contrary, Captain, it is I who strive to be his equal."

"Then he must be quite a man. May you have a long and happy life together."

Although his words could not be faulted, the tone with which they were delivered left Mercy shaking with anger. With a few innocent utterings, Starbuck managed to belittle—or so it seemed to her—both her marriage and her mate. The others seemed not to have noticed. Indeed her father was inviting Starbuck to take some refreshment with them.

"Sarah's carried a basket down from the house," Captain Randall explained. "I'm sure the girls would enjoy a gam with you. And so would I."

Starbuck refused with a curt shake of his head. "Thank you, but there's work to be done. At your convenience, I'd like a word with you, sir." He left the office quickly, and in a moment the Randalls heard the outer door close with a bang.

Not trusting herself to speak because of the man's unfathomable behavior, Mercy cleared a space on a worktable and unpacked the basket. Out came plates and cutlery, oranges, a cheese tart, poppy-seed cake. She concentrated on the tangible objects, but her fury with Sam Starbuck did not diminish. How could her father have so much affection for a man who was insolent and rude? Only Starbuck's oft-proved prowess as a whaleman could explain it.

Contrary to Mercy's supposition, however, the encounter with Captain Starbuck had affected her family. While serving themselves from the impromptu board, each of the Randalls retreated into thought.

Benjamin Randall ruefully remembered the evening before Starbuck had left on the voyage he had just completed. He and Sam had talked late into the night, and, overcome by what he could think of only as a wave of sentiment, he allowed how happy he would be if Sam and Mercy married. He had spoken unwisely that night, but perhaps he had even more unwisely allowed Mercy to marry a man of whom they knew so little. His sister-in-law Elizabeth had, of course, vouched for the boy and his family, but then she remembered so little of Nantucket ways, which were not Boston ways. Had Mercy married Sam, at least she would have heard from him when he was at sea. But Mercy had never cared for Sam, any more than Sam cared for Mercy. That was plain enough. Sam had laughed at his proposition that night, laughed till the tears rolled down his face....

Caroline thought of how she preferred Captain Sam's forthright, if rough, manner to her brother-in-law's ways. By contrast, Nathaniel was too polite, almost fawning. Although he seemed to be concerned for others, she suspected he was truly concerned only for himself. A minority of one, she had never cared for Nathaniel. But no one knew that. For once she had kept her opinion to herself....

Sarah thought about how to draw the loneliness in someone's eyes. Despite Uncle Sam's protests, she was sure of what she had seen. This afternoon she would practice. She thought she could draw his face from memory, but she was not certain she could get the eyes right....

And Mercy thought about Nathaniel, with a tender nostalgia now instead of the fear and worry that so often colored her thoughts of him. She had always felt so calm and cared-for with him. Not challenged and confused, the way she felt with Sam Starbuck. How lucky she was to have visited Aunt Elizabeth in Boston and met Nathaniel when she did. The daughters of many Nantucket captains married men who sailed on their father's ships. Marriage to her father's most trusted captain would have been a most natural—indeed almost the expected—thing. Especially since Mercy was then well past twenty and still unmarried. Had her father desired and pressed for such a match, she would have found it difficult to refuse, no matter what her feelings for—or against—Sam Starbuck.

As soon as the family had served themselves and were seated, Caroline, whose thoughts had quickly moved to a prospect more pleasant than her errant brother-in-law, made a proposal. "We must have a party to celebrate the *Meribah*'s homecoming."

Captain Randall was the first to agree, and with a great deal more enthusiasm than he usually displayed for social gatherings. "A splendid idea, Caroline. I would enjoy sharing our good fortune with our friends and neighbors."

Caroline jumped up, plate in hand, and gave her father a resounding kiss on the cheek. "Thank you, Papa. Oh, it will be such fun. I shall learn all the new music, and we'll sing and dance until midnight."

"Belay there a moment, miss. Let's check with the mistress of the house first. How do you feel about a party, Mercy? I know the burden of the preparations will fall on you."

She had enjoyed herself so little since Nathaniel sailed, Mercy thought. A party and its preparations would be a welcome respite from her routine. "I would be happy to see to it, Papa. If Caroline and Sarah will help me, of course." Not until she had spoken did Mercy remember that Captain Starbuck would have to be invited. "It's been such a long time since we've entertained our friends. Let's make it a large party," she suggested, thinking to lessen the impact of Starbuck's presence.

"Yes!" Caroline agreed. "Then we shall have to get new dresses."

"Will I have a new dress, too? Will I be allowed to stay up?" Sarah clamored, looking to her papa.

Captain Randall was accustomed to deferring all such decisions to his eldest daughter. In these matters, she knew far better than he what was appropriate. Still, he was relieved when Mercy nodded her approval. He would have been loathe to exclude Sarah from the evening's entertainment.

"A new dress," Mercy confirmed, "and as you are nearly twelve, you may have supper with our guests and stay up until ten o'clock."

Sarah responded with a prim thank-you, so pleased she could not say more. Immediately Caroline leaned over to her younger sister and began to describe exactly the sort of dress Sarah must have.

With Caroline and Sarah engaged in that important task, Captain Randall took the opportunity to speak privately with Mercy. "Captain Starbuck brought a letter from the *Abishai*. It had been left in the Western Islands by another ship." The hope shining in Mercy's eyes made Randall wish sorely that the letter had been the one she pined for.

"The letter is from Nathaniel," she said with quiet certainty.

"No, my dear, from Captain Hussey. It took quite a long time to reach us. It was written over a year ago, from the Samoa Islands. He says that Nathaniel is well."

Mercy's mouth was dry, her breathing shallow. "Was there no other news, Papa?"

"I'm sorry." Randall shook his head and patted her clumsily on the shoulder.

Ascribing the worry in her father's eyes not to herself but to the scant news of the *Abishai*, Mercy put aside her disappointment and sought to console him. "The *Abishai* will send a shipment home soon. I am certain of it, Papa."

But even as she spoke, her fears for the *Abishai*—and her husband—were mounting.

Chapter Two

For the next three days, the house on Orange Street was fitted for the festivities with the same meticulous care that one of Benjamin Randall's ships was fitted for sea. Emily and the daily helper, Mary, had scrubbed the house from stem to stern, beat the Turkish carpets as if they were mutinous sailors and rubbed the furniture until it glowed like a ship's beacon. Provisions were laid in; a hearty meal planned.

On the night of the party, a score of lamps set the place ablaze with bright, clean light from the finest whale oil. When the grandfather clock in the entry hall pealed the quarter hour before eight o'clock, Mercy was removing the last of the curling rags from Sarah's hair. Once brushed, she pinned three fat sausage-shaped curls firmly into place on each side of Sarah's head.

Sarah, dressed only in her chemise, pantalets and two petticoats, shivered and squirmed nervously under Mercy's ministrations. "Can I look now?" she pleaded.

"Why don't you wait until Caroline has done your ribbons? They're in her room, along with your dress. She'll do them so much better than I." Mercy wrapped a shawl over Sarah's shoulders and hurried her across the hall. "I must go down and see if everything is ready. Don't let Caroline tarry too long. And enjoy yourself tonight, pet. I'm sure Papa will be very proud to see you looking so grown-up."

She suspected that their father would be a bit sad, too, to see Sarah looking so much the young lady. That was a feeling she understood well. Each time she looked at Sarah, so close to womanhood, Mercy was reminded that soon the house would no longer have a child in it. What a comfort Nathaniel's child would have been to her. But she would have to wait until her husband's return for that—and the other comforts, physical and emotional, she was denied by his absence.

Turning left at the bottom of the stairs, she entered the front parlor. Extra ladder-back chairs had been placed around the room to complement the usual seating arrangements. A roaring fire crackled invitingly in the hearth. Finding all in order, Mercy moved to the back parlor, a less formal room where the family often gathered. Here, too, extra chairs stood in readiness for their guests. On Caroline's spinet, a stack of music sheets awaited the singing and dancing that would commence after supper. The sparkling ebony and ivory keys of the instrument seemed to grin at Mercy, as if anticipating the evening's merriment. Even though she had no talent whatever for music, she struck a few keys at random and left the room humming—in a manner of speaking—the air they suggested to her.

Crossing the hall to the dining room, she inspected the stacks of blue-and-white Canton china arranged on the sideboard, using her handkerchief to rub a fingerprint off the bowl of a silver spoon and smoothed a wrinkle in the heavy damask cloth on the table. Following her nose into the kitchen, she found Emily stirring a giant pot of seafood stew. The long oak table at the far end of the room was laden with fresh loaves of bread, cold meat pies, wheels of cheese, spice cakes and apple tarts. She complimented the cook.

"Thank you, ma'am," Emily replied. Although Emily had known Mercy practically from the moment she was born, now that Mercy was mistress of the house, Emily insisted on addressing her as such. "Would you care to taste the cider?"

Spiced cider was a favorite household drink, of which her father was particularly fond. A pity Nathaniel had not come to like it, Mercy thought as she sampled a small dipperful. He had often complained, jokingly of course and in the privacy of their bedchamber, that he preferred his cider well fermented to well spiced. But strong drink was not served in Benjamin Randall's household, even if it was allowed, in strictly limited quantities or as a medicinal aid, on his ships. Although he no longer adhered to the Quaker persuasions of his forebears, he had held to some elements of their faith, especially the prohibition on spirituous liquors. How that prohibition had plagued her husband, Mercy remembered. She also recalled how diligently he had struggled to abandon more than this one worldly habit in hardworking, God-fearing Nantucket Town. Though it was difficult for him, he often told her how glad he was to do it for her sake.

The sound of the door knocker shook Mercy out of her reverie. She replaced the dipper as Emily dispatched her helper to answer the door. Then she issued her final instructions to Emily and proceeded to the front parlor to greet her guests.

The Mitchell family was the first to arrive. William Mitchell was the cashier of the Pacific Bank, which Benjamin Randall patronized. He was accompanied by his wife and two daughters. Mercy greeted the entire family warmly, but reserved an especially affectionate greeting for the elder daughter, Maria. She and Maria were friends and confidantes, and theirs was an alliance forged on the strength of their mutual interest in matters of the mind. Devoted to astronomy, Maria had a small observatory in the tower of her father's bank, one of the town's tallest structures, and she often invited Mercy to join her in her observations.

Maria Mitchell's disregard for the demands of fashion was evident in her sturdy blue cashmere dress, so simple it could have been worn by any proper Quaker lady of the previous century. The modest gown made Mercy's dove-gray-and-lavender-striped silk look almost gaudy by comparison, which it by no means was.

Mercy's gown, with its balloon sleeves and rounded off-the-shoulder neckline, though elegant and becoming, would not have been featured in the latest fashion plates. Of this, however, Mercy was well aware. Unlike her friend, she knew that styles had changed, that sleeves were worn straight and tight now, that necklines were vee shaped. But she had eschewed a new dress in favor of this old one because it had been made for a very happy occasion—her engagement party. It reminded her of a happy time, as did the pearls—Nathaniel's wedding present—that graced her neck and the gold-and-pearl-drop earrings that had belonged to Nathaniel's mother.

"I can't stay long," Maria whispered to Mercy as the group entered the front parlor. "You know I only came because of you."

Mercy smiled fondly at her friend's frankness. "Surely you will stay until the meal is served. Even you have to eat."

"Unfortunately," Maria replied dryly.

At that moment, Benjamin Randall entered the room, extending a heartfelt welcome to his friends. The knocker sounded again, and the guests began to arrive in quick succession—Swains and Coffins and Folgers and Gardners; Starbucks, Hadwens, Macys and Mayhews. There were more women than men, as usual at Nantucket gatherings, but this did not serve to dampen spirits. The safe and profitable end of any whaling voyage was an event to be celebrated. Soon both parlors were full of people engaged in sipping cider and talking animatedly.

The last to arrive was Captain Samuel Starbuck. The moment he entered the parlor all attention focused on him, as inevitably as a rolling wave heads for shore. Even Mercy's eyes were drawn to him as he moved easily through the room, clasping the hands of the men and flirting audaciously with the women. All responded favorably, even eagerly, to his attentions, and yet again Mercy tried to un-

derstand the regard with which others universally beheld
him.

Lest you begin to wonder, gentle reader, why Mercy was
so out of step with her community on the issue of Sam
Starbuck, let me inform you that Sam had not always been
so admired. As a boy, he had terrorized Nantucket Town.
If there was mischief abroad, Sam was its instigator. His
widowed mother could not control him. The citizens of
Nantucket shook their heads and said that the boy took
after his father, for whom he had been named, a notorious
privateer who had been killed in the War of 1812, leaving
his widow and year-old-son penniless and dependent on the
charity of the Starbuck clan. Since the elder Sam Starbuck
had done all in his power to disgrace the family name, this
largess was dispensed grudgingly at best.

For reasons Mercy still could not fathom, her father had
befriended Sam as a boy and when he was fifteen, had
taken him aboard the *Meribah*. From foremast hand, Sam
had worked his way up to captain. He had earned the respect of his peers, the obedience of his men and the ado-
ration of females from eight to eighty. Mercy knew of only
two women in Nantucket Town who had not fallen under
his spell—herself and Maria Mitchell. Maria was too bound
up in her studies to succumb to any of the usual female
preoccupations with the male sex. As for Mercy, she found
it impossible to be sympathetic to a man who treated her as
if he knew something about her—some secret, even scan-
dalous, thing—that she herself did not know.

Suddenly Mercy realized that Captain Starbuck had seen
her observing him. Without interrupting his conversation
with the venerable and slightly deaf Mrs. Mary Gardner, he
returned her attention, catching her eye and nodding almost imperceptibly. The look in his eyes was smug and self-
satisfied, reminding her of Jim—the well-fed tomcat who
was Emily's companion in the kitchen—as he lapped his
morning bowl of milk after returning from a long night on
the prowl. She did not care for that look in a cat, much less
a man.

Well schooled in a lady's proper decorum and the art of disguising one's feelings in public, Mercy acknowledged Starbuck's glance with one that held no more interest than that of a hostess for a guest. But he misinterpreted that, too—or pretended to do so—taking it as an invitation, no, a summons, to conversation. With a bow, he excused himself from Mrs. Gardner and headed purposefully toward Mercy.

Fortunately, Caroline chose that moment to make her entrance. Caroline always entered a room with the air of a princess to whom undivided attention and uncontested devotion were naturally due. Tonight the effect was heightened by having enlisted Sarah in the role of lady-in-waiting. The two stood poised on the threshold: Sarah, the uncut marble; Caroline, the finished work of art.

There was a moment in which everyone gazed admiringly at the *tableau vivant*. Then, with a nudge from behind, Sarah, timidly charming in blue velvet the color of the evening sky in winter, came into the room. Caroline followed in deep rose satin shot with silver. Suddenly the place was alive with motion as the gentlemen competed with one another to bring Caroline a glass of cider, to find her a chair. Only one gentleman did not rush to pay court to Caroline. Sam Starbuck offered his arm to Sarah and led her to a chair beside the fire. His gallantry prompted an exchange of broad approval between Mrs. Mary Gardner and her neighbor, Mrs. Mayhew.

Trust him, Mercy thought, albeit somewhat unkindly, to draw attention to himself by attending the cygnet instead of the swan. Still, she was grateful for his courtesy to Sarah at her first adult party. Eyeing the pair again, however, she was struck by an unwelcome bolt of jealousy. She missed her husband, with his courtly manners and his concern for her comfort. Much as she loved her father and sisters, she longed to be hostess in her own home, with her own children sleeping peacefully upstairs. Time, she counseled herself as she made her way across the room, all that will come to you in time.

In the kitchen, Mercy asked Emily to serve supper in fifteen minutes. On her way back to the front parlor she found Maria in the hall, plucking her cloak from a peg. "You can't go before supper," Mercy pleaded.

"I must. The night is too fine and clear to waste." Maria wrapped the garment around her and removed her gloves from her reticule. "No one will miss me."

"I shall miss you," Mercy declared.

"I doubt that. You'll be far too busy. How you do it, Mercy, I don't know. I could never have the patience for all this housekeeping."

"You have another kind of patience. You are disciplined and work until you find the truth. You wait as long as you must to make a discovery. I, on the other hand, find waiting very difficult. So please don't tell me I am patient."

"And don't tell me I am patient, either. What I have is not patience, my friend, it's something quite different. Rather like a hunger I must feed. Oh, I know everyone thinks me a queer sort. But I'm not, really. It's only because I'm female that anyone thinks twice about my telescope and my books. Had I been my brother no one would have noticed me in the least. And now," she finished bleakly, "I must be off."

"But you haven't eaten anything."

Maria waved her hand dismissively. "I shall find something cold in the pantry at home."

"I know you too well," Mercy admonished. "You'll sit up the entire night without any nourishment at all. Let me have Emily fix you a basket."

"Thank you for your concern, Mercy, but I must not tarry any longer."

Mercy acquiesced. There was a certain look in Maria's eyes that told her she would be wasting her breath to continue her entreaties. "Will you visit me tomorrow afternoon? I've missed your company lately." She pressed her friend's hand.

"Yes, I will," Maria agreed. "*That*—" she gave a side-long glance into the parlor "—is something I would enjoy very much."

Full of admiration for her friend's single-mindedness, Mercy watched her safely down the front steps and into the street. Had I not met Nathaniel, she thought, I might have followed her lead and applied myself to the study of medicine the way she has applied herself to astronomy. But I did meet Nathaniel, and that has changed everything.

Mercy's thoughts were interrupted by the cheerful noises emanating from the parlors, reminding her that her guests required their hostess. She turned to enter the front parlor but was stopped on her way into the room by Captain Starbuck. "Has Miss Mitchell deserted us? I suppose we mortals are no match for the heavens," he said mildly.

Mercy's reply was cold. "I greatly admire Miss Mitchell's devotion to her work." She would permit no man to belittle Maria for her thoughtful pursuits.

"As do I, Mrs. Wright."

He laid undue stress on her name, as if it were not her legitimate title but one she had stolen. "Do you, Captain?" she asked with a similar emphasis.

"I do, indeed. In fact, were society not so rigid on such points, I would invite her to sail with me on the *Meribah*, so that she could continue her studies with no obstacles between herself and the heavens. I am certain Mr. Mayhew would not mind giving up his quarters to such a worthy endeavor."

"What wouldn't I mind?" Valentine Mayhew, mate of the *Meribah*, stepped up beside Starbuck.

Grateful for his timely arrival, Mercy smiled warmly at Val. She and the *Meribah*'s mate shared an aunt—his mother's sister was married to her mother's brother, Thomas Pearse. Their friendship, begun in childhood, had continued into adulthood.

Seeing the two men side by side now, Mercy was struck by their physical contrast. Sam Starbuck was all darkness—hair, eyes, skin, disposition. Val, on the other hand, was all light—blond hair bleached even lighter by the sun, translucent blue eyes, skin more freckles than tanned by long months at sea, and an even-tempered manner. Despite these great differences, the two men got along famously.

Sam repeated his proposal to Val, who took it in with the air of one accustomed to another's eccentricities. "The cabin is hers. Far be it from me to hinder the pursuit of scientific truth," he replied generously. "Besides, having Miss Mitchell aboard would raise the level of conversation in the officers' mess."

"I'm sure it would," Mercy agreed pointedly.

"Perhaps Val will tell you what he thinks is wrong with the conversation aboard the *Meribah*." The disapproval in Starbuck's voice was clearly directed at Mercy.

Val came gallantly but diplomatically to her defense. "Aside from your foul moods, Sam, nothing more than what the conversation of any whaler lacks: a woman's tempering influence."

With that the dinner bell rang, allowing Mercy to excuse herself and hurry across the hall. Starbuck watched her intently, continuing to stare into the hall long after Mercy disappeared into the dining room. She had been often in his thoughts since his return, and he searched now for an explanation of his preoccupation with her. She was no more beautiful than she had been. In fact, she seemed pale and strained. But neither was she the cool, detached young woman he remembered. There was heat in her now. It was buried deep, like embers in an apparently cold hearth, but it was there. Not only did he sense the spark, he found himself wanting to probe for it, too, to see if it could be fanned into a flame or if a strong gust of wind would blow it out. This desire disturbed him. In fact, the whole business of noticing her and thinking about her disturbed him. Perhaps, he reasoned, it was merely the change in her that intrigued him.

He turned to his mate, who knew her so much better than he. "Do you find Mrs. Wright much altered since her marriage, Val?"

Val studied his friend for a moment. There was definitely a bee buzzing in Sam's bonnet, but Val had no intention of swatting it. You never knew with Sam—you might shoo the bee away, or you might get stung. He decided to keep his distance. Although he had noticed a difference in Mercy—a certain hardness, a tautness she had not had before, he loyally kept that observation to himself. "I believe she is finding the separation from her husband difficult."

Sam grunted and gave Val a narrow-eyed look. "Your manners are too damned good."

"Old habits die hard, no matter what company one keeps." Val ignored Sam's guffaw and edged away. "I must hurry or someone else will be bringing Caroline her supper plate." He turned to gaze at Caroline, who was holding court from a small upholstered armchair. "Have you ever laid eyes on anything more delicious?"

"You haven't seen the food yet, man."

"Or tasted it," Val replied with longing.

Sam laughed and shook his head at his mate. Ah, to be that young and innocent again, instead of the crusty barnacle he'd become. But then, he reminded himself, I was never that young and innocent. He hung back as the others filed into the dining room. When most had returned with their plates to the parlor, he entered the dining room, where Mercy was watching over the supper service.

He waited until everyone was served to approach her, not sure himself why. He had never particularly cared for Mercy Randall, nor she for him. If he'd had the slightest interest in that direction, he would have pursued her and married her, for Ben would have liked nothing better and had once told him so. But he had not been so inclined.

There had been a time when it was important for him to know he had the admiration of every female he encountered, and Mercy Randall's indifference had once rankled him. But surely by now, at the age of thirty-two, he should have outgrown that need.

"I will fill a plate for you, Mrs. Wright. You must be quite tired—and hungry—after your efforts on behalf of your guests."

"Thank you, but there are things I must attend to in the kitchen."

Her tone was firmly dismissive, but he persisted nonetheless. "Your guests are all served, madam. You must take some rest and refreshment yourself."

"Some who command at sea, Captain, relinquish the habit of giving orders on land."

"And others are tyrants no matter where they are!" he countered.

Mercy flashed him a fiery look and seemed about to speak again, when she excused herself and hurried from the room. Her exit was dignified enough, but Starbuck had not mistaken the heat in her glance or the spots of angry color on her cheeks. So she is not as implacable as she tries to appear, he thought. His triumph, though minor, was enjoyable nonetheless. He took a plate and began to fill it, but as he worked his way through the dishes on the sideboard his spirits dampened. What triumph had he achieved? He had been rude and had offended a friend's hospitality. The glum truth was that Mercy Randall brought out the worst in him. She always had.

Mercy waited in the kitchen until she regained control of her temper. Perhaps she had reacted too strongly to Captain Starbuck, but she would not be ordered about in her own home. Why, her own father did not speak to her in such a tone. She peered into the dining room and, finding it empty, filled a plate for herself and carried it into the front parlor. She sat in the empty chair beside Isabelle Macy, who was so enamored with talking that it was unnecessary for her partner to utter a single syllable.

By the time the party finished their supper, it was nearly ten o'clock. Mercy was about to instruct Sarah to say her good-nights when Val brought out his fiddle and asked

Caroline to join him at the piano. He also begged Captain Randall's permission to clear the back parlor for dancing. Randall agreed with alacrity, but Caroline demurred prettily and had to be cajoled before she took her seat at the spinet. Mercy caught Sarah's pleading eye and relented with a nod. She would let the child watch one dance.

"Mercy," Caroline cried. "You and father must begin the dancing with a reel."

"Oh, no, daughter," Captain Randall countered. "I am too old and too clumsy for dancing. I must call on my friend Captain Starbuck to take my place. Sam?"

Starbuck stepped forward gallantly. "It would be my very great pleasure, sir." He faced Mercy and bowed.

Though still smarting from their exchange in the dining room, Mercy could not refuse the summons. Reluctantly she took her place facing her partner. The pair stood poised to begin, gazing uneasily past each other's shoulders as they waited for the music. Finally Val and Caroline struck up the lively rhythm.

Pulling Mercy along behind him, Starbuck dove into the dance like a baking-hot man into a cool, refreshing sea. Her only choice was to sink or swim. She swam. He spun her around in the small space with such verve that the others did not get up to dance, but began to clap their hands with the music. Encouraged by his friends' enthusiasm, Sam whirled Mercy around more and more vigorously, so that she had all she could do to stay upright and follow his lead. But follow him she did, in a billow of gray-and-lavender silk.

The men began to whistle and cheer. Mercy's head swirled, her heart thumped, her cheeks burned. She was dipped and twirled like a storm-tossed ship, steadied only by a firm-handed captain at the helm. But once she got the feel of the waves, she began to weather them with confidence. No matter how tricky or fancy his footwork she stayed solidly in step. She clung to him tightly and threw back her head, laughing with the excitement of it all.

The wind that drove them stopped suddenly with a loud chord and a long bow stroke, and Mercy found herself breathless and panting in Sam Starbuck's arms. A chorus of huzzahs and applause greeted the dancers. The captain bowed to his partner, and she returned the favor with a curtsy.

For a moment, Mercy felt only the pleasurable tingle of vigorous exercise and the headiness of a challenge well met. During the dance, all her cares had receded and she felt a sense of lightness and freedom such as she had not known since she first danced with Nathaniel in Aunt Elizabeth's parlor.

But the moment passed quickly, and reality washed over her like a gray, chilly mist. There was Sarah to see to, and her guests. Caroline to chaperon, her father to attend. And her cold, empty bed to retire to. It would take more than one whirlwind dance to make her forget all that.

Quickly she looked away from Captain Starbuck. Keeping a light note in her voice, she called for Val and Caroline to continue the music and encouraged the other guests to join in the dancing. Without another glance at Starbuck she went to Sarah. "Come and say good-night to Papa."

Starbuck, however, did not look away from her. He had enjoyed their dance more than he cared to admit and kept his eyes on his partner. At sea, when the whaling was slow he often searched the horizon, as if by mere looking he could will a whale to appear. Now he peered at Mercy, as if by staring he could force the motive for his new fancy to emerge. He was much chagrined by his reaction to her. Why should he be so excited by a woman he couldn't have, when there were so many he could?

Perhaps it was simply that Mercy seemed different—unpredictable now, when once he had found her tame and tiresome. The South Atlantic weather is hardly more changeable, he thought of her transformation after their dance. One moment she was a laughing, carefree girl, the next a proper hostess looking older and far more serious than her years deserved.

Or perhaps he was drawn to her simply because she was unavailable. It was long past time for him to marry, and he should have been setting his sights in that direction. Despite his scornful laughter, little Sarah had been right to see the loneliness in his eyes. This last voyage had made him yearn for a home to return to. The places—and beds—where he was welcome around the world no longer satisfied him. And yet he was still reluctant to settle, to be tied to a woman and a family.

The music struck up again, fast and gay, and Sam banished his gloomy ruminations. He tore his eyes away from Mercy and quickly scanned the room. What he needed was to dance and to laugh, and with a partner who could make him think of nothing but moving his feet in time to the music. He made his bow to Susan Hadwen, a frivolous maiden of eighteen, who accepted his invitation with a gleeful giggle.

Across the room, Captain Randall accepted a good-night kiss from his youngest girl and wished her sweet dreams. To his eldest daughter he said, "It's grand to see a bit of color in your cheeks, Mercy. I must have the young people in for dancing more often."

That innocent remark revealed to Mercy that her melancholy feelings had been showing lately. She could not, would not burden her family with her private worries. "Yes, Papa," she answered quietly, resolving to keep her emotions more firmly in check in the future.

As Starbuck danced with Susan Hadwen, his eyes were once again drawn toward Mercy. Susan was a lively lass, but her inconsequential chatter was not enough to keep his thoughts from straying. He found himself wanting to dance with Mercy again, wanting to recapture the elusive part of her that had surfaced so briefly and sounded so quickly. Then a sharp shaft of recognition stung him: his feelings for Mercy were the same ones he experienced when he was tantalized by a fugitive whale. So that's it, he thought with no little relief, it's the pursuit I'm after, not the fish.

Before the dance was over, Starbuck noticed the Randalls' housekeeper enter the room. With obvious discomfort, she went to Captain Randall, her attempt to be unobtrusive making her all the more conspicuous. As she spoke to him, the captain became agitated, and by the time he pushed himself out of his chair and followed her across the room, everyone was watching, although with sidelong glances and every appearance of polite indifference. Starbuck felt no such reticence. He disengaged himself from his partner and left the room. As he crossed the threshold into the hall, he saw Ben ushering Captain Matthew Folger, a Martha's Vineyard man, into the library. What the devil? he wondered as he followed the two into the room.

Upstairs, Mercy brushed out Sarah's curls and helped her out of her clothes and into her nightdress, while the child chattered on like a bird at first light.

"The best part was seeing you dance with Captain Sam," Sarah declared.

"Was it?" Mercy turned back the covers on Sarah's bed and settled the girl beneath them.

"You were like someone else, someone I'd never met before."

"Your wicked old sister disappeared, hmm?"

"I didn't mean that!" Sarah said quickly. "I only meant that I'd never seen you look the way you did then."

And just how had she looked, Mercy wondered as she explained to Sarah, "Dancing can have that effect on you. It carries you away from yourself. I guess that's why so many people are set against it."

"I know some people think it very wicked, but I don't see why."

"That's a very difficult subject, pet, and we can talk about it tomorrow. But now I must return to our guests. Do you think you can close your eyes and go to sleep? Will you try?" Mercy smoothed the covers one last time and dimmed the lamp. She stood by the bed until Sarah's breathing had quieted and then whispered a final good-night.

In the back parlor, the music and dancing continued, but the room seemed curiously empty to Mercy. Looking around, she noticed that neither her father nor Captain Starbuck were there. With a twinge of annoyance, she hoped they had not sneaked off to discuss some business about the *Meribah*. She also noticed that the cider bowl was nearly empty and went to the kitchen to request more refreshment for her thirsty guests.

"I felt it best to come as soon as I could," Matthew Folger said.

"Then you must bring me bad news, sir," Randall replied.

"How bad?" Starbuck put in.

Folger, a tall dour man with a manner that matched his steel-gray hair and eyes, looked to Randall before continuing. Randall indicated that he should proceed. "Captain Starbuck will know everything soon enough."

There was no love lost between Starbuck and Folger, who had clashed two years previously over the behavior of their crews in the Sandwich Islands. Folger tried to control his men's recreations, while Starbuck allowed his men to do as they pleased, as long as they did not wreak havoc or harm anyone. Folger thought Starbuck a reckless libertine; Starbuck thought Folger a sanctimonious prig. Neither man was likely to change his opinion of the other.

Folger nodded gravely. "My news concerns the *Abishai*."

"She's lost." Captain Randall spoke with certainty and resignation.

"I fear so."

"All hands?"

"Yes."

Randall grimaced. "My daughter's husband was on board, Captain Folger. He was the mate, Nathaniel Wright."

Starbuck thought he saw Folger flinch, but then decided he must be mistaken. Whatever he was, Folger was not a

man to shy from or be shocked by the harsh realities of the
whaling life. But when Folger began to speak again, he
stammered on his first word. Starbuck began to feel some
alarm. If Matthew Folger was shrinking and stuttering, the
news must be very bad indeed.

"I—I did not know Mr. Wright was your son-in-law, sir.
Your loss is very great indeed, then. Er, perhaps you may
find comfort, as I often have, sir, in the words of—"

"The sermons can wait, man," Starbuck interrupted
impatiently. "Tell us what the devil has happened!"

Folger glowered at Starbuck, and Starbuck glowered
back.

"Please, Sam," Captain Randall importuned quietly.

Starbuck turned to look at his friend. He was pallid and
seemed unsteady on his feet. Sam immediately regretted his
outburst. While he cared not a whit for Matthew Folger's
opinion of him, his gratitude to Benjamin Randall was
great, and he wished he had not embarrassed his friend with
his rude behavior. "Excuse me," he said, "I spoke out of
turn."

Captain Randall recovered himself and suggested that
they all sit down. "I take it we are not in for a pretty tale,
Captain Folger, but delaying won't make it any the pret-
tier."

As he took his seat, Starbuck noticed that the sounds of
the party seemed to be coming from a distant place. The
parlor across the hall might have been as far away as Nantucket from the South Seas. The music and laughter were
much like the phantom sounds—the peal of a church bell,
the tinkle of a child's laugh—he sometimes heard when he
had been too long at sea, too long with only the lapping of
waves and the creaking of timber.

Matthew Folger began his tale without introduction. His
words were plain and unadorned, and his manner of
speaking extremely restrained. "More than six months ago,
in early June it was, I was in the Bay of Islands, fitting my
ship for the voyage home, when the *Mary Grant* put in to
the harbor there. Her captain is my cousin, George Folger.

Learning I was on my way home, he asked me to bring you word of the *Abishai*.

"About two months before George and I met—that would be late in March of '42—the *Mary Grant* was cruising in the South Seas, among the Black Islands, my cousin taking great care not to draw too close to land and risk attack by the fierce, godless inhabitants of that place. Then one day the lookout spotted a tattered white flag on a small, barren atoll. A whaleboat was dispatched and two sailors found, both near dead of sun and lack of food and water. They were carried aboard the *Mary Grant,* but lived only long enough to tell my cousin what had happened aboard the *Abishai*."

"And what exactly did happen?" Starbuck exploded. Despite his desire to consider Ben's feelings, he found Folger's circumspection unbearably infuriating. "Sorry," he muttered.

Pointedly ignoring him, Folger continued in the same careful, controlled manner. As the story unfolded, Starbuck came to see why Folger had schooled himself so strictly. For many long months, he had shouldered the burden of the tale alone, unable to reveal what he knew to another living soul. Only such an emotionless delivery could have made the telling possible.

Starbuck thought himself a hardened man: he had killed whales for profit and sport, he had flogged rebellious sailors, he had killed men when necessary. But as he listened he felt his entire body slacken, as if his strength were actually quitting his bones, leaving them weak and brittle. The flow was stanched only by a bright, burning anger that enabled him to fend off despair. For what could a man feel but utter despair when he learned that the human race could spawn such creatures as could create the dire circumstances into which the *Abishai* had fallen.

Unlike Sam, Benjamin Randall was beyond anger, beyond even the disbelief that comes before anger. He heard and understood everything Matthew Folger said. He knew that the community had been robbed of many fine men and

that he would be the one to tell their wives and families. He
also knew that his financial loss was great. But he had a
problem greater than that, a dilemma that distressed him
more than anything in his life so far, except perhaps the
death of his dear Lucy. Whatever would he say to Mercy?
How would he tell her that Nathaniel Wright was dead?
What would he tell her about his death?

"Mercy," he murmured. "How can I...?" Randall
turned desperately to Folger. "Is it possible, Captain, that
anyone survived?"

"I cannot believe it," Folger answered gravely.

"Then my daughter is a widow."

Feeling clumsy and inadequate to the task, Sam tried to
offer what solace he could. "She is not alone in her loss,
Ben," he said quietly.

"I know that, son, but can we offer her no hope?"

"Why should we?" Sam felt his anger rising again.
Nathaniel Wright's behavior in this sorry affair was despicable. If anyone had survived, by all that was right it should
not be him. For Ben's sake, however, he stifled his fury.
"There is no hope we can offer anyone in this grim business," he finished.

"But we can soften the blow somewhat, for everyone.
Can we not, Captain Folger?"

"You well know, Captain Randall," Folger replied,
"that I do not countenance lies. But I have had much time
to contemplate this matter and have concluded that we will
not do a disservice to the truth if we keep certain aspects of
these events among ourselves."

"Yes," Randall agreed gratefully.

Starbuck's natural inclination was to broadcast the whole
bloody tale, to bellow out his rage against the stupidity and
venality of some men. But even he recognized the need for
discretion. "Something must be said, so we'd better agree
among ourselves what it will be."

"The *Abishai* ran aground in the Black Islands," Randall began in a dull voice. "She was attacked by hostile
natives. All were killed, except two sailors who escaped to

a nearby atoll. They were rescued by the *Mary Grant,* but died shortly after they were taken on board. As far as it goes, that is the truth. Will this version satisfy your conscience, Captain Folger?''

"It will save many pain and grief." His business concluded, Folger stood and said that he would see himself out.

When the library door opened, the sounds of the party crashed into the room like thunder. The noise catapulted Starbuck out of the dreadful world he had inhabited for the past half hour, but Captain Randall seemed hardly to notice that Folger had gone or that a party continued across the hall.

Gentleness did not come easily to Starbuck, but he softened his voice to speak to his friend. "We must tell the others, Ben. I'll do it if you like."

Randall took such a long time to reply that Starbuck was about to repeat his words. "No," the older man said at last. "I'll do it. I'm the one who is to blame. What was I thinking of? Sending an inexperienced city boy out as first mate. Even an honorary one."

Silently Starbuck agreed that his friend's gamble had not been a wise one. But he well remembered another gamble taken on another young man. "You couldn't have known," he said loyally.

"I'd prefer it if you told me what you really think, son. I've known you too long and too well to suffer politeness or platitudes from you."

But Starbuck would not rise to the bait. Nor would he let Ben shoulder the blame for the fate either of the *Abishai* or of his son-in-law. Benjamin Randall should have nothing on his conscience: he had not acted out of greed or laziness or any other unworthy motive. Perhaps his judgment had been poor, but it was more than likely that he had been swayed by other considerations. If Sam knew Mercy Randall at all, she had had some hand in securing her husband's position aboard the *Abishai.* "You took a chance, Ben. You once took a chance on another young man, one who was much less promising. Not every whale stays fast to the line.''

A ghost of a smile crossed Randall's face. ''No, that's true.'' He looked intently at Starbuck. ''You must promise me one thing.''

''Name it.''

''Mercy must never know how Wright died. She worships—worshipped him.''

''The more reason to tell her, then,'' Sam protested. ''Why should she live a lie for the rest of her life?'' Worship indeed. The word galled him. Why did men and women have to worship each other? Could they not simply accept one another for what they were? He could see no reason to spare Mercy's feelings. She had married Wright, had joined him for life. She should know the truth of his death. ''I think she should know everything,'' he counseled.

''No!'' Randall underscored his vehemence by slamming his hand onto the arm of his chair. ''Losing him is sorrow enough. I couldn't bear to see her suffer any more than she has to. She's taken on so much since Lucy died— the house, the girls, me. I wanted her to be happy.''

''She made her own choice,'' Sam argued. ''She should know the consequences of it.''

''No!'' Randall reiterated staunchly. ''You must promise me she'll never know what really happened. I've never asked you for anything, but I ask you this one thing now: your word that you will never tell Mercy the truth about the *Abishai*.''

As much as he would have liked to, Starbuck could not refuse his friend. Nor could he override a father's wishes for his daughter. Reluctantly he acquiesced. ''I do not agree with you, sir, but you have my word.''

''Thank you, Sam.'' Randall rose wearily. Since Lucy's death he had often felt his age, but what he felt now was something worse than that. Life had not merely aged him, tonight it had defeated him—decisively, irreversibly. ''I must tell the others.'' He dragged himself toward the door, as heavily as if he were towing the *Abishai* and her crew behind him.

Tragedy and disaster, dear reader, are the dark side of Nantucket life. They are never far away, lurking behind every sunny day and every happy gathering, and we Nantucketers learn as youngsters to recognize the arrival of bad tidings.

As soon as her father entered the room, Mercy knew that something was desperately wrong. The others sensed it, too. Val's bow rested on the strings of his fiddle in midstroke; Caroline's hands halted in midmeasure. Even Isabelle Macy stopped talking, although a second or two after everyone else.

"I fear I have bad news for you, my friends," Captain Randall began. "News that is especially sad coming as it has on a night when we have gathered to celebrate the safe homecoming of the *Meribah*. Another of my ships has not met such good fortune. The *Abishai* is lost." He looked helplessly to his daughter. "Mercy, my child, I am sorry."

Mercy did not faint. She did not weep. Caroline was the one to burst into loud tears, to rush to her sister and cling to her, sobbing. Gently Mercy pushed her sister away, whispering to her that she must save her grief for a more private time. In a voice that was clear, if not as strong as usual, she addressed the guests.

"I am sure you will understand that our family wishes to be alone now. We thank you for coming to us this evening, and we offer our sympathy and prayers to all of you who are also bereaved by the loss of the *Abishai*." Then she stood by the door of the front parlor and accepted the kind words and condolences of the departing guests.

Benjamin Randall watched his daughter with awe and trepidation. Her self-mastery was prodigious, but he feared that it masked a grief so great she did not dare acknowledge it.

Starbuck was impressed, too, but not as favorably as Mercy's father. He had never seen a woman, even a naturally stoical Nantucket woman, control her feelings so rigidly; it chilled him to the bone. Faced with such a display of strength, he regretted his promise. Mercy should know, he said to himself. She'll make a saint of Wright now. The mere thought brought a bitter-tasting bile to his mouth. But he had promised. He would not be the one to tell her.

When everyone was gone and she had convinced Caroline to go upstairs to check on Sarah, Mercy joined her father and Starbuck in the front parlor. She wished Starbuck had gone with the others, but unwelcome as it was to her, she knew his presence was a comfort to her father. "You must tell me what happened, Papa. I want to know everything." During his brief recital, her mind worked with speed and clarity. The news was not entirely hopeless, she determined. "Two men survived, so others may have. It is possible that Nathaniel is still alive."

"If he is, I pity him," Starbuck put in bitterly.

A stab of hatred pierced Mercy's heart. In that moment she hated Sam Starbuck for the breath he drew as much as for the cruel words that came on that breath. "Captain Starbuck, because of my father's attachment to you I did not ask you to leave with the others. But if you persist in making untoward remarks I shall be forced to ask my father if he can spare your company."

Starbuck rose stiffly, hardly allowing himself to breathe. His desire to tell Mercy every wretched detail of the attack on the *Abishai* was overwhelming. "I have no wish to overstay my welcome, Mrs. Wright. Ben, I trust you will send for me if I can be of any service." He left the room as quickly as he could, breaking stride only to allow his hand to rest briefly on his friend's shoulder.

"I'm sorry, Papa, but I could not allow—" Mercy broke off. Her father had touched her with a hand so icy cold and trembling it robbed her of breath and speech.

"Mercy, I beg you, don't cling to false hopes. Nathaniel is dead. You must accept that and mourn him. It is impossible that anyone could have survived. Impossible. Impossible."

Her father spoke so fervently that for a moment Mercy believed him, and a noxious, suffocating cloud of sorrow began to close around her. Then she remembered. Two had survived. "I cannot give up hope. Not now. Not yet. Please don't ask me to do that." The miraculous power of hope dispelled the evil cloud, leaving her calm, even tranquil. "Why don't you try to get some rest, Papa? There will be a great deal to do tomorrow." She rose, her legs strong and steady beneath her, and kissed her father lightly on the forehead. "Do you want anything? No? Then I'll have a word with Emily before I go up. Good night, Papa."

When his daughter was gone, Benjamin Randall slumped in his chair. He had failed Mercy miserably. Perhaps he should have taken Sam's advice. If he had told her the truth, she could have no doubt that Nathaniel Wright had perished. But he had not told her, and what was more, he did not believe he would ever again have the strength to make himself do so.

He had lost much more than a ship this night. He had lost his will. It was gone, vanished as irretrievably as the *Abishai* and all her crew.

Chapter Three

If he is, I pity him. I pity him. I pity him. The refrain ran rampant in Mercy's mind all through the endless, dark night. What could have occasioned Sam Starbuck's malicious remark? He was a brash and headstrong man, and she disliked him, but she had never known him to be guilty of deliberate cruelty. What could be pitiful about Nathaniel being alive? She could think of only one explanation. The demise of the *Abishai* was more terrible than her father's dull recital of the facts allowed, and something particularly horrid had happened to Nathaniel.

She wished now she had not let her temper get the better of her. Of course her father would try to shield her, but why should Sam Starbuck be party to such cosseting? She did not flatter herself to think he held her sensibilities in that high a regard. Still she had not questioned his remark. Instead she had as good as ordered him from the house. Had she spoken rationally, she might have learned more, known more.

Mercy was much concerned with knowledge. She believed in it unreservedly and deplored the female propensity for being swayed by feelings instead of facts. Yet throughout the stormy night she was beset by feelings she could neither explain nor dismiss. They were strong, and they buffeted her reason to the point that she began to doubt its continued existence.

Beyond all rationality she believed that Nathaniel was alive. Her belief exceeded her understandable hope and desire that Matthew Folger had been mistaken about the fate of the *Abishai*. It was more, too, than a natural human impulse to impose her wishes on a world beyond her control. Anyone locked in a battle with grief makes these attempts. But this conviction was something else. It was like her knowledge that the stars are not mere points of light in the sky but huge, hot orbs burning brightly millions of miles from earth, something she believed without actually having been to a star to see for herself. As sure as the stars were blistering balls of fire, Nathaniel was alive.

Through the long night she wrestled with these thoughts, until at long last the first rays of light stole into her room. With the dawn of day, she waited for her reason to return, for the renegade idea to disintegrate, to shoot across her mind and disappear like a shower of meteorites. But the notion did not fade away in the light, and so she tried to push it out of her head instead. Like all suppressed rebellions, however, it gained force and power in its struggle for ascendancy, giving rise to a corollary notion that a Nathaniel who still lived was somehow different from the courtly young man with whom she had danced in the ballrooms of Boston. The man who had dispelled the shyness of their wedding night by reading her poetry, who had treated her with the utmost courtesy and deference was no more. That was a ludicrous proposition, she chided herself. If Nathaniel was still alive, he was still Nathaniel.

The longer she stayed abed the more these ideas preyed upon her. And so she rose. She washed and removed from her wardrobe a black satin day dress, a proper, even severe, number intended for occasional use on somber occasions. She greatly disliked wearing black, not only because it robbed her hair and complexion of their warm lights but because it was as harsh and unrelenting as death itself. But now it was to be her color for the next twelve months.

She laid the dress on the bed and considered it as she donned her undergarments. It seemed like a costume. Instead of proclaiming her true feelings, it hid them, wrapped them in convention. She felt no widow's loss, no bereavement, the weight of "never again" did not press heavily on her shoulders. She had not shed a single tear nor uttered a single cry of anguish. Instead she felt much the way she had the day before, when she was merely a wife enduring a long separation. She felt so unchanged that she very nearly sat down to write her daily letter to Nathaniel, lingering hesitantly beside the desk as she held in her mind the conversation she would have had with him on paper.

Dearest Nathaniel—last night we had a party to celebrate the safe homecoming of the Meribah. *We had a lovely supper, followed by music and dancing, and then Father announced that the* Abishai *was lost and you were dead. But I do not feel that you are dead, my darling. I feel you are only what you have been for so long—far away and silent....*

Nathaniel, Nathaniel, she railed. Why did you abandon me? The pincerlike pain deep in her heart let her know she had reached the real source of her pain. If Nathaniel was dead, she could accept it. But never could she reconcile herself to his silence without knowing the reason for it.

Her eye fell once again on her black dress and she considered it with distaste. Though it was in every way unlike the gown she had once worn to a fancy dress ball in Boston, it reminded her of that costumed event. At Nathaniel's suggestion, one that was applauded by Aunt Elizabeth and all their friends, she and Nathaniel had dressed as Rowena and Ivanhoe. Their appearance as the unattainable lady and her faithful knight was an unqualified success. Now their situation mocked that past triumph. The lady, it turned out, had not been unattainable, and the knight not so faithful.

Stop it, she ordered herself. No more. She would not stoop to bitterness and irony, both of which she considered weaknesses of demeanor to be resolutely eschewed. She would wear the dress as she must, with dignity, and she would become accustomed to it. Like so much of life, wearing this badge of widowhood, even if she felt it a false emblem, required only practice. With the diligent application of her will and intelligence, she would come to accept and adjust to her new state, as well as to the sudden and irrevocable change in her status and expectations.

While Mercy was thus ruminating, Caroline was making her way, with some trepidation, up the stairs with a breakfast tray. The events of the previous evening had thrust her into the role of mistress of the house. Mercy could not be expected to give orders to Emily or to do anything else today, so she had taken up the post, but she was unsure exactly how to execute her reluctantly assumed duties.

Cradling the tray with one arm, Caroline knocked tentatively on her sister's door and, without awaiting an answer, pushed it open a crack. "Why, you're up and nearly dressed," she exclaimed. She had expected to find Mercy still in bed, pale and haggard, her eyes dull and rimmed with red. Except for a barely perceptible loss of color in her cheeks, her sister looked much her usual self. By comparison, Caroline herself was the more careworn and drawn.

"Of course I am," Mercy replied briskly. She took the tray and, placing it on the desk, inspected its contents— milk, hot coffee, buttered bread and jam. She took a portion of each and, although she was not the least bit hungry, sat down and began to eat. "Is Papa up yet? We must begin visiting the families. And what about the church service, and relief baskets—"

"Surely you won't go out with Papa today, Mercy. You must stay home and receive callers." Caroline was shocked by more than Mercy's intention to be away from home this morning. Where had Mercy found such an appetite, she wondered, averting her eyes. The mere thought of food this morning had her feeling slightly unwell. Only sisterly devotion and compassion had enabled her to transport the tray from the kitchen. She never dreamed Mercy would touch anything more than a sip or two of the coffee, but there she was, fairly devouring the bread and butter and drinking down a whole glass of milk.

"You and Sarah can accept the condolences on behalf of the family. I can't let Papa do this dreadful job by himself. I must go with him. Don't forget, dear Caroline, there are others whose losses are far greater than mine. Eliza Goodwin has three young children to feed and clothe. Mrs. Hastings, who bore nine children, has lost her sole surviving son. What is my loss compared with theirs? My life has changed little since yesterday." Outwardly, that is, she said to herself. "I still have you and Sarah and Papa. Our circumstances are reduced, but Papa is not ruined by the loss of the *Abishai*."

"But you'll never see Nathaniel again, Mercy. How can you—"

"You needn't look at me as if I've lost my reason."

"Haven't you?" Suddenly Caroline felt a rush of scalding tears gathering in her eyes. "Your husband is dead, Mercy, and all you can think of is parish visiting, as if this terrible tragedy had happened to someone else, not to you, not to our family." The tears spilled over now, and Caroline fumbled in the pocket of her morning dress for a handkerchief. She didn't know why she was crying, really. She hadn't even cared for her brother-in-law. Still he was a member of the family. And there was dear Papa to think about. He had lost so much.

"We each must grieve in our own way," Mercy said quietly, and laid a comforting hand on Caroline's shoulder. Those of us who can grieve, she added to herself. The fall of footsteps sounded in the hall. "Papa," she cautioned, and went to the door.

Now it was Mercy's turn to be shocked. Her father seemed to have aged twenty years overnight. His posture was stooped, and his sun-darkened skin had turned an ashen gray that gave him a peculiar waxy look. He seemed to be tugging his body forward, as if dragging a heavy weight behind him.

Mercy advanced into the hall and bade her father a good-morning. Benjamin Randall lurched to a halt and looked up at her, staring for a moment as if he weren't sure who she was. "Ah, yes, Mercy. I must see Mr. Murchester and then Mr. Mitchell at the bank. Mr. Chase has already sent word that he will hold a service at four o'clock. I suppose that will give me enough time to visit all the families."

"I will go with you today, Papa," she said. He responded with a gesture as if to shoo her away. "Please, Papa, it will be a great comfort to me. But I need a few moments to speak to Sarah. She doesn't know yet."

"I've told her. You've been spared little enough in this. But I don't know if I made it any easier for my poor little one...." He trailed off helplessly.

"Caroline will go in to her," Mercy assured him. "She'll be all right. She's a strong, resourceful child."

Caroline, who had been watching the exchange between her sister and her father with a feeling of helpless horror, willed herself into action. She found her voice and came into the hall. "I'll go right now. Then we'll both dress to receive callers. You get your cloak and hat, Mercy. I'll see to everything here—refreshments and meals." She managed a small, brave smile. "Don't worry about anything. For once I shall be the efficient, single-minded sister." Then she threw her arms around Mercy.

Mercy returned her sister's embrace and thanked her.

"Your mother would be proud of you both," Captain Randall mumbled weakly, "if not of me."

"Now, Papa," Caroline chided, "you know that's not true."

"Do I?" her father responded.

The day was a long and grueling one. Mercy and her father walked first to his office. While her father attended to business matters, Mercy wrote letters to the families of *Abishai* men who were not from Nantucket. The officers and petty officers aboard the *Abishai* had been Nantucketers to a man, but the common seamen came from all over the world. Some were Nantucket men, and others came from nearby Salem, New Bedford or Martha's Vineyard, but a few hailed from the farming villages of western

Massachusetts or New York. One letter would go to a family of free Negroes living in Philadelphia, another to the Western Islands, a third to the far-off Marquesas Islands in the South Pacific. Two of the forecastle hands had no fixed addresses. They were drifters, rough men apparently without family ties. Still, they had been someone's sons, someone's brothers, perhaps even someone's fathers, and Mercy regretted the fact that their deaths would go unnoticed and unremarked.

Nathaniel himself had no family. He was an only child whose parents had died when he was an infant. His father's half sisters had raised him, but these maiden aunts had both died, within weeks of each other, the year before she and Nathaniel married. Of course, she would have to write to Aunt Elizabeth, who had been her closest confidante as a married woman. To her only could Mercy reveal her private conviction that her widowhood was a hoax. But that task was best left for another time, perhaps this evening when she was alone and could examine her mind thoroughly and choose her words with meticulous care.

Business concluded and letters posted, Mercy and her father set off on their rounds. They began by calling on Isabelle Hussey, wife of the *Abishai*'s captain, and then worked their way down through the ranks until they had walked Nantucket Town six times over and offered such words of consolation as they could to the bereaved families. As they left each desolated household, it seemed to Mercy that the weight her father towed grew heavier. He struggled more with each step, and by the time they reached the church he seemed to be using all his strength to fight it.

Mercy sat dry-eyed through the service, despite Mr. Chase's eloquent sermon and the muffled sobs, all the more affecting for their restraint, that now and then disturbed the otherwise still air in the church. Though she had passed the day in the presence of grief, Mercy had yet to feel any herself.

After the service the Randall family made their way slowly back to Orange Street, where they sat down to a simple meal of beef and vegetable soup. No one made more than a perfunctory attempt at eating, and when the barely touched plates had been cleared, the family retired to the back parlor where Caroline stared at the pages of a book, Sarah took out her sewing unbidden, Mercy sat lost in thought and Captain Randall dozed uneasily in front of the fire. At seven o'clock Mercy announced that she was going to order tea and then retire to her room. Emily brought in the tray shortly, and Mercy commenced to pour. She handed cups to Sarah and Caroline and then brought one to their father.

But when she reached his chair, she saw immediately that the dear man was past needing tea or anything else from the mortal world. Quietly she set down the superfluous cup and whispered to Caroline that she must take Sarah to her room and send Mary to fetch Uncle Thomas. "Papa is not ill. He is at peace now," she explained.

When her sister's meaning became clear, Caroline felt herself begin to fall into a faint. She forced herself to stay upright, ordered her head to clear and did as she was bid. Sarah, too stunned by the day's events to protest, left the room docilely, calling a soft good-night to her papa on her way.

That innocent farewell was more than Mercy could bear. Quickly she shut the parlor door behind her sisters. She turned and started toward the chair where her father was, but before she reached the middle of the room, the grief she had evaded all day accosted her, like a vicious and greedy highwayman who comes from behind, bent not just on robbery but on the destruction of everything good in life. She struggled mightily against the thief, but he was too strong, too determined to overcome her, and she succumbed to a bout of silent but inconsolable sobbing.

Through her despair she was vaguely aware of the door knocker, of Emily admitting a visitor. How like Uncle Thomas to come so quickly, she thought with relief. She felt a pair of strong arms surround her from behind, and she collapsed into them. She was so tired of being brave, of waiting, of thinking of everyone but herself. In that moment she wept for the loss not only of her father, but also of her youth and her innocence. She had always thought life essentially good, but could it be so when she had been robbed of her father, when she longed to know why her husband had been silent for so long, when she could not accept his death in a godforsaken land halfway around the globe?

She clung tighter and pressed closer to her uncle, giving up all pretense of strength and taking much-needed succor from the powerful embrace. Not until she felt a clean-shaven cheek brush lightly against her hair did her overwhelming wave of self-pity recede. Uncle Thomas had whiskers, she thought in a moment of sudden clarity. She wheeled around and looked up—into the shining black eyes of Captain Sam Starbuck.

"What will you do now, Mercy?" Maria Mitchell asked her friend when they were alone late the following evening. Benjamin Randall had been buried that afternoon, and Caroline and Sarah, exhausted, had gone to their rooms. After two nights without sleep, Mercy was beyond exhaustion. She doubted she would ever sleep again and was grateful for Maria's offer to spend the night with her.

"I don't know yet. Nathaniel and I had nothing but what Papa settled on us at our marriage. What's left of Papa's money will come to me, with provisions for Caroline and Sarah, of course. Uncle Thomas is the executor, but he says I must do as I please. Perhaps," she said on a whim, "I shall take over my father's business."

"And perhaps I shall take a trip to the moon. I would very much like to see what it looks like up close."

Mercy smiled lightly. "Actually, it's not as preposterous as it seems. Indeed, why shouldn't I? I need something more than domesticity to occupy my time, and why should I pay someone to do a thing I can do perfectly well myself? My father confided in me a great deal about his business dealings. It's not as if I am totally unschooled."

"I do not doubt your ability to manage a whaling business, Mercy. It is the gossip business I wonder about."

"I am a childless widow of twenty-three, Maria, with two unmarried sisters to care for. What could anyone say to me or about me that could hurt more than the loss of my parents and my husband?"

"The coldness and disapproval of one's neighbors can be more painful than you suspect, dear Mercy."

Mercy reached for her friend's hand. "And I always thought it didn't bother you."

"Bother me? You think I don't even notice it," Maria rejoined.

"So you do see what is not at the end of a telescope?" Mercy asked playfully.

"It's good to see you smile again, Mercy."

The next morning Mercy and Maria left the house on Orange Street, Maria to her observatory atop the Pacific Bank, Mercy to her father's office on the wharf. There was much to be decided now that the *Abishai* was lost, and Mercy spent the next several hours poring over the account books and legal documents. Finally, figures swimming in her head like schools of fish, she went to the window and looked out on the wharf. Her hold empty, the *Meribah* bobbed high in the water, the only ship at the pier not the object of feverish activity. All the others were being unloaded or repaired for the next voyage, but the *Meribah* stood idle, her fate uncertain for the moment. Should she sell her or have her fitted out for another voyage, Mercy wondered.

She could not sell, she decided. That would be like parting with a portion of her father's memory. The thought, however, of spending the rest of her life in this office was not a comforting one, either. She would never marry again. How could she when she doubted Nathaniel's demise? Even if she was sure of her widowhood, any Nantucket man she might marry would be a whaling man, and how could she again endure the loneliness and uncertainty of such long separations?

What I would like to do, Mercy thought suddenly, is sail on the *Meribah* myself. She was weary of living through others. Why should she not see the world firsthand, and know the thrills and dangers of chasing a leviathan? Why should she accept the secondhand and, she suspected, partial tale of the *Abishai*'s undoing? Why should she not go to the Black Islands herself to see if Nathaniel had escaped, like the two seamen picked up by the *Mary Grant?*

At that moment Mercy saw a dark figure hurry down the *Meribah*'s gangway. Driven by the wind of her musings, she flew through the outer office and out onto the wharf. "Captain Starbuck! A word with you, if you please."

"Mrs. Wright," he said evenly, despite his surprise at the summons. Since the night of her father's death, Mercy had barely looked at him. He suspected she was more than a little embarrassed by her loss of composure that evening. If truth were told, he himself was somewhat chagrined. In Benjamin Randall he had lost the closest thing he'd ever had to a father. His embrace of Mercy on that occasion had been far too familiar, far too full of emotion, on his side as well as hers. They had clung to each other with a need that went beyond seeking solace in mutual bereavement. "Can I be of some assistance?" he asked when they were installed in Ben's office. He kept his voice carefully casual and avoided looking at Mercy.

She didn't answer for a moment. "Were you serious when you said you would offer Maria Mitchell a berth on the *Meribah?*"

A curious sense of relief poured over him. Was that all she wanted? "Why do you ask? Has she requested one?"

"Would you say yes if she had?"

"I hold no superstitions about having a woman on board, if that's what you mean."

"Good. Because you *will* have a woman on board when the *Meribah* next sails."

"And who might that be, Mrs. Wright?" He was fast tiring of this cat-and-mouse game.

"Me."

"What?" he exploded. "What possible reason could you have for wanting to go a-whaling? Miss Mitchell I can understand, but you?"

"I intend to search for my husband, Captain."

"You're mad, madam. Your husband is dead."

"Perhaps. Two men from the *Abishai* lived. Is it reasonable to suspect that others may have survived, my husband among them?"

Starbuck's entire demeanor darkened. "In this case, it is entirely unreasonable."

"How can you be so sure? Do you have information I do not?"

"I know the Black Islands, Mrs. Wright. I know the treachery of the natives, the perfidy of their ways. They do things you cannot even imagine."

"Do you mean they eat people, Captain?"

"That is the least of it." Starbuck took a deep breath. He must somehow convince Mercy to abandon this madness, without breaking his promise to Ben. "I beg you to reconsider, Mrs. Wright. I understand the depth of your grief—"

"Do you, Captain?"

"Yes, damn it, I do. My connection to your father was the only close one in my life. I have no sisters, no home, no family that cares a whit about me except that I do not sully the Starbuck name. Stay home, Mrs. Wright. Tend to your sisters. Find another husband. Live in the world as you find it, instead of chasing around the world after a ghost."

"A pretty speech, Captain," Mercy returned hotly, "but one that does not sway me. I sail with the *Meribah,* whether or not you are at her helm."

Starbuck opened his mouth to protest, but found himself laughing instead. "I have always admired a man—or a woman—who fights to win." He himself was one of them, and now, he sensed, was the moment to call her bluff and take his prize. "All right, if you still want to go when the *Meribah* sets sail in July, I will not object."

To his surprise, however, *she* called *his* bluff. "In April, Captain."

"Impossible," he countered.

"When you have killed a whale, do you stop work at nightfall? Do you allow your crew to sleep? No, you light the cresset lamps and double the watch until the whale is tried and the oil stored. That is what we'll do here. Hire two crews and work both from first light until curfew."

Though he liked winning, Starbuck did not needlessly expend energy on a fight already lost, and he could see that Mercy's determination was unshakable. Why not ready the *Meribah* and sail, even if it meant taking her along? He had found little enough pleasure in Nantucket this homecoming. Idling away a summer here was only slightly more appealing than a month becalmed in the broiling sun at the equator. "Then I advise you to protect your hearing, Mrs. Wright. Between the roar of wagging tongues and the noise of the saws and hammers and anvils, you may go quite deaf. We all may." He rose and strode purposefully out of the office.

Mercy allowed herself a moment for exultation, but before her resolve could be weakened by the enormity of what she was about to do, she sat down to begin her preparations. First, she must write to Aunt Elizabeth, asking if Caroline might come to her. Then she must call on Uncle Thomas and Aunt Lavinia to ask if they would be so kind as to take Sarah into their home. She thought these arrangements would suit her sisters. Caroline would get her long-dreamed-of taste of Boston society, and Sarah would continue among familiar friends and surroundings.

There were other letters to write, as well, to solicitors and banks, insurance brokers and creditors. Mercy reached into the top drawer of the desk for writing paper, pulling out all of the few pieces that remained. The bottom three had gone astray from the rest of the small pile, and as she attempted to straighten the stack she noticed there was writing, in her papa's hand, on the errant pages. Two were orders for paints and a piano. The third was a sketch of a house. At the top of the page was written, "Siasconset Cottage. For Mercy."

Mercy's eyes blurred with tears. Poor Papa, he'd written the orders the day the *Meribah* docked, but had been too busy to send them. She blinked and wiped away her tears from the back of one hand. With the other she held Papa's sketch away from her, so as not to mar the ink should she start to weep again. How dear of him. He had been going to build her a cottage on the ocean side of the island, a place she loved for its wildness, its starkness. She felt her resolve to leave Nantucket waver as she studied the plans. Four square rooms, two downstairs, two up, all facing the sea.

Papa had never envisaged her leaving Nantucket, but then Papa had never thought she would be alone and responsible for the family. He had expected Nathaniel to be with her. Her world had taken an entirely different turning now, and she must spin with it or forever regret her timidity. Carefully she put away the drawing and the orders, preserving them between the folds of a larger sheet of paper. Someday, when she returned, she would show them to Caroline and Sarah.

Chapter Four

To continue my tale I must introduce a change of venue. We must leave Nantucket Town, cross Nantucket Sound, skirt Martha's Vineyard, sail over Buzzards Bay and land in New Bedford, Massachusetts, another place where the whaling industry is paramount.

We'll skip the clatter and clang of the wharf and business district and go straight to a modest dwelling on Cook Street. In the kitchen of this house, two women—one about fifty, stocky and spry, the other seventeen, lean and willowy—are working. They are the women of the Harding family, Jane and her mother, Kate. The eight men of the Harding family, from James at the head to young John at the foot, are all a-whaling, no two on the same vessel. Tacked up on one wall of the room is a map of the world, stuck in various places with colored pins. As letters are received, Jane and Kate move the pins from one location to another. It is their only way of keeping track of their men.

On the fine April afternoon to which I refer, Jane and Kate were engaged, as usual, in the chosen enterprise of the distaff side of the Harding family—fine laundering and finishing. They mend, wash and iron fancy linen from the grand houses owned by whaling captains and other maritime industrialists. Their work is much admired by the ladies of these houses, who declare to a one that a lace shawl or tablecloth mended by Kate or Jane looks as good, or better, than when it was new.

Having finished with the small tear in the lace gloves that Miss Abigail Quincy absolutely had to have for that evening, Jane reached for her shawl. "I'll just deliver these, Mother, and be right back."

"Fine, dear," Kate replied without looking up from her work on the intricate trim of a linen bedsheet. "Will we be entertaining Mr. Culpepper this evening?"

"He did say he might stop by after supper." Jane picked up the gloves, wrapped them in a clean cotton towel and headed quickly for the door. But her mother kept talking. Jane waited impatiently.

"Then you must serve him some of your pecan cookies. It never hurts to show a young man you're a passable cook."

"Yes, ma'am," she replied dutifully. "I really must go now. Miss Quincy will be 'prostrate with worry,'" she mimicked Miss Quincy's dramatic delivery, "if I don't get there soon."

Actually Jane didn't care a fig for Miss Abigail Quincy or her silly gloves. Whatever was the point of wearing gloves except to keep your hands warm? She was in a hurry because she had finally saved enough money to buy the last necessary item—a pocketknife—for her seabag. Everything else was ready: shirts and trousers made from her brothers' castoffs; a pea jacket, cap and muffler; a wide band of canvas that, when wrapped tightly around her breasts, concealed them; thread, needles and scissors; a tin cup, plate and spoon. Once she had the knife she would be set to go.

After months of careful scheming—hiding anything from her mother was the devil's own work—it was hard to believe she might actually be setting her plan in motion soon. But it could happen any day now. Then she too would be going to sea, as all her brothers had done, as she would have done if she hadn't had the wretched luck to be born a girl.

Her errand completed and a dandy knife stowed in the pocket of her sturdy cotton skirt, Jane hurried home,

stopping a block from the house to catch her breath. She
had to be especially cautious now. She must not do anything to set her mother's all-too-active mind to work.

When Jane sauntered in the back door, Kate had already put away the irons and kettles, packed the threads
and shuttles in their cases and begun cooking the evening
meal—fried oysters and boiled potatoes with bacon. Jane's
appetite, always hearty, was honed sharper by excitement
tonight. As she laid the table she inhaled hungrily, trying to
memorize all the tantalizing smells. Her mother's fine food
was one thing she knew she would miss at sea. Father and
the boys complained interminably about the food aboard
ship—the salted meat known as salt horse; the hard biscuits that were often moldy or worse; coffee so strong it was
the color and consistency of mud; and drinking water that
was slimy and foul. But to Jane this seemed a fair trade for
endless days on the open ocean. She wouldn't need to eat,
she would be nourished by the salt air itself.

After the meal, Jane and her mother tidied up the kitchen
quickly and settled themselves in the parlor. Kate picked up
her sewing, but Jane could do nothing productive. Even the
latest installment by Mr. Dickens failed to capture her
imagination. She was vastly relieved when Tommy Culpepper finally knocked at the door. After a few minutes of
polite chatter over cookies and milk, Tommy proposed they
go for a stroll. Usually Jane had to be the one to suggest an
activity that would get them out of her mother's earshot,
but tonight—as soon as he'd drained his milk and eaten
half the cookies on the plate—Tommy brought up the idea
himself. Permission secured from Mrs. Harding, Jane and
Tommy walked out into the cool of the spring evening.

As soon as they turned the corner, Tommy grabbed
Jane's hand clumsily. "I know this is sudden, Jane, but I'm
leaving tomorrow. I don't know when I'll be able to send
for you, but I will, as soon as I'm settled in Ohio. You still
want to come, don't you?"

"Of course I do." Jane was grateful for the cover of
darkness. She hated lying, but it was a necessary evil if her

plan was to succeed. She knew she could never live a contented life until she had at least tried to get to sea. If that meant deceiving Tommy Culpepper, well, she was very sorry, but that's what it meant. She would have felt somewhat less guilty if the task had not been so easy. But Tommy was not one to delve too deeply into things. He believed what he saw and what he was told. On the other hand, she hoped he also would not be hurt too badly by what she was about to do.

"I'll write every week," he promised.

"Oh, no, don't do that." Jane thought quickly. She couldn't have Tommy sending letters. Her mother's heart was going to be broken as it was. "Don't write me until you're settled. It'll make me miss you too much."

Tommy pulled her close and fumbled for her mouth before planting a hasty, breathless kiss on it. He'd never taken such a liberty before, and Jane was too stunned to do anything but let him. But it was over soon enough and as harmless as an affectionate lick from a frisky puppy.

"Will you visit my mother once I'm gone? She had such high hopes that I'd be the son to stay home with her. And I would have, until you started talking about going west. I know now it's what I'm meant to do. I could never stomach the thought of going to sea and being cooped up on a ship for years on end. That's why I apprenticed myself to a carpenter. But now that I've been thinking about those wide open spaces in the West, even New Bedford seems small and cramped. I just wish Ma didn't rely on me so much. She's got my sisters close by, but since Pa's ship was lost she wants me to stay right here."

"Try not to worry about her, Tommy. She'll get used to you going. The women around here have to get used to their men being away. There wouldn't be a single one of us left alive if all we did was sit around and pine." She never had been able to see the justice in the men being the ones to go away all the time. Now she was going to see what it was like on the other side of the fence.

Tommy squeezed her hand. "That's what I like most about you, Jane. You're so practical. I don't care much for a fainting kind of woman."

"Neither do I, Tommy." She spoke so forcefully that she had to laugh at herself, and Tommy joined in. Then they started back to the house. "You've got to act as if nothing is going on," Jane admonished when they reached her corner. "My mother mustn't suspect. I'll never get her to consent to my going out to meet you if she thinks we had it all planned."

"You do think of everything, don't you?"

"I try to."

Tommy took both her hands in his and pressed them to his chest. "I'll be thinking of you, Jane. All the time."

"Don't you waste your time mooning over me, Tommy Culpepper. You just keep your mind on getting to Ohio."

"All right. I'll only think about you now and again. But you can't stop me from doing that."

This time when he embraced her, Jane embraced him back. It wasn't as if she was forcing him to go west. She'd only planted the seed in his mind. Tommy himself was the one who'd watered it and made it grow. If she wasn't sure he'd be happy there, she'd never have let things go this far. But there was no turning back now.

Tommy said good-night to Mrs. Harding and asked if he might call on Jane again on Saturday. Then he winked at Jane and left. Jane stood at the open door, listening to him whistle softly as he disappeared down the street. Then she turned to her mother and with an ostentatious yawn said she was going up to bed. Kate bade her a pleasant night.

Upstairs Jane sat on the bunk in the tiny cubbyhole she had inhabited since she was a child of three or so. It fit snugly in the hall between the two upstairs rooms—the one where her parents slept and the other, larger room, stacked with bunks, that had served as a dormitory for the boys. Even after her younger brother John had vacated the dormitory, she remained loyal to her little space. She liked the coziness of it, the way she kept her belongings in a chest at the foot of the bunk, as if she were at sea.

Digging deep into the chest, she pulled out her breast band, shirt and trousers, put them on and slipped her nightgown over the whole outfit. She checked her canvas seabag one more time, looking twice to be sure she had the scissors with which she would lop off her thick honey-blond braid. Then she stuffed the bag with as many of her clothes as it would hold. These she could sell in Nantucket to supplement the few pennies she would have after she paid for her passage out of New Bedford and for her room and board until she could sign a ship's articles.

Her preparations complete, Jane climbed under the covers and pretended to sleep. She listened for the sound of her mother's footsteps on the stairs, for the creaking of her bed, for the even, soft breaths that meant she was asleep. Lying absolutely still, she waited as the minutes dripped by like cold treacle. Finally, when the parlor clock struck three, she rose, doffed her nightgown, hefted her seabag in one hand and her brogues in another, and in her bare feet crept down the stairs.

The next moments were much different than she had imagined. Jane wanted desperately to go to sea, but as she took her last look around the downstairs rooms, she felt a sudden pang. Call it doubt or conscience, fear or excitement. Whatever it was, it kept her from dashing out the door immediately. Her home was more dear to her than she had realized. True, she had been bored to distraction by learning and practicing her mother's trade, but she would miss this house and her mother. She stopped for a moment to pack a few final items: memories of her favorite things. There was the brown earthenware crock on the table, which in summer was often filled with wildflowers from the surrounding meadows; the clock shaped like a mermaid, ticking away in the parlor; the rich, buttery smell of her mother's breakfast biscuits.

Her memory stuffed as full as her seabag, she dug from the pocket of her pea jacket the note she had written to her

mother, explaining her elopement to Ohio with Tommy
Culpepper and apologizing for leaving her alone. This she
propped up against the crock. Then she wrapped a ration
of bread and cheese in a clean cloth and slipped away into
the night.

The scene Jane encountered on the dock in Nantucket the
following afternoon was much the same as the one she
knew so well from home, with one distinct difference. The
smell. The air was saltier and sharper here, all sea, with
hardly any smell of land at all. Racing down the gangplank, Jane reveled in the feeling of freedom that came
from wearing trousers. Without skirts and petticoats flapping around her ankles, she could take long strides,
stretching out her legs as far as they would go with each
step. Not that she had ever affected a mincing female gait,
like Miss Abigail Quincy and her gaggle. Still the simple
ability to move from one place to another without en-
cumbrance was exhilarating.

As she wandered along the wharf, dodging wheel-
barrows, drunken sailors, men carrying sacks and lengths
of timber and women hawking bread and buns, she tried to
imitate the male carriage. She stuck out her chin as if it were
a sail and moved as if the wind were at her back. Her neck
was a movable mast, craning and swiveling to catch the
wind. Keeping her legs well apart, she let the top half of her
body sway in concert with the bottom half, and swung her
arms back and forth in an easy rhythm. It felt more like
rolling than walking to her, so effortless after years of at-
tempting to limit her movements to those deemed proper
for a female. Growing up had taught her many painful les-
sons, but throwing off the carefree deportment of childhood had been one of the hardest. Assuming the rigid back
and slightly downcast eyes expected of an adult woman had
been difficult, but abandoning such behavior was a joy.
Soon she was swaggering down the dock as if she'd been
doing it for years.

"Looking for a berth, sailor?" Jane saw the unkempt, wooden-legged man approach her, but for a moment did not realize he was speaking to her. "Not deaf, are you, boy?"

"No!" she declared, remembering to deepen her tones. "Do you know of a place? Is there a ship going out soon?"

"It's only the green ones are so eager. Old Billy-Boy can spot one every time." The man gave a cackling laugh, somewhere between protest and resignation, which reminded Jane of a chicken that knows it's about to become your supper. "The *Meribah*'s leaving tomorrow. They're a hand short. Follow me."

Jane was rather dismayed that she had been spotted so easily as one who'd never been to sea. She thought the clothes she'd chosen and the seabag gave her an authentic air, and that she might have been thought a former cabin boy. On the other hand, the man hadn't asked why a girl was trying to get to sea, although she had to admit the reek of strong drink on his breath suggested that his powers of observation might have been dulled.

The wooden peg was no impediment to Billy-Boy's movements. He navigated the crowded dock like an experienced captain in waters he knows so well he doesn't need to consult a chart, and Jane soon found herself inside the offices of Benj. Randall and Co., Whaling Merchant. "This one's greener than a new cabbage, Mr. Murchester," her benefactor said with another raucous squawk. "But as willing as a Taheeti maiden." He held out a hand darkened by sun and dirt in equal proportions. "I'll take my wages, if you please."

"If he signs, Billy-Boy." Grumbling, Billy-Boy withdrew to a corner of the room.

Jane stood stock-still under Mr. Murchester's scrutiny, forcing herself to meet his eyes. "How old are you, boy?"

"Seventeen," Jane replied, exulting to herself. This one wasn't drunk. She'd be surprised if Mr. Murchester had ever smelled liquor, except on a sailor's breath, much less tasted it.

"Barely," Murchester said baldly. "Where are you from?"

"New Bedford, sir." She'd already decided to stick as close to the truth as she could without giving herself away.

"Then why come all the way to Nantucket to find a berth?"

Jane was ready with her tale. "My father and my seven brothers are all at sea, sir. My mother didn't want me to go, too, and Pa promised her I wouldn't. She thinks I've gone west, but all I've ever wanted to do was go a-whaling."

"Then you know what you're getting yourself into, eh?"

"Oh, yes, sir," Jane replied eagerly.

Murchester gave her one last appraising look, then handed her a piece of paper. "Can you read, boy? What's your name?"

"Harding, sir. John Harding. It says I'm signing the articles of the ship *Meribah* as a foremast hand and that my lay is one two-hundredth of the ship's profits."

"If there are any, and less any purchases you make from the slop chest. Sign here." Murchester dipped the pen into the inkwell on his desk and handed it to her. She took it and signed the articles firmly and proudly. "And here." She wrote John Harding again in the ship's book. Murchester blotted both signatures and handed the papers. "That's the *Meribah*. Be on her at first light." Then he reached into his waistcoat pocket, extracted a coin and tossed it in Billy-Boy's direction. The one-legged man caught it and thumped rapidly out the door. "I might as well give the money directly to the saloon keeper," Murchester complained. "That's all, Harding. What are you waiting for?" He waved his hand at her impatiently, as if she were an annoying insect.

"Nothing, sir, I don't know, sir." Without looking, Jane started for the door, when she felt herself collide with a large moving object.

"Watch where you're going, lad," it shouted gruffly.

"Captain Starbuck," Murchester piped up in his thin, reedy voice. "The *Meribah*'s got a full complement now. I've just signed young Harding here."

The black-eyed, black-haired man narrowed his eyes and inspected her dispassionately, as if she were a barrel or a bucket. It was harder to stand still this time. The captain's scrutiny was not as quick or as superficial as Murchester's. Jane felt a telltale blush rise to her cheeks. She cursed herself silently. Of all the foolish female things... But she forced herself to meet the captain's look as he took her measure. "Face as smooth as a girl's," he observed.

I'm finished, Jane thought. This man was no fool, no office cipher looking for an easy end to the day's work.

"Let me see your hands," he demanded. She held them out and with some difficulty kept them from shaking. Luckily the hot water and heavy irons of her trade had roughened her hands. "You may not have set a sail yet, Harding, but you've worked at something." A broad smile creased the captain's face. "We'll soon toughen you up, my lad." But suddenly he stopped smiling and gave her a stern look. "Make no mistake," he warned.

Jane swallowed hard. I won't. Not on your ship. I don't judge you'd look kindly on that. "No, sir, Captain. I mean yes, sir, Captain. Thank you. May I go now, sir?"

Starbuck threw back his head and let out a thunderous laugh, so loud Jane almost jumped. "Where in creation did you find a polite sailor, Mr. Murchester? Oh, what a voyage this is going to be!"

With that the captain stomped off into the inner office, and Mr. Murchester picked up his pen. Jane took it that she was dismissed and hurried back outside. But once she was outside she stopped rushing. What reason had she to rush any longer? She was free as a bird until dawn. She slowed her pace to an amble, surveying the scene with new eyes. Now she belonged. She was an articled seaman. Or seawoman, she thought with a giggle. Ravenously hungry, she parted with a few precious pennies to buy an orange and a roll stuffed with fried sausage. Forcing herself to eat slowly and savor her meal, she walked back and forth in front of the *Meribah*. Jane had heard enough cautionary tales from her father and brothers to know that the condition of a whaling vessel was a clue to the quality of the voyage and the disposition of the captain. With some relief she saw that the ship that was to be her home for the next three or four years was clean and well fitted. And apparently well provisioned. From the skids above the deck, where rested two of the *Meribah*'s whaleboats, hung scores of cabbages, as well as two sides of beef. Not that Jane expected to taste any of that. Fresh meat would be served to the officers and petty officers, not the foremast hands.

As she finished her sausage roll, taking minuscule bites to make it last as long as possible, she turned her attention to a carpenter and his helper, who were putting the finishing touches on a tall, narrow structure on the larboard side of the foredeck. Jane had never seen such a thing on a whaler before, and she had stared at it for several moments before she realized what it was. A head for the sailors! Attending to her bodily functions had been one of Jane's greatest worries, but it was no more. She tossed her orange gleefully into the air. Having met Captain Starbuck, she couldn't believe he was *that* solicitous of his men's welfare. But whoever Benj. Randall was, he was a generous and farsighted owner.

Taking off down the dock again, Jane peeled her orange, stowing the strips in her seabag. As the peel dried, it would keep her clothes smelling fresh. She passed a merchant schooner, a whaling bark and then encountered a Boston-bound mail packet receiving its last cargo and passengers. At the foot of the gangway a compelling scene was taking place. Two young women and a girl, remarkably similar in person despite their divergent ages, were huddled together on the dock. The younger of the two women, wearing a traveling suit of maroon serge that even Jane recognized as stylish, was weeping. The older, all in black, was fighting tears. The girl was dry-eyed but from the look on her face was perhaps the most disturbed of the three. Finally they embraced one last time and the woman in maroon mounted the gangplank. She looked back every other step, calling out tearful messages about Aunt Elizabeth and long letters. The others waved and smiled bravely.

In that moment Jane was acutely aware that no one would be sending her off to sea with tears and embraces. She regretted not having bade her mother goodbye and thought with a sting of conscience of her mother alone in the house on Cook Street, tatting and washing and ironing from morning till night. Her mother was not one for idle chatter, but her many sharp and amusing observations would now find only an occasional audience. The feeling of guilt was so strong that Jane had an urge to charge down the dock, seeking a boat bound for New Bedford. She stood still and waited for it to pass, which it did, but only after the girl and the woman in black had disappeared down the dock.

Following this incident, Jane began to realize that she was very tired and as yet had no place to pass the night. She inquired from a passing sailor and was directed to a boardinghouse on Whale Street run by a Mrs. Betsy Bostle. There the coldly efficient landlady supplied her with a bowl of fish chowder—hot but more water than milk and more fish heads than fish, relieved her of seven cents and sent her upstairs to a minute, airless chamber that contained a narrow bed and two rough chairs. The bed was already occupied by a large dark-skinned sailor who reeked of something. Not of drink, however. It had not the sour, used smell of drink. It was sharper, more penetrating and yet sweeter, though in a sickly way it seemed to Jane. It put her in mind of onions, but was yet quite unlike the mild and pleasant odor of that useful vegetable. The creature was also emitting loud, gurgling snores that seemed to set the bed and the walls of the tiny room vibrating.

Jane looked longingly at the bed. Weary as she was and as much as she would have liked to spend her last night on land in a bed, the prospect of many hours' close proximity to the menacing figure already in occupancy prompted her to draw the two chairs together. It was not the fact that he was a man that made her cell mate menacing. The day's experiences had left her secure in the efficacy of her disguise. She feared no untoward advances in the night. Rather it was the man's bulk, his strangeness, his face that looked more like a mask than the pliable visages she was used to seeing on human beings.

You'll see stranger than this, she warned herself, plumping her seabag into a pillow. Which is precisely what you wanted. This stern reminder failed to allay Jane's uneasiness, but sheer exhaustion carried her away from it, and despite discomfort and apprehension, she slept heavily and without dreams that night.

Several blocks away on Orange Street, Mercy too was in a disquieting environment. With Caroline sailed, Sarah already settled in with Uncle Thomas and Aunt Lavinia, and Emily dispatched to a new position with Mr. and Mrs. Coffin, she had the house to herself. She was spending the first night of her life alone. She had always found the night a comforting, friendly time when the soul was set free in unrestrained thoughts and dreams, but tonight she saw in the dark hours the fearsome, diabolical nature many claimed for them. Unbidden images rose in her mind— Nathaniel as a haggard, near-crazed fugitive, Captain Starbuck as a kind, gentle healer—turning her well-ordered world upside down. Ascribing her confusion to loneliness and apprehension, she let the exhaustion of the last days pull her into sleep.

Chapter Five

Just before dawn Jane woke with a start, momentarily surprised not to find herself in her bunk at home. But a rumbling snore and the odor of onions gone mad reminded her where she was. She leaped off the chair, tipping it over in the process, but the noise did not disturb her slumbering companion. Indeed she vacated the room without him ever having known of her existence. Downstairs her landlady chided her for the noise and handed her a mug of hot coffee and a plate of leaden biscuits coated with a thin layer of fatty bacon gravy. Jane downed hers silently, as did the other guests, and hastily took her leave of Mrs. Bostle's poor establishment.

Despite the lingering darkness, the dock was beginning to bustle. The activity served only to whet Jane's appetite to be under sail. She boarded the *Meribah* with alacrity and was told by a petty officer to go below to the fo'c'sle, pick a bunk and stow her gear. She hurried to the forward hatch and scurried down the ladder.

It was at the moment that she reached bottom Jane had her first moment of true doubt about her adventure. The forecastle, a small semicircular room wedged into the prow of the boat, was ringed with a double tier of twenty small berths. It was lit by a single smoking lantern, which cast a gloomy, forbidding light. Although only about half the foremast hands had arrived, the place was already packed with bodies, most of whom had only a passing, if any, acquaintance with the cleansing properties of soap and water. The only air to be had was whatever blew down the hatch, when it was open. The ship was newly cleaned and freshly painted, but the atmosphere below was already musty smelling and uncomfortably warm.

Jane hesitated on the threshold, unwilling to enter but knowing that she had no choice. She had signed the ship's articles; there was no chance of being let off the *Meribah* now. She might as well swallow her medicine. Waiting would not make it more palatable, she decided. Before she could take a step, however, she heard a voice, large and deep but also cheerful and lilting, call out to her.

"Don't be shy now, young sir. It's not such a bad place once you get used to it." Peering among the shadows, Jane determined that the voice was coming from a huge, square figure of a man. When her eyes had adjusted to the gloom, she saw the speaker was the largest Negro she had ever seen, so tall that he could not stand to his full height in the fo'c'sle and so broad that his shoulders spanned double the width of the two grinning, giggling brown-skinned fellows who flanked him. This pair was large by any standard, except when measured against the gigantic Negro. The tops of their heads pressed against the ceiling, and their shoulders strained the worn seams of the twilled kersey shirts they wore. "I am Big Jack," the Negro continued, his words fairly bouncing around the crowded space like India rubber balls. "And these are my friends, Pete and Sweet, or so we call 'em, from the island of Tahiti, one of the most beautiful spots on God's green earth."

In comparison to Big Jack's, Jane's normally clear, audible voice sounded weak and trifling. "My name is John Harding. I'm happy to make your acquaintance."

"Happy to make your acquaintance," a mocking voice replied in such a high tone that Jane feared its owner might suspect her true nature. "What is this, some damned social club?" the man growled. Locating the speaker, Jane saw a tough, stringy sort of fellow. He reminded her of a rooster, long past his prime, who refuses to give way to the younger, handsomer birds in the barnyard.

"John Harding," Big Jack said, a hint of menace replacing some of the sunshine in his voice, "meet Crebbs. He's a hardworking tar, so hardworking he likes to make everything harder than it has to be." A crash of laughter followed these words, and the others in the fo'c'sle joined in, as did Jane.

"At least I'm not always laughing my head off like a fool," Crebbs rejoined in such a tone that the others who were laughing stopped immediately. Jane was not so quick to stifle her merriment, though, and Crebbs glared at her meanly. The look was so malicious that Jane averted her eyes, then immediately regretted her display of weakness. Crebbs was a type she recognized, a man who bolsters himself by preying on the disadvantages of those around him.

Disregarding the sullen Crebbs, Big Jack continued with the introductions. There were Pedro and Francisco, who reminded her in person and in aroma of her cell mate at Mrs. Bostle's. They were, she learned, from the Western Islands, the Portuguese outpost that would most probably be their first port of call. There were two more green hands, Aaron Cole and Owen Weeks, and a golden-skinned native of the Sandwich Islands whose long and unpronounceable name had been shortened to Kay. The remaining ten, as they arrived, proved to be a motley assortment of Americans, mostly from seafaring towns in Massachusetts, Rhode Island, Connecticut and New York.

The foremast hands were a rough lot, and Jane guessed that she was not only the solitary female among them, but the only one who could read and write more than her name. But, apart from Crebbs, they seemed courageous and congenial, and willing to pull together and make the best of whatever came their way.

At Big Jack's urging, Jane took the bunk directly above his. She recognized in this act that he was proclaiming himself her benefactor, and she was grateful. She could already see that as the youngest, weakest member of the crew, she would do well to cultivate the friendship of a stronger, more experienced seaman. She only hoped that her instinct about Big Jack was correct and that he would turn out to be friend indeed and not foe.

Not many blocks away, on Orange Street, Mercy was awake long before the church bells pealed. Sleep had dispelled the frightening uncertainties of the previous night, and she awoke with a clear head and a heart less burdened than in recent weeks. She dressed quickly in one of the simple black skirts that were to be her uniform on board the *Meribah,* topped it with a black blouse and packed her few personal items in a small tapestry bag. This morning she was glad she had insisted on saying goodbye to everyone the day before. Distancing herself from Sarah, from Uncle Thomas and Aunt Lavinia, from her friends, the Mitchells, before actually leaving *had* made the break easier. She felt quite ready to go now.

Mercy walked rapidly through the empty house, which, as her last duty, Emily would close later today. She was beginning to feel a kind of freedom and a growing impatience finally to embark on the mission she had taken upon herself. Saying a hurried goodbye to the only home she had ever known, she locked the door behind her, and made her way swiftly to the offices of Benj. Randall and Co. There she gave her final instructions to Mr. Murchester and went into her father's office to await the arrival of Captain Starbuck.

As she waited, her mind strayed to the sequence of events that had led her inexorably to this morning. She was deeply engrossed in contemplation when the door burst open, and Sarah, flushed and breathless and lugging a laden basket, flew in. "I've brought you a basket of food," she declared, "even though I was forbidden. I have a right to say goodbye to you, in my own way, even if you don't think it's good for me."

Taken aback, Mercy recovered her composure. "I only wanted to spare you pain, dear Sarah."

"You wanted to spare yourself! You can leave the basket here if you like, but I wanted to bring it." Sarah's fury softened. "It has all your favorite things. Just like we used to bring to Papa."

Mercy took Sarah in her arms. How she would miss her sister's fierce determination, her pride. "All right, pet," she soothed. "We'll stay together until I board."

An hour passed, in which Mercy and Sarah took new measure of each other. Sarah lost some of her anger at being left behind, and Mercy was assured of Sarah's ability to adjust to her new circumstances. Although outwardly unremarkable, this meeting changed the basis of their relationship, leaving them to part more as sisters than as surrogate mother and daughter. After the first few strained moments, they had begun to chat, aimlessly, as if they had time to spare. As they spoke, Sarah took up pencil and paper and began a likeness of Mercy seated at their father's desk.

When Captain Starbuck came upon the scene, he could not believe the calm of it. In the past weeks, as the *Meribah* drew closer to readiness, he had more and more regretted his decision to sail with Mercy aboard. What had he been thinking of? Nothing more than his own pique and restlessness. And what had he done? Invited a full-blown disaster aboard the *Meribah*. He should have given up his place rather than agree to this crazy scheme.

The placid scene he encountered in the office, far from quelling his reservations, served only to fuel them. Had he encountered weeping and wailing, he would have been much more confident. This quiet, however, seemed to him like the lull before a storm, a storm that would now break aboard his ship, damn it all. Not bothering to conceal his irritation, he informed the sisters that the time had come to board and unceremoniously hustled them out of the office.

Mercy was appalled by Starbuck's crude disruption of her and Sarah's farewell. Had he no shred of consideration—if not for her then for Sarah? She planted herself firmly in the middle of the dock, causing Sam to stop just short of treading hard on Sarah's heels. "Captain," she declared defiantly, "my sister and I will be one moment more."

"Do as you like now, Mrs. Wright," he allowed, "for as soon as you set foot on that gangplank, my word is law. Do we understand one another?"

"All too well," Mercy replied coolly. But she understood neither Sam Starbuck nor herself. She had always thought of herself as a sensible woman, but here she was, drawn only by the merest thread of hope, about to embark on a voyage around the world to find a man everyone said was dead. And what was more, for reasons she could not fathom, Sam Starbuck was allowing her to do so under his command. She very nearly asked to have her trunk removed from the ship, but instead she shelved her doubts and turned to her sister.

"Grow strong and true, pet, while I'm gone." She reached out and smoothed an errant lock of Sarah's chestnut hair. "And write to me often, as I will to you."

"Of course I will," Sarah promised. "I'll send sketches, too. Would you like that?"

A sudden, unbidden pang of sadness assailed Mercy as she was reminded of a similar pledge made on this wharf at the base of the *Abishai*'s gangplank. Only one participant in that pact had adhered to it. She turned her head aside so that Sarah would not see the pain in her face. "Of course I would like that." She formed her lips into a smile and faced her sister again. "Goodbye, Sarah." She took a last long look at the child she would never see again. When she returned, if she returned, Sarah would be a young woman. She hugged that child close for a moment, then pulled herself away. "I must go now."

"I know," Sarah said bravely. "I hope you find what you're looking for, Mercy."

"So do I, pet." With that, Mercy turned and mounted the gangplank.

Starbuck followed her, pausing to pinch Sarah's cheek and give the child a final wink. "I'll bring your sister home, little Sarah. That's my promise to you."

The child regarded him gravely. "You won't be so lonely with Mercy on board."

Starbuck had to laugh. "Perhaps you're right about that, little Sarah." Still chortling, he followed Mercy up the gangplank. *I may be less lonely*, he thought, *but I'm sure to have my hands full*. Then he straightened his shoulders and prepared to command the *Meribah*.

Below in the fo'c'sle, Jane had settled down to unpacking her few possessions and stowing them in her sea chest, which was one in a row lashed to the floor in front of the berths. As she worked she noticed a queasy feeling in her stomach, which she put down to the grim reality of the fo'c'sle. It couldn't be seasickness. After all, the boat was still in dock, and she had been out to sea fishing with her father and brothers hundreds of times, albeit in a much smaller vessel, without the merest twinge of seasickness.

Soon enough, though, Jane had more to think about than the state of her stomach. The hands were called on deck, and the process of dividing the men into watches began. The first mate was a Mr. Mayhew, and he was as handsome and refined a gentleman as Jane had ever seen. His golden hair sparkled in the sun, and his eyes were the color that she had always imagined the sea of the South Pacific to be. His figure was fine, too, straight and narrow and strong. Although his demeanor was serious and commanding, he had a ready smile and seemed to be a man with much feeling and compassion. The second mate, Mr. Hunter, was not so admirable a person. He was short, bald and from the down-turned corners of his mouth, appeared to be quite without humor.

Beginning with Mr. Mayhew, mate and second each chose a man from among the common seamen, to serve on their respective watches. Mr. Mayhew's first choice was Big

Jack. Mr. Hunter took Crebbs. Being chosen first was an honor, putting Big Jack and Crebbs in line to join the ranks of the petty officers should anything happen to those men. Despite his unappealing character, Crebbs must be a brave and seasoned whaleman, Jane reasoned.

Mayhew and Hunter continued to choose until only Jane and the other two green hands were left. Both officers examined the three closely, pacing back and forth before them until Jane began to feel quite uncomfortable. Mr. Hunter would have the first choice, and Jane found herself hoping that he would pass her over with a fervor that went beyond believing him to be the less understanding officer. When Hunter did choose the young man on her right, she felt a further sinking in her intestines and a concomitant rise when Mr. Mayhew pointed at her and said, "You!"

As she stepped forward to join the others in the mate's watch, their eyes met. For a split second Mr. Mayhew looked at her as if to say, *Who are you, and what are you doing here?* And Jane responded with an unreasonable urge to tell him. She felt herself redden, appalled at her behavior. How was she ever to maintain her guise if she let her thoughts turn to female foolishness at a mere glance from a handsome man? She had never engaged in this kind of inanity back in New Bedford, and this was certainly no time to start.

When the watches had been chosen, the men were assigned to a whaleboat crew headed by one of the four mates. Jane was again chosen by Mr. Mayhew, and again she rejoiced in her good fortune. When the *Meribah* encountered her first whale, she would go into battle with both Mr. Mayhew and Big Jack at her side. What other young woman in America, in the entire world, had ever been on such an adventure? At the thought her stomach rode another wave of happy turmoil.

With the men divided into their watches, it was now time for the captain to board, and up the gangplank he came. But he was not alone. Captain Starbuck was accompanied by the very lady Jane had seen on the dock saying goodbye to the traveler in maroon the previous afternoon. She stood beside the captain, surveying the deck as if assessing another woman's parlor for the efficiency—or deficiency—of her housekeeping. Could she be the captain's wife, Jane wondered. But they seemed a strange pair—the ebullient, unrestrained Captain Starbuck and the self-contained, even remote, lady. Perhaps they were only recently married and she was so subdued because this was her first time away from home. Still, there was another woman on board, and even though Jane could not reveal their sisterhood, there was surprising comfort in knowing that another of her sex was so near.

All was quiet on the deck as Captain Starbuck inspected his men. He greeted the officers and petty officers by name, which struck Jane as liberal but not shockingly so. However, when he addressed as many of the common seamen as he knew, including her, by name, Jane knew she was on an extraordinary vessel. A foremast hand was usually known to all except his fellows in the fo'c'sle as, "You!"

"Those who have sailed with me before know the way things are done on the *Meribah*. Follow orders and work hard, and you'll be treated fairly. Make trouble and you'll wish your parents had never laid eyes on one another, much less had the misfortune to give life to you." Starbuck passed by each man now, looking him in the eye, making sure he understood—and agreed to—the terms just stated. When her turn came, Jane did not dare even to blink until he had passed on.

"There's another reason to be on your best behavior on this voyage. Mrs. Wright, the *Meribah*'s owner, is traveling with us. And we will not disappoint her—or her purse. There will be *no*—" he fairly shouted the word "—grumbling about bad luck on this voyage because there's a woman aboard. I don't believe in luck where whales are concerned. It's labor and discipline that beats the great beasts. Nothing more, nothing less." The sound of his boots on the planks of the deck cut loudly through the quiet as he walked back and forth, waiting for the men to digest this latest morsel. "I have only one more thing to say before we're off. A short and greasy voyage!" he shouted.

A chorus of cheers went up. "A short and greasy voyage," the men echoed. Jane's hurrah was loud and long, given out as much in relief that she had not been found out before they'd left the dock as in excitement at the start of the journey.

Starbuck gave the order to weigh anchor and signaled for the start of the camel, the barge that would tow the *Meribah* away from the dock, over the sandbar that blocked Nantucket Harbor and out to the open sea. Then he left the men in the able hands of Valentine Mayhew and escorted Mercy aft and down the companionway.

The mate's cabin, the rearmost on the larboard side, contained a berth, a porthole and a small wooden desk with a bookshelf beside it. The desktop opened, providing a space to store pens and ink, and there was a brass oil lamp fitted into the wall above it. It was the mate's duty to keep the log, and the desk was provided to assist him in this duty. Mercy's trunk had already been brought on board and lashed to the deck beneath her berth.

"Is there anything further you require, Mrs. Wright?" Starbuck asked when they had reached the door of the cabin.

"I am fine, thank you, Captain," she answered, even though her words were patently untrue. The sight of the small cabin that would be her home for the next three or four years made her acutely aware of the comforts, both physical and emotional, she was leaving behind. "Please don't feel you have to entertain me, or even pay any attention to me. I shall try to keep as much as possible to myself, so as not to interfere with the running of the ship."

"I would prefer you not to make promises you can't keep, Mrs. Wright." Though he spoke evenly, there was an unmistakable challenge in his voice, as if he were daring Mercy to try to interfere.

"I am aboard the *Meribah* for one purpose," Mercy responded tightly. "To look for my husband and to find out exactly what happened to the *Abishai*. That is all."

This was precisely the Pandora's box that most concerned Starbuck. Mercy's presence in itself was of little moment one way or another to the operation of the ship. The root of his discomfort, he realized, lay in what might happen when they reached the Black Islands. "It is not too late to return to shore," he said. "I can easily have the camel turn us around."

Mercy's answer was hot if restrained. "I realize I have forced myself upon you, Captain, but I have no intention of turning around, or of being dissuaded from my mission. I suggest we speak of it no further, until in the course of our journey we have reached the Black Islands."

With a clipped, "As you wish," Starbuck turned away, leaving Mercy to her own devices.

She busied herself unpacking her trunk. She stowed her medicine chest and the brass spyglass given her by Maria in the cupboard above her bed; her pens, ink and paper beneath the lid of the small desk, and lined up her books on the shelf. Her clothes—a supply of black skirts and white blouses; one winter frock, a plum-colored challis, and one summer frock, a sprigged muslin, for those few occasions when they were in port; several nightdresses; a dressing gown; and various undergarments—she left folded in her trunk. For the sake of simplicity and comfort she had decided to abandon her mourning clothes once they left shore. On land she had naturally bowed to convention, but what was the point here, especially when she was making the voyage precisely to know if she was or was not a widow.

As she completed her simple task, she thought on her relations with Captain Starbuck. If they were to survive their enforced proximity they would have to learn to accommodate each other. She would have to learn a deference that did not come easily to her, and he would have to accept her as she was, without trying to change her. In a private moment she would have to discuss this with him.

Suddenly the ship stopped with a jolt, and Mercy grabbed on to the side of her berth to steady herself. The camel must have brought the *Meribah* over the bar. She shut her cabin door and climbed up to the deck. As she emerged from the companionway, she heard Starbuck give the order to set the sails. The sailors scampered up the ropes to the yardarms on the three vertical masts and out onto the jibboom. Balancing themselves on the foot ropes looped beneath each yard, they bent their bellies over the yards and hauled up the sails, which puffed out in the wind like so many arrogant men. In a short breath or two, the *Meribah* moved forward on her own. A cry went up from the officers on deck, "Greasy luck!" which the sailors echoed as they made their way back down the ropes.

Mercy too sent up the cry, for she also longed for a successful voyage. The loss of the *Abishai* had made a severe dent in the Randall family coffers, and if she was to provide for Caroline and Sarah, the *Meribah* needed to meet and master many whales. But she also felt a shiver of excitement as she made her shout. There was freedom in leaving Nantucket, in following the dictates of her heart, in leaving behind uncertainty in the quest for knowledge. She thought of Nathaniel and wondered if he had felt a similar loosening of strictures at the first billowing of the *Abishai*'s sails. Had the sacred tie that bound him to her been cut then, at that first moment of freedom, or later when time and distance intervened? Or had he lapsed into silence because he was so unhappy aboard the *Meribah* that he had no words to express it. She must find out, or never live another peaceful day.

Jane's departing cry was a feeble addition to the lusty chorus, for her trip up the ropes, if only to the lowest yard on the mizzenmast, had done nothing to soothe the riotous condition of her innards, the contents of which she had almost lost as she was bent in half over the yard unfastening the mainsail from its bindings. She was happy to have reached the deck without embarrassing and calling attention to herself, but that feeling dissolved in a few seconds when she realized that the swaying of the ship was more pronounced now that the ship was under sail. Her distress was so great that she found it hard to rejoice as the *Meribah,* driven by a favorable wind, cut steadily through the waves.

Once the ship was well under way, Jane and the rest on her watch were put to work readying the whaleboats. Jane's task was coiling rope inside a tub, rope that would be played out when a whale was fast to the line. A shoddy job could mean a lost whale, so she bent to her task with diligence, but the constant circular motion she was required to make served only to increase her internal churning.

The evening meal was a stew of fresh meat and vegetables, likely the last fresh food she would be seeing for a while. It was bland and pasty with flour and potatoes, but she forced it down. Sailoring was hard work, she had learned. And so was keeping her meal in her stomach until her watch was released to the fo'c'sle at eight that evening. She thought she would feel better in the secure surroundings of her bunk. She might even be able to pretend she was in her bunk at home. But lying down intensfied her queasiness. She tried a variety of positions—on her side with her knees drawn up, on her back, on her stomach, sitting propped up against the partition between her bunk and the next. But nothing helped.

The other green hands seemed beyond help, too. Both were assigned to Mr. Hunter's watch and should have been up on deck, but most of the second mate's men had been sent below for their last full night's sleep, owing to the lack of duties to be performed on deck. The fo'c'sle, then, was unusually full, with sixteen of the twenty berths occupied. The sleep of all was interrupted by the grunting and groaning of the sick boys, sounds that increased in volume with every toss of the ship.

One young man vomited, and a vile stench filtered up to Jane. It was so foul that she could no longer control herself and retched, too, making a mess of herself and her bunk. This loss of control affected Jane so greatly that she felt herself about to weep. That, above all, she must not do. So instead she cried out, moaning loudly, like the others, to release some of her pain and frustration.

At the other end of the lower deck, Mercy was trying to write down her impressions of the day. She had determined to keep a journal of her life aboard the *Meribah,* both to preserve the events and to help her endure the confinement and monotony of life at sea. But the plaintive sounds emanating from the opposite end of the ship made it impossible to keep her mind on her task. Why is no one doing anything? she thought as she described the terrible moaning in her diary. Her next thought was, Why am I not doing anything?

She rose and took from her stock of medicines a bottle of powders that would soothe the heaving stomachs of the afflicted men. Then she crossed the officers' mess on her way to the steward's pantry in search of water, encountering the captain and Val, still seated at the mess table. Starbuck asked her if she needed anything, and she explained her purpose.

"You needn't bother, Mrs. Wright," he said with a chuckle. "They'll get over it in a few days."

"No doubt, Captain, but why must they be miserable in the interim when I have the means to alleviate their discomfort?"

Starbuck's tone acquired a sharp edge. "When a man is sick, I will doctor him, Mrs. Wright. These men are not sick."

Just then the ship pitched, and a particularly gruesome chorus of groans issued from the fo'c'sle. "And those, I suppose, are the sounds of healthy men, Captain?"

"I've heard worse, Mrs. Wright."

"So have I, Captain, and that is why I intend to do something about them. Unattended sickness only feeds on itself." She continued on to the pantry to mix her powders.

Starbuck was now forced to make a decision. He could forbid her to visit the forecastle, which would only increase her resolve, or he could let her go—on his terms. That she assume all responsibility for doctoring the men for the rest of the voyage. Surely she would balk at that. When she came out of the pantry, he said, "You may have my permission to attend to the men on one condition. That you agree to assume all responsibility for doctoring for the remainder of the voyage. This means setting broken bones, removing gangrenous limbs, putting a tin tube in a man's throat when it has been crushed by a whale—"

"If you seek to frighten me, you waste your breath. I am more than willing to assume whatever responsibilities you deem necessary on this voyage, sir. As well you know, I have no wish to hinder or encumber this ship."

"I am happy to hear it, and I am happy to appoint you hereby our medical officer. Val, accompany Mrs. Wright on her rounds of mercy." He smiled smugly at his play on her name, and waved them both away.

As there was no way through the steerage, where the petty officers were berthed, it was necessary to ascend to the main deck and walk forward to the fo'c'sle hatch to reach the sick men. Val carried a lantern to light their way. "He's testing you, Mercy," he said softly when they had reached the main deck.

"I know that, Val. But what am I supposed to do for the next four years? Sit quietly and write in my diary? Knit and sew? I can be tested, but I will not be bested by Captain Starbuck."

"And if I know Sam he won't be bested by you, so you'd better call a truce."

"Which is just what I was thinking this afternoon. But for a truce to be effective, both parties must be willing to enter into it."

"And Sam needs to be made more willing?" Val ventured.

Mercy merely smiled into the darkness. They had reached the fo'c'sle hatch, and Val called down to the men. "Ho, there. I'm bringing Mrs. Wright to tend to the sick men."

Gathering her skirts around her, Mercy descended the narrow ladder into the gloom. Her nose was immediately assailed by the sour, pungent smell of vomit, but it did not cover the equally unpleasant odor of human waste. How were men to remain healthy in a festering hole like this one, she wondered angrily. She let her ears guide her to the sick men—boys really. She asked Val to send for water and empty basins, as well as soap and towels. Val whispered that he could manage the former but not the latter. "Then take them from my own stores," she ordered.

She set about ministering to the ailing men, wiping their feverish brows with her handkerchief and feeding them portions of medication. When a sailor arrived with the supplies she had ordered, she set him about cleaning the bunks that the sick men had fouled. The men were quiet as she went about her work. She asked the boys their names— John, Owen and Aaron they were. All three were embarrassed to be cared for as if she were their mother or sister, but they suffered her ministrations politely, if with manly reserve. Poor John Harding was the only one to betray any other sentiment. Mercy felt a gratitude from him that was not forthcoming from the others, a refinement that permitted him to understand difficulties inherent for her in this mission.

She was in the fo'c'sle for the better part of an hour, until her three patients had quieted down and were sleeping, if only lightly and fitfully. She left the fetid hole tired but full of determination to improve the place. Back in her cabin she busied herself with plans for better sanitation, ventilation and other schemes to promote a more healthful life for the foremast hands. Some in the forecastle, however, were not as purposefully employed.

No sooner had Mercy and Val departed the fo'c'sle than Crebbs was off his bunk, whispering into the ears of Hayward and Flubb, two among the crew who admired and sought to imitate his sly, crude ways. The three mischief makers each picked a sick boy and sidled up to his bunk, then commenced to taunt him for being a weakling, or tied to his mother's apron strings. Crebbs took Jane for himself and, standing on a sea chest, thrust his face into hers, so that the smell of his rancid breath woke her from her doze. When she saw who it was, she wished she could retch all over him, but unfortunately the potion supplied by Mrs. Wright had stilled her stomach into an uneasy submission.

"Any sailor worth his salt wouldn't have let himself be mollycoddled that way." Crebbs leered at her, and she closed her eyes and turned away from him. "You like it, don't you? Maybe you're one of *those* sorts of boys—who wishes he was a she." He made obscene kissing noises and grabbed her roughly by the shoulder, pulling her back to face him. Frightened, weakened and appalled though she was, Jane mustered all her strength and wrenched herself away again.

Then she felt the bunk shake under her and heard Big Jack emerge from his berth. She turned to look and saw him push Crebbs aside with one swipe of his paw. "Leave him alone," Jack ordered.

"Don't you push me around, you big ape," Crebbs came back. "I'll teach you to talk that way to a white man." With that he pulled a knife from the waistband of his trousers and brandished it at Big Jack.

Jane cowered in her bunk, wondering what to do. Plead with them to stop? Keep her mouth shut? Before she could decide, Sweet and Pete had come up behind Crebbs and pinioned him, one on each of her malefactor's arms. Crebbs's cronies attacked Sweet and Pete, and the melee began in earnest. Soon everyone except the three sick boys was swinging his fists, throwing punches, kicking and shouting salty epithets. The noise was fearsome, and Jane's already-aching head began to throb.

The fracas grew in volume and velocity until it was finally ended by the captain's shouts of "Belay there!" and his orders for all hands on deck. By that time, there were several bruised faces, a bloodied nose and a man with a gash in his thigh from passing too close to Crebbs's drawn knife.

The crew was assembled hastily on the foredeck, and Captain Starbuck lit into them. "There will be *no* fighting on board my ship. When one man even tries to fight, all men must suffer. For one week, no foremast hand will use tobacco on this vessel. If any man is found with tobacco on his person he will be punished, whether or not he is found smoking it. You will all relinquish your tobacco to me now. At the end of a week, if there have been no infractions of this order, your supplies will be returned. If *anyone* has disobeyed, the ban will be extended for one week for each infraction."

Before he sent the men into the fo'c'sle to give up their supplies of tobacco, the captain called on the sickest looking of them for an account of the trouble. "You, Harding, what went on?" he demanded, thinking to get the most information from the least hardened of the crew.

Jane's head was spinning from the sickness and the rapid succession of events, but she considered her answer carefully. She had to tell the truth and yet preserve her place among the foremast hands. "Some of the men were joking about myself and the others Mrs. Wright took care of, sir. Others of the men took exception to the jokes. Words were exchanged, and a fight broke out."

The captain glared at Harding. Hardened he might not be, but smart he was. "A very pretty and discriminating account, if altogether vague. But I won't press you for details. What I want you to remember is that fighting on this ship does no man any good. And I'll tolerate no more of it!" With that he ordered the men, except the one with the wounded thigh, below to relinquish their tobacco to Mr. Hunter. The wounded man he left on deck to await the attentions of the medical "officer."

Returning to the officers' quarters with his temper barely contained, once again he found Mrs. Wright seated at the mess table, her face drawn with worry. As he spoke, he circled her like a hawk stalking his prey from above. "I believe the Hippocratic oath importunes healers first to do no harm."

"And I have done none," she retorted.

"The sailor with the gash in his thigh may not agree with you."

"Is it any wonder that men penned up like animals fight like animals?"

"I've never before had a fight aboard a vessel of mine on the first night away from shore. The men fought because some of them were taunting the green hands for letting you tend to them."

"Am I to be held responsible for the behavior of a handful of ruffians? I did not make these men what they are."

Starbuck pounced on her. "Did you not just say that men who live like animals will fight like animals? Why do they live like animals? Is this not your ship? In your father's time, did it not earn the money that bought your comfortable house, your soft bed, your fine clothes?"

She remained unbending under his attack. "It did," she declared, "but until tonight I was unaware of the true conditions here. I am ashamed, but as you say, Captain, this is my ship, and I will see that the situation is rectified."

Starbuck threw up his hands and let loose a thunderbolt of laughter. "And how, madam, do you propose to do that in the middle of the Atlantic Ocean?"

"I am not yet certain, but I will think on it," she replied evenly.

"You do that, Mrs. Wright. But in the meanwhile, I must insist that you neither further interfere with discipline on this vessel nor neglect your other duties. There is a wounded man on deck."

"I will see to him directly, Captain."

During her exchange with the captain, Mercy had controlled her fury, but once on deck she found herself cleaning the sailor's wound with unnecessary vigor, so that he winced and called out. She reined in both herself and her emotions before continuing to apply salve and dress the deep cut. But her thoughts could not be so constrained. Who, really, was the most to blame in this incident? She for her ignorance and misunderstanding of the conditions in the fo'c'sle? Or Sam Starbuck, for both knowing about them and allowing them to remain?

Mercy pondered these questions, and her answers to them, deep into the night.

Chapter Six

The following morning, Jane swung her feet slowly over the edge of her berth, not at all sure she would be able to stand upright when she eased herself onto the floor. To her amazement, her knees did not wobble, her head did not spin, and she was able to stand straight with only the slightest feeling of fuzziness in her brain. This, she suspected, was more the result of her newly imposed sleeping patterns than anything else.

After the ruckus in the fo'c'sle, Jane wanted only to sleep, but her watch was required on deck in the hours from midnight to four in the morning. The captain had rescinded his order to delay the crew's strict adherence to the usual watch schedule. There had been almost nothing do— the sails had long been hauled in for the night, the deck was clean and tidy. Except for the helmsman and the lookout, the rest were free to doze or think or dream or even whisper among themselves. After her dose of medication, she had had little choice but to doze. A nap sitting up in the open sea air was no substitute, however, for a proper night's sleep. At four o'clock she'd returned to her berth and went out like a snuffed candle, without so much as a sputter.

Now Jane tested her balance on the deck for a moment. The *Meribah* was rolling and rocking, but the movement seemed familiar now. Each swing and sway did not send her head into a spin and set her stomach churning. With an almost jaunty spring in her step she went up through the fo'c'sle hatch, carrying her mug, bowl and spoon. In her pocket she had a nub of soap and strip of flannel, a remnant of the nightdress she was wearing the night she left home.

On her way up she grabbed her washbasin from the row of tin bowls hanging beside the edge of the hatch cover and took it to the water butt. The day was bright and fresh, with a strong breeze and a cloudless blue sky. She had to blink rapidly against the glare of sun until her eyes adjusted to it, but the clean, brisk air further enhanced the almost giddy sense of well-being that comes when an illness, no matter how transitory, has passed. After procuring her ration of salt water—only the officers had fresh water for washing—she scrubbed her face and neck and then repaired to the head for the luxury of a private wash. Following her ablutions, she felt quite restored, replaced her basin, retrieved her eating utensils and walked aft to the galley, where she presented herself to the cook for her ration of porridge and coffee. By eight o'clock, when her watch was called, she felt ready for anything.

Except what was required of her. Now that the *Meribah* was on the open sea, the crow's nests were to be assembled and manned. Jane and Aaron Cole—her fellow green hand also appeared to have responded well to Mrs. Wright's ministrations—were given two wooden planks, two metal hoops and a few brief words of instruction. They were then sent to the top of the masts—mainmast for Jane, foremast for Aaron—to set up the lookout posts where two men, an officer and a foremast hand, would scout for whales in two-hour-long watches.

Refusing the order was impossible, even asking for clarification of her instructions would mark her a coward. But it was more than one hundred twenty feet to the top of the mainmast, a very long way indeed for someone whose sea legs were wobbly at best. All Jane could do, however, was pick up the planks and hoops and without a moment's hesitation set out on her task.

Despite the planks roped to her back and the hoops around her shoulders, Jane made it to the first yardarm with little difficulty. Getting past the yard presented a challenge because of the wooden platform that made a half circle around the mast. Before proceeding, she studied the problem, trying to ignore the jeers—some good-natured, some not—coming from the men left on the deck. Because of her encumbrances, the maneuver would require her to balance herself with one hand and one foot on the rope ladder while extending her remaining two limbs to their utmost in an effort to negotiate herself over the yard, past the platform and onto the next stage of the ladder. At the last possible second she would have to let go, heave herself over the bar and reach blindly for the tarred side bar that would ensure her safety. Until she felt her fingers curl around it, she would be suspended in thin air, life and limb dependent upon her own momentum.

Knowing what she had to do, however, was not the same as doing it. She practiced the moves slowly in her head, imagining exactly what she would do when. Once she was sure of them, she took a deep breath and leaped. A second of pure agony came next, but then she felt her fingers secure on the hardened tar and she knew she had made it. From below came a round of encouraging shouts and whistles.

The next yard was no easier simply because she knew what she had to do. She was that much more tired, her muscles that much more tense. But she stopped, engaged in a mental practice session and then negotiated the second yard. More calls and whistles reached her ears, but they were dimmed by the pressure building up in her ears. She was breathing hard now and deathly scared to look anywhere but up, yet she kept going. Repeating the maneuver twice more, she reached the appointed place at the top of the mast. The ropes here were no longer fashioned like a ladder, and she clung to her single support like a monkey on a stick.

She allowed herself to rest and catch her breath for a moment, then slowly disengaged one hand. With infinite care she eased first one plank and then the other out of the sling on her back and fitted them between the slack loops of rope that awaited them. Then, using her last ounce of strength, she shinned further up the rope and eased herself down on the planks, keeping her hands firmly on the rope while she tested their steadiness with her feet. They wobbled at first and she feared she had inserted them improperly and that they might sail down to the deck, injuring someone or damaging the vessel, or even sending her crashing to her death. With another couple of pushes, though, they set firmly between the ropes.

Breathing more easily now but without daring to stop, Jane turned to the final portion of her task—fitting the metal hoops into the planks and fastening them to the ropes. Her practiced eye, trained by years of reconstructing the intricate designs of damaged lace, quickly saw how the pieces fitted together, and with a shudder of relief she performed the required actions.

The second she had completed her job, Jane started back down the ropes. With nothing to carry she felt as if she were almost coming down a slide instead of a ladder, so easy was the descent. When she landed on the deck, she was greeted with a chorus of cheers, the loudest coming from Big Jack, who reached out and clapped her on the back. "Well done, Little John," he cried. "Only one other green hand I know ever put up a crow's nest on the first try. And he was a big man. Those planks were nothing but twigs on my—I mean his—back." He grinned modestly.

"And you no give back breakfast."

"Like other young fella," Pete, then Sweet, added.

Jane looked around the deck and found Aaron Cole, propped up against the foremast, Mrs. Wright holding a cup to his lips. His color gave the term, green hand, new meaning. Another seaman was swabbing the deck forward of the windlass. She began to smile and then to laugh—in her own relief and not ridicule of poor Aaron. But her merriment was cut short by a sharp shout directed at her.

"You!" Captain Starbuck pointed an angry finger at her. "Did I call alow from aloft? Back to the nest with you!"

Immediately Jane jumped up on the ropes and climbed for all she was worth, reaching the nest before she realized she didn't know what she was to do when she got there. Look for whales, she knew that much. But was she to shout out for anything else? By this time she had secured herself inside one of the metal hoops, her feet resting solidly on the planks, and all thoughts in her head were stilled by what she saw. She hadn't noticed anything on her first trip up the mainmast, but now she looked out and saw nothing but sea. The water was a deep blue-gray, cut with silver sparkles from the sun. Here and there was a fillip of white as a wave rose and crested. At the edge of the sea was the sky, a purer blue, without depth but with the promise of infinity instead. The sound was pure, too, not quiet, for the sea swelled, the wind blew and the sails flapped, but there was no human caterwauling, none of the internal or external chatter that informed the human condition. Jane was awestruck and as perfectly happy in a single moment as she had ever been.

But how could her happiness have been perfect if the next moment she was even happier? Her joy increased, but the perfection was marred, for in this new happiness there were grave impediments. Suddenly she was aware of a presence beside her. When she saw it was Mr. Mayhew, she smiled radiantly at him, forgetting that he was among the highest of the high and she was the lowest of the low.

For his part, Mr. Mayhew found himself unexpectedly moved by the innocent joy in young Harding's face. He remembered his own first time in the crow's nest, his own first glance at endless sea and sky, and the feeling of being in league with the Creator, a favored soul granted a glimpse of heaven. He said nothing, not wanting to intrude on Harding's privacy, but his own thoughts continued without restraint. In his years at sea, he'd passed hundreds of watches in the crow's nest with scores of sailors, but never before had he felt that a single other one would have understood had he been so bold as to try to describe his feelings during his first watch from aloft. But one look at Harding's smile just now told him this young sailor would know.

Many silent moments had passed when Jane realized that she had greeted her officer with only an idiotic grin. She had better stop mooning about, she warned herself, or she was going to be found out for the fraud she was. "Good morning, Mr. Mayhew, sir," she said shyly. Expecting nothing more than a grunt, she was surprised by Mr. Mayhew's incisive response.

"I believe you already like it up here, don't you, Harding?" he asked kindly.

"Yes, sir," she agreed, endeavoring to conceal much of the enthusiasm she was feeling at the moment. She longed to burst forth with all she was thinking and feeling—about her morning's feat, the fears and close calls, her amazement at being here at all. But she controlled herself.

Val found himself inexplicably disappointed by Harding's short, proper response. Although he could not fathom why he had this sudden and unusual penchant for conversation with a green hand, he attempted to draw Harding out. "I'm fond of being up here, too," he admitted. "That makes us a breed apart, you know. Most seafaring men loathe these watches in the crow's nest. They're bored and uncomfortable way up here, but I've always thought it a reward for the hardships we endure on a voyage."

Jane could not believe an officer, especially one for whom she felt such an unmistakable affinity, was addressing her in such intimate and personal terms. She wanted to answer him, but a fear of revealing what she must not kept her diffident. "Yes, sir," she repeated. It was hard to say just those two words when so many others were fighting to tumble from her mouth. She avoided looking at Mr. Mayhew again, keeping her eyes strictly on the sea. The officer continued to question her, about her origins, her family, her schooling. She kept her answers short, giving as little information as she could without a breach of manners or respect, all the while longing to elaborate, to tell him more than he asked for, and not less.

Then suddenly she saw a flash of light on the horizon. It disappeared so quickly she was uncertain of what she had seen. But then there was another and then another—silvery arcs shooting out of the sea, across the sky and back into the sea. "What's that?" she cried, pointing toward the ephemeral shimmers.

"Where away?" Val asked, scanning the horizon. Then he saw the silver flashes, too. "It's a school of porpoises, Harding," he said excitedly. He cupped his hands and yelled to those below. "Porps! Porps!"

"Where away?" came Starbuck's answering cry.

"One point off the leeward bow," Val shouted back.

Jane and Val had the best seats for the show that then began. Starbuck ordered the third and fourth mates to lower their boats and give chase. To the boat that killed the most fish he offered freedom from duty during the second dogwatch that evening. Two hours of leisure were a powerful inducement, and the two teams hurried to lower their respective boats from the davits. Once the boats were in the water, they rowed feverishly in the direction of the school. Only the helmsman and the lookouts remained at their posts as the race began in earnest.

Mercy, who had been sitting quietly on deck, taking in a measure of the day's activities, raced to the bulwarks with the others, and soon she too was mesmerized by the jumping fish. They were now close enough to the *Meribah* that she could marvel at their exquisite grace as they dove in and out of the water. They seemed such happy creatures, frisking and leaping like lambs at play. Scanning the crowd on the deck, she saw that to a man all were taking pleasure from the aquatic antics.

But when the boats reached the porpoises and a harpoon pierced one of the beautiful creatures in midarch, she felt an unexpected surge of anger. Why should the porpoises be the object of such wanton sport? Although she had no qualms whatever about killing animals to serve the needs of men and women, this seemed to her a different proposition altogether. Was it right, in the absence of whales, to catch and kill what crossed the *Meribah*'s path? She rushed over to the captain. "Why must they be killed?" she demanded. "What is the purpose of this brutal exercise? You must stop it at once!"

In the heat of the moment, she had raised her voice, and now all eyes were trained on her and the captain. The race to the porpoises was no longer the most interesting spectacle unfolding before the men. Starbuck turned slowly to face her. His tone was quiet but none the less menacing for its softness. "The men need practice in the whaleboats and fresh meat, madam. Now I will thank you to remain silent or I will have you escorted to your cabin."

A string of peppery salvos gathered on Mercy's tongue, but she fired none of them into the charged air. On the faces of the men around her, she saw an excitement that frightened her. They hardly dared to breathe, so eagerly were they waiting to see if she could put a chink in the captain's armor. She had to disappoint them. Any further argument on her part might undermine Starbuck's authority, perhaps even make him appear weak. Whatever he was, Sam Starbuck was no weakling. No one who commanded the respect of such an ill-assorted group of men, as he obviously did, could be thought spineless. She must be seen to bend to his will, also. "My apologies, Captain," she said. "My heart spoke before my mind had considered the consequences."

He turned from her without a word, but she thought she detected a barely perceptible softening in his face. Not forgiveness perhaps, but an acknowledgment that something had been understood between them.

Mercy watched the rest of the competition without enthusiasm. She could not help but be impressed by the skill of the men in approaching, harpooning and capturing the fish, but she did not share in the glee that prevailed when the boats had returned and the catch hauled aboard. Both had caught two porpoises, and in view of the equal score, the captain magnanimously granted the promised liberty to all the men who had participated in the hunt.

There was feverish activity on the *Meribah* that afternoon as the porpoises were butchered, their blubber boiled down in the try-pots and stored in casks and the equipment in the whaleboats cleaned and set to rights again. Mercy made herself useful assisting Doc, the cook, in making sea pies—flour dumplings stuffed with minced porpoise meat. During the first dogwatch, between four and six o'clock, the sails were trimmed and the deck cleaned of gurry, as the men called the slime and blood that accompanied the butchering of a fish. During the second dogwatch, from six until eight o'clock, the sailors at liberty celebrated loudly, with yarns and songs, cavorting rowdily, while the day's work was finished. Then everyone feasted on fried porpoise steaks, sea pies and boiled cabbage, the men on deck, the officers and petty officers in their own messes.

At eight o'clock the larboard watch, Mr. Hunter's, were free to go to their berths, but the captain said they could remain on deck if they chose. He asked Val to bring out his fiddle, and those men who were not too weighed down by the sumptuous meal danced to the music. Within the hour, though, the merriment had played itself out. The men were tired and sated, and the larboard watch retired to the fo'c'sle while the starboard watch lethargically undertook their few nighttime duties.

Despite all the excitement around her, Mercy's mood was subdued and pensive. During the meal, admittedly tasty yet unpalatable to her for the method by which it was obtained, she and Captain Starbuck maintained a studious politeness, neither addressing nor looking at one another directly. Afterward she retired quietly to her cabin, sitting alone with her thoughts for some time. She had so much to learn about life on this vessel. It was a far cry from the genteel society she was used to, but it had its own rhyme and reason, which she must do her utmost to understand.

She still believed she could bring improvements to the *Meribah,* but now she knew she must do so without clashing or even seeming to clash with her captain. Her beliefs did not admit the unquestioning deference of any one man or woman to any other, but someone had to be in charge of the *Meribah.* By dint of his experience, bravery and dexterity with the men, that person must be Sam Starbuck. He must be her captain, too. She could not set herself apart in this regard without causing harm to the vessel and its inhabitants.

Her ruminations concluded, Mercy took in hand the small spyglass that had been Maria's parting gift and climbed up to the deck. Standing by the stern railing, she put the glass to her eye and began to study the heavens. The night sky was as clear as the day's had been, and with no obscuring clouds to hide behind, the stars were blazing in their full complement. Mercy could not help but think of Maria, who could undoubtedly interpret better than she the formations of this army of twinkling lights. Still they were pretty to watch, and she found comfort in the knowledge that these staunch battalions could not be felled by any earthly foolishness. Whatever mistakes men and women made, this host of stars would remain.

At the fall of footsteps behind her, Mercy lowered her glass and turned around. "Good evening, Mrs. Wright," the captain said, pausing at the top of the companionway. He made as if to continue on his way, but then changed course and approached her. "Have you found anything of interest in the heavens this evening?" he asked with a distant and impersonal cordiality, as if they were acquaintances in a drawing room.

"Only confirmation of my own ignorance."

"And how is that? I would have thought your friendship with Miss Mitchell had taught you a great deal about the stars."

"No," she said, "despite my closeness with Miss Mitchell, I understand only the rudiments of astronomy. As, despite being my father's daughter, I understand only the rudiments of whaling." Her companion remained noncommittally silent. "I have come to see how wrong it was of me to fly at you this afternoon, Captain."

"How very astute of you, Mrs. Wright." He intended some irony in this comment, but it was tempered by his recognition of the bravery and humility in Mercy's admission.

"It won't happen again," she promised.

Having spent just over twenty-four hours on board ship with her, Starbuck could not believe, no matter how devoutly he might wish it, that she could keep this vow. "I trust," he said mildly, "this means you will spend the rest of the voyage in your cabin, coming out only for meals and a breath of air now and then?"

With light provided only by the stars and a small sliver of moon, it was difficult to see his face, and Mercy missed the jesting twinkle in his eye. "It most certainly does not!" she retorted hotly.

He responded with a hearty laugh. "I didn't think so."

She then saw that he had been teasing her and went warm with embarrassment. "I meant," she said primly, "that whatever disagreements I have with you, I shall air them only in private."

"Then we are certain to disagree? On any particular matters, may I ask? Just so that I may be prepared."

This time Mercy did not miss the banter in his tone. "There is the matter of the sick bay."

"And what sick bay is that?"

"The one I propose to establish in the storage room in the steerage." With his encouragement, she described her plans more fully and then, driven by her own mounting enthusiasm, moved swiftly on the additional measures of sanitation and cleanliness she would like to institute, without pause from one topic to the next.

While she spoke, Starbuck was captured less by her plans than by the purpose and animation with which she informed them. She was full of the life and energy he had seen only once before, when they had danced together in the parlor on Orange Street. An unfamiliar feeling welled up in him, a longing that led him to the awareness of a tiny chamber deep inside himself. It was a locked and empty place, echoing with the words little Sarah had spoken to him on the morning he had returned from his previous voyage. "You've changed, you're lonely," she had said. Perhaps the innocent girl had been wiser than the experienced man, he now thought.

In the wake of these musings, he was seized with an overpowering desire to take Mercy in his arms and kiss her, to draw her liveliness and her warmth inside him and let it fill that empty place. He fought this impulse for the dangerous action it was. A lover of danger, however, dear reader, is not always the best person to spurn it, and Captain Starbuck did then what any lover of danger might have done. He pursued it, caught it and faced it. Not with the raw and violent power some men would have used, but with stealth and gentling.

"Mrs. Wright," he interrupted her softly, "you are tiring me with your ambition. A discussion of your worthy projects is much more suited to the light of the day. A night such as this is better spent considering its many pleasures."

"And what might those be, Captain?" Mercy inquired, taken aback by the sudden change in his demeanor.

He edged closer to her and held out his hand for her glass. "May I?" He put his hand on the object and gently extricated it from hers. Then, circling behind her, he held the glass up to her eye and pointed toward the heavens. As he spoke of the stars above them, he felt his breath hot on her fragrant chestnut hair, felt the tantalizing nearness of her.

With Starbuck's arms encircling her, Mercy began to feel an uncomfortable but not entirely unpleasant prickling on the back of her neck. She tried to keep her mind on what he was saying, but her attention remained riveted on the man himself. She could sense the strength and solidity of his body behind her, could feel the radiant heat emanating from it. An exchange of charged energy was taking place between them, as if a ray of some strange and strong emotion were beaming down on them from the stars and they were compelled to pass it back and forth from one to the other.

Starbuck's arms closed around her. He lowered the scope and, holding the instrument firmly in one hand, turned her slowly toward him. She knew what was about to happen, and the sensible part, rational part of her wanted to forestall it, but she was unable to control the rapturous, magical power of starlight. He brought his mouth down on hers and crushed her to him, and she returned his burning kiss with a hunger she had not known she possessed.

Now, reader, this was not, of course, the first time that Mercy Randall Wright had been kissed. A married woman, she was not unacquainted with the pleasures of the physical act of love. Though it was difficult for her to speak to me of these matters, she did intimate that she was quite startled by the intensity of the captain's embrace and by her equally strong response. Only when she began to compare the feeling of being in Starbuck's arms to that of her husband's caresses did she remember herself.

The thought of Nathaniel streaked across her brain like a shooting star, and she wrenched herself away from Starbuck with such violence that she heard her precious spyglass fall to the deck with a clatter. She paid it no mind, however, for all she could think of was fleeing to the safety and solitude of her cabin. She flew down the stairs, closed and locked her door and threw herself, panting and on the verge of shedding a torrent of hot guilty tears, onto her berth.

Starbuck, still on the deck, bent to retrieve the spyglass. Examining it with his hands, he found only one small dent in the brass casing. All in all not much damage had been done, one way or another, he assessed. Unused, though, to the frustration of interrupted passion, he accepted it with an equanimity that surprised him. None of the women he had been with in his travels would have fled him at the juncture he and Mercy had reached. On the other hand, none of them would have displayed the guileless response he had just evoked from Mercy.

There was danger in what he had just done, but that peril did not frighten him. It sharpened him and drove him to a willingness to open and explore the locked and empty room within him. He felt stronger and more capable than he had in many a month. There was a spring in his step as he tripped lightly down the companionway. Before retiring to his own cabin, he rapped softly on Mercy's door. "It's Captain Starbuck, ma'am. You left your glass on deck."

"Would you please keep it until morning?" came the muffled response.

"I think it will be safer with you."

A moment passed before Mercy opened the door a crack. With a shaking hand she accepted the object from him. "Thank you, Captain," she said hoarsely.

"Oh, no, Mrs. Wright. Thank *you*."

Chapter Seven

When day broke, Mercy wanted nothing more than to stay in her cabin, but she knew she must not succumb to her desire to hide. She had been rash and imprudent with Captain Starbuck the night before, but refusing to face herself in the light of day would only increase her discomfort. So she dressed and seated herself at the table in the mess, trying to concentrate on her bread and butter and tea and not on the unavoidable fact of Sam Starbuck, who sat opposite her, calmly consuming ham and cheese and bread. Among the officers there was talk of weather and work. Mercy tried to interest herself in the conversation, but her mind wandered like a rudderless ship.

Halfway through the meal, Val turned to Mercy and asked solicitously, "Are you quite well, Mrs. Wright? You seem unusually quiet this morning."

"Thank you, Mr. Mayhew, but I am fine."

Val gave her a private, questioning look, and she sought to reassure him with a subtle shake of her head. "Captain, have I your permission to proceed with setting up the sick bay this morning?" As she spoke she looked not directly at the captain, as was her custom, but slightly to the right of his right ear.

"If you will tell me what you need, I will arrange it."

Mercy felt rather than saw that his eyes bore down on her as he answered. Still without looking at him, she replied,

"The services of the carpenter, please, and one other man. Perhaps one of the green hands could be spared."

"Yes, all right," he decided. "But not this morning. After dinner you can have the carpenter and one man. You'd better have the one with the manners. What's his name, Val?"

"Harding." Although there was no reason he should not know Harding's name, Val felt somehow shy of saying it, as if merely speaking it would reveal their intimate conversation in the crow's nest the day before.

"Aye. A spunky lad, too. You don't see many like him," Starbuck allowed generously. "Keep an eye on him, Val, we might be able to turn him into a decent sailor. I trust waiting until afternoon will not inconvenience you too much, Mrs. Wright." He spoke as if to dare her to quibble with him.

"Not at all, Captain." Only twenty-four hours before she might have taken up his dare, but now she would not. Fervently she wished that she had not let him kiss her. By that, she had irrevocably altered the balance of their relationship, unfortunately tipping the scales in his favor.

After breakfast, Mercy retired to her cabin and spent the morning drawing up a list of plans she wished to have implemented aboard the *Meribah*. The activity was a welcome distraction, but it did not entirely prevent her from ruminating on the events of the previous night. Even if she and the captain never passed so much as another second alone, they now each possessed secret knowledge of the other. She knew that Starbuck found her desirable, so much so that he had been moved to act on his desires. While he could be impulsive, he also well knew how to discipline himself, and although he may not have planned to kiss her, neither did he stop himself from doing so. For his part, the captain knew that she was not above allowing herself to be kissed. Although she was shocked by her own behavior and would not commit such an indiscretion again, he knew that she had enjoyed the kiss sufficiently to let it continue.

Whenever they looked at each other now, they would know these things, and inevitably that knowledge would color their every exchange. Her only recourse was to meet the challenge squarely instead of shrinking from it as she had at breakfast. When they spoke, she would look him in the eye and communicate to him, if not in so many words, that she had every intention of restoring an equal balance in their relations.

Val spent a long, tedious morning, first recording the uneventful progress of the *Meribah* in the log and then conferring with the captain and the steward on various matters of inventory and supplies. He felt unusually impatient for the beginning of a voyage. He was always eager at the start of a journey, but there seemed to be the promise of something more than whales and adventure fueling his uncommon restlessness.

After the midday meal, Val sought out Harding himself, although he could well have appointed a petty officer to the task, and escorted him to the storage room where Mercy was to have her sick bay. "The captain was much impressed by your performance yesterday," he said to the boy as they descended into the steerage.

Jane tried to hide the warm flush of pleasure that arose not only from the captain's compliment, but also from hearing it from this particular bearer. "I only did what anyone would have done, sir, tried my best."

"And very good it was indeed, Harding." Not known for his volubility, Val felt he could talk endlessly with Harding, a feeling that contrarily produced a silence that was most uneasy on his part. He felt rather like a boy who has just discovered that girls were not the silly, despicable creatures they once seemed. He had much to say but lacked the means of expression. Why did Harding have such an effect on him, making him feel not a man of twenty-six, but a boy of twelve or thirteen. "Did you enjoy the festivities yesterday evening?" he asked clumsily.

"Oh, yes, sir," Jane declared. "Especially your fiddling," she added shyly. "What was that song you—" At that moment Mrs. Wright entered the storeroom, and Jane cut off her sentence, as if she and Mr. Mayhew had been talking about something private. "Good afternoon, ma'am."

Mercy smiled at the boy. "Did I hear you declare yourself an admirer of Mr. Mayhew's music, John? It is excellent, is it not? I have long admired it myself."

"Mrs. Wright and I are childhood friends," Val explained, then wondered why he had felt compelled to justify his relationship with Mercy, something that was no more the business of this foremast hand than charting the vessel's course. With hasty compliments to Mercy, Val then hurried away, wondering about his behavior with much consternation. It was very worrying to be so drawn to a common seaman, no matter how able and quick and amiable. He was very confused and not a little concerned.

Jane remained with Mrs. Wright through the afternoon watch, acting as apprentice to the carpenter, who had begun the construction of a double-tiered berth where sick men might be nursed and recuperate. She expected to be dismissed at the start of the first dogwatch, but Mrs. Wright inquired if she had any skill at sewing. "A little," she admitted reluctantly. "As the youngest and wanting any sisters," she explained, hoping her excuses would be found plausible, "I was often pressed into my mother's service, and so I learned to do things that most boys do not." When asked then to assist in the preparation of bandages, she could not refuse, and accompanied Mrs. Wright to the upper deck, where she was supplied with strips of cotton cloth and asked to hem them. She tried to appear maladroit as concerned the use of needle and thread, but her skills were too ingrained, and Mrs. Wright marveled at her dexterity.

"Your mother must be a fine seamstress indeed to have taught you to be so quick and sure with a needle, John."

"With seven to clothe, there was always something to make or mend," Jane mumbled. Just then she looked up from her work, only to see Crebbs, passing by in the course of his duties, cast a disdainful, mocking glance her way. She forced herself to stare him down, refusing to give in to the intimidating sneer. Still the experience left her shaking inwardly for several moments. Crebbs, she had realized, was one of those people who are angry all the time, and she feared he had chosen her as an easy mark on whom to vent his violent feelings. In fact he had chosen well—she was smaller and weaker and she had something to hide. She also knew that, as is the way with such men, the more she backed away from his challenges, the more he would prey on her. She would have to be both vigilant and tolerant where Crebbs was concerned. She could not afford to let him provoke her.

The exchange between John Harding and the ruffian Crebbs was not lost on Mercy, and she was most impressed by his behavior on that score. Boys of his age tended to have both hot heads and strong impulses, two attributes that do not necessarily mix well. But John Harding seemed to have himself well under control. He had been unfailingly helpful and polite through the long afternoon, tackling each task assigned to him intelligently and assiduously. That evening, after the meal, Mercy mentioned his exemplary assistance to Val as they were strolling the deck together. "Still, I can't put aside the feeling that he is out of place here," she commented. "Why would a boy with his advantages choose to article himself as a common seaman?"

"We all have to start somewhere, Mercy. I was a foremast hand on my first voyage."

"Under your uncle's command. It was your apprenticeship. You and everyone on the ship knew that."

"Including Uncle Tobias. He never treated me differently from the rest."

Val gave the word *me* a peculiar, bitter emphasis. "What do you mean, Val? That Captain Starbuck has been too favorably disposed to Harding?"

He hesitated. "No, I mean that I have."

"Is that so very perturbing?" Mercy asked solicitously.

"Of course it is," he answered sharply. "An officer who shows favoritism is asking for trouble."

"Favoritism is one thing, and duty another. Is it not in the best interest of the ship and the whaling industry for an officer to nurture and promote a promising seaman?"

"Of course it is, but—" Val lowered his voice to a bare whisper. "My feelings for Harding already go beyond that duty. I want to make a friend of him. It confuses me, Mercy, and frightens me, too."

"Why should it be frightening to want to make a friend, Val? There is no officer aboard the ship whose temperament and talents match yours, no one with whom you could have a true friendship."

"Sam is my friend."

"Yes, but not a friend of the heart, the way Maria is for me, for instance. The captain is not someone to whom you can say anything and know he will understand. He has not your sensibility, for one thing."

"I think you overrate me, Mercy, and do Sam an injustice. Sam may not have my pretty manners or my temperate disposition, but I lack his passion and determination."

"Perhaps you confuse arrogance for passion and intractability for determination."

Val chuckled softly. "I think our captain must have crossed you in some way, for you to speak so harshly of him."

Mercy relented with a laugh. "I fear I have been mistress of my own house for too long to submit gracefully to another's domination. But we have strayed from the point. I will admit to your friendship with the captain, but I still maintain that he cannot be the one friend on whose love and counsel you can utterly depend. Your only problem with your inclination in young Harding's direction is the discrepancy in your situations. He sails before the mast, you are the ship's second officer. Were he the fourth mate you would feel no such qualms."

"You may be right, Mercy," Val agreed. "At sea one's feelings at times become almost unbearably intense, especially at the beginning of a voyage when the memory of family and friends left behind is so vivid. One seems to feel things so much more. Thoughts that never would have occurred to you on land possess you. Things you never would have considered doing begin to seem possible, even normal and natural...."

His voice faded away, and Mercy replied only with a murmur of understanding. Val had given her the key to explaining her incomprehensible behavior with the captain the previous night. It had been occasioned by nothing more than the strangeness of being at sea, the sudden, enforced intimacy, the task of adjusting from one way of life to another. She had nothing further to fear. Now that she understood the phenomenon she could control it.

Mercy spent the remainder of the week in final preparations for the sick bay. John Harding, when he could be spared, was her helper. The green hands had passed through their seasickness and there had been no accidents or other illnesses, so her infirmary was yet to be used. But the work had been demanding and she was glad when Sunday arrived. Because they were not yet on the whaling grounds, Sunday was a day of leisure. Only necessary work was done, although the crow's nest was manned on the off chance that a whale or more likely some porpoises might be sighted.

In the morning the captain and some of the officers read from the Bible, a few prayers were offered and a hymn sung. After that, as the day was fine, the men turned to washing their clothes, giving one another haircuts or shaves and other more enjoyable pastimes. As there were yet no whale bones or teeth, only one or two men who had such material from previous voyages worked scrimshaw, using a sharp thin blade to draw images that were then darkened with India ink to make them stand out. Rope was in abundant supply, however, and some of the men worked strands of it into ornamental knots that they used as handles for their sea chests or to hang small items—both decorative and useful—from their bunks. Others had flung fishing lines over the bow, in pursuit of a tasty dinner. Nearly all the men would have enjoyed a smoke or two, but the captain's ban on tobacco was still in force, so those who were not inclined to industry sat idle.

For Jane, the day could not have been more pleasant. Duty in the crow's nest caused her to miss the morning service, but this disappointment was allayed by the company of her fellow lookout, Mr. Mayhew. Snatches of the readings wafted up to them, and they ventured guesses as to the passages being quoted. Voices raised in song reached the crow's nest more easily, and she and Mr. Mayhew joined in the hymns, their voices lost in the open air like two small birds in the rafters of a vast cathedral. After that, their conversation came in fits and starts, with topics taken up and pursued with enthusiasm, then broken off abruptly when Jane felt a shy reserve overcome her or Val recalled the impropriety of so warm a relationship with the young seaman.

Down from aloft Jane turned her hand to washing her extra set of clothes. She went rather pink at the thought of her cotton drawers drying in the sun, but hers were no different from other such garments that littered the decks, and Mrs. Wright seemed unconscious of her own petticoats and pantalets drying on a line strung up aft by the steward. Still it brought Jane an uneasy feeling—that some mark or other on her clean clothes would give her away. But no one paid her things any mind, and she happily prepared a line and threw in her lot with the others who were fishing. While waiting for the fish to bite, she threaded a needle and set to mending a tear in one of her two shirts.

Jane was not the only sailor sewing that afternoon. Two or three others were also mending, but their use of thread and needle was laborious compared to Jane's, despite her efforts to appear less skilled than she was. Absorbed in her task—it is always difficult to seem clumsy at something when one is not—Jane was unaware of being watched, until she smelled a foul breath, rank with tobacco and strong drink, close to her face.

"Look at this, boys," Crebbs cried. "Our young gentleman's sewing would put your mothers' to shame."

Moving past Jane, he "accidentally" knocked her hand with his knee so violently that she stabbed herself with her needle, drawing blood. Instinctively she put her finger into her mouth, then decided she'd best keep it there. It would help her hold her tongue. When Crebbs moved away, she examined her forefinger. The wound was nothing, the bleeding already stopped. It was slightly tender but nothing more. She went back to her sewing, pleased to have escaped the encounter unscathed.

But Crebbs was soon back for more. This time he sat close beside her and bent his head down over her shirt so that his head was almost in her lap. "Never did see a *man* make such dainty stitches," he taunted. "Ain't we lucky to have such a wonder on board? Not only climbs to the top of the rigging, but *he's* as clever as a girl with a needle, too."

By now Jane was beginning to feel a bit frightened. Was Crebbs just taunting her, or had he discovered her true nature? Despite her alarm she tried to think clearly. Whether or not Crebbs knew, her best course would be to move out of harm's way. She made a move to swing her legs around and put her back to him, but at the same moment Crebbs grabbed for the shirt in her lap. She heard the sound of tearing fabric. "Now see what you've done!" she cried before she could think the better of it.

Crebbs was on his feet instantly, pulling her up after him. "Want to make something of it, boy?"

The blow he delivered along with his words hit Jane squarely in the stomach. The air was knocked out of her, and she doubled over, fighting back the tears that stung her eyes. In a moment, however, she had straightened up, in time to see Mr. Mayhew charge across the deck, grab the back of Crebbs's shirt, swing him around and punch him squarely in the jaw. Crebbs returned the favor, and the two men fell to the deck. Mr. Mayhew seemed wild with rage. He was bigger than Crebbs and stronger, but not nearly as wily or as experienced a scrapper. His punches were fierce, but poorly aimed. Crebbs avoided most of them and landed a few himself, including one to the first mate's chin that resounded with the loud crack of bone on bone. Still Mr. Mayhew would not be subdued. He lashed out at Crebbs time and time again, finally delivering a blow to Crebbs's temple that knocked him out cold. Bleeding from cuts on his forehead and his chin, the mate rose and glared with satisfaction at his unconscious opponent.

The quiet on the deck was broken by the captain's voice, low, controlled but unmistakably furious. "I don't like to repeat myself, and I don't intend to say this again. There will be no fighting on the *Meribah!* Not among the crew, and certainly not by the officers." He glared at Val. "You, Harding! In the middle of it again, I see. What the devil was going on?"

Jane could think only of protecting Mr. Mayhew. "It was my fault, sir. Crebbs wanted to look at the sewing I was doing on my shirt, and I moved suddenly, and the shirt tore, and I made an angry remark."

"And?" Starbuck demanded menacingly.

"And he hit me," Jane answered in a small voice.

"Why?"

"I don't know, sir." She looked doubtfully at the prone figure of Crebbs, still lying motionless on the deck. "You'll have to ask him." From behind her Jane heard a low rumble, the beginning of a laugh from Big Jack, frozen on an intake of breath after a mere glance from the captain.

"Did you threaten him?" Starbuck continued his interrogation.

"No, sir."

"Did he threaten you?"

"No, he just punched me."

This time Jack could not hold in his laughter. He gave a great guffaw, which would have set the whole crew off but for the captain's stern look and nearly whispered admonition, all the more effective for its quiet delivery. "This is no laughing matter," he said, then bellowed for Mrs. Wright. "Bring some smelling salts. I want this demon to hear what's going to happen to him."

Mercy did as she was told without comment or hesitation. As she held the vial of aromatic salts against Crebbs's nose, she could not help but notice the strong odor of both tobacco and drink. She must unconsciously have wrinkled her nose and recoiled, for the captain yelled at her, "What do you smell, Mrs. Wright? Has that blighter been using tobacco?"

"I believe it may be possible, Captain," she replied.

Starbuck charged over to the now partially revived Crebbs, grasped him roughly by the shirt and brought his face close to his own. He sniffed, muttered something so foul that Mercy could only infer its meaning and unceremoniously let Crebbs's head drop to the deck. "Get up!" he ordered the downed man. "Leave him alone now, Mrs. Wright." As Crebbs struggled to his feet, Mercy went to Val and offered a clean cloth to stanch the blood that still flowed from the cut on his chin. "Him, too!" Mercy jumped at the order, but obeyed it immediately. Then Starbuck turned his attention back to Crebbs, who was on his feet but so unsteady that the possibility of him remaining upright seemed quite slim. Mercy feared he would be knocked over by a strong wind—or the force of Captain Starbuck's voice.

"You! For no apparent reason you hit this sailor," he gestured to Harding.

Crebbs peered out from under one swollen eyelid, seemingly incapable of opening the other eye at all. "Got no use for them prissy types," he answered defiantly.

"And I've got no use for bullies, you shiftless son of a whore. This man is to be manacled to his bunk for one week, except when he is on duty. His rations are to be halved for the same duration, and his possessions are to be searched for tobacco and drink. No man will speak to him, except when necessary for the completion of a task. The next man who lays so much as a finger on another will be flogged. I don't care what the provocation is. The ban of tobacco will continue for another week. Now get this pile of manure out of my sight. Mr. Mayhew, I'll see you in the officer's mess!" With that, Starbuck stalked off.

Mercy immediately turned back to Val to see to his wounds, but he pushed her away. "Not now, Mercy," he said, and hurried after Sam. She had of course realized that Val was in serious trouble for fighting with Crebbs, but until that moment she had not realized how serious. She knew better than to follow Crebbs into the fo'c'sle to see to his bruises—she would please neither the man himself nor the captain with such an attempt—and so approached John Harding. "Are you all right?" she inquired. "Is there anything I can do for you?"

"No, thank you, ma'am. I was more startled than anything else. I'm all right."

"That's good," she said, patting him gently on the shoulder. "But if you should feel unwell later, please do not hesitate to send for me."

Mrs. Wright's touch was almost more than Jane could bear. The voyage was less than a week old, and there had already been a few moments when her lark had turned into a perilous escapade. "Yes, ma'am," Jane promised weakly as Mrs. Wright moved away. She bent to retrieve her spare shirt, which had been further damaged and dirtied in the scuffle. As she examined it, Big Jack came up to her. His broad grin bewildered her. There seemed little to smile about just now, but he insisted she follow him forward of the windlass, to the spot where she had thrown her fishing line over the bow. He tugged on one of the ropes dangling there and asked if it was hers. When she responded affirmatively, his grin widened. "Then the day's not entirely lost. 'Cause I found this—" he bent down and produced a bluefish large enough to feed ten men "—on the end of it."

Jane started to laugh, then clutched her belly, wishing it didn't hurt so much.

Jack paid no attention to her ills. "I baited your line again and threw it back over," he said. "So you could have a fish, too. This one is just about enough for me." He patted his ample stomach and licked his lips in gustatory anticipation.

His antics brought another smile to Jane's lips, and she was about to join him in jesting when, out of the corner of her eye, she thought she saw her line move. She watched it closely. Yes, something was definitely tugging on it. She played out a little more line in order to take a measure of the fish. The answering pull was strong. This was must be even larger than the first one, she thought as she started to haul it in. The fellow on the other end of the line had other ideas. Pull as she might, the line began to slip through her hands. She called out for Jack, and together they wrestled their catch—another big, fighting blue—out of the water. The hands all gathered around as the duo brought the fish up over the bow, cheering when it finally landed on the deck with a mighty thud.

Doc appeared in an instant, his sharp knife at the ready to gut and clean the catch. "It's another decent meal for you worthless lubbers tonight," the stringy, sinewy cook declared with relish. Doc's glee at the prospect of preparing a good dinner succeeded in breaking the grim atmosphere that had settled over the crew after the fight. An air of joking camaraderie replaced the downheartedness, and Big Jack and John Harding became the objects of much good-natured ribaldry.

Below deck, however, the air was not so clear. Alone in the fo'c'sle Crebbs listened to the shouting and laughter, a bitter bile forming in the back of his throat. Why should green Harding walk away from every challenge unscathed while he, a seaman whose ten hard years had been rewarded with precious little, was beaten near to a pulp and left to be a hungry outcast for a whole week? His hatred of John Harding grew, feeding on the pain in his body and the ache in his belly.

Nor was the scene in the officers' mess a pretty one. Starbuck lit into his mate with the ferocity of an Indian Ocean squall. "What the hell did you think you were doing up there? I have enough trouble keeping the men in line without my first officer using his fists instead of his brains, too. What got into you, man?"

How could Val explain to Sam his feelings when he saw Crebbs strike John Harding? He could never say to Sam the things he had said to Mercy about John Harding. "It seemed unfair, sir. Crebbs is years older than Harding and ten times as nasty."

"Fair? You dare to use that word? What is fair about an officer beating a man as if he were a savage? You're supposed to break up a fight if you see one, Mr. Mayhew, not get into it."

"Yes, sir," Val answered contritely. "I know that, sir."

Starbuck was silent for a moment. He looked at Val intently and then turned away. "I won't have it," he said quietly.

"It won't happen again, sir. I give you my word."

"That's not what I mean, Val. It pains me greatly to have to say this to you. I value you as an officer and as a friend. But I will not have any unnatural attachments on this vessel."

Val blanched. The words pounded in his ears, as if he were caught inside a pealing bell. But they rang with truth, too. This was the awful reality he had tried to explain away in his talk with Mercy. All their talk of sensitivity and friendships of the heart was only a cloak for Val's deepest fears—that he had for John Harding feelings he had never had for a woman. There. He had said it to himself. He steeled himself and faced his captain. "I promise you there are none, nor will there be any," he vowed, meeting Sam's eyes squarely, avoiding neither his own nor his friend's pain and discomfort. Whatever sentiments John Harding stirred in him, he must keep them to himself and never allow them to interfere with his responsibilities to the *Meribah* and to Sam. The captain continued his merciless scrutiny, but Val remained silent, knowing that anything he said further would be superfluous. Their eyes unlocked only when they heard the sound of Mercy's boots on the stairs.

Coming upon the scene, Mercy felt the atmosphere of tension immediately. "Am I interrupting, Captain?" she ventured.

With her question the strain broke, leaving the room with a drained, sodden air. "No," Starbuck said wearily. "Mr. Mayhew and I are finished."

"Then may I see to Mr. Mayhew's cuts?"

"As you wish, madam." The captain gave her a per-functory bow and retreated to his dayroom. Shutting the door behind him, he unlocked a small cabinet above the sofa and poured himself a liberal ration of whiskey, which he tossed down in a single burning gulp. He waited for the anesthetizing power of the liquor to take hold, but the strong drink brought no release.

Every whaling captain must have one officer he trusts indubitably, implicitly, and for him, Valentine Mayhew had always been that person. But tonight, Val had behaved unconscionably. Starbuck still could not quite credit it: his first mate beating a common seaman to a pulp, and over another foremast hand? He feared for the *Meribah* should disaster befall him, especially on this voyage, when there was Mrs. Wright to consider. He was no longer certain Val would be equal to the task. Were he a superstitious man, he just might begin to take some stock in the notion that a woman aboard *did* bring bad luck. But Mercy had nothing to do with Val's wretched behavior, he reminded himself. John Harding's presence was none of her doing. Except that she had made rather a pet of the boy. He would have to mention that to her, but not now. Tomorrow, or the next day, when he wasn't so overwhelmingly tired, would do. He was so weary that he could no longer hold himself erect. He sank onto the sofa and let his eyes close, wanting only to block out the whole bloody episode. Or to have someone else black it out for him.

In the mess area, Val waited numbly for Mercy to come to him with hot water, towels, soap and salve. His cuts were deep and it hurt mightily when she washed them, but he barely registered the pain. He was too caught up in his own shame and remorse. How had he allowed himself to lose control in that way? He had betrayed every bit of training and good sense he'd ever had. He had disgraced himself, his captain, his fellow officers, the *Meribah* herself. But the worst of it was that should a similar situation arise, he knew he would do the same thing again. How could that be, when he knew all too well that he was at fault? From where did his blind need to protect John Harding spring? And to what sorry place would it lead him, he wondered.

"I'm finished, Val," Mercy was saying gently. "See if you can get some rest now." Dully he looked up and thanked her, unable quite to meet her eyes, then slunk away to his cabin.

Poor Val, Mercy thought as she cleared away the basin and towels. And yet she could readily understand his humiliation and contrition. He had been clearly in the wrong and should regret his actions. A far greater quantity of her sympathy, however, extended to Captain Starbuck. Not only had there been a grave infraction of discipline on his ship, but his faith in his chief officer had suffered a severe blow. For a man who dealt in absolutes, as Starbuck often did, this evening must have been painful indeed. She was deliberating the merits of going to the dayroom to inquire after him when she heard the sound of shattering glass.

She hurried to the door of the dayroom and knocked, bracing herself for an angry growl or a shout. Instead she heard a flat voice telling her to enter. Opening the door, she found the captain sitting on the sofa. He did not rise or even nod when he saw her, only stared at her blankly. "Are you all right?" she asked quietly.

"I dropped a glass, Mrs. Wright. That is all."

His voice was raw and hoarse, and he seemed not only tired but bewildered, as well, as if he could not understand how the glass came to be broken or indeed what to do about it. She had no doubt that should an emergency arise he would leap up and conquer it without a second's hesitation. But this small mishap defeated him. "Shall I send for the boy to sweep it up?" she offered.

"No. Leave it."

There was a moment of awkward silence while Mercy wondered if she should go into the room or leave the captain to his own thoughts. It was best not to thrust herself upon him, she decided, but she would make one more overture. "Can I do anything else for you, then?"

He shook his head and she turned to go, but a sharp command pulled her back into the room. "Talk to me, Mrs. Wright. Tell me anything. Take me away from this godforsaken vessel."

Quickly and instinctively, Mercy responded to his appeal. She shut the door behind her, sat beside him and began speaking quietly. "I don't know what made me think of this today, but for some reason I remembered something Caroline did as a child. When you think of what my sister has become, it is quite amusing." The tale she proceeded to relate was one in which the captain would ordinarily have had not the slightest interest, but she told it with all the skill she possessed. When she was about eight, Caroline had secretly sewn herself a grown-up lady's outfit from scraps purloined from their mother's sewing basket. When the apparel was finished, she had dressed in it and stolen out of the house to go a-calling, looking more like a beggar woman than the fine lady she imagined herself to be. They had found her grandly taking tea with Mrs. Mary Gardner, who could barely keep a straight face as she poured out into her best china cups.

Starbuck listened with his eyes closed, and Mercy painted the scenes as delicately as she could. She spoke in pastel watercolors, not dark-hued oils, and little by little the lines on the captain's face eased. When he reached for her hand, she did not withdraw it, but continued her recollections. And when he wrapped her in his arms she did not move away, but let him draw comfort and succor from her.

His embrace demanded nothing more than this from her tonight. Far from the turbulent feelings his touch had aroused in her before, now she felt only warmth for the man. He bore a great burden, admirably and without complaint, but in this moment he needed respite, a single hour when he did not have to play Atlas to the *Meribah*. And Mercy was only too glad to provide that hour for him.

Chapter Eight

After that stormy Sunday—which both Mercy and Jane have oft marked as a milestone on the voyage—life aboard the *Meribah* moved into calmer waters.

Relations between Mercy and her captain were much improved, one might even describe them as cordial. Mercy had proposed and received permission to institute a number of changes in the sanitary practices aboard the ship—a daily scrubbing of the fo'c'sle with salt water and vinegar; vessels for night soil placed in the fo'c'sle with strict instructions to the men to use them; the construction of a canvas tube which, when attached to the rigging and inserted in the fo'c'sle hatch, caught the breeze and diverted fresh air into the sailors' quarters.

Mercy did endeavor not to find herself alone with Captain Starbuck in the few dark, lonely recesses the *Meribah* offered at night, but they did spend many evening hours talking or quietly reading or writing together. There developed between them a mutual respect and, given the closeness in which they necessarily lived, even a small degree of affectionate regard. But the passionate incident of the first night at sea was not repeated, even though its memory did linger prominently and somewhat distressfully in the minds of both participants.

No whales were sighted—the North Atlantic grounds having long ago been depleted of the gigantic beasts—but the whaleboats went out frequently, both for practice and when porpoises and blackfish were sighted. The oil gleaned from these missions would later be mixed with lesser grades of sperm oil, but this was not the principal profit of these expeditions. That lay in the proficiency the men gained from working their boats.

Jane's prowess as a sailor grew, as did her reputation among the men. She was very much different from the rest—she did not smoke, swear or fight. Despite Captain Starbuck's ferocity on this point, there was the occasional altercation and attendant fisticuffs to settle it in the fo'c'sle. These incidents the men kept to themselves, to protect both their sport and themselves from the wrath of their captain. But she was also seen to be brave, capable and cooperative, this last an unusual quality in the fo'c'sle of a whaling vessel. Even Crebbs seemed to be swayed by the opinion of the majority and ceased his harassments, treating her with such grudging civility as he was capable of.

Jane's happiness was marred only by the coolness of Mr. Mayhew's behavior toward her. He avoided her at every opportunity, and when they were thrown together by duty in the crow's nest, he was silent almost to the point of rudeness. Yet she would catch him staring at her in the odd moment's leisure, just as he would catch her from time to time. But for these furtive looks and the longings that accompanied them, Jane would have counted herself the most fortunate young female on earth.

Six weeks and two days after setting out from Nantucket the *Meribah* made her first port, Ponta Delgada on the Western Island of São Miguel. The islands were a colony of Portugal and prospered by serving ships and sailors, providing every commodity a sailing man—from captain to foremast hand—could desire. For Mercy their chief charm—aside from the novelty of setting foot on firm land—was the letters that would be waiting for her there, carried by faster merchant ships.

They landed on a fine but hot morning in early June for a stay of twenty-four hours. So eager was she to fetch her mail that she would have dashed down the gangplank on her own and somehow made her way to the post office. But Captain Starbuck had made it clear to her, in a rather warm debate the previous evening, that she was not to negotiate the streets of Ponta Delgada unaccompanied. The steward, Mr. Carmody, had been assigned to escort her first to the post office and then to the home of Dom Diego Sobral, a maritime merchant who had been a favorite acquaintance of her father. For some years she had corresponded with Dom Diego's daughter Manuela and was hoping to meet her pen friend on this visit.

Except for the fact that most people were speaking Portuguese, a more musical and higher-pitched tongue than English, Mercy found the wharf of Ponta Delgada different only in degree from the scene she knew so well in Nantucket. It was more crowded, with more people whose origins she could not fathom speaking more languages she did not recognize. The smells were stronger, some unidentifiable to her, but the richness in the air was not at all unpleasant. The architecture was more haphazard than she was used to. Most of the buildings seemed to be wooden shacks, hastily constructed for expediency and not meant to withstand time and tide as the structures at home. But its vibrancy was apparent and most attractive to her.

Until she set foot on dry land she did not realize how deprived her senses had been on board the *Meribah*. The sights and sounds and smells of the open sea varied little from one day to the next, and she found the sudden influx of sensation was stimulating, not at all frightening or threatening, as the captain had predicted. She would have to chasten Sam for so underestimating her reaction to the scene.

The postal depot was crowded with men and women of all sorts—from shabbily clad sailors to fashionable ladies attended by female servants in black dresses. Waiting one's turn was apparently not the custom here, so Mercy, along with the rest, pushed her way to the counter and vied for the attention of the proprietress, a large dark-skinned woman wearing an extraordinary blouse of full-blown red roses against a bright blue background, the effect of which was to make her appear to be a walking garden on a hot late-summer day.

Through her correspondence with Manuela Sobral she knew a few words of Portuguese, but she soon learned this was not necessary as the proprietress spoke a kind of universal polyglot tongue that enabled her to understand and be understood by all. When the lady finally deigned to serve her, Mercy was presented with a large stack of lovely letters, which she clutched to her bosom with absolute joy and delight. While Mr. Carmody asked on behalf of the others aboard the *Meribah*, Mercy leafed through her treasures and deciphered the handwriting on the envelopes. There were two or three each from Caroline, Sarah, Aunt Elizabeth and Aunt Lavinia. Maria had not neglected her, nor had her Uncle Thomas. Other friends had also been generous with their time and ink, and she could barely restrain herself from ripping open all the envelopes and rifling through them, like a hungry alley cat in a tantalizing scrap heap.

Mr. Carmody came away from the counter with a very large number of letters for the officers of the *Meribah* and even a few for those fortunate sailors who had home ties. Their business concluded, Mercy and her escort struck out for the villa of Dom Diego Sobral. The distance from the commercial district to the residence was not great—Ponta Delgada was a small place—but the change in scenery was remarkable. The Villa Lara was a large stone house, built of the island's black granite and surrounded by a wall of the same dark stone. The effect was not at all forbidding, but it was highly dramatic. Stopping at the wrought iron gate, Mercy gazed through it into the lush gardens with their pebbled walks, pools and banks of blooming shrubbery. Mr. Carmody rang the bell, and in a moment a woman servant clad all in black appeared. Nearly exhausting her knowledge of Portuguese, Mercy gave her name and asked for Senhorinha Manuela. More from gesture than understanding, Mercy divined that her friend was absent but Dom Diego was at home.

Mr. Carmody waited outside while she was shown into a cool, spacious marble-floored hallway. In a moment the carved wooden doors of a room on the right of the corridor flew open and a very small gentleman with a very large mustache appeared. In musical if not perfect English, Dom Diego Sobral greeted her as if she were a long-lost daughter. "Ah, the girl of my good friend Benjamin Randall. The sad news has reached us here, and I make very sorry to hear it. Both sad newses—your dear father and your dear husband. But to see you! For me how pleasing is this. As if one of my own has traveled home. Please, come."

Mercy allowed herself to be led into a large library, its walls covered floor to ceiling with shelves crammed every which way with books. There was a sea of red-and-gold Turkish carpet on the floor, flanked by a flotilla of leather armchairs and sofas. In the center of all this reigned the flagship—a long table with elaborately carved legs, piled high with papers and maps and drawings.

She had just thanked Dom Diego for his expression of sympathy and his warm welcome and was about to remark on the beauty of Villa Lara when there was a knock at the library door. Before Dom Diego could reply, the door opened. The visitor at the portal did not observe the formality of waiting to be invited in. Nevertheless he too was greeted like a long-lost offspring. "Samuel, my excellent friend," Dom Diego cried. "In one morning so much surprises."

Starbuck stood a full foot taller than Dom Diego Sobral, but what the smaller man lacked in height he made up in ebullience. He scurried to his friend and pumped his hand vigorously. "But do you travel together? Upon the *Meribah*. But of course you must. It could not be so much a, how do you say it, a coinciding?"

"Coincidence," Sam supplied. "Mrs. Wright has graciously joined me for the voyage," he said smoothly.

Dom Diego looked speculatively from Sam to Mercy and back again. "Then she is a very brave woman," he said slyly, and the two men burst into raucous laughter. Mercy failed to see what was so funny.

Dom Diego then clapped his hands together loudly and to the servant who responded issued an animated series of orders. "We will drink coffee now and I will say all the news of Ponta Delgada and you will say all the news of Nantucket."

"The coffee I will accept gratefully, but I cannot tarry for gossip," Starbuck replied, arranging himself comfortably upon one of the large leather sofas. "I must see to the provisioning of the ship. I only came now to be sure Mrs. Wright was safely delivered into your hands. But I will gladly accept your invitation to dine. As will Mrs. Wright."

Mercy could not help but cry out, "Captain! You presume too much on Dom Diego's hospitality." Not to mention my own good will, she added to herself. What was the occasion, she wondered, for this astounding rudeness?

"No, no," Dom Diego assured her. "The next word I was to say was this very thing. You will both come and eat tonight. I am alone for many weeks now. In Lisboa are my wife and daughters. I welcome your company. To entertain Captain Starbuck is a very great novelty. Each time he is here I ask him to come to me, but always he has other engagements. This time—" and again Dom Diego looked at Mercy and then back at Sam "—I believe he spends himself more profitably."

"Much more," Sam agreed.

Coffee was served, from a silver tray, in sparkling gold-rimmed cups, a fragrant, delicate brew that bore only a passing resemblance to the muddy liquid served up on the *Meribah*. Mercy savored every sip, as well as every bite of a fluffy sweet roll fragrant with cinnamon. Sam took his refreshment and his leave directly, expressing regret at the absence of Dona Maria and her charming daughters.

As they finished their coffee, Mercy questioned Dom Diego about Manuela and all her activities. The trip to

Lisboa had been undertaken, she learned, to allow Manuela and the young man her father had chosen for her to become acquainted before their wedding. Dom Diego let it be known that this was a great concession on his part and one to which he had acceded only because of Manuela's strong sentiments. "I fear that living in so unconventional a place and meeting with so many peoples has given my daughter some dangerous ideas."

Mercy's view of arranged marriages was much different than her host's, but she kept her own "dangerous" ideas to herself. Instead she broached the topic of her dining attire. "I am afraid I have no suitable gown," she apologized.

"In this house there are enough gowns to clothe all the womans in Ponta Delgada. You pick what you like. I send the seamstress to fix it for you."

Mercy demurred at this generosity, but Dom Diego would not relent. He put his entire establishment at her disposal. He was sorry, he explained, but business called him away for most of the day, but in his absence she was to have anything she wanted. He was so warm and insistent that the only gracious course open to Mercy was to accept.

Thanks to Dom Diego, Mercy spent a wholly indulgent day. She remained in the library, sipping another cup of coffee and reading each of her letters through quickly, to glean the news. Then she was shown to the room that was Manuela's, and a bath was drawn for her. While awaiting her bath, she chose, with some difficulty, a gown of rosy pink organdy from the enormous stock of the Sobral women. She was hardly able to imagine what they had taken with them if they had left so much elegant clothing behind. When the seamstress had finished fitting the gown, Mercy settled down for a long, leisurely soak in a floral-scented tub.

Her rare excursion into a world of sybaritic pleasures sent her thoughts spinning off in unusual directions, too, although they started in quite an ordinary place. Gazing around the beautiful bedchamber, with its regal canopied bed, its dressing table crammed with exquisite crystal jars and bottles of creams and scents and potions, she had been struck by how easily she could imagine Nathaniel wandering through it. Indeed he would fit quite comfortably into any of the rooms of the Villa Lara, each of which was arranged for the comfort and ease of its occupants and meant to be enjoyed with all the senses. She could not help but contrast these luxurious chambers with the spartan cubicles aboard the *Meribah*, in which she found it difficult to place Nathaniel at all.

Given his love of sensuous pleasures, it was strange that Nathaniel had wanted so much to live on Nantucket, where utility, not excess or beauty, was the arbiter of life. She would have remained in Boston, had he desired it, but he had insisted on making their home on Orange Street. Considered in this light, it was strange, too, that he had even married her, a woman who could appreciate an occasional foray into indulgence, but who neither desired nor needed it as a daily diet. He must have loved her very much to abandon such pleasures, and to make further sacrifices by going whaling. But then why, why, since his departure, had he acted as if she had ceased to exist? She simply could make no sense of his behavior.

With these thoughts her delight in her bath cooled, and she finished her ablutions in a businesslike way and dressed in a lace-trimmed morning gown. Leaving her speculations firmly behind—they could only serve to ruin her pleasure in her day, which she had no intention of doing—she repaired to the sitting room that adjoined Manuela's bedchamber. There she retrieved her batch of letters and retired to the balcony to read them through again, slowly this time, lingering over each word. At midday she was served a meal of vegetable soup, fresh-baked bread and an assortment of fruits and cheeses, and she spent the remainder of the afternoon replying to her correspondents. After the close quarters aboard the *Meribah*, she found the solitude delicious, and in responding to her sisters and her many friends felt almost as if she were home with them. The rest of the day passed all too quickly.

While Mercy was thus engaged, the other of the *Meribah*'s women was seeing a wholly different side of Ponta Delgada. Each watch had been granted twelve hours' liberty, Mr. Mayhew's from seven o'clock in the morning, Mr. Hunter's from seven o'clock in the evening. As they lined up to leave the ship, Jane was approached by Big Jack, who suggested they spend their leave together, and in his company Jane had her first taste of a sailor's onshore haunts.

They first repaired to a tavern packed to bursting with drunken sailors, where Big Jack drank several glasses of raw, dark rum. Jane resisted the importunings of her friend and took only ginger beer, not because she objected to strong drink in principle, but because she was aware, although she had never tasted a drop, that one of its chief effects was a loosening of the tongue. She feared that under its influence she would say or do something to give away her true identity. Watching Jack imbibe, she was a bit leery of what so much liquor would do to him, but unlike the rest of the men, who were shouting and jostling and pushing and boasting, the rum seemed only to widen his smile and produce a slight glistening of perspiration on his round face.

"Ah," he sighed. "That's better. Are you sure you won't join me, young John? It's not your purse you're worried about, is it? Because if it is, Big Jack will gladly stand you to a glass or two."

"No, no," Jane assured him. "I have enough money to get into trouble, if I choose."

"Then you must be saving it for some other recreation, eh?" He gave her a crafty grin. "Ponta Delgada is a very good place for that. Every port is, for that matter." He clapped her on the back so hard that she nearly fell into her ginger beer. "I know a good house—where the women are young and pretty and very obligin', if you know what I mean."

Jane did and felt herself turn a deep, dark red. "No, no," she stammered. "I mean, yes, I do know what you mean, but I don't—"

"There's boys, too, if that's what you want," Jack said matter-of-factly. "No, I guess not," he replied to her gasp. "Then what are we going to do all day, my friend? You don't drink, smoke, fight or do anything else that's fun," he said merrily.

"You don't have to stay with me," Jane said haughtily. "I can take care of myself."

"Oh, I don't doubt that. It's myself I'm worried about. You see, I like to do all those things and I might get into trouble without you."

"In that case," she relented, "I suppose I'll have to stay with you."

Jack let out one of his booming laughs and pulled Jane away from the counter. "Come on, at least we can get a good meal. I know you eat."

They made their way through the crowd on the wharf to a dilapidated shack that had a few rough tables and chairs in front of it. Soon they were eating big bowls of something delicious—a kind of fish stew but unlike any Jane had known. It had no milk in it, the fish was floating instead in a broth of its own juices, a heavy oil, a sweet red vegetable and a pungent herb, something like an onion but stronger. It reminded her of what she had smelled that night in the boarding house in Nantucket, except that her tongue found it much more palatable than her nose. She asked Jack about it.

"In these parts they put it in everything. Tastes good, but it leaves you with a powerful breath afterwards, especially if you chew it raw. The folks hereabouts think that keeps you healthy. I expect we'll be smelling it in the fo'c'sle now. Pedro and Francisco will have laid in a supply." He grimaced and held his nose.

Jane grinned. "Maybe we can get them to give it to Doc to cook."

"That would be something to taste. Salt horse Western Island style." Jack slapped the table, enjoying his joke as much as Jane. Then they both ordered another bowl of stew. Jack had a third for good measure, and between them they polished off a loaf of crusty bread.

They spent the rest of the day walking and feasting and talking, buying a trinket or two. There was a sideshow every minute—a brawl here, a flirtation there, musicians, jugglers, acrobats and mountebanks, a grand lady picking her way through the mud and garbage in her finery. All too soon, however, their twelve hours of walking on dry land and doing as they pleased were over, and they made their way back to the *Meribah*'s slip, where they found Mr. Mayhew, waiting to count his watch and see they all returned to the ship on time.

Val's day had been spent much less eventfully than that of his men. After assisting Sam in securing provisions for the ship—fresh water, wood, fruits and vegetables, a hog, a battery of chickens—he had visited the one decent hotel in town for a bath and a large, excellent meal. He had posted some letters, purchased a few necessary items and taken a long, solitary walk. Though he had tried to banish them, his thoughts had been much on John Harding. What was he doing? Was he faring well? Had he met harm at the hands of a thief or cutthroat? But now, as Val saw Harding sauntering down the wharf beside Big Jack, he knew the young man had been in good company.

Big Jack was in a voluble mood, having drained a large flagon of rough red wine with the last of their many meals. He hailed Mr. Mayhew jauntily and embarked on an account of the day's activities. "Now, did you ever hear of a more harmless day for a sailor in port? I was all set to satisfy the devil in me today, but I took up with young John here this morning, and that put old Mr. Satan right behind us." He cuffed John playfully on the shoulder. "Did you ever see such a good sailor, Mr. Mayhew? How do you suppose young John Harding got that good? And what's more," he roared with hilarity, "how do you suppose he stays that way, spending all his time around people like me?''

Jane smiled sheepishly at Mr. Mayhew, flustered by Jack's forward behavior. A foremast hand did not address an officer so intimately, and an officer did not accept such behavior—unless he was making allowances for the end of a liberty. And apparently Mr. Mayhew was—for Jack. The allowances did not extend to her, for he looked away from her sharply and ordered them both to board. Jane could see that Jack, who loved to talk even without liberal doses of spirits, was about to deliver another speech, so she tugged hard on his arm and pulled him along with her, up the gangplank. It was hard work, this with Jack stopping every other step to air another thought or opinion.

At one point she turned around to glance at Mr. Mayhew and caught him looking at her. She smiled wanly, feeling that familiar ache that she had come to associate with seeing him. And then a dreadful thought struck her. Poor Mr. Mayhew! For all he knew, she was a young man and if he was feeling for her anything like what she was feeling for him . . . She remembered how confused and embarrassed she had felt in the tavern this morning when Jack had suggested— Mr. Mayhew must be in a terrible quandary indeed. She wished there was something she could say, but the only way to ease his mind would be to unmask herself. Oh, dear. Poor Mr. Mayhew, she thought again. And poor Jane Harding. She was in quite a state of agitation as she lay in her bunk that night. Could she really keep up this charade for *years?*

Even as Jane was lying awake, Mercy, cool and rested and resplendent in her rose-colored gown, was descending the marble staircase at the Villa Lara. At the landing, she was met by her host, who offered his arm and escorted her into the drawing room. There Captain Starbuck, freshly groomed and dressed in his finest suit, was already enjoying a glass of Dom Diego's excellent sherry.

Starbuck bowed to her and bade her good evening, his demeanor and tone unusually formal. He seemed almost to have rehearsed his part, as if he—and she—were actors in a play. She also saw that he was enjoying the engagement with all the zest of an enthusiastic amateur. Mercy caught his amusement and added an acknowledging smile to her greeting. Given their unusual costumes and the setting in which they were placed, they could well be on a stage together.

Dom Diego led her to a dainty armchair upholstered in pastel-green brocade. The room itself was as feminine as Dom Diego's library was masculine, all lights and mirrors and shimmering fabrics. The furniture required a straight back and a small hip, and Mercy perched herself prettily on the edge of her chair and accepted a glass of sherry. Surveying the room, she thought how different the decor was from Aunt Elizabeth's drawing room. That place was all velvet and heavy horsehair settees, and yet she was reminded of her time in Boston, where much of life was also devoted to such frivolous pursuits as were possible in a room like this. It was hard to imagine settling into any of the chairs here to read or think or to do anything but converse and observe the others in the room, always of course with an eye toward protecting or enhancing one's social position.

Her first introduction to that particular parlor game had come in Boston, and while it had interested her at first—it was new and for that reason diverting—she had soon grown impatient with it. Though very much a part of that world, Nathaniel had often told her how weary he was with people who were not acutely aware, as he was, that there were more important things in life. Their shared view on this subject, he said, had drawn him to her. And her to him. Or had something quite different actually occurred? Had they both been acting a part? He of the insider longing to be free of stifling convention? She of the outsider longing to be part of the wider world outside her small, if comfortable, community? If so, the drama had taken a sharp, unexpected turn. Could it ever end happily now, she wondered, or was tragedy inevitable?

Dom Diego's voice brought her back to tonight's play, a drawing room comedy in a much lighter vein than the one that occupied her thoughts. "Is she not a vision?" her host was asking. "Even my own Manuela is not so lovely in that dress."

"That is a pretty compliment indeed," Mercy said, "from so doting a father."

Captain Starbuck found himself gazing at her with undisguised admiration. Her unexpectedly dazzling appearance made him realize how much he had come to take her beauty for granted. In the plain garb she wore aboard the *Meribah,* it was merely there. Tonight it shone radiantly, like a full moon suddenly cleared of an obscuring cloud. "But not a compliment that exceeds its bounds," he assured her. "You do look splendid, Mercy."

"Why, thank you, Sam." She returned the use of her Christian name archly. Although they did now in private address each other familiarly, she was surprised by his lapse. Perhaps his day of liberty had made him unheedful of the bounds of propriety. Or perhaps he simply felt welcome and at home with Dom Diego, as she did. Or perhaps he sought to advance the plot of the evening's drama, she thought with dismay. But what if he did? She should pay it no mind. It was only a few hours' diversion. When they returned to the *Meribah,* they would revert to their usual roles.

She sipped at her sherry, a drink for which she had acquired a liking in Boston but had not tasted since. She had forgotten how warm and flushed it could make her feel, and how pleasant that feeling could be. The ensuing conversation was lively and wide-ranging, as it can be when people in sympathy with one another and also in want of stimulating company gather together.

Dom Diego spoke of the maritime trade, the political situation in Europe, his hopes for Manuela and her younger sister Isabella. Mercy recounted the news from home in her letters—Caroline's balls and teas and dinner parties; Sarah's joy in the easel and oil paints that had been Mercy's parting gift; Maria's studies; the various goings-on reported in her other letters. Sam spoke of his day's activities provisioning the *Meribah;* of conversations he had had with other captains in the town and news gleaned from around the world. Before Mercy knew it, a sumptuous dinner of five courses had been consumed and it was time for her to withdraw and leave the gentlemen to their port and cigars.

Dom Diego begged her to remain with them. "For your company I will gladly forego my tobacco."

"But I will not give up my port," Sam declared emphatically.

"Let us compromise then," Mercy proposed gaily. "A few breaths of night air will not go amiss. Instead of sitting alone in the drawing room, I shall take a turn around the garden."

Dom Diego protested briefly. He could not permit her to think him so poor a host that he would send her out-of-doors alone. She assured him that she preferred to go alone, but only when Sam added his voice to hers did Dom Diego consent to the plan. She must, however, be accompanied by one of the female servants. Now Mercy was inclined to protest, but realized he was only offering her the same courtesy and protection he would afford his daughters. With a servant following discreetly behind, she took her stroll.

And a lovely walk it was. Mercy memorized the balmy touch of the air, with only a hint of salt sting in it, the sweet fragrance of the roses, the rustle of the wind in the trees, the muffled neighing of the horses in the nearby stables. She had taken land sounds and smells such as these so much for granted in Nantucket. Now they seemed very rich and precious. Time had hardly seemed to pass when she heard the crunch of footsteps on the pebbled walk, and in the dim light spilling through the windows of the house, made out Sam's figure. How straight and tall he walks, she thought as he approached her.

They took their time returning to the house, for Sam too was in need of the night air and a bit of exercise after so much rich food. Mellowed by the meal and the wine that had accompanied it, Mercy took his arm when he offered it, never once thinking to be wary of this closeness. She felt an unusual warmth for Sam this evening, the result she suspected of the combined effect of their warm welcome at the Villa Lara, the food and wine, the luxurious change from their usually Spartan routine. They were talking and laughing softly as they returned, still arm in arm, to the house.

"My friends," Dom Diego cried when he greeted them at the door, "it is so charming to see you together this way. I am having great sentiment to look at you. Please, do not go now. Spend the night with the Villa Lara. There is plenty of rooms. And," he glanced sideways at Sam, "you will find your host a very sound sleeper."

To Mercy this last seemed an odd thing to say, and it was a moment before she understood Dom Diego's inference: that she and Sam should spend the night here—together. She felt the blood drain from her face, not in outrage but for doubt of her own performance. Had she acted and spoken in such a way that her father's friend would believe her capable of such behavior?

"That is very kind of you, Dom Diego," Sam was saying. "But we must get back to the ship. We must catch the outgoing tide as soon as the second watch returns."

Dom Diego then insisted they take his carriage, and a flurry of arrangements began, with servants gathering up Mercy's things, orders for returning the gown in the morning and gifts pressed upon them both. Though grateful for Dom Diego's hospitality, Mercy found it hard to face him squarely during the leave-takings and to thank him properly for his generosity. Finally all had been said and done, and Sam handed her into the carriage.

Mercy sat silently, immersed in thought, minutely reviewing her every word and action in respect to the captain over the course of the evening. Her reverie was shattered by a loud burst of laughter.

"You'd better stop being so nice to me," Sam said with a chortle. "People seem to get the wrong idea.'

"I am trying to remember," she said in a small, tight voice, "what I could have said or done. Or—" her voice hardened "—what you said or did to give such an impression."

"What I said or did! I behaved in the most gentlemanly fashion all evening."

"You did call me by my first name."

"And you followed suit. For heaven's sake, Mercy, we've known each other all our lives. Your father was the best friend I've ever had. It's ridiculous for us to be captaining and missus-ing each other in the home of a mutual friend."

Mercy was silent for a time, not so much accepting his argument but still thinking, recalling every word, every gesture. "But why? Why?" she mused. "What could draw Dom Diego to such an unwarranted conclusion?"

Sam turned to her. "Perhaps our friend merely sensed what is there beneath the surface, Mercy."

"There is nothing beneath the surface," she said flatly, although her insides were zinging with unwanted excitement.

"Are you saying you'd as soon be hung for a sheep as a lamb, then?" He wrapped his arms around her and brought his face close to hers. "Tell me, Mercy, tell me there's nothing between us."

She tried to turn away, but he caught her lips with his and pressed himself to her. Her head was swimming—the night air, the wine, his touch, the soft, sweet smell of his breath—they all swirled around her, drawing her deeper, deeper into the vortex. Even as she kissed him, she wondered why it was like this. With her husband she had never felt these strong, compelling urges for physical fulfillment. With Nathaniel she had felt nothing more than a gentle longing. Their embraces had never been feverish. Even in the intimacy of marital relations she had never felt the insistent passion Sam called up in her.

Sam crushed his lips to her throat. "Tell me," he demanded again. "I want to hear you say there is nothing between us." He brushed the back of his hand across her body, just above her bosom where flesh and fabric met. His touch burned her, but she felt herself shiver. There was that kind of perversity in her feelings. Hot was cold and cold was hot. She could not accept it, but neither could she reject it. Nor could she say the words he challenged her to say. She could only lean against him, breathless and spent.

The curtain had not yet fallen, she feared, on the final act of the evening's play. They finished the journey in charged silence.

Chapter Nine

The greatest enemy aboard a whaling ship is not storms or an enraged wounded whale bearing down upon the vessel; it is boredom. And that, dear reader, is what took root aboard the *Meribah* a week after she left the Western Islands. The novelty of starting the voyage was over; the excitement of making the first port was fading fast. Day after day the *Meribah* headed south toward the equator, virtually in a straight line, hugging as close as possible to the line of 30°0 west latitude. Day after day there was only sea and sky. A bit of rain was an event of great moment, every aspect of which was discussed—how the sky changed, how the wind came up, where the clouds formed, what type of clouds they were, how large or small the drops were, how forceful was the downpour, how long the rain lasted, how many barrels of rainwater were caught, how quickly or slowly the sky cleared afterward. A group of women could hardly have done better justice to the engagement or wedding of a near relative or friend. But for men whose world could be traversed in fifty paces in one direction and ten paces in the other, who needed employment and excitement, a fifteen-minute rainstorm could provide only so much occupation.

Though lookouts were posted all day, not a single whale was sighted for the whole of June or July. Starbuck kept his men busy and in line, but without the arduous work of catching and butchering and boiling down whales the men had not sufficient demands upon their energy. There had been no fighting among the men—at least no serious fighting that came to the attention of the officers—but the incidence of sniping and snarling gave the captain cause for concern. The men needed some diversion.

And so at the officers' mess one evening when they were about three or four days' sail from the equator, he proposed a crossing-the-line ceremony, where all hands who had not previously crossed the equator would be initiated into the fold and proclaimed followers of the sea god Neptune. Preparations began immediately. Mercy was enlisted to create costumes for Neptune—the captain—and his associates—the officers. Mr. Hunter was to work with the carpenter and the cooper to construct the dunking vat. And the captain and the mate would plan, in secret, the form and content of the ceremony. There was, as well, some discussion about whether to announce the festivities ahead of time or to keep them a surprise. Mr. Mayhew's opinion, that there was much to be gained in morale from the anticipation of the event, prevailed. The mates were to announce it to their watches the next day.

The difference in the men was evident by afternoon. They carried out their duties with alacrity; even the most sullen and disaffected displayed occasional smiles as they went about their work. The green hands—Jane, Aaron Cole and Owen Weeks—were subjected to many tantalizing and terrifying accounts of what would happen to them on the night of the ceremony, and talk among the men was now animated. What would the initiates be required to do? Would there be a special meal? And a ration of rum?

On this last point Sam sought the opinion of his officers, and the issue was debated heatedly. Sam himself, most unusually, vacillated in his thinking. Finally, however, he decided that one portion of rum per man would enliven the ceremony and gratify the crew without any drunkenness or disorder.

Besides lifting the mood of the men, the ceremony had another benefit. In the hours they spent alone making plans, the captain and his mate at last were able to recapture some of the warmth that had once characterized their relationship. Since the incident with Crebbs and Harding, there had been considerable restraint on both sides, each man behaving with unfailing correctness toward the other and both regretting the loss of their former intimacy. But the sheer glee of concocting pranks together restored some of their mutual ease, especially when they hit on a particularly devilish surprise.

Mercy thoroughly enjoyed her part in the preparations. She sewed robes for Neptune and his court out of bedsheets, made colorful sashes from scraps of cloth, even fashioned a wig for Neptune out of a mop head. With the carpenter, she planned Neptune's trident—three harpoon irons fastened to a mop handle. And she assisted Doc in the preparation of a dozen dried-apple-and-raisin pies.

The closer the *Meribah* got to the line the more the ship seemed to buzz and hum with excitement. The men were like a group of overactive children on their way to an outing, asking every ten seconds, "Are we almost there?" Finally, late in the afternoon, word was brought to the captain that they were.

Sam ordered the sails shortened and the ship's course altered. Until the green hands had been initiated, the *Meribah* could not cross the line. Jane, Aaron and Owen were ordered into the fo'c'sle, with the hatch closed so they could not hear the preparations taking place on board. When all was ready, one of the harpooners was dispatched below, three blindfolds in his trouser pocket. The sightless trio were then led onto the deck.

Despite efforts by the experienced sailors to strike terror into her heart, Jane trusted that the evening's activities would be more fun than frightening. When the blindfold was tied around her eyes, she first felt a shiver of excitement and then just a small tremor of alarm. Suddenly deprived of her sight, her complacency vanished in the utter darkness.

The three were led onto the deck and greeted with absolute silence, which went on for a very long time and served to increase Jane's apprehension. She could hear people padding about on tiptoe, but could make out nothing definite except the normal sounds of the sea and the ship. Then there started up such a racket that she nearly jumped out of her shoes. Beside her she sensed Aaron and Owen twitching nervously, too, as all manner of things were banged and crashed about their heads. The clang of iron on iron soon set her own ears ringing and left her feeling dizzy and lightheaded. Then suddenly the noise stopped, and there was another long silence.

Three ominous raps—wood against wood this time—finally broke the silence. "Hear ye! Hear ye!" She recognized Mr. Mayhew's voice. "The great god Neptune has risen tonight from the depths of the sea to judge these three men."

"Men? You call these sorry specimens men?" the Captain's voice rang out, and the crew echoed Neptune's disapproval of the initiates. "Is this the best you can offer?"

Mr. Mayhew again. "I fear it is, O great one."

"This is an insult to my powers," he roared. "Take them away. Toss them overboard. I abominate them."

"As you command, great Neptune."

Suddenly Jane felt herself caught up in two pairs of strong arms and lifted into the air. She was carried somewhere and put down on what seemed to be a narrow plank. "Go forward," Neptune commanded. She extended both her arms, searching for something to hold on to, but found nothing but thin air. "Go forward!" the command came again. Jane advanced cautiously, feeling carefully with her toe before putting each foot down. Soon she reached the end of the plank. Again she tested her surroundings, dipping one foot and then the other all about and finding nothing solid. Again she was commanded to move. She dared not tarry any longer, so she walked off the plank, expecting a long fall and a splash when she did. But her fall was shockingly short, onto something soft, a pile of mattresses she judged from the rustle and the smell. As she struggled to her feet someone clamped a hand over her mouth so she couldn't spoil the surprise for the others.

After Aaron and Owen had walked the plank, Neptune grudgingly declared them not as cowardly as he had originally thought. But then said he thought them all rather stupid. To alleviate this condition they were made to eat what Neptune called the brains of his smartest creatures, so that they would be wise in the ways of the sea. Jane doubted the concoction that was shoved into her mouth was fish brains, but it was foul smelling, slimy and foul tasting all the same.

The last test was one of perseverance. They were given a needle and thread and had to connect one with the other, without benefit of eyesight. The jokes and gibes of the crew did not make the job any easier, but finally all three mastered it.

At last satisfied with the performance of his initiates, Neptune proclaimed them fit—barely, of course—for his service. "You must now prove your worthiness by descending to the bottom of the sea."

Jane felt herself hoisted up again and placed precariously in a rope sling. Then the sling was hauled up and up and up. Clinging on for dear life, she called out, "What are you doing? This is the way to heaven. The sea is in the other direction!"

Over the guffaws of the men, Neptune thundered, "Insolence! I will not tolerate insolence! Send this sailor down."

The sling went down so fast that Jane's breath was taken away, and before she could get it back, she was underwater and fighting her way to the surface. Finally, gasping and sputtering, she reached it. Ripping the blindfold off her eyes, she found herself not in the sea but in a large vat on the deck. Big Jack offered her a hand and helped her over the edge. Exhausted and dripping wet, she stood on the deck proudly. She had crossed the line. She was a real sailor now. Soon there were two more sopping sailors beside her, and Neptune was about to close the ceremony.

"But wait!" he cried. "Something is amiss here. Do I detect another on board this vessel who has never crossed the line?" Suddenly he bore down on Mrs. Wright. "This woman! She is not one of us. The ship cannot continue until she is."

Before she knew it Mercy found herself in the sling. Though entirely surprised, she recovered quickly and took her punishment as gracefully as she could. She waved to the men on her way up, held her nose on the way down and was greeted by hearty applause as she surfaced.

"I hope you didn't mind," Neptune whispered as he and his chief courtier helped her out of the dunking vat. "It was all his idea." He pointed an accusing thumb at the first mate.

"It was not," Val protested.

Mercy looked at them both coolly. "As I recall, Captain, your youthful reputation as a mischief maker exceeds that of Mr. Mayhew, who himself has not a few childish pranks to his credit. In fact, I seem to remember being the butt of a number of them," she finished.

"They were all in good fun," Val defended himself.

"As this was," Sam put in.

"I know," Mercy relented with a smile. She pushed a stray strand of wet hair out of her eyes. "Actually, I'm flattered. I feel as if I really belong on the *Meribah* now."

"Aye, that you do," Sam said quietly.

Suddenly Mercy was aware of the captain's eyes on her and of the fact that her clothes were clinging closely to her body. She felt unaccountably flustered and shivered despite the warmth of the night. "Excuse me, I must change into some dry things." She hurried aft and down the companionway.

While she was gone, the men were given their single portion of rum and the health of John Harding, Aaron Cole and Owen Weeks was drunk. Doc was just dishing up the supper of fried fish and boiled potatoes and turnips when

Mercy returned to the deck. From then on, general merriment prevailed—with fiddling and singing and dancing and storytelling and pie eating. In fact, the atmosphere was so relaxed and uproarious that the steward committed a serious lapse of duty. He did not immediately lock up the rum butt after the dole, a fact that did not go unnoticed by sailor Crebbs and his friends, Hayward and Flubb.

Shortly after eight o'clock, Sam ordered the men back to their usual duties. Mr. Mayhew's watch was on deck; Mr. Hunter's retired to the fo'c'sle for a few hours' sleep. After clearing away the remains of the festivities, the first watch settled in for an easy night. With their backs resting against the windlass, Jane, Aaron and Owen compared notes about their initiation. What was the most exciting? When were they the most scared? What was really in those "fish brains" that they ate? After such a time and the rum and the food it was no wonder that Neptune's newest followers should drop into a light doze, even the one who had given her portion of rum to her good friend Big Jack.

The trio's awakening was rough and rudely accomplished. They found their hands being tied behind them with stout ropes and their ankles hobbled with a longer line. A rough hand stuffed a wad of cloth into Jane's mouth and tied a bandanna around it. Then she felt herself tossed over someone's shoulder like a sack of meal, to the accompaniment of an evil whisper. "No one's truly crossed the line until they've been keelhauled. Now we'll see what stuff you're really made of." Even in a strangled whisper, she recognized the weasellike croak of Crebbs. Hampered as she was by her bonds, she did her best to cause a disturbance. She thrashed and grunted and kicked and flailed. But to no avail. Her captor held her securely and no one came to her aid.

It was Big Jack who first noticed something amiss. The green hands had been sitting in front of the windlass and now they were gone. He scanned the dark deck but saw nothing in the shadows. Then he heard a muffled scuffling and raced aft to alert his officer. Going aft without permission was a serious offense, but Jack didn't think of that. He thought of keelhauling, of how he'd almost drowned when it had been done to him on his first voyage. How were these three boys, all smaller and less hardy than himself to survive such a stunt? It was a perfect night for mischief—dark and moonless, everyone sated and woozy.

"Mr. Mayhew," Jack whispered urgently, and explained his errand. Val thought immediately of John Harding and raced forward with Big Jack, ordering his two petty officers to follow them and the third mate to raise the captain.

Jane, meanwhile, was terrified. She was upside-down, being lowered inch by painful inch down the side of the ship. She could see the black water looming before her and desperately tried to think of a way to save herself, to keep herself from drowning as she was dragged in the wake of the ship. But she was securely trussed and powerless, and her mind was a blank. What could she do but pray?

Back on the deck the rescue party had discovered Crebbs and his cronies amidship on the larboard side. Only one keelhauling had begun. The other two green hands were still on deck, while the third—John Harding—dangled overboard. Jack pinioned Crebbs while Val took hold of the rope securing the third sailor. The two petty officers took charge of the other culprits.

Val hauled the rope up, hand over hand, carefully so as to make sure the stranded sailor was not sent crashing into the side of the ship. Finally he pulled the wriggling bundle over the bulwarks, saving John Harding from a harrowing fate that could have ended in serious injury or even death. The joy he felt at seeing the boy's face was nothing compared to the joy he saw in it. He lowered Harding to the deck and unleashed his bonds, containing his fury with the utmost difficulty. He did not dare look at Crebbs, for the sight of the man would have sent him into a frenzy. He wanted to tear the brute limb from limb. "Are you all right?" he asked the shivering young man.

"Yes, sir, I think so, sir," Jane stammered. Tears did not come easily to her, but she felt a hot stinging in her eye. She wanted to be held and comforted—by Mr. Mayhew for preference. But that was impossible. "Thank you, sir," she managed a small smile. "The water was getting rather close."

"What in the name of Beelzebub—?" The captain had arrived on the scene, Mrs. Wright hard on his heels. Val explained while Mercy bent over Jane, first rubbing her ankles to restore the circulation and then inspecting the rope burns on her wrists.

"Order all hands on deck, Mr. Mayhew. These men are to be flogged. And light the cresset lamps. I want everyone to see clearly." Starbuck then turned his wrath on Crebbs. "You! You reek of liquor. Where did it come from?"

"Ship's stores, sir," Crebbs mumbled. "Steward left the rum butt out. Will he be flogged, too?" He flashed a defiant smile at the captain.

Starbuck grabbed Crebbs by the front of his shirt. "You've just earned yourself an extra five stripes, sailor."

The sailors were rousted from the fo'c'sle, petty officers and idlers from the steerage. While all watched, the three offenders were stripped to the waist and hung by their thumbs from the rigging. "Engaging in a prohibited practice is a flogging offense," the captain warned the assembled crew. "These men have further disgraced themselves by stealing rum. And one of them has added insolence to the charges against him. Their punishment will be swift and harsh, as will yours be should you emulate their actions. Hayward and Flubb are sentenced to five lashes, Crebbs to ten." Mr. Hunter stepped forward to hand Starbuck the cat-o'-nine-tails, but he was waved away. "Mr. Carmody," the captain summoned the steward, who stepped forward, head bowed. "For carelessness you will be confined to your quarters outside your duty hours for two weeks. For that period you will relinquish your tobacco and such other privileges as are afforded you as a petty officer of this vessel."

"Yes, sir. Thank you, sir." Mr. Carmody stepped back into line with the other petty officers.

Starbuck now took the "cat" from the second mate and without further hesitation began to administer the punishment. Hayward would be first then Flubb. He would leave Crebbs for last.

Mercy, standing beside Val and discreetly supported by his elbow, averted her eyes as the leather strips played over the men's backs, but nothing could keep her from hearing the horrible smack of rawhide against skin. She fixed her eyes firmly on the distance and counted the terrible strokes, wishing that there were not so many spaces between five and one. As the number mounted, though, her concern for the captain pulled her eyes in his direction. His face betrayed nothing but grim determination. He was not enjoying his task, as some might, but neither was he shrinking from it. He flogged Hayward with his full, and considerable, power and might.

The act reviled her. To see men beaten like animals was abhorrent. Yet it was also hateful to realize that these men deserved their punishment. They had tried to harm others grievously, had stolen, had employed stealth and deceit, and for no end but their own entertainment. She had once believed that left to their own devices, men would behave honorably and sensibly, but she had proof before her that this could not be depended upon. As captain, Sam required the rules of the ship to be followed to the letter and without objection, but he was not unduly harsh. Men were not beaten for minor infractions, rather privileges were revoked. The men were not baited; they did not live in terror; they were not degraded and made to cower before their captain like dogs before a cruel master. As long as they did their work well and behaved with respect toward their officers, they were left alone. There were many whaling captains who would not agree with this philosophy, but it had been her father's way and had always been the way upon his vessels. But when men did behave abominably, what recourse did a captain have other than swift, sure punishment? She wished the world could be otherwise, but it was not.

Yet what effect did such punishment have, not on the men who, by their actions, had called it upon themselves, but on the man forced to deliver it? Sam was a difficult and complex man, but not an unthinking one, not an unfeeling one. What was he thinking behind that iron countenance?

Just then a sudden pressure on her arm alerted Mercy to another drama that was taking place. The end of Hayward's punishment had come—the final assault, a bucket of salt water thrown over the wounds on his back. Throughout the flogging he had not made a sound, but this final stinging attack elicited a gasp and a groan. She herself winced and stifled a moan, then glanced up at Val. His face was openly pained, but the object of his sympathy was not the flogged sailor. He was gazing across the deck at John Harding, who was ashen and seemed about to crumple. His posture was like that of a scarecrow—upright only for the pole at his back, limp at all other points.

Jane, for her part, could barely remain standing. Her whole body felt weak and shaken, the result, she was sure, of her narrow brush with disaster. It was not so much the nasty prank that ate away at her, but the knowledge of her own vulnerability. Had she survived the keelhauling, she would no doubt have been taken to the sick bay and tended by Mrs. Wright, who would naturally have removed her wet clothing—and discovered her. Was her freedom, her lark, worth all this trouble? Not only was her own peace of mind affected, but Mr. Mayhew's, too. She had seen in his face the hatred he harbored for Crebbs, as well as his deep concern for her and the conflict that rent him whenever he was in her presence. Even now, as she peeked surreptitiously across the deck, he was watching her closely. For his sake, as much as her own, she willed herself to remain on her feet and to watch impassively the brutal punishment of her tormentors.

This minor drama affected Mercy no less than the principal play. Into what sort of a society had she put herself, where there was no room for compassion between two men simply because one was an officer, the other a foremast hand? Where it was necessary to chastise wrongdoers in a way that had been long abandoned by society at large? If such questions affected her so greatly, how had Nathaniel felt aboard the *Abishai?* She at least had a broad practical streak, the ability to see things as they are and not as they should be. But Nathaniel, with his romantic, poetic sensibilities, his ignorance of cruelty, how would he have fared on a night like this? Not well, she ventured to guess. But she couldn't let herself think of him now, when it could be many months, even years before she could investigate his fate.

Finally all three floggings were finished. The crew, silent and subdued, was dispersed—Mr. Mayhew's watch to continue on duty for another hour, Mr. Hunter's to the fo'c'sle until midnight. Before going below, the captain admonished his mates, "I've had enough for one night. Make certain I am not required on this deck again before morning."

Starbuck's voice was flat, without any depth or color, which Mercy found more disturbing than anger or sarcasm or any of the expressive intonations he usually employed. She wavered briefly before approaching him, but she had to ask his permission to treat the miscreants. Not to do so would be to flaunt his authority. "May I see to the men's wounds, Captain?" she asked, so quietly that only Val and Mr. Hunter might hear her. Sam did not answer, just stared at her blankly, as if he had never seen her before, as if he did not know who she was or what she was doing there.

"Sir?" she prompted.

"As you wish," he said in that same flat voice. Then he turned and was gone.

She made her way down through the booby hatch to the sick bay, where she collected, in a basin, strong soap, salve, towels and bandages. After fetching some warm water from the galley, she attended the ailing men. It was the first time she had been called on to minister to men whose pain called forth a feeling other than compassion in her. She had to remind herself that these men felt pain like any others, that their sufferings were not less because they had committed a crime. She tended the men in the order of their flogging. Hayward took his treatment gratefully, moaning in relief as she applied the cooling salve. When she was finished he muttered his thanks, although he could not look her in the eye. Flubb was stonily silent throughout his treatment, accepting it without either protest or thanks. But when she moved on to Crebbs, he pushed her away roughly. Surprised, she recovered quickly and declared, "I will not leave until I treat you."

"Get away," Crebbs snarled.

Ignoring him, Mercy began to clean his wounds with warm water and soap. Blindly he swatted at her, flailing his arms behind him as if she were an annoying bee. She moved out of his reach. "You might as well save your strength," she said, and continued her work. But his arms shot out for her again, and this time he made contact, knocking the basin off her lap and sending it clattering to the deck. The noise brought Val running to the scene.

"Mrs. Wright? What has happened?"

"This sailor seems to have a fear of medical treatment," she said staunchly, using a ruse Uncle Thomas often employed—usually on patients under the age of reason, however.

"I don't want your pity," Crebbs defended himself.

"I offer no pity, only salve," Mercy returned.

Val looked at Crebbs with naked loathing. "If it were up to me, I would let your wounds fester, but the captain has consented to Mrs. Wright's ministrations. If you value your hide, Crebbs, you'll take your treatment and be quiet. There won't be much left of it if I have to fetch the captain."

Mercy hid her shock at Val's threats and quickly returned to her work on a now-silent but still unyielding Crebbs. The man did not so much as flinch at anything she did, even when she cleansed the deepest and rawest of his wounds. Val stood by until she was finished, then escorted her to the booby hatch.

"Hatred does not become you, Val," she said gently when they stood apart from all the others. "You are not John Harding's only friend. He has others on the *Meribah,* myself included. No harm will come to him, but it will come to you if you let this venom seep into your soul. Cast it out, Val, I beg you."

"Would that I could," he said bitterly.

"You can. If I have the power to nurse the man you have the power to treat him like every other sailor on this ship."

"Do I, Mercy? I doubt myself greatly these days."

Mercy laid a comforting hand on his forearm. "I don't doubt you, my friend." With that, she disappeared down the hatch and into the sick bay. When all was put to rights there, she returned to her stateroom, noticing as she entered the officers' quarters a faint light coming from beneath the closed door of the captain's dayroom. She rapped softly, calling for the captain. When there was no answer, she opened the door a crack.

"I don't believe I granted you leave to enter," he said sharply.

"I'm sorry." In the dim glow of the lamp, Sam's face was haggard and dark with weariness. "Is there anything I can get you? A cup of tea? Something stronger?"

"If I want anything I'll call the cabin boy, Mercy."

"Then may I come in?"

"For what? A chat?" He turned his head away disdainfully. "I'm not in the mood for conversation tonight, I fear. It would not satisfy me."

"And what would satisfy you, Sam?"

Starbuck looked back at her now, squarely in the eye. "Something more than you can offer," he said coldly.

Mercy felt the harsh sting of his words. "And what is it you feel I am withholding?"

"What the devil do you think, woman? I'm a flesh-and-blood man. I need flesh-and-blood comforts, not cups of tea or even whole bottles of whiskey."

Drawing in a deep breath, she said, "There is more to comfort than that, Captain. I am sorry that what I am able to give is less than what you will take. I won't trouble you any further this evening, sir. Good night." She closed the door and stepped hurriedly into her own stateroom. This current that flowed between them was dangerous, like an undertow that kept a tired swimmer from returning safely to the shore. Tonight he was the swimmer, she the shore. She could offer the warmth and solid ground he needed, but he could not negotiate the current.

In the dayroom Sam heard the sound of Mercy's door closing and cursed himself for a fool. She had offered him succor and solace, but he had wanted only crude, physical comfort from her. And so he had sent her away, like a child who refuses a toy because it is not the one he wants and is left with nothing. Now he had nothing, and only himself to blame.

He hated having to flog a sailor, not so much because it inflicted pain—he had hurt plenty of men in fair fights—but because the act gave one human being absolute power over another. That power was seductive and easy to abuse. It inflamed a man and gave him a false sense of his own strength and worth. He was not immune to it and needed someone to temper its effects on him. For this—and for much else—he needed Mercy. But he could never admit that to her. He could barely stand to say it to himself or to sit with himself having thought it. So he blew out the lamp and hastened to his cabin, where he abandoned himself to the numbing embrace of sleep.

Chapter Ten

The atmosphere aboard the *Meribah,* as she continued south, was subdued, yet crackling with tension. The men spoke to one another only when necessary. Even so there were raised voices, and heated looks passed frequently among them. Conversation in the officers' mess was static and constrained. Mercy, never one for gossip or idle conversation, longed to talk freely with someone, anyone, without the need to measure every word, every gesture. Jane too found herself longing for the easy tedium of her mother's kitchen, the two of them working steadily, passing the odd comment from time to time, their words carrying no subterranean meanings, no veiled threats.

But all that changed in one glorious instant.

"Blo-o-o-ws!!! There she blo-o-o-ws!" The high-pitched cry plummeted to the deck like a tasty morsel, and the hungry sailors scooped it up like gulls.

Starbuck cupped his hands and pointed his face to the heavens. "Where away?"

"Four points off the windward bow," the answer drifted down.

Work halted and all attention was riveted at the sight of the magnificent beast cutting through the water, spewing a gray, misty lava like a black volcano. Time and the *Meribah*'s men stood still for only a few brief seconds. At the captain's order to clear away, the deck swarmed with activity.

The four crews raced to their respective boats, removed the stowed articles, double-checked their gear and made sure the boats were prepared for lowering. When all was secured, Starbuck ordered them to lower away, and the crews released the fall ropes that lowered the boats from their davits. When the boats were level with the bulwarks, the mates and their harpooners jumped in and guided the boats into the water, pushing against the sides of the *Meribah* to keep the boats from banging against her. As the boats neared the water, the remaining crew members scrambled into them as best they could, shinning down the fall lines or scrabbling down the side of the vessel.

The first mate's boat led the party of four. Val's position was at the stern of the graceful double-ended whale-boat. Standing and facing the crew, he manned the long steering oar and, aided by semaphore signals from the captain, determined the strategy of the chase. Jane, seated on the starboard aft thwart, facing Mr. Mayhew, had the first oar. It was her job to keep time for the rest of the oarsmen and to bail the boat when necessary. At the next thwart, seated larboard, was Sweet, the tub oarsmen, who was responsible for the boat's two tubs of whale line, the main one stowed in front of his seat and the spare behind. Big Jack sat directly behind Jane on the third thwart. As the strongest man, he had the longest oar and would give the boat its power. The fourth rower, Pete, at larboard, was the harpooner's assistant. At the fifth oar, on the extreme forward thwart, was the harpooner himself, Mr. Jenkins, who, when they reached the whale, would dart his iron to fasten the great fish to the whaleboat.

They had rehearsed this so often that Jane did not have to think of what she was doing. At the captain's order she removed a bolt of canvas and some other stored articles from the space in front of her thwart; then checked the cuddy, the cubbyhole beneath the stage where Mr. May-hew would stand to command the boat, for her bailing piggin, two hatchets, two sheath knives, the lantern keg and the water breaker. She made sure her oar was there and that her oarlock was working properly, then helped the tub oarsman get the spare rope tub aboard. Then she and the tub oarsman stood ready to work the two lines that would swing in the cranes once the boat, which rested on them, was raised a few inches. The two remaining crewmen took charge of the fall lines that lowered the boat. When the boat was nearly in the water she left just enough slack to finish the job, tied off her rope and shinned down the fall line to the boat. Once it was in the water, she helped unhook the fall line davit, then took her seat and put her oar in place.

When all were seated and ready, Mr. Mayhew gave the command to row and shouted out the cadence. Picking up the rhythm, Jane dipped her oar into the water. The others followed suit, and together they pulled for all they were worth. At that moment they were worth quite a lot—months of pent-up energy and emotions made their boat cut through the calm waters like scissors through silk.

Up until that second it had not occurred to Jane to be scared. But now, watching the *Meribah* recede, she noticed that her heart was pounding vigorously, her mouth had gone dry, and there was a hard lump at the base of her throat that made swallowing difficult. She looked up at Mr. Mayhew, tall and straight before her, his blond hair turned to sparkling white in the glare of the sun. He chose that moment to look down at her. Some combination of awe and fear slowed her reactions, and her gaze remained fixed on his for a time, just long enough for both of them to recognize that familiar feeling of being attracted and repelled at the same time. They were like two magnets, placed north to north and fighting each other, when they longed to be placed north to south and clinging to one another.

She lowered her eyes quickly and concentrated on her oar. Except for the rhythmic dip of the oars in the water, the men were silent and would remain that way. Only Mr. Mayhew would speak, softly, to issue the necessary orders. Any noise would gally—or frighten—their prey and send him swimming away so fast he could not be caught. Or else he might sound and they would have to wait for hours, with no way of knowing where he might surface.

Jane felt another rise of fearful excitement. She longed to look around and see the faces of her fellow sailors. What were they thinking and feeling, she wondered. Were they frightened, too, or merely excited? Were they aching for blood and victory? For these precious few hours of hunting, they all endured the boredom, confinement and loneliness of years at sea. That thirst for action was sure to override their fears, as it was her own, she decided, putting all her newly honed strength into her oar.

Back on board the *Meribah,* Starbuck was marshaling his few remaining men. The "idlers"—cook, cooper and carpenter—had been set to work on the essential business of keeping the *Meribah* moving along after the boats. The steward was elevated to mate for a few hours, and the cabin boy sent up into the rigging with a waif, the red flag through which the captain would communicate instructions to the mates. For the most part he would let the mates make their own decisions, but from his vantage point he could sometimes see things they couldn't. He could also get a sense of the whale itself, how it moved, when it moved, its strengths and weaknesses.

Mercy had stayed well out of the action, hopping atop the skylight, where she sat with her legs folded under her skirts. Though only a spectator, she too had welcomed the blessed relief that had followed hard on the lookout's cry. She had seen the boats lowered many times, but never all four at once and so quickly, the men performing like a complicated machine in perfect working order. It had been a most impressive spectacle.

Now the boats were bearing down quickly on the whale, who was swimming on a course perpendicular to the *Meribah*'s. Though she had heard the tales many times, she had not understood until now just how large a whale was. Even at a distance the beast was a fearsome, if beautiful, object—fast and strong and solid, a formidable opponent for the tiny men in the small, fragile boats.

She was so involved in watching the chase that she did not realize Sam was standing beside her until he spoke. "I had half a mind to leave Valentine in charge and take his boat out myself," he confessed. "It's not nearly as much fun staying behind." During his speech, he never took his eyes off the action.

"Or nearly as dangerous," Mercy reminded him. "I can't get over how big it is."

"He. We're chasing no forty-barrel cow, Mercy. This monster is a bull—ninety or a hundred barrels at least. And I wouldn't say we're out of danger just because we're on the ship. If we get too close he could charge and dash it to pieces."

"And will he?"

"This one looks wily, not mean. But it's hard to say with a whale."

"If you're trying to frighten me, Captain," Mercy said with a laugh, "it won't work. I am my father's daughter."

"Aye, that you are," he agreed.

By now the boats were closing in on the whale. Val's was in the lead, the others close behind. Mercy imagined she could almost see the beads of sweat on the men's brows as they pulled their oars, could see the blisters rising on even those callused hands. Then suddenly the whale changed course, taking a sharp turn away from the boats. "Damn!" Starbuck exclaimed. "He knows they're there now. One of those blighters must have crossed the glip," he said, referring to the stream of weak oil a whale emitted in its wake. Disturbing the glip, it was believed, somehow sent a danger signal to the whale. The captain stalked away and began bellowing orders to the boy in the rigging, who turned them into signals with the red waif. The boats immediately adjusted their course, and the chase continued.

Due to his skillful steering, Val's boat was the first to recover from the change of course. This was their chance to leave the others behind and be the first to reach the whale. His crew was rowing as hard and as fast as they could, but he urged them on, and they dug down deep and found the extra ounce of strength and determination he knew they had. He kept his eye trained on the whale, glancing away only occasionally to watch for signals from the *Meribah,* steadfastly resisting the temptation to turn to see how far he was from his fellow mates' boats. But he strained his ears for the sounds of their oars, and it seemed they became more faint with his crew's every pull.

The whale had settled down again, swimming steadily but not too fast, bobbing gently from side to side, believing himself safe now. Because of his extremely limited sight a whale would not see a boat until it was nearly upon him, but his hearing was so acute that it would be necessary to abandon the oars for silent paddles when they were within one or two boat lengths of the animal.

They were approaching the whale from the rear, and Val watched his giant tail now—easily as wide as the boat was long—pitching up and down with each stroke of the flukes that propelled the beast forward. The trick was to approach swiftly with the oars and switch to paddles at exactly the moment that their bow came even with the whale's tail. Then they could move quietly along the whale's right side, until they had passed the midsection and the harpooner, at the front of the boat, was in a position to stab the whale's head with his irons.

Val counted his crew's strokes, trying to judge the number necessary to cover the remaining distance at the speed the whale was traveling. A quick calculation yielded twenty-four as the magic number. He whispered this to the crew and began to mark the strokes silently, using his fingers to indicate the number elapsed. The men strained at the oars, their faces etched with pain and concentration.

Twenty-two, twenty-three, Jane counted to herself, feeling as if her arms could not pull the oar another time. One more, one more, she had been telling herself with each stroke for the last hundred. And now they had reached the last. She wanted to grunt and groan when they stopped rowing, and take a well-deserved rest, but there would be no rest for quite a while yet. So she silently shipped her oar and grabbed her paddle. On Mr. Mayhew's signal, she put it in the water and pulled back with all her rapidly dwindling might.

The boat surged forward. After doing one thing for so long it was a relief to use her drained muscles in a different way. She was infused with energy again, for this change of instruments could only mean they were very close to the whale. She could hear the flopping of the great beast as it rolled from side to side, sense its warmth and smell its acrid odor, but she didn't dare take her eyes off Mr. Mayhew for a second lest she miss an important command.

Then all of a sudden something huge and black loomed in the corner of her eye. It was like a wall of solid ebony rising high above her, sleek and shiny and vast. She and the others continued to paddle, but the wall seemed to have no end. She could already see one boat-length's worth of it in front of her, and still there was no command to go wood to blackskin with the beast. That would happen when the boat had passed the midpoint of the leviathan. Finally Mr. Mayhew signaled Mr. Jenkins to ready his harpoons. They paddled on, the black wall beside them rising and falling, the boat pitching further and further and further to this side or that with every stroke of the huge flukes that were now directly beneath them. Jane held her breath. Then the sign to go wood to blackskin came. They stopped rowing and allowed the boat to bump into the great wall of greasy flesh.

There was a tremendous thump and recoil when the boat hit. His eyes poised on Mr. Jenkins, Mr. Mayhew raised his hand. When the boat stopped moving and was steady for a split second, the hand came down. Quick as a flash Jenkins darted first one iron and then the other into the whale. While this was happening, the others dropped their paddles and unshipped their oars. The instant the second iron hit home, Mr. Mayhew gave the command, "stern-all," and they began rowing backward with all their might.

With the prick of the irons the whale reared. His enormous head shot up out of the now-white, churning water, then he bent his gargantuan body so that his hump rose out of the sea. Rolling back on the arched hump, he turned his great head and snapped out at the boat with his fearsome jaws. Jane could not see what was going on, but the rush and roil of the water, the gush of spray that rained down on them, the ear-splitting crack and not least of all the intent, wide-eyed look on Mr. Mayhew's face assured her it was an awesome scene. She took seriously his importunings to row faster and faster.

The boat rocked precipitously again, and there was another deluge and a second thunderous crash. Her heart raced, as if trying to get out of her body and make it to safety alone, but she continued to row. Then suddenly her oar was almost knocked out of her hand as the boat took off like a shot in the opposite direction. Mr. Mayhew tightened his grip on the steering oar and ordered the crew to face forward. "Hang on tight," he yelled. "We're in for a Nantucket sleigh ride."

The whale had taken off in a rage, trying to rid itself of the nasty encumbrances fastened to its neck by two prickling irons and a length of rope. The line played out of the tub so fast that it had begun to smoke. Jane grabbed her bailing piggin and began to toss water on the line. Mr. Mayhew used the steering oar to try to make the boat more difficult for the whale to pull. Jack and Sweet pulled back on the line, also trying to slow down their catch. Meanwhile, Mr. Jenkins fastened the drogue to the line and tossed it overboard. This square of stout wood caught the water in the whale's wake, creating a counterweight. But all these measures, combined, were no match for the force and fury of the whale. He pulled them along with no discernible slackening of his pace.

Jane had once been caught on a runaway wagon for a hair-raising ride through the streets of New Bedford, but that event had been a Sunday stroll compared to the ride she was on now. The boat skidded and skipped and lurched and lunged. They were entirely at the mercy of the whale, unable to do anything more than hang on and hope he tired very soon. But he didn't. He drove on and on into the horizon, leaving the *Meribah* and her other boats far behind.

As suddenly as it had begun, the ride ended. The whale sounded, disappearing beneath the waves, and the boat skidded to a dead halt. For several minutes all the six could do was lie back panting. When normal breathing was once more possible, silence reigned for a moment. It was shattered by the rip of laughter that tore from Big Jack's throat. "I guess we got the Big Jack of the deep attached to this boat. Somebody prick me with a sharp pin, I'd get mighty mad, too." The rest laughed along with him, as much in relief as at his sally.

Val enjoyed the merriment, too, but without taking his eye off the point where the whale had sounded. He gave the order for them to ship their oars again, and they took off for the spot. Once they reached it, however, there was nothing to do but wait and pray that they were close to the whale but not right over him.

While he could still be reasonably certain the whale was too tired to surface, Val ordered the lantern keg opened, and each man was rationed a sea biscuit and a half cup of water. Knowing this was all they would have for who knew how many hours, the men ate slowly and carefully, wasting not a crumb or a drop. The position of the sun said that midday was past. They had been at sea for more than four hours and needed to relieve their bladders, Jane included. The men simply turned their backs and urinated over the side of the boat, but for Jane this was not possible. Her modesty was well-known by now, so there were no comments as she discreetly eased herself over the side of the boat into the warm sea. The salt water soothed her aching muscles and stung her broken, bloodied blisters, but she kept her hands under water, knowing that it would cleanse and begin to heal her wounds. When she had rearranged her clothing, she hopped back into the boat.

The meal concluded, the mate and the harpooner changed places, and Val seated himself in the bow, the razor-sharp lance with which he would kill the whale readily at hand. After the exciting morning, all the men were keyed up and eager to get on with the business of killing the whale and triumphantly dragging their quarry back to the ship for cutting in and trying out. Everyone was restless and edgy and hot in the blazing afternoon sun, and the minutes passed by torturously. There was nothing to do to while away the time—they could not sing or shout or tell yarns for they had to be ever on the alert for the moment the whale sounded. If they were carrying on noisily or napping or daydreaming, they might fail to kill the whale before he realized he was still attached to the boat. Then it would be another sleigh ride and more hours of oppressive waiting.

Jane tried to keep her mind on the whale, but all her thoughts gravitated to Mr. Mayhew—his bravery, his skill in sizing up their noble adversary, his good humor. Throughout the arduous morning he had not once lost his temper. She simply could not imagine him in the kind of foul mood she had sometimes seen in the captain. Mr. Mayhew was so evenhanded, so—

Jane had no opportunity to finish these thoughts, for suddenly she was heaved out of the boat and into the water with a violent force. She caught a mouthful of water on the way down and felt her windpipe closing off as she struggled to find and break the surface. Her feet hit something hard, and she tried to use the object to give her a push to the top. Her ploy worked and she rose, but the thing itself moved and she was catapulted up and out of the water. Coughing and sputtering, she gasped for air and waited to hit the water with a thwack. But when she came down, it was on something solid and thrashing about wildly. She blinked the stinging water out of her eyes and looked down. All she could see was a vast expanse of gleaming, glistening blackness. She was riding the back of the whale!

The surface of the beast was slick and oily, with no place to gain a hand or foothold. She was tossed and tumbled, rocked and rolled, but somehow, if only by sheer resolve, she stayed astride the beast. In those few instants when she was not blinded by salt spray or suspended in midair, she looked around for her boat mates. Finding the first one spread a chill through her hot and sweat- and sea-drenched body. It was Mr. Jenkins. Or what was left of him. His head was gone, and she recognized him only by the clothes he was wearing. She muttered a quick prayer and added a plea to God to save the others and please, to spare a moment to keep an eye on her, as well.

Down in the churning water, Big Jack cast his eyes around for his young gentleman friend, but Harding was nowhere to be found. Jack was surrounded by flotsam, mostly pieces of the stove boat, but the severed head of Mr. Jenkins bobbed by, too. He nodded in respect to his fallen comrade, then continued to search the seething foam for the others. The first he spied was Mr. Mayhew, and he rejoiced that at least one other had survived. As near as he could figure out, the whale had risen right under the boat and slapped it into pencil-thin strips with his tail. Big Jack waved frantically to his officer. Through the obscuring spray, he thought he detected the glint of a lance in the mate's hand. Wiping the salt from his eyes, he looked again. Yes, he believed it was a lance. There was still a chance to kill the beast. He cut through the waves, shouting until he garnered the mate's attention. The two swam to meet each other, and with hand signals and half-heard cries, devised a plan of attack, even as the whale continued to thrash and snap at them with his great jaws.

Then Jack looked up. There was something on the top of the whale. No, it was someone. Harding! "Jumpin' Jenny!" he cried, stabbing the air with his finger, pointing toward Harding. "Hold on!" he screamed. "Hold on!" The screeching captured Val's attention, and he too looked up. The whale had to be killed—and quickly before John Harding had his neck broken by the savage beast. A look of agitation and renewed resolve passed between Jack and Val.

They worked in concert now, rescuing the largest piece of the boat and positioning it near the ear of the bucking whale. Calling up his last shred of strength, Jack steadied the flotsam, creating a small wooden stage. By this time, Sweet and Pete had appeared, and they helped Val climb up onto the narrow strip, then aided Jack in keeping it afloat. Val carefully noted the vulnerable spot he had to pierce in order to kill the whale, knowing he must reach it with the first thrust. If he missed he would only enrage the whale more, and Harding would surely be killed. Aiming at a moving target from a wobbling, unsteady stage was almost impossible, but Val narrowed his eyes, fixed them and his mind on the spot, and delivered as hard a blow as ever he had. Then he tumbled backward into the sea.

Up atop the whale, Jane was suddenly covered with a spray of fetid, hot, red liquid. She spluttered and spit and gagged in surprise and revulsion, but then she heard a faint cry. Chimney. Someone was yelling something about a chimney.

"His chimney's afire! His chimney's afire!" Big Jack's voice rang out on the now-quiet sea. She recognized it and realized that the whale was thrashing no longer. Crawling cautiously forward on her stomach, she looked over the edge of the whale's back. Beneath her she saw Jack and Mr. Mayhew and the two other crewmen. They were gesturing for her to come down. Carefully she turned over and sat up, then let herself slide down the side of the whale with a scream of glee. The water was warm, filled with stinking blood and oil and pieces of the stove boat, but the five survivors clustered beside the carcass of their catch could have been at a fancy ball at the best hotel in New Bedford. The loss of Mr. Jenkins was the only damper on their joy.

Jane grabbed onto a piece of floating wood and treaded water with the others, babbling excitedly about what had just happened, demanding to know every detail of the kill. She was so happy she wanted to shout to the whole world that she was a woman and that she was here, with the body of a whale she had helped to chase and capture. But she held her tongue, because she wanted to be able to do this again and again and again.

In less than an hour, Mr. Mayhew's crew was rescued by the three remaining whaleboats. The survivors scrambled into two of the boats, and the body of Jenkins, now covered in canvas, was tied to one of these. The third boat was left to tow the whale, and the party made its way back to the *Meribah*.

When they reached the *Meribah*, and the boat in which she was riding pulled up beside her, Jane made her way up the ropes easily, as if she were doing no more than climbing a short flight of stairs. She wasn't the least bit tired—only exhilarated and eager for the next hunt. As they came on board, the captain welcomed each of Mr. Mayhew's men with a handshake and a hearty slap on the back. I've done it, Jane thought as Captain Starbuck pumped her hand. I'm a real whaleman—the world's first and only whalewoman—now!

But Jane and the others in Mr. Mayhew's boat had little time to savor their victory or to recover from their exertions. The first order of business was to say a few words over the canvas-wrapped body of Mr. Jenkins and consign his remains to the sea. That done, the sailors lined up at the galley for plates of bean-and-bacon stew, followed by plum duff, a steamed raisin-and-suet pudding that was a favorite of all the men. This special meal was the only concession to celebration. Otherwise the taking of a one-hundred-barrel whale meant only work.

Although it was already late afternoon, the cutting stage, a long, narrow plank, was lowered on the starboard side of the *Meribah*, and a section of the bulwarks removed to facilitate bringing the whale aboard. The first job was to sever the whale's head, or case, from the body. This job fell to the captain, Mr. Mayhew and Mr. Hunter, all of whom balanced themselves on the cutting stage, armed with the sharp spades with which they would carry out their task. Once severed, the whale's head would be hoisted on board and the case bailed for spermaceti, the valuable substance that made smokeless candles and served as a base for fine cosmetics.

After that the whale's blubber would be cut into strips and peeled away from the body. These blanket pieces, as they were called, were then lowered through the main hatch into the blubber room, where they were cut into smaller horse pieces. On the mincing block, back on deck, these were cut into thin slices, although not all the way through, so that they resembled the pages of an opened book. These "bible leaves" were then thrown into the iron try-pots and melted down. The remaining fibrous material was used to fuel the fires.

It took a dozen or more hands to man the windlass, supplying the power to manipulate the ropes that secured the whale and to lift the head and the blanket pieces on board. The others were engaged in cutting the blubber, operating the tryworks, bailing the oil into copper vats for cooling, sharpening the equipment necessary to all these tasks or clearing the deck of gurry, the blood and slime and offal that naturally accompanied such an operation.

Until the case was heaved on board, Jane was one of those who sweated and pulled at the windlass, but once the mammoth head lay on board she, along with two of the smaller hands, was assigned to bailing spermaceti, a task best accomplished by standing inside the case. Her fellow bailers immediately stripped to their drawers and jumped in, but Jane obviously could not.

The others on deck were not long in noticing her consternation. There was a chorus of chortles, and then Crebbs called out, "Why so modest, *Miss* Harding? Afraid we'll peek?" The men's refrain was a stanza of snickers, and she felt herself grow hot with anger. The third mate, Mr. Allen, who was in charge of the deck operations, commanded the men to quiet down and sharply ordered her to get on with her work.

"Begging your pardon, sir," she ventured, "but it's against my convictions to remove my clothing in the sight of others."

"I don't care what you wear or don't wear, Harding," Mr. Allen snarled. "You can borrow one of Mrs. Wright's dresses for all I care, if she'll oblige. Just get on with it!"

This remark garnered a round of guffaws from the men, but this time Jane didn't mind the laugh at her expense. Breathing a sigh of relief, she hopped into the case with the others and began to bail. The spermaceti was thick and viscous and warm, and being in the case was like standing in a huge vat of melted wax. She could see why the others had removed their clothes—she'd never get the greasy, penetrating substance out of hers.

By now it was growing dark, but the work continued in the dim glow of the cresset lamps and try-pot fires, which cast the scene in a ghostly, eerie light. The deck was treacherously slippery, and the men were beginning to sag with fatigue. But there was to be no rest for the next four or five days, until all the blubber was melted, cooled and stored in the hold, until the case had been thoroughly bailed and the whale's intestines inspected for ambergris. By boat crew, the men were sent off to sleep, but for no more than four hours in twenty-four. The rest of the time they worked.

Mercy had little to do, other than help the cook and the steward, the only members of the crew who kept more or less to their regular duties, and patch up the nicks and cuts the men got from their sharp instruments or from slipping on the oil-slick deck. There were no regular meals in the officer's mess, and no one to talk with. Her eyes smarted from the smoke rising constantly from the try-pots, and her usually strong stomach was in a permanent state of upheaval from the stench of burning whale blubber.

For the majority of the five days it took to try out the huge whale, Mercy was alone with her thoughts. The excitement of watching something she had heard about for so long quickly paled, especially when she thought of Nathaniel, as she often did during this time. The scene on deck was chaotic. There was dirt and grime everywhere. The work was tedious and unrelenting, the atmosphere rank and fetid. How would he have fit in, her meticulous, fastidious husband? What had she and Nathaniel and her father been thinking of when they approved the scheme of him going aboard the *Abishai* as the honorary first mate?

As she thought about those days, when the plan was broached, discussed, refined and settled upon, she recalled that it was Nathaniel who had been so insistent on going. Her father originally felt his new son-in-law needed to learn only the land-based aspects of the business. But Nathaniel had talked endlessly about how the other owners and investors would never accept him, how the captains and mates and men would never respect him, how Mercy herself might someday think him inferior—less brave, less qualified—to her father if he did not have first-hand experience of all aspects of the whaling industry. No matter what she or her father had said, he would not be dissuaded from the plan. Not only that, but he'd ended up convincing them it was the most sensible, indeed the only possible course of action open to them.

But she couldn't imagine that Nathaniel had enjoyed himself. His romantic notion of going a-whaling must have been much more palatable than the experience itself. But perhaps she was wrong. Perhaps he had reveled in the grit and grime of the whaling life. Perhaps it had been a release from the genteel, constrained life he had always led, a real-life adventure for a man who had passed so many of his hours in a drawing room or sequestered with a book. Perhaps it had even been a release from her, from a marriage he found tedious and dull. When they were together, he had seemed so loving, so attentive, but she no longer knew what to think. She had known him so little, really, and he had disappointed her so deeply, and now he was probably dead and she was worlds away from home, family and friends trying to find out what had happened to him.

Why had her father refused to give her all but the barest details of the fate of the *Abishai*? Usually he told her everything, confided in her, unburdened himself to her. But this time, she suspected, he'd had something to hide. What

dreadful thing had befallen the *Abishai* and Nathaniel?
Why had Sam said he pitied Nathaniel if he were alive?
Both Sam and her father seemed convinced that her hus-
band was dead, but somehow she had not been convinced.
What had they concealed from her? And what was Sam still
concealing from her?

The more she thought about these things, the lower in
spirits she became. She had begun to doubt her mission, her
marriage and even herself. Forgotten by the others in the
bustle and bother of trying out the whale, her doubts fed on
one another, like the hungry sharks that had gathered
around the whale's carcass during the cutting in, and
gnawed away at the certainties she had once held easily at
her core.

This was an unusual and highly uncomfortable state of
affairs for Mercy. Unlike most females of her time she had
never been plagued with self-doubt. Her first experience of
it was not at all pleasant, her anxieties compounded by her
lack of confidantes. Writing to Caroline or Maria or even
to her journal, as she did, was no substitute for a face-to-
face encounter in which nuances of voice and posture said
as much as words. There was no one here in perfect
empathy with her, no one to help her anticipate the hidden
and dangerous curves along the emotional road on which
she had embarked. And so she careened along it, moving
deeper and deeper into unknown, uncharted territory.

Finally the work was finished. The casks of oil and spermaceti and the precious chunks of ambergris were stored in
the hold, the try-pots empty and scrubbed, the decks clean
and order restored. Everyone was exhausted and filthy and
hoping for a few days' respite before any more whales were
sighted, the captain included. Having hardly slept, eaten or
washed since the whale was sighted, Sam ordered the steward to fill the tin basin that served as the *Meribah*'s bath-
tub and to put a decent meal on the table for the officers'
mess. Scrubbed and combed and dressed in clean linen, a
large, hot meal in his belly, he felt restored, even energetic,

and invited the mates not on duty and Mrs. Wright to join him in the day cabin after the mess for a glass of Dom Diego Sobral's fine port. Mr. Hunter and Mr. Chase drank their wine quickly and then retired, Mr. Hunter to his cabin, Mr. Chase to the steerage, leaving the captain and Mrs. Wright together on the tufted velvet sofa.

The captain too drank his first glass of port quickly and rose to pour himself another. "Now that you've seen it all, Mercy, what do you think of whaling?"

"I think," Mercy answered honestly, "that it is dangerous, difficult, dirty work."

"None dirtier," Sam agreed. "But the chase is splendid, is it not? It makes up for all the rest."

"Does it?"

"You sound doubtful."

"Perhaps it is because I've never been in a whaleboat, never been eye to eye, so to speak, with a whale. From the *Meribah* it looked rather like a *tableau vivant*—entertaining but not quite real."

"Oh, it's very real when you're there, I assure you," Sam said with a chortle.

"Yes, I'm sure it is."

Sam took a moment to look closely at Mercy. She seemed subdued and saddened, somehow, even a bit pale. "What is it?" he asked, sitting down beside her. "You seem unusually pensive this evening."

"Do you think Nathaniel ever took a thwart in a whaleboat, Sam?"

Sam's face hardened. "I haven't the faintest idea," he said in a tone meant to put an end to the subject.

Mercy was not deterred. "I've spent the whole of the last days trying to imagine Nathaniel in the midst of a scene like that. But I couldn't do it, no matter how hard I tried."

Sam could see Mercy was troubled, but the mere mention of Nathaniel Wright's name set him seething. He tried to control his wrath by speaking lightly. "Knowing Captain Hussey, your husband pulled his weight on the

Abishai, or he'd have been left in the Azores and sent home on the first available berth."

"What happened aboard the *Abishai,* Sam?" She reached out and touched his arm. "What are you keeping from me? Why did my father take the loss so hard it killed him? I must know. What happened to Nathaniel?"

As she spoke, her fingers tightened around him. The heat of her grip permeated the fabric of his sleeve, warming the flesh beneath it. The warmth spread wildly throughout his body. Her eyes bore into his, rife with apprehension and uncertainty. He wanted to change that look—to one of certainty and fulfillment. "Forget about Nathaniel Wright," he said roughly. "He's dead, Mercy. I am alive." With that he swept her into his arms and pressed his mouth to hers.

Mercy felt all too clearly that Sam Starbuck was alive. His kiss was demanding, insistent yet tender and searching. He was like a scholar of ancient history, deeply hungry for knowledge yet aware that the texts he must study are fragile and dusty from lack of use. That he must treat them with care, or he will destroy their secrets before he can decipher them.

Yes, she was frail and dry, brittle and close to crumbling, and she had secrets to yield—that she sometimes wanted to believe that Nathaniel was dead; that she had on occasion even hoped he was dead. But the deepest secret of all was that she lusted for Sam as he lusted for her.

Sam pulled his mouth away from hers. He took her by the shoulders and looked hard into her eyes. "I'm going to get up and lock the door. You can leave now, but once I've locked it, we will finish what we've started." He released her and sat back, waiting.

Mercy understood her choice—accept him freely and to the full extent of their passion, or forsake him forever. Leaving would require her to quell the wild, rebellious desire pounding inside her like the feet of a thousand Amazons charging into battle. Staying would make her an adulteress, or at best a fornicator. So what was she to be? A dry, desiccated parchment using the last remnants of her strength and pliancy to safeguard her secrets? Or a sinner, tainted in the eyes of God and her fellow man? She thought, and she prayed.

Could she abandon the habits and beliefs of a lifetime? Could she live with herself afterward if she did? Could she betray Nathaniel, as he perhaps had betrayed her? This point she considered closely. She would be very wrong to accept Sam if her motive was to hurt Nathaniel. But she did not want to hurt the man she had married. What she wanted was fulfillment of her own needs—for love, for passion—needs she had barely acknowledged since the *Abishai* sailed and Nathaniel was gone. Once acknowledged, however, these long suppressed needs clamored for attention. She wanted to look at them squarely, to know them and nourish them, for if she did not, she sensed, they would prey on her, perhaps even devour her soul with bitterness and regret. This last was a consequence she could not accept.

"Lock the door, Sam," she said with certainty. He did.

Later, as they lay happy and spent in each other's arms, Mercy whispered Sam's name over and over, as if it were a magic incantation that could preserve the joy and the wonder of their union.

Softly he echoed her refrain. "Mercy, Mercy," he murmured.

"Are you saying my name, or asking for what you wish me to grant you?" she asked playfully.

"Both, you rogue." He tousled her hair and kissed her lightly. "Ah, mercy me, Mercy, will you believe me now?"

"About what?"

"That Nathaniel Wright is dead."

Suddenly Mercy's eyes filled with tears. To lie with Sam had seemed such a rational decision. But now in the aftermath, she felt no such certainty. "Why did you say that? You are cruel and thoughtless," she accused.

"Would you have me pretend, Mercy? That we are nothing but young and innocent lovers, with no past and no future, alone at sea forever? Face up to reality, woman."

She fought to extricate herself from him and fumbled for something to cover herself. "And what reality is that? That I am an adulteress?" Sitting up, her back toward him, she began to dress.

"No, that you are a widow, and that you have finally found a man who can match your passion. Leave that pale excuse for a husband behind. He is dead."

"And what if he isn't?"

"Do you want him to be alive so that you can taunt him with your infidelities? I warn you, Mercy, I will not be party to such a game."

"I play no child's game with you, Sam," Mercy rejoined hotly. "Or with myself. I came to you from my own desire, and to please or harm no one but myself."

"You harm me with your refusal to accept your husband's death." He pulled her round to face him. "Would I have lain with you if I believed you were still another man's wife?"

"Then you know Nathaniel is dead?"

"I believe he is dead."

"They are not the same thing." She rose from the couch and finished arranging her clothing, hands trembling, fingers fumbling.

"Only in your stubborn brain, woman! I want all of you, Mercy, not Nathaniel Wright's leavings."

"So I am a parcel to belong to one or the other, am I? You have misjudged me, Sam. I was never that, nor will I be for any man. I have misjudged myself, too. I see now I am not fit for such a liaison as this."

With that, Mercy fled the dayroom. She craved air and space and solitude and raced up the companionway. Until she reached the deck and took a large, reviving draft of sea air, she did not realize she had stopped breathing.

Chapter Eleven

When the summons to see the captain came, Big Jack racked his brains, trying to think of what it was he'd done wrong. It must have been real bad, or else the captain wouldn't have been bothered about it. But no matter how hard he thought, Jack could not come up with a single thing. Still, he was feeling mighty nervous as he stood beside the wheel, waiting for the captain to emerge from the companionway.

"Captain, sir," he acknowledged nervously as soon as Starbuck came on deck.

The captain greeted him with a hearty smile. "Good day, Big Jack. Is that all you go by? Haven't you a surname, man?"

"No, sir." Bewildered, Jack searched the captain's face for signs of displeasure.

"Then you shall be Mr. Jack."

"Pardon, sir?"

"Mr. Jack. You're a petty officer now, harpooner in Mr. Mayhew's boat."

Jack started to laugh uneasily. There were plenty of men willing to play a joke on a black man, but he hadn't pegged the captain for one of them.

"What's so funny about being made harpooner, Mr. Jack?"

"Nothin', sir. I just kind of thought maybe you were havin' a bit of fun with me."

"Not at all," Starbuck assured him. "I need a harpooner. You're the best man I've got. You'll move your things into the steerage right away, and I'll have you make your mark on the papers. Your lay will be increased, of course."

Jack felt as though a rainbow had just sprung up over his head. He was as proud and as excited as he could be, but there was a dark cloud hovering up there, too, a very dark cloud. "If it's all the same to you, sir," he said, looking Starbuck square in the eye, "I'd rather stay where I am."

Starbuck was surprised. He'd never had a man refuse a promotion before. "Why?" he asked.

"I don't want to cause trouble on the ship, sir. There's sure to be some aboard who don't take to having a black man as an officer, even a petty officer."

"You will command the same respect as every officer on this vessel. I'll see to that, Mr. Jack. The first man who steps out of line with you—or with any officer—will be duly punished."

"Sometimes it ain't that easy, Captain. Sometimes it's more a feelin', a look, a tone in the voice."

"And you can't take it?" Starbuck challenged.

"Oh, I can take it all right, sir—"

"Then what's the problem?"

Jack broke into a grin. "No problem, sir. Looks like you got yourself a new harpooner. Mr. Jack," he tried the name on for size. It was big, but so was he, and it fit.

On the way to clear his things out of the fo'c'sle, Jack sought out John Harding to tell him the news. Jane was enormously pleased for her friend but knew she would miss him. Their friendship would of necessity take on a different cast now. They were separated by the strong, if invisible, barrier of power, which somewhat dampened her pleasure in Jack's success. She tried not to let him see that, but Jack sensed something amiss.

"You have any problems—any at all—you let Jack know. Just 'cause you call me mister, doesn't mean I'm not your friend."

But it wasn't his protection she would miss the most; she had little need for it now. The others seemed to accept her unequivocally, and since the attempted keelhauling, Crebbs had avoided her as if she were a leper. What she would really miss was having a companion. One of the things she had noted, now that she was living as a man, was how much she depended upon friendship. Her need in this regard seemed to be markedly different from those of the other men in the fo'c'sle. She was, she admitted reluctantly, more of a woman than she had thought. Still, she could explain none of that to Jack, or to anyone, so she smiled broadly and thanked her friend for his reassuring offer.

It did not take long, however, for her to find out she was wrong on one score. She *had* depended on Jack's protection. For as soon as he left the fo'c'sle Crebbs started in on her again. The harassment wasn't too bad at first—a cutting comment here, a poke in the ribs there, a small possession missing, a clumsy "accident" on deck that made her look foolish. Then the incidents escalated—a dead rat in her berth, a tool dropped from the rigging that missed her by inches, a bared scrimshaw knife stuck blade side up in her mattress. Luckily she only brushed her arm against it, coming away with a nasty cut, but had she landed hard in her berth that night she might have impaled herself through the heart. She found herself tense and wary all the time. She knew that Crebbs and his friends were responsible, but she could prove nothing and therefore could say nothing.

With each incident, however, it became harder and harder to keep silent, especially on those days when she and Mr. Mayhew were in the crow's nest together, or when she was facing him at her oar in the whaleboat. Make it stop, she longed to say to him. But Crebbs was clever, and vigilant as she was she could not catch him in the act. If Jack was still living in the fo'c'sle and working with the crew, he might have been able to help her lay a trap for Crebbs, but Jack was no longer a foremast hand. She could confide in him, but she had no proof that Crebbs was behind the attacks. The burden was becoming too heavy to carry alone, however. Mrs. Wright sometimes asked for her to help in the sick bay, perhaps one day she could say something to her. But what could Mrs. Wright do? Tell the captain or Mr. Mayhew? They too would not act without proof. By speaking to anyone, she showed herself a tattletale or a coward, and such an action was not likely to either stop the harassment or endear her to the rest of the crew.

Then the *Meribah* hit a patch of luck, catching five whales in succession. Crebbs was too busy for pranks, and she was too busy to worry about them. Soon after this, toward the end of August, the *Meribah* reached Tristan da Cunha. There was no reason to grant the crew liberty, for there was nothing to see or do on the barren volcanic island, which was hardly more than a large black crag rising out of the sea. Its few benighted natives were happy to trade wood, fresh water, meat and vegetables for cloth, lamps, pots, oil and other manufactured goods, and there was a cove where the *Meribah* could put in and make some necessary repairs, but it offered the men no respite from their daily drudgery.

Mercy was impatient with the delay at the island, as she had been impatient with everything since her night with the captain. Seeking love, without conditions on her side, she had been met by Sam's demand that she "belong" wholly to him. Why was it not possible for a woman to love and be loved in return without this business of belonging? She did not want Sam—or any man—to belong to her. Why did she have to belong to a man? But while Sam's claim tested her sorely, she was most perturbed with herself. She should have foreseen the complications that lay ahead and forsworn her renegade passion. Worse still, since that night, her attraction to Sam had only grown stronger. It seemed that the more thwarted her feelings were, the more they grew.

What she wanted now was simply to know what had happened to Nathaniel. She wanted either to speak a ship that had news of the *Abishai,* or to reach the Black Islands. This last goal, however, was still many months distant: the

Meribah had yet to round Cape Horn and reach the Pacific Ocean. And every whale they caught slowed them down, but each kill meant money added to the sorely depleted family coffers. She must not be selfish. She must think of Caroline and Sarah and their well-being. But each day dragged on interminably. No matter how many projects she undertook she still had too much time to brood, to ache, to doubt.

For his part, Sam was glad of the work, for he found it impossible to rest, to stop. Had the hunting been slow he might have gone mad. Why did he always have to say everything that came into his head? Why after his exquisite coupling with Mercy had he brought up Nathaniel Wright? Why throw it in her face, bait her as if she were a whale, a prize to chase and capture? He had known captains who had spent their whole careers searching for the legendary white killer whale, Mocha Dick. He had always thought them fools, buffoons who had lost sight of reality. But now he knew what drove them, now he knew obsession. For all he could think of was how to win Mercy back, how to recapture those few perfect moments when she was his and he was hers.

He refitted and restocked the ship as quickly as possible. It was midwinter in the South Atlantic, and the weather was perpetually inhospitable. The damp and cold seemed to seep through his clothes and burrow beneath his skin. He was chilled all the time. The sooner he put Cape Horn—always a treacherous spot—behind him and headed north, to the temperate waters of the equatorial Pacific, the better. The whaling would be easier there, too, as the grounds were not so depleted. And the faster he filled the *Meribah,* the faster he could sail her back to Nantucket. Perhaps this time there would be enough profit to set himself up in business on land. Never attractive before, the charms of being anyplace, as long as it was not the *Meribah,* were beginning to multiply.

The taking of two small cows between Tristan and the Strait of Magellan slowed their journey somewhat, but finally in mid-September the *Meribah* entered the strait. The sky that day was a leaden, ominous gray. The wind stung and the air was frigid. Believing the quickest way through the strait was the best, Starbuck ordered all canvas hoisted, but with the added precaution of all hands on alert and he himself keeping a sharp eye on the weather, which could change in less time than it took a man to breathe in and out.

Twenty-four hours passed without incident, and Starbuck pressed on hard, thinking only of getting through, of cruising up the coast of South America and heading west. Like many captains, he always tried to make Honolulu for Christmas. Although he did not care for the place himself, he found that a stop there improved the morale of both officers and men. Mercy, he was certain, would also appreciate the amenities and female company she would find there. Perhaps she would even have tired of the *Meribah* by then and decide to return to Nantucket by clipper ship. That would surely simplify life.

His distracting thoughts continued for only a few seconds, but in that short space of time the *Meribah* sailed into a raging snow squall. Though only midday, it was suddenly dark. Blinding gusts of snow-filled wind swept the deck, making it impossible to see more than a few inches in any direction. The wind howled and screamed, drowning Starbuck's frantic orders to reef all sails. All hands on deck were forced to grab anything they could to avoid being swept up by the wind. They clung to the rigging and the lash rail; they hugged the masts as the deadly wind filled the sails, tipping the *Meribah* further and further to starboard until she was in danger of keeling over. Only two things could save the ship: a miraculous end to the squall or reefing the sails.

To a man, the crew realized this, but no one was in a position to act. The *Meribah*'s situation was critical. Hugging the lash rail with one arm, using the other to wipe the stinging snow out of her eyes, Jane assessed her chances for making it to the mainsail halyards. She was just larboard of the tryworks. If she could somehow make her way there and climb atop the brick wall, she might be able to reach the ropes and unfasten them. Or she might be pitched into the angry, swirling sea. But if she didn't try, the chances were excellent she would end up there anyway.

Crouching low to the ground, trying to cheat the wind, Jane let go of the lash rail. She was immediately flung to the ground and catapulted across the slippery deck. She put her arms out in front of her, both searching for something to grab on to and hoping to protect her head. Something sharp ripped her leg, and she winced at the biting sting as salt water washed into the wound. The wind suddenly died and she skidded to a halt, her back ramming into a solid object. When she had cleared and opened her eyes, she saw she had landed beside the brick step that led up the try-works.

This bit of luck spurred her on and she groped in front of her for the grate fronting the works. Finding it, she used it for purchase to get back onto her feet. These two maneuvers had cost her a great deal of time and strength, and she stood panting, trying to recover sufficiently enough to go on. Suddenly a hard thump on the back knocked the breath out of her. With a gasp, she turned to see what had happened. Squinting against the pelting snow, she made out a piece of loosened rigging and ducked just in time to avoid being hit by it again.

As she cautiously came to standing, she noticed a quivering form clinging desperately to the rope. She reached out for it, but a wave of icy water knocked her hand away. Coughing and spluttering, for she'd taken a mouthful of water, she wiped her face and eyes and again reached for the dangling rope. This time she caught it and was able to make out the face of the man clinging to it. Crebbs. For a fraught instant the snow and spray cleared and they could see each other. Even with his life in her hands Crebbs did not relent. He glared at her defiantly, as if daring her to fling the rope away and send him to a watery death.

But she could not. She had to try to save him. Abandoning the security of her spot on the tryworks, she grabbed the rope with her other hand, too, and began to lash it to the nearest secure piece of rigging. The wet rope lined her hands. There was little slack to tie up, and between the weight and the wind it took an interminable time—even for her now-nimble fingers—to fasten it securely. When she was done, her strength was nearly gone—and she had yet to attempt what she had set out to do.

Again she flung herself toward the tryworks, belly against brick, and gained a foothold a second time. Now, working against the snowy turbulence, she raised one knee and hoisted herself up onto the front of the works. Balanced precariously on her knees, she extended first one hand, then the other across the deep holes where the iron pots rested when the works were in use. Clinging to finger holds in the bricks, she pulled her body forward until she was crouching against the back wall. Again she rested and reached deep inside herself for the strength to go on, for her hardest trial was yet to come.

She started her climb onto the back wall of the works, first relinquishing her finger holds and then rising to her feet with infinite care. Once erect, a gust of wind assailed her, and she was forced to drop to her knees again. She waited for a moment's respite, listening intently to the wind, trying to anticipate its movements. As soon as she sensed a lull, she shot up and reached blindly for the mainsail halyards. Miraculously she connected. Her hands clumsy with numbness, she fumbled with the knots that held the halyards fast. Since boarding the *Meribah,* she must have untied such knots a thousand times, but now her fingers would not obey her commands. She was close to swearing when she felt the ropes loosen. Above the cries of the wind she heard the sail flop down. In another moment the *Meribah* began to right herself.

The sudden motion toppled Jane, bouncing her off the brick wall and onto the carpenter's bench that sat back to back with the tryworks. She was rolled onto her stomach and nearly off the bench and onto the deck, but she managed to grab the edge of the bench and maintain her precarious perch. In this inelegant but reasonably secure position she rode out the rest of the storm.

The squall abated as precipitously as it had begun, and suddenly the *Meribah* was sailing more or less smoothly under the same dull sky that had turned to charcoal darkness only thirty minutes before. Without the throbbing gash in her left shin, a painful and all-too-real souvenir of that eventful half hour, Jane might have thought she had dreamed the entire episode. With great effort, she rolled over and sat up to inspect her memento. The ragged cut was about two inches long, but not deep. The bleeding had already stopped, but the skin around the wound was swollen and tender.

Suddenly she was aware of someone standing over her and looked up into Mr. Mayhew's concerned face. "Are you all right, Harding?"

"Yes, sir," she stammered. "Just a cut, sir."

Val quickly called for two other sailors. "Carry this man to the sick bay immediately," he ordered. "And send for Mrs. Wright."

The last thing Jane wanted was to be carried. One of the men might notice the curves in her body and become suspicious. She hopped off the bench in a hurry, wincing as she landed on her wounded leg. "I'm fine, sir." She took a step and felt a searing pain in her left leg, but plastered a grin on her face, hoping it covered the grimace. "I can get down to the sick bay on my own. Honestly."

By now the captain had approached. As he peered at her leg, Jane reminded herself not to blush and prayed he did not touch her. "If that's our worst injury, we've much to be thankful for. How did it happen?"

Jane recounted her trip to the tryworks and how she'd unlashed the halyards, omitting any mention of Crebbs in her account.

"So it was you who saved us, Harding," the captain realized. "Well done, lad. Very well done."

"Thank you, sir," Jane replied modestly. The pain of standing on her wounded leg was becoming quite intense, so much so she found it difficult to breathe normally. "With your permission, sir, may I get down to the sick bay?"

"On your way then. What are the rest of you gawking at?" He gave orders for the mainsail to be raised again, for the rigging and the deck to be inspected for damage. When he finished, Val was still by his side. "What is it, Mr. Mayhew?" he asked impatiently.

"I think Harding deserves to be recognized for his bravery, Captain," Val said. He knew his request might throw him open again to charges of favoritism, but whatever his feelings for Harding—and he still had them—it was an officer's duty to see his men praised when they deserved it.

Sam looked at him darkly for a moment, then the cloud cleared. "Aye. It was quite a feat for a green hand, never in the strait before. Summon all hands when the watch changes."

"Yes, sir," Val replied with zest. Sam had been moodier than he'd ever seen him these past weeks, but at least this was an indication that he himself was not the entire source of the captain's ill humor. On that score, he did have a theory, but it was as yet little more than a glimmering, and totally unproved.

Meanwhile, below in the sick bay, Mercy was attending to John Harding's leg. She snipped off the bottom of his left trouser leg to facilitate her examination and could not help but notice how smooth the leg was, and how surprisingly slim and shapely. While her uncle had trained her to treat all patients with a firm but gentle hand, she found herself trying to be especially gentle as she washed the jagged tear and applied salve and a dressing to keep it clean as it healed. For some reason, John Harding elicited a great tenderness in her, and she had to fight off an urge to comb his tousled hair and stroke his grimy cheek as part of the treatment. Instead, she simply patched him up and sent him on his way with an admonition to keep the wound clean. She said that to all the men she treated, but smiled knowing that Harding was one of the few who would pay any attention to that instruction.

When Jane emerged from the sick bay, she expected to be sent back to work, but Mr. Allen, who was on duty, sent her to rest on her berth until the watch changed. She was both surprised at this preferential treatment, for there was much to do in the aftermath of the storm, and somewhat apprehensive of it, for it was no favor for her to be singled out in any way, but the dull ache in her leg made her grateful all the same. She retired to the fo'c'sle, where she fell fast asleep almost as soon as her head hit the mattress.

She was awakened by a loud summons. Startled out of sleep, she grabbed her mug, plate and spoon and climbed onto the deck, thinking it was mealtime. But the scene on deck was not the usual dinner-hour commotion, with men roving back and forth to the galley and sprawled hither and thither spooning down their food. The crew was standing in an orderly row, starboard of the main hatch, with the captain and the officers facing them. Even Mrs. Wright was on board. What was going on, Jane wondered. Then she heard her name called again, only this time it was the captain who hailed her.

"Yes, sir!" she responded.

"I've gathered the men here so we could all thank you for saving our sorry hides this afternoon."

Surprised but exceedingly pleased, Jane felt her chest puff out with pride. "Thank you, sir," she responded. Stealing a glance at Mr. Mayhew, she caught his eye. They both looked away quickly, but not before they had exchanged a flash of unspoken but well-understood mutual admiration.

"To most men on this ship I could offer tobacco or rum to show our appreciation of your bravery. But with you, I am at a loss. Perhaps something from the slop chest would interest you."

"A length of calico would do nicely," she said eagerly, then realized her gaffe. What would a sailor want with a length of calico? "I—I understand you can barter it for trinkets—and things—in the South Sea Islands," she stammered.

"Indeed you can," the captain agreed with a hearty laugh. "But you don't want to get the native girls overexcited, Harding, so I'm throwing in a new pair of trousers, too."

The men began to chuckle and guffaw, and Jane looked down self-consciously. She reddened thoroughly when she realized she had not changed into her other pair of trousers, and flushed even more when she thought of Mr. Mayhew seeing her nearly naked leg. Oh, why did things have to be so complicated, she railed to herself.

"All right, that's enough," the captain continued. "Fill your bellies, and get on with it. We're still in the strait, and we've already had one close call too many today."

The crew was dismissed and dispersed, either to their duties or their dinner, and Jane, swaggering with pride, made her way back to the galley. On her way forward, with a full plate and mug, she saw Crebbs coming her way. She swerved to avoid him, but he still came at her.

"I didn't ask you to do what you did today," he rasped, "and I don't owe you nothin'."

Determined not to let him spoil her triumph, she looked him straight in the eye. "Who said you did?" she asked roughly and turned on her heel.

This scene did not go unnoticed by the *Meribah*'s newest petty officer, who called out for Harding. "Is that man bothering you?" Mr. Jack asked quietly, but not so quietly that others might not overhear him.

"No, sir," she answered, making sure her reply was audible, too. She stood silently, offering nothing further, keeping her face blank. It pained her to behave this way with Jack, but the less said the better. There was no reason for anyone to know she had saved Crebbs's life. Despite his threatening manner, perhaps his speaking to her a moment ago was his way of acknowledging his debt to her. The harassment might stop now, but it surely wouldn't if she spoke of it to an officer. She could see from Jack's face that he didn't believe her, but she held his gaze and her tongue, and he dismissed her.

But Jack too was distressed. This damned officership was coming between him and his friend, who, he suspected, was very much in need of his help. He only hoped he could keep an eye on the situation, in case he was ever needed.

Below, in the officers' mess, the talk was livelier than it had been for weeks. The insouciance that often follows a narrow escape loosened tongues and lightened spirits. Mercy and the captain even exchanged a few civil words, phrases not fraught with submerged meaning and unspoken emotion. After the meal, Mercy, who had been below all day, indeed in her stateroom as much as possible these past weeks, accepted Val's invitation to take a breath of air on the deck. Though icy and raw, the air was welcome, and she swallowed it down with deep, hungry gulps.

She felt as if she had survived more than near disaster this afternoon. During the storm, when confronted with the possibility of imminent demise, she had gained a sense of perspective about her lapse of judgment. It had been the temporary triumph of hurt, resentment and pure animal lust over moral training and good common sense. But she had survived it, as she and the *Meribah* had survived the storm. She was battered perhaps, but alive. Her deep sigh of relief was audible.

Val responded with an equally heartfelt echo. "We never cherish life so much as when we nearly lose it, eh, Mercy?" he asked. "Just as you're wondering how in heaven's name you can keep going, something happens to remind you that the alternative is not desirable."

"No, the alternative is not 'a consummation devoutly to be wish'd,'" she agreed. "But why this malaise of spirit in you, Val?" She had been so wrapped up in her own troubles that she had not paid much attention to her friend's state of mind.

"I don't seem to know myself anymore," he said quietly, tautly.

Mercy rested her hand lightly on his sleeve. "Nor do I, Val. But perhaps it is merely a stage through which we are passing."

"The Strait of Magellan of life?" he proposed mischievously.

It took a second for his sally to sink in, but then she could not help but laugh. "Yes, indeed, exactly so." His answering laugh rang clear and true in the sodden, frosty air.

Chapter Twelve

Mercy was enchanted. From her vantage point on the deck of the *Meribah* the island seemed to be swaying in the sea. She knew it was an illusion, but it was still delightful, watching the jagged heaps of rock dance in the distance. They were approaching Santa María, or Charles as it was known on the charts of English-speaking sailors, in the Galápagos Islands, off the coast of Peru. Although the island was uninhabited by humans, she had been told there were wonders of nature there that could be seen nowhere else on earth.

Even if the place were reputed to be the dullest place in the world, Mercy would have welcomed the sight of it. November had begun and five months had passed since her single day of liberty in the Western Islands. Any change of scene would have met her approval, but Charles Island had additional appeal—its post office. In a sheltered cove where whaleboats could land sat the upended shell of one of the giant tortoises—who lent their Spanish name to the islands—which served as a depository for letters. Starved as she was for word of her family and friends, and possessed of a thick packet of missives she wished to send on their way, she had begun to dream of the shell. Each night it appeared, overflowing with envelopes, carved all over with cryptic forms and designs, their meanings, like ancient hieroglyphs, long forgotten or lost.

Just as she was. Or so it had begun to seem. It was difficult to remain connected to those so far away while on
board a ship with no fixed destination and no fixed date of
return. Even the dangers of the chase and the backbreak-
ing work of cutting in and trying out had become routine
by now. There was little to look forward to, except that the
whaling should continue, for the days without it, when
there were more than two or three in a row, hung long and
heavy on all. Spirits were raised only by the promise of such
few breaks in the monotony as were possible—hunting
turtles on Charles Island, putting in to Honolulu for
Christmas or a gam with another whaler. One was forced
always to look ahead, and yet the ever-present dangers
could make any day one's last. It was an odd, disjointed
sort of existence, one that made any land—even a lonely
hunk of lava and rock rolling in the middle of a vast sea—
seem an enchanted land.

It was late afternoon when the *Meribah* came as close to
Charles Island as she could without ripping her bottom on
the shoals, and Captain Starbuck ordered the anchor
dropped. The next morning, after a night of almost palp-
able restlessness, straws were drawn to see which unfortunate men and officers would stay behind on the ship while
the rest piled into the boats and rowed ashore.

Mercy asked to be taken ashore, and her request was
granted by the captain with a perfunctory grunt. She cared
little for the feel of solid land beneath her feet, for the sight
of the giant turtles sunning themselves on rocks like ossi-
fied old men or for the caterwauling of strange birds. These
interesting phenomena were eclipsed by the more compelling thought of news from home. She had made out the
bleached-white post office shell even before the whaleboat
was pulled ashore, and waited impatiently for the boat to
be secured on the rocky beach.

The moment she alighted she went directly to the shell,
knelt down in front of it and scooped up the pile of letters
with both arms. Then she let the precious papers trickle
through her fingers, like sand, back into the shell. She did

this a couple of times, laughing like a child at play, before sorting through the letters. Many were for ships and people she knew, and she rejoiced for each recipient and hoped they would soon discover this priceless treasure. When she found the first envelope with her name on it, she whooped aloud for joy. The letter was from Caroline. She held it close for a moment before continuing her search. By the time she had finished, she had three letters for herself and several more for others aboard the *Meribah*.

As soon as the mail had been distributed, the captain ordered the landing parties to proceed with their searches for fresh water and firewood. When these essential stores had been replenished, he would allow the men to hunt for turtles, and there would be fresh meat which the men had not seen in months.

Mercy had expected Sam to order one of the men to stay with her on the beach, as he had assigned Mr. Carmody to her in the Western Islands, but today he gave no such order. Perhaps he had simply ceased to care what happened to her. With some trepidation she took a good look around her, finding a world unimaginably strange but apparently benign. Contritely she banished her caustic thoughts, which she ascribed more to her own frustrations than any motive of Sam's. He knew this place well; he had left her to her own devices because he had no cause to be concerned for her welfare.

When the men departed, she found a flat rock in the shade where she sat to savor her letters—one from Caroline with an enclosure from Aunt Elizabeth, one from Sarah with a note from Aunt Lavinia, and one from Maria. She pored over every word, every comma, every dash, and was transported so completely to Boston and then to Nantucket that when she heard Val's voice calling her name she thought she was imagining it. She was sure she was on Orange Street, and he was hailing her there. But then she realized she *was* hearing his voice and that his shouts were filled with alarm. She looked up. Val, Mr. Jack and several sailors were hurrying toward her.

She jumped up and ran to them. "What is it? What's happened?"

"It's the captain. He's been bitten by a snake."

"Take me to him," she ordered without hesitation, "and send a man back to the *Meribah*." Val chose Mr. Jack, and Mercy told him what she needed and where to find it. The men dispatched, Val led her over the rocky beach and into a stand of trees that soon deepened into a tropical forest, dark and dank, redolent of decay and renewal. When they reached Sam, they found him unconscious and drenched in sweat. His heart was pounding wildly, his breathing rapid and shallow.

Mercy demanded a knife and a match. John Harding's hand shot out with a sharp pocketknife. Val produced the match. She wiped the blade, then seared it clean with the flame, proceeded by instinct and dim memory rather than training. Snakebites were unheard-of in her uncle's surgery, but she had read of their treatment.

First she lifted her skirt, tore off a strip of her petticoat and tied the cloth tight around the thigh of the affected leg. By cutting off the circulation, she hoped to stop the further spread of the poison. Then she bent over Sam's clammy leg and made a deep cut where the snake had attacked his shin. She began to suck the wound, drawing up the venom and the blood and spitting out each horrid mouthful. Her mind stopped. She thought of nothing but draw in, spit out, don't swallow, keeping up the desperate measures until she heard Sam stir.

He began to thrash around wildly, trying to kick her away and to sit up. She ordered the men to hold him down. "You must not move," she told him. "Try to lie absolutely still." But Captain Starbuck was not so easily subdued. "Wha' happa?" he asked. His speech was slurred, and he tried to raise his head and look around as he spoke.

She covered his forehead with her hand, wanting to hold him still and comfort him at the same time. "You were bitten by a snake." His head was burning. "You *must* lie still," she told him again. But he had lapsed out of consciousness once more.

She could do nothing but wait, yet waiting was intolerable. Her uncle had schooled her well in the value of patience in the practice of medicine, but this was no ordinary patient before her. This was Sam, whom she had once taken for her lover. Though she had struggled mightily with the many conflicting feelings that act had engendered, she had lost her battle not to care so deeply for him.

Among her medicines, she had no antidote for snakebite, but she did have powders that would reduce his fever and quell the wild beating of his heart. If he was strong enough to fight off whatever poison had entered his system, he would live. If not, he would die. She did not know how to read his state—should she be encouraged by the fact that he had regained consciousness, however briefly, and that he was not raving and delirious? Or was his stillness a sign that the poison had already taken hold? She knew only that there were no guarantees, and that Valentine Mayhew might soon be the captain of the *Meribah*.

When Mr. Jack and his men returned with supplies, she set them to work, fetching fresh water, building a fire to boil it. She covered Sam with the blankets they had brought and bathed his face with a wet cloth. When the water had boiled and cooled, she prepared the medicines and fed them to him. Then she and Val sat in vigil beside him. The rest, except John Harding, whom Mercy asked to be left behind, could be of no use and were dispatched to their original duties. Whatever happened to Sam, the *Meribah* must continue her voyage, and for that she needed fresh wood, water and meat.

"Time is so peculiar," Mercy remarked, as much to herself as to Val and young Harding. "This morning the minutes flitted past like graceful dancers. Now each one drags itself by as if attached to a ball and chain. As I was reading my letters—" She stopped short. In her haste she had left her precious letters on the rock. "My letters!" she exclaimed.

"I'll go find them," Jane volunteered. It was torture sitting here with Mrs. Wright and Mr. Mayhew, watching over the captain. There were so many things she wanted to say, so many times she wanted to reach out and comfort both of them, but as John Harding she could not do that. "If I might, sir," she requested, trying to temper her eagerness.

"Of course," Val agreed with alacrity. Sitting so quietly and so close to Harding had made him more nervous than he already was under the circumstances. When Harding was out of earshot, he confessed to Mercy, "I don't think I'm ready to captain the *Meribah*."

"God willing you won't have to, Val," she answered fervently. Often, in the past months, she had wished for Sam to somehow miraculously disappear. She didn't want him dead, of course, but since their night together her life had become so complicated. Now, with him lying pale and silent beside her, she realized that she had not wanted the man to disappear at all. She had only wanted the situation to disentangle itself. Faced with it now, the possibility of life without Sam seemed bleak and barren indeed.

A moan escaped Sam's lips and Mercy hastened off the fallen log where they were perched and knelt beside him. His forehead seemed a degree or two cooler, but his color was worse, or perhaps it was only the sallow light wending its way through the dense trees that made it seem so. The island that had seemed so enchanting from afar was forbidding and full of foreboding up close. But appearances so often deceive, Mercy thought as she bathed Sam's face again and put her ear to his chest to listen to his heart. It was still beating fast but had steadied some, and his breathing seemed less jagged and forced than it had an hour or so ago.

"It will be nightfall soon, Mercy. We must decide whether to try to take him back to the ship or not."

Mercy looked around her, listening to the raucous shrieks of the birds and the rustlings and scratchings of the creatures on the ground. The forest was an ominous place, not a spot for recuperation. The poisonous snake had es-

caped; it could return at any time; there could be scores
more lurking about. "I think it is safer to move him than
to stay here through the night."

"I agree." Val whistled for the men to halt their tasks and
reconvene. They improvised a pallet and the sad, solemn
procession wended its way through the forest and across the
rocky beach. The trip through the choppy waters to the
Meribah was a long and silent one.

The strain of being moved caused Sam's fever to rise
again, and as they carried him aboard he began to rant and
rave and to thrash so wildly that the men could hardly
transport him down the companionway and into his cabin.
Finally he was laid on his berth, still moving about violently, babbling and confused. Mercy had to ask the men
to tie him down, a humiliating moment for all of them.
Their captain was so reduced by fever that he had to be restrained like a madman to protect himself.

For three days Mercy stayed by Sam's side, leaving only
for occasional forays to the deck for a few breaths of air.
Charles Island still danced in the sun, but Mercy was neither enchanted nor fooled by its beauty. John Harding had
brought her bits and pieces of her letters, the few pages that
had not been taken up by the wind, washed out to sea or for
all she knew eaten by a giant tortoise. As she sat by Sam's
bed she had used the fragments to reconstruct the letters,
but it was like trying to reknit a much-loved shawl on which
the moths had been feeding all summer. She might patch
the pieces together, but the garment would be forever
flawed and not the one she had loved.

Sam moved in and out of delirium, his fever rose and
abated, rose and abated again, and her hopes followed its
course up and down, up and down. Then on the fourth day,
after Mercy had been briefly on the deck in midmorning,
she returned to Sam's cabin to find him sitting up in his
berth, looking around in bewilderment.

"What the devil is going on and what the devil are you
doing here?" was his greeting.

"Sam!" she cried.

Starbuck cringed. "No need to shout, Mercy. My head feels as if it's been stuck inside a ringing church bell for a week." He slid back down on his berth, exhausted by the effort of speaking and moving.

Mercy went to him and put her hand to his forehead. It was blessedly cool. "How do you feel?"

"Like Jonah after the whale spit him out," he answered with a feeble smile. "What happened? Where are we?" Mercy explained and Sam was incredulous. "Five days ago! Get Valentine down here! Tell him to get this tub moving!" He made a move to get off his berth, but fell back panting and in a sweat.

She sat beside him on the edge of the berth. "You must rest, Sam. You've been very ill."

He reached for her hand. "Have you been here the whole time?" When she nodded, he continued. "Were you merely filling Hippocrates's shoes, or do you hate me less than I'd imagined?"

"I don't hate you," she answered softly, tears welling in her eyes.

It took all his strength, but he brought her hand to his lips and held it there for a long moment. "I'm glad," he whispered, "very glad." With that he dropped off to sleep, still clutching her hand. She stayed where she was, smoothing his brow with her other hand, running her fingers through his matted hair. Then, exhausted too, she let her head drop to his chest in relief. The long siege was over.

The *Meribah* put to sea again, with the captain still in his stateroom and Mr. Mayhew at the helm, but the mate was running a merry chase between taking care of the ship and satisfying the captain's need to know every last detail of events on deck. Mercy stayed close by, making sure that Sam rested and ate properly and did not overtire himself. Under her tender and watchful eye he grew stronger—and more like his usual bellicose self—each day, until finally, after two weeks, his full energy and vigor were restored. Not even Mercy could keep him in his stateroom any longer.

At the end of his first day in command, Sam felt, to his combined delight and relief, remarkably well, only somewhat more than usually fatigued for a relatively uneventful day at sea. Following the evening meal, he retired to the day cabin for a rest, asking Mercy to accompany him. His long recuperation had given him much time for thought, most of it about Mercy. With vanity and arrogance, he had demanded that she choose between him and Nathaniel Wright. He had wanted her to acknowledge his "victory" over Wright, and to claim her as his spoils. But love, he had come to see, was not about winning and losing. It was about giving—as Mercy had given unstintingly to him in his sickness. He wanted now to try to give to her as she had to him. For this, he would need some instruction and some practice.

Mercy was not surprised by Sam's summons, for in the course of his recovery, a comfortable intimacy had been established between them. Before reaching the Galápagos Islands, she had avoided being in the small sitting room with him alone—or at all if possible—but tonight, as he closed the door behind them, she felt no sense of panic or foreboding. On the contrary, she was profoundly calm and composed. For in those days of nursing Sam, she had also come to an acceptance of her most unusual situation.

Her family and friends were worlds away. Her marriage had failed. No marriage, even under the duress of a long separation, could be counted a success when one partner made no attempt to bridge that separation with letters or messages. Why Nathaniel had abandoned her, she might never know. But now that she had lived aboard a whaler, now that she had seen for herself that it was possible to maintain connections, even across vast distances, she had to accept that that was what he had done. Had it not been his intention to be rid of her, he would have kept his promise. He would have written, perhaps not every day, but he would have sent her messages one way or another.

Perhaps she had come on this journey not so much to find him, as to find out why he had left her and also to recapture the piece of her heart he had taken with him. But, she had realized, she might never accomplish these things. She might die first. One man had already been lost; the *Meribah* had nearly sunk in the strait; Sam had almost died. Death was immanent on a whaler.

And so was life. Despite vagaries of sea and weather, despite countless near-calamities, the *Meribah* had survived. The ship and her crew had bested many formidable adversaries. Now she, Mercy, must embrace the force that made those victories possible and use it to carve out whatever life she could with Sam, here in this small sphere, in whatever time was allotted to them.

Observing her former patient as they sat beside each other on the sofa, Mercy was deeply satisfied to see him once again with ruddy cheeks and gleaming eyes. "Compared to a fortnight ago, you look like a new man," she said.

"That's because I am," he replied with a jaunty smile. "Or almost new," he amended. "I lack only one item to complete the transformation."

"And what is that?"

"Your love."

She blushed with happiness, yet withdrew her hand from his. "My love, and not me?" she questioned seriously.

"I now know the difference, Mercy," he assured her, "and it is your love I seek."

"Then I must ask you to be very sure, Sam, that you are not seeking it merely out of gratitude to me."

"I am grateful to you, Mercy, but I am a new man not because of your care—without which I might have perished—but because of a new understanding, which I have come to on my own."

"And what have you learned?" she prompted.

He paused, preparing his answer carefully. "My life has been one of pursuit. For me, there is great excitement in the chase, in the wanting and the conquering. But you are not a trophy to be won, not through craft or camouflage or deception. Nor are you a prize to be owned and displayed on my mantelpiece. I want to be with you, Mercy, but I am not certain I know how. Perhaps you can teach me.''

"I would like to try," she replied solemnly, "but only if you will endeavor to teach me that life is in the living of it, and not in the planning and the waiting.''

He held out his arms and invited her into them. "I will endeavor as never before," he promised. Without hesitation or doubt she went to him, allowing his warmth and strength to envelope her, enhance her. She felt a new pliancy in him, a new tenderness, just as she felt a new contentment and receptivity in herself.

"Will you come to me tonight, my love? We shall have to be very discreet," he murmured.

"I know," she answered. "And I shall have to remind you to be gruff and discourteous to me from time to time, so no one will suspect. But that won't be so very hard, will it?" she asked mischievously.

"Probably not," Sam admitted ruefully. "Although I feel like a new man, I will more than likely behave like the old Sam Starbuck.''

"Don't throw the old Sam completely away, please? I rather liked him."

"Now and then."

"Yes, now and then."

He kissed her affectionately, caressing her face and smoothing back her hair. "I will leave you now. But not for long.'' He rose and opened the door of the cabin. "Good night, Mercy,'' he said neutrally.

"Good night, Sam,'' she said, just as evenly. She remained in the dayroom for half an hour or so, pretending to read a book, then retired to her stateroom, where she prepared for the night ahead as she had never prepared for her wedding night. For tonight she was no girlish bride. She was a woman going against all she had ever known, toward something she did not and could not know. She prayed for guidance and the strength to see her choice through, whatever the future held.

Chapter Thirteen

The *Meribah* cruised west and north, hunting for whales, but without much deviation from the direct course to Honolulu. There were already over eight hundred barrels in the hold, a sizable catch to send home to Nantucket. The men and officers well deserved the reward of a few days on land for their hard service. With the money derived from the sale of this oil, Mercy would be able to satisfy some of her father's creditors. She looked forward to her sojourn in the Sandwich Islands—there would be fresh food, clean sheets, letters, companionship—but the urgency she had once felt to arrive there was gone. Indeed, she felt little urgency about anything these days, basking as she was in the glow of Captain Starbuck's tender attention.

The need for discretion allowed them far fewer private moments than they wanted, but it made those they did have sweeter and more intense, like strawberries that have stayed on the vine a shade too long and have ripened just slightly beyond their peak. But she did not long for the season to be over. Now the *Meribah* seemed cozy rather than confining, the monotony of the voyage comforting rather than tiresome.

Mercy spent much of her time on deck, sitting in the shade under the skids where the spare whaleboats were stored, reading or writing or sewing or simply watching the goings-on. She no longer felt a need to be profitably occupied every waking moment. It was quite acceptable to her to sit and enjoy the warm, tangy breezes, the swell of the whitecaps, the soft bobbing of the ship, the sight of Sam taking a reading or inspecting the rigging.

One especially fine, balmy morning Val paused in his duties and came to stand by her chair. "I just had to tell you how well you are looking these days."

"It's all the fresh sea air I'm getting," she answered gaily.

Val eyed her skeptically. "I'm getting as much sea air—more—than you, and I don't look, or feel, so happy or content. What's your secret?"

Judging it time to change the subject, Mercy looked closely at her friend. "You don't look well, Val. You're drawn and careworn. What is it?"

"I don't know," he fibbed. "But I'm out of sorts all the time. Sam and I seem to have changed personalities. He's purring like a cat in the sun, and I'm barking and snapping like an ancient cur. What do you make of it?"

"Perhaps the captain is glad to be alive," she said lightly.

"He's had narrow scrapes before—we all have. Usually it makes him more irascible. I don't understand it."

Mercy said nothing more but concentrated intently on her knitting, and before Val could pursue the subject further, he was called away. Although he had said nothing about any relationship other than captain and owner, between herself and Sam, he obviously had noted the change in both of them. If he hadn't already made a sum from those numbers, he soon would. And so would others. He was not the only observant man on board. She must mention this to Sam, and they must continue to be very careful. She wanted to do nothing to compromise discipline and morale aboard the *Meribah*.

But when she spoke of the matter to Sam, he was less concerned about Val's observations than about Val himself, although he said nothing of this to Mercy. His mate's downheartedness was beginning to worry him, especially as he suspected it related to young John Harding. He couldn't put Harding off the ship in Honolulu on suspicion alone, and besides a sailor that good was hard to come by. Mercy seemed fond of him, too, and he had to admit that he liked the lad, as well. For now he would leave things as they were, keeping a careful eye on the situation. He set Mercy's mind to rest about the other matter, assuring her he'd had no insolence or innuendos from the men and that even if they did sense anything going on between the two of them, it was causing no problems. Then he changed the subject to their imminent arrival in Honolulu.

Although he did not let on, Sam had little enthusiasm for Honolulu. He found it a strange, hollow place. It was neither one thing nor another, but an unfortunate combination of foreign port and American town, with the worst aspects of both—the seaminess of the one and the small-minded righteousness of the other. But now as he spoke of it to Mercy, he saw it in a different light. How she would enjoy sailing the *Meribah* proudly into the crowded harbor, seeing the fabulous flowers, tasting the exotic fruits, and how he would enjoy squiring her about the town, making sure she had her fill of the amenities of civilization.

Mercy was amused by his schoolboy animation and assured him that she would enjoy the change of scene but she was perfectly content as she was aboard the *Meribah*. On the morning of the twentieth of December, however, when they finally sailed into Honolulu harbor, she was unexpectedly moved to tears by the sight of so many whalers, nearly all with American flags flying and familiar names emblazoned on their sterns.

"There's the *Industry*," she cried to Sam, "and the *Mary Mitchell!*" She wanted to throw her arms around him but checked herself. "Isn't it exciting, Captain? It's almost like coming home!"

"Almost, Mrs. Wright," he agreed, so impatient now for his holiday with Mercy to begin that he had thoughts of abandoning the care of the ship to Val and absconding with her. But these aberrant ideas passed quickly, and he turned his attention to the many details of anchoring and liberty schedules and lists of supplies to be purchased and repairs to be ordered. Finally all was in readiness and he ordered a whaleboat lowered, with himself, Mrs. Wright and her valise in it.

On the swarming dock, in her plain black skirt and white blouse Mercy felt like a drab sparrow lost among a pack of preening egrets. The dock was abuzz with ladies in bright muslin and cambric, their straw bonnets decorated with vibrant flowers and feathers. She searched the crowd for faces she knew, but while everyone looked familiar—she had not realized how much she missed seeing people, their various faces, expressions and modes of dress—she recognized no one with whom she was actually acquainted.

The scene reminded her somewhat of the Nantucket dock in a summer season gone ariot. There was the same mixture of people, although there were many more exotic types here, and the same chaotic bustle, but the trees were palms instead of maples and oaks, the flowers frangipani and hibiscus instead of roses and tiger lilies. The smells were richer and warmer and the air soft and languid, lacking the bite and tang of the Nantucket atmosphere. After so many months of sameness, her senses were overwhelmed by the profusion of sights and sounds and smells. She held tight to Sam's arm, exclaiming over this or that, demanding to know what one or another strange fruit or flower was called.

The New Pacific Hotel, a large white stucco mansion, was happy to accommodate the daughter of Captain Randall in one of their few remaining rooms. The manager himself served her, apologizing for the lack of rooms with a sea view, but assuring her she would enjoy the view of their gardens. Mercy told him happily that she had seen quite enough of the sea lately and would very much enjoy the tropical foliage. Once he was certain of her comfort, Sam, who would be staying on the *Meribah,* excused himself to conduct some business, arranging to dine with her at the hotel. She would have the rest of the afternoon to herself.

Her room was spacious and airy, with a small balcony. The walls were covered with pink flowered wallpaper, the curtains and bedcover made of a complementary chintz fabric. It was sweet and demure and girlish and exactly suited her mood. She only wished Sam could see it, even share it with her, but of course that was impossible. The first thing she did was order a bath drawn for her, and she soaked in it until the water was cold and her fingers and toes were wrinkled. Then she dried off, dressed her hair and put on her sprigged muslin gown. It seemed odd, at Christmas time, to be donning a summer frock rather than a dark gray challis or a claret-red velvet, but the brilliant sunshine and balmy breezes demanded the untraditional attire.

It was late afternoon by the time Mercy completed her ablutions. Not having been filled since breakfast, her stomach was demanding attention and she decided to take tea in the hotel dining room. There were many other ladies and gentlemen engaged in a similar pursuit, and she scanned the room for acquaintances. When she recognized Josephine Gardner, seated with a woman she did not know, her reaction was one of excitement and pleasure, though hardly unmitigated. Josephine, a woman about five years her senior, was the daughter of Josiah Hussey, the captain of the *Abishai*. Mercy had always found her rather humorless and severe, but still she was a Nantucketer, and now they shared a common if tragic bond. Thoughts of her father and the *Abishai* saddened her, but she composed herself and approached Josephine's table.

"Good afternoon. It is so good to see you, Josephine."

While she had expected Josephine Gardner to be surprised—that was natural—Mercy was unprepared for the confusion and even embarrassment with which she was greeted. Josephine stared at her for a moment as if she were an apparition, and an extremely unwelcome one at that. "Good afternoon," she said finally, without a smile or any degree of warmth, not to mention an invitation to sit down. The situation rapidly became uncomfortable, for Josephine's companion as well as for Mercy. That other lady looked at Josephine expectantly, her curiosity obviously piqued. At last Josephine made the necessary introductions, but with the barest possible civility. Mercy strove to rescue the conversation.

"Do you live here in Honolulu, Mrs. Hastings?" she asked.

"No, Mrs. Wright. I am aboard the ship *Polaris* with my husband. We sail from New Bedford." An awkward pause followed. "And you?"

"I am aboard the *Meribah*."

"I don't believe I know a Captain Wright. Does he sail from Nantucket?"

"Captain Starbuck heads the *Meribah*," Mercy explained. "I am the ship's principal owner, and I am searching for my husband, who was aboard the *Abishai*. I believe he—and others—may have survived the disaster."

"You cling to a fairy tale of your own making, Mercy," Josephine put in sharply. "I have long ago reconciled myself to my loss. It would be better for all concerned if you did the same."

Mercy felt her temper rising. Josephine Gardner had never been known for an easy sociability, but by any standards, hers was extraordinarily rude behavior. She had no intention of letting it pass. "I hope you can also reconcile yourself to joy if I discover that all upon the *Abishai*, your father among them, were not lost. Good day, Josephine. Mrs. Hastings. A pleasure to have made your acquaintance." With that she turned away and summoned the maître d'hôtel.

Once seated at a table on the other side of the dining room, Mercy replayed the scene, seeking some explanation for it. Why should Josephine Gardner imply that she should abandon her search for Nathaniel? Would it not profit everyone bereaved by the loss of the *Abishai* to know as much as possible about the fate of their loved ones? But perhaps Josephine was unduly distressed over the loss of her father. As Mercy well knew, losing a father was a sharp blow. Could Josephine have become unbalanced in her grief? It was the only explanation that made any sense.

When her large and sumptuous tea was served, she determined to put the peculiar encounter out of her mind and enjoy her meal. But the luscious fruit and sandwiches and cakes were not enough to totally dispel her uneasiness. Following the meal, she decided on a stroll in the gardens and then a rest before dressing for dinner with Sam.

At about the same time that Mercy had descended to the dining room, Sam was rising from a long luncheon at a gentlemen's club frequented by merchants, diplomats, naval officers and whaling captains. Much news and gossip had circulated among the half dozen in Sam's party. With his usual careful consideration, he had sorted the useful intelligence from the self-serving, ferreted out the truth from among the exaggerations, but when one particular story was told he had been too shocked to do anything but listen. It was a tale of survivors of the *Abishai,* of sensational misdeeds and frightful immorality, of treachery, betrayal and murder, and its central character was Nathaniel Wright. After the meal, he took the talebearer aside and questioned him closely. He came away with the impression that, though vastly inflated, the story had some basis in truth. It followed the general lines of Captain Folger's chronicle, but with a great many embellishments, not all of them necessarily true to the original, reminding him of a simple cottage made grandiose and ostentatious by additions made as the owners increased their wealth and pretensions in the world.

Throughout the afternoon, in the offices and warehouses he visited and in chance meetings with old acquaintances, Sam inquired after and heard several variations of this same story. Depending on the propensity of the speaker, the tale was more or less fantastic or given more or less credence, but one common thread stitched the accounts together. Nathaniel Wright was a base and vile blackguard. That, of course, was no surprise, given what he and Ben had been told by Matthew Folger. What shocked and outraged him, however, was that despite all odds, it appeared that Wright *could* still be alive.

This possibility weighed upon Sam like an unpleasantly heavy meal on the stomach—difficult either to digest or to dismiss from one's mind. More unpleasant, and more serious, though, were its implications. Should the stories turn out to be true, and Wright was alive, Mercy would surely leave Sam, and he would have to let her go. He could not continue to be with her if he became convinced she was still married. Not that he was such a saint himself. He could not pretend that he had never pursued or bedded a married woman, but he had restricted himself to those who made clear they welcomed the pursuit. Mercy, however, was not one to engage in such entertainments. Nor did he consider their relationship merely a pleasant pastime. His feelings for her were far more profound than that, and even the idea of losing her pained and saddened him greatly.

More disturbing, however, was the thought of how Mercy would suffer were she to learn the extent of Wright's transgressions. With much chagrin, he remembered the night when he first learned the fate of the *Abishai,* remembered his insistence that Mercy should know all, remembered his impatience with Ben Randall when he refused to tell his daughter everything. Now Sam was in Ben's position, and he understood only too painfully his old friend's dilemma.

A further worry also gave Captain Starbuck several fretful moments. That worry was intuition. Now, my friends, in Mercy, as in many of our sex, this was a highly developed sense. Indeed, it was this very power that had caused her to come to certain conclusions regarding the fate of her husband. I need not remind you that the captain was not the first, or the last, man to take issue with the Lord's decision to settle this capability on womankind. But, from his point of view, it had already caused a great deal of trouble. Had Mercy not put so much trust in her intuition she never would have thought of coming along on the *Meribah.*

For that eventuality, our brave captain had more to curse than intuition. He piled blame on his own shoulders, too. Without his selfish need for adventure and challenge, he would never so much as entertained the notion of Mercy traveling on the *Meribah,* never mind assented to it. While changing the past was impossible, in the present he could act to protect Mercy from the stories that would undoubtedly cause her much heartache and anguish. The way to do that—and not an unpleasant task when he considered it— was to stick close by her side, to act literally as a buffer between her and the rampant rumors, rumors that might lead her to even greater and more dangerous intuitive leaps.

He found, however, when they met for dinner that evening that he had already left her too much on her own. Upon hearing of her encounter with Josephine Gardner, he tried to convince her that she was making too much of the lady's behavior. They both knew, he said, that Josephine had been a sour child who had grown into a sour woman, just the type to blame her own misfortunes on someone else. Though Mercy appeared to acquiesce to his point of view, he could tell she retained some reservations, not only about his explanation but about his vehemence. He must remember, he noted to himself, to act more naturally with her.

And then he changed the subject. He had had many invitations that day—to dinners and receptions and for Christmas lunch at the American consul's home. Mercy had been included in all of them, and he convinced her of the need to spend some of the *Meribah*'s oil on a gown or two. He also required her counsel on various matters of business and presented her with a plan for the next several days that left her with little time alone, except when she was asleep in her hotel room.

At first Mercy thought Sam was merely contriving ways to spend time with her, but he stuck to her like a burr, an irritant who would not be dislodged. She encountered much coolness among the people she met, both socially and in the course of business, but perhaps, she reasoned, that was the way in Honolulu, although the climate and the setting would seem to encourage an excess rather than a want of feeling. But when the coolness extended to people from home, she began to be suspicious again. Men and women she had known, or known of, all her life refused to make more than small talk with her. They treated her like a stranger, and one whose acquaintance they did not care to make.

Could they suspect her relationship with Sam? In public neither had behaved with anything other than complete propriety, but perhaps word had somehow filtered off the *Meribah,* spread around by one of the officers, not maliciously but carelessly, a casual speculation between one friend and another. But if that were the case, someone would have made an allusion, some veiled if pointed comment. In her experience, people could not long deny themselves the satisfaction of revealing their reasons for holding themselves superior.

By Christmas Eve, Mercy was thoroughly dispirited. Even a gathering to sing carols at the home of John Kingsley, a merchant with whom her father had had the most cordial dealings, served only to deepen her sense of frustration and bewilderment.

"You're merely feeling the effects of being away from home at Christmas," Sam assured her when she confided in him in the carriage on the way home from the Kingsleys. "I've spent many a Christmas in a warm climate, and it still seems strange. Not real."

"No, it's more than that. Much more."

"Then, it must be that you are missing me," he whispered.

"Missing you! You've hardly let me out of your sight during a single waking moment since we arrived."

"I was thinking more of your nonwaking moments. Leave the balcony door ajar tonight, Mercy. I'll come to you."

"I couldn't, Sam," she demurred. "What if—"

"The *Meribah* sails the day after tomorrow. Let us have one night in each other's arms before that. Who knows when we'll have another chance?"

They had never spent a full night together, only a few furtive hours locked in the day cabin or in Sam's stateroom. What a luxury to stay together in the wide bed in her hotel room, and how she needed comfort after the social strains of the preceding days. She acquiesced.

How much she had changed in a few short months, she mused as she undressed and put on her nightclothes. She could never so much as imagined giving herself to a man to whom she was not married, especially when she might still be married to another, but here she was, entering freely, even joyously, into such a relationship. And without hating herself or the man, and with full cognizance of the troubles that would ensue if she and Sam conceived a child. She had made her choice—to live for today—but she often questioned that choice as a convenient disguise for pure, unadulterated hedonism.

Her ruminations ceased, however, the moment she heard the soft fall of Sam's footsteps on the balcony. She quickly turned out the lamp and let him into the darkened room. Their long-checked passion was not slow in asserting itself, and soon they had abandoned themselves to a night of unbridled passion.

At dawn, Sam untangled himself from her arms and, with a prolonged shower of kisses, stole from her room. Turning over lazily to plump her pillows after he was gone, she discovered a small velvet-covered box hidden amidst the rumpled bedclothes. She smiled, thinking how Sam would find the small memento she had hidden in the pocket of his coat. Slipping out of bed, she made her way to the window, where in the pale light she untied the ribbon and opened the box. The cameo brooch, exquisitely carved and encased in filigree silver, brought tears to Mercy's eyes. From the starkly pragmatic Captain Starbuck, such a gift could only express the many delicate sentiments he seemed unable to put into words. She smiled serenely, pressing the precious packet to her bosom.

When Sam called for her later that morning, he made a point, as she crossed the hotel lobby to meet him, of checking the time on his watch. She saw, dangling from the chain, the gold fob, in the shape of Neptune's trident, that she had left in his pocket. She laughed silently at his gesture, returning it with her own casual touch of her hand to the cameo at the throat of her sprigged muslin gown. From the mischievous look he returned her, she suspected that he was enjoying their secret as much as she.

They left the hotel arm in arm and procured a carriage from the line in the road. As Sam handed her into the carriage, he whispered a thank-you and an endearment, and they proceeded to church, to celebrate the birth of Christ. Riding through the bustling streets, Mercy felt at peace and secure in the knowledge that her love for Sam would help her offer good will to the others they met today, even though little enough of that commodity had come her way during this Christmas season.

When they alighted in front of the church, there was already a throng milling about in the brilliant sunshine. Sam was immediately pulled aside by John Kingsley, and Mercy, left alone for a moment, was pushed by the crowd in the other direction as it made way for the unloading of yet another carriage. She found herself pressed against a tight knot of chattering women, none of whom she recognized.

"And did you hear, Isabel," one said in a conspiratorial whisper, "she is actually here in Honolulu? Anne Hastings met her in the hotel, and Elizabeth Grant met her at the Kingsleys last night. Mrs. Grant thinks she cannot possibly know anything about her husband, because she is perfectly composed in company."

"She must be nothing more than an actress," another put in. "What other sort of woman would marry a man like that and still be able to hold her head up?"

A third piped up, her voice louder and more penetrating than the others. "I hear she is very beautiful—slender, with a fair complexion and dark chestnut hair. Perhaps she really means to find him, and—"

"Do keep your voice down, Mary," the first chided. "Someone will hear."

"Then they won't hear anything they haven't heard before," the loud lady rejoined. "It's all people have been talking about for the last three days."

Beneath her straw bonnet, Mercy burned with shame. Obviously she was the subject of this unpleasant discussion. But at last she had an inkling of what was going on. These women—and apparently everyone in Honolulu except herself—knew something about Nathaniel that she did not. And that Sam was sure to. That was why he had been keeping so close to her—to protect her. She was furious with him. She had a right to know everything about her husband, even if it was unpalatable, as it must be from the tone of the discussion she had just overheard. How dare he set himself up as her protector, she fumed. She wanted no protection from him in this matter, only tolerance and guidance.

Suddenly he was at her side again, but in one flashing look he knew something was desperately wrong. The contentment had vanished from Mercy's face and was replaced by anger or even contempt. He cursed himself for letting Kingsley waylay him. She must have overheard something in the crowd and was certain to be furious with him for not telling her himself. Damn, he railed, he thought he had succeeded. He thought that on Christmas, of all days, people would have something else to talk about. But he had been wrong. The gossip was too fascinating, too lurid to have abated on even this holy day.

Mercy sat rigid, staring straight ahead throughout the service. The words of the preacher flew over her head like migrating birds. She heard them and then they were gone, making no lasting impression on her. She mouthed the hymns, neither the words nor the music erasing from her mind the scathing comments she had overheard. After the service she whispered to Sam as they were filing out of the church that she wanted to go immediately to a place where they could talk privately. He had the carriage take them back to the hotel, and they strolled to the furthest reaches of the gardens. There Mercy told him what she had heard.

"You must tell me the truth, Sam."

"I don't know the truth," he responded. "And I will not repeat rumors. They are nothing more—fantastic, unproven stories. You know how starved people are for excitement. They will make a feast out of every smallest morsel."

"I am profoundly disappointed in you," Mercy said quietly. "I thought that you, of all people, would have the courage to say to my face what everyone else is saying behind my back. But apparently you do not."

"I do not lack courage, Mercy. What I lack is the capacity to cause you pain. That I refuse to do."

"And how do you know my pain is not the greater for not knowing? Am I not the only one who can tell you which is worse? How do you presume to judge what is best for me? You are neither my father nor my husband. Such a connection might entitle you to determine what I shall know and what I shall not, but we are not related in that way."

It was a cruel truth. He was nothing to her except what she allowed him to be. "In my heart, Mercy, I am yours. You must know that by now."

From a proud man like Sam such an admission was nothing less than startling. Perhaps he was really trying to protect himself and not her, she thought. "Is Nathaniel alive? Is that what you refuse to tell me? In my heart, Sam, I too am yours, but if my husband is alive I will have to let that portion of my heart die, no matter what the cost, to either of us."

"I tell you I have no proof he is alive. That I would not withhold from you, Mercy. I swear it."

"But still you will not tell me what others have been saying?"

"No."

"Then I must find someone who will," she rallied.

"And who might that be?"

"Valentine. He will tell me."

"Not if I order him not to."

"And will you do that?"

"If I must."

"Then you would be wise to see him before I do."

Another woman might have cried or blubbered or blustered or badgered a man in such a situation, but Mercy simply turned and walked away from him. Another man might have run after, importuning her, seducing her, but Sam stood his ground. You see, reader, the lovers had reached an impasse that their feelings for each other could not overcome. For sexual and emotional connection is a potent thing, but it is nothing if one or the other of the partners must sacrifice his or her dignity and integrity. Many people, of both sexes, do make or demand such sacrifices—often out of ignorance, laziness, weakness or a desire for power. But you will not find any such characters in this scene. You will find only two determined people, who must now navigate the capricious currents that separate their strongly held but widely divergent positions.

Chapter Fourteen

You may be wondering, reader, how our friend Jane fared over this time in Honolulu. Her natural curiosity and taste for adventure kept her roaming in town during her hours of liberty. If anything, Honolulu seemed both more foreign and more like home than Ponta Delgada. She found the scenery lush almost to the point of indecency. Illicit pastimes—brothels where the favors of persons of either sex could be purchased, gambling dens, intoxicating substances to drink or even smoke—were so readily available that she imagined some of the pleasure these held for the rougher elements might be diminished by the openness with which they were pursued. Thieves and procurers of every size, shape and disguise roamed the wharf, trying in one way or another to come between her and her few pennies.

But there were also familiar sights that set her longing for home—the sight of so many whalers in the harbor, the American flags flying, and curiously enough the sight of so many American women in so many American dresses. She never thought she would see the day when she longed to be out of trousers and back into a skirt, but there now seemed a freedom in wearing a dress, or at least in taking off the tight corset that bound her breasts. The effort of concealment was wearing her down. She had proved herself a worthy sailor. It seemed vastly unfair that she could not reveal herself for what she was. Would it make her any the less a sailor? Of course not, but she was certain no one else

aboard the *Meribah*—or anywhere else, for that matter—
would see it that way.

But still she enjoyed her liberty. Her body seemed starved
for the luscious fruits that were everywhere available, and
she spent much time downing mangoes and papaya and
breadfruit. She made up a game she played with herself
while touring the town—who were the people she saw,
where had they come from, what were they doing in
Honolulu, were they what they seemed or had they a secret
life, too? She took long walks beyond the town and bathed
in the sea and basked in the sun, washing and bleaching
away the musty, near-rancid smell of whale oil that seemed
to permeate not only her clothing but her skin and hair and
flesh, as well.

She was at liberty for three of their five days in port, and
although not strictly necessary she chose to return to the
Meribah to sleep, unlike most of her fellow sailors, who
spent their nights in taverns or brothels. On Christmas Eve,
at dusk, feeling rather lonely and homesick, Jane decided
to make her way back to the ship, there being no place else
she wanted to go. The taverns and brothels were not for her,
nor were the missions, where saving drunks and gamblers
and fornicators from the error of their ways was the paramount activity.

Her low mental state diminished her usual vigilance, and
instead of watching with one eye for danger, she was engaged in thinking about what her mother would be doing
on Christmas Eve, and whether her father or any of her
brothers would be there. With so many brothers it was not
outside the realm of possibility that she would meet one of
them here, another reason to maintain a watchful attitude
on the docks. But she was equally relieved and dismayed
not to have seen, even from afar, a single one of her much-
beloved siblings.

Caught in such a maze of thoughts, she continued down
the wharf, entering its most uninhabited and ramshackle
stretch, where a dory could be hired to take her back to the
Meribah. Suddenly a hunched form materialized from the

shadows, a pointed dagger in its upraised arm. For a second Jane was too startled to do anything, but she recovered and ran, heading back toward the part of the dock where there would be a crowd or a tavern into which she could disappear. But her assailant had surprise on his side. He caught hold of the billowing back of her shirt. She yanked herself free and fumbled for the pouch, tucked inside her waistband, that held her money. She tore it out and scattered the coins behind her as she ran. But this was not a thief. He laughed derisively and let the coins roll where they would, continuing his pursuit.

Then she heard a loud crack, the sound of bone against bone. Still racing, she swiveled her head. There was Mr. Jack, standing alone. The cutthroat had disappeared. She stopped running and let a series of long, ragged breaths escape her bursting lungs.

"A Merry Christmas to you, John Harding," Jack hailed her.

"And the same to you, Mr. Jack," Jane managed.

"Looks as though you've dropped your money," he said, bending down to search the wooden planks.

Jane approached him. She was still shaken, but tried to enter into his jaunty mood. "I thought the man was collecting alms."

He handed her the few coins he had salvaged. "This is no place and no time to be alone," he admonished.

"I was on my way back to the ship, sir," Jane said.

"What! On Christmas Eve? You'll come with me, Harding. That's an order."

Together the two repaired to the home of Lalaheini, a one-armed Sandwich Islander who had once been a foremast hand with Jack. On the voyage, he'd lost his arm to a whale—but had gained the ability to converse in English and many Pacific Island tongues and now was assistant to a whaling merchant in Honolulu. There they ate Sandwich Island food—starchy poi and roast pig—and sang English carols until their bellies were bursting and their throats raw.

For several merry hours, Jane forgot all about her narrow escape and her longings for home. It was not until she and Jack were curled up in thin, rough blankets in front of Lalaheini's grass-thatched hut that she had time to think about either. She replayed the Christmas Eve celebration over and over in her mind, memorizing every detail, for this would be something to tell her parents and brothers when she got home. And her grandchildren, if she ever had any. But just as she was dropping off to sleep she heard the raucous cry of a gull, and suddenly the derisive laughter of her assailant was ringing once more in her ears.

Another nighttime memory surfaced, too. She was hanging upside down over the edge of the *Meribah,* dangling from a rope, her head inches from the black water. She had heard that same contemptuous cackle then. Crebbs. It was Crebbs who had tried to kill her tonight. Her stomach knotted in fear and frustration. She thought after the incident in the Strait of Magellan she was done with all that madness. For that's what it was. Sheer and utter madness.

She was never going back to the *Meribah*. She would hide here in Honolulu until the *Meribah* had departed, then she would find a berth on a ship headed for home. In a few months she would be finished with this masquerade. Only one thought stopped her. Mr. Mayhew. If she jumped ship now she would never see him again. But what good was seeing him now, when he did not know and could not know, who and what she really was. Perhaps it would be better for her simply to disappear. The strong feelings that passed between her and the first mate could not be denied, but at least she knew the truth of their situation.

She had never thought of it this way before, but how would she have reacted had she suddenly found herself with an overwhelming attraction to another young woman? Would she not have been confused and doubtful and anguished? So, what must Mr. Mayhew, Valentine—she hardly dared to think of him by his given name lest she slip someday and use it on board—be thinking and wondering? These disturbing thoughts settled the issue for her. She would jump ship. She would return to the *Meribah* tomorrow, collect her seabag and be gone. She had had her adventure. She had proved herself as able a sailor as her brothers. She would start for home as soon as she could.

Extricating herself from her host and her friend on Christmas morning was not easy, but by adhering firmly if politely to her plan she managed to get away after breakfast—but not without accepting a sack laden with fruit and slices of roast pig. Her plan was to go back to the *Meribah,* pack her seabag and somehow get it and herself past Mr. Chase, who along with a skeleton crew of two or three others would be on duty today.

She did not go straight back to the wharf, however. Instead she took a detour by the church, hanging about the edges of the churchyard until all the finely dressed people—she spotted Mrs. Wright and the captain among them—had gone into the church. Then she slipped in and stood by the back door during the service, slipping out again before the final hymn was finished. On the way back to the *Meribah,* she thought about the rest of her plan—where she would hide until she found a homeward-bound ship. She even had a wild idea of heading for Ohio and finding Tommy Culpepper....

Meanwhile, the *Meribah*'s mate was also passing an uneasy Christmas morning. A handsome, respectable bachelor like Valentine Mayhew was a great prize among the mamas of Honolulu—the wives of the merchants, diplomats and navy men charged with procuring suitable husbands for their marriageable daughters. Throughout his liberty Valentine had not lacked for invitations or entertainments. Together with his cousin Abner, the mate aboard the *Industry,* who was similar in age, looks and temperament, Val had been to luncheons, teas, dinners and receptions, where the beautiful and not-so-beautiful, the charming and not-so-charming daughters of Honolulu society had been paraded and presented. Abner took up his assigned role with relish, filling a plate with cakes for Miss

This and replenishing a punch cup for her friend—and rival—Miss That. Valentine tried, but even the prettiest, most sensible and accomplished girls did not interest or amuse him, and the dull or insipid ones tried his patience mightily.

Abner attempted to discover why his usually gay cousin was not enjoying himself, why he seemed distant and uninterested in the festivities, but he heard no plausible answer to his questions. Val was not unwell, he claimed not to be pining for Caroline Randall or anyone else Abner could think of. There had been no especially dramatic occurrences aboard the *Meribah* thus far in her journey. The rumors about the *Abishai* and Nathaniel Wright were disturbing to everyone who heard them, but as far as Abner could tell, while Val was concerned, especially for Mercy Wright, he was not unduly upset by them.

Abner, who had been overjoyed to see the *Meribah* sail into Honolulu, was finding his cousin a distinct social liability and so was not disappointed when he was asked to convey Val's regrets to their host and hostess: Mr. Mayhew had been unexpectedly called back to his ship and would be unable to attend Christmas lunch.

Val was in a melancholy state when he left Abner. He vehemently wished he could shake his lassitude, but nothing seemed to help. Upon arriving in Honolulu, he hoped that with the work to be done refitting and restocking the vessel, the change of scenery and the festive atmosphere, he would recover his normally high spirits, but over the five days on shore he had fallen lower and lower, until he would rather have been doing anything—sweating at the tryworks, riding out a snow squall—than sitting in a drawing room watching other people enjoy themselves.

Mr. Chase was surprised when the first mate came on board, and even more surprised when he was told he was at liberty for the rest of the day. But Mr. Chase was not one to question a favorable turn of fate, and he was soon on his way to the town. The skeleton crew—two sailors and the harpooner, Mr. Adams—were taking their ease, as there was nothing to do. The only purpose of their presence was to discourage enterprising thieves, and this they could do by merely staying visible and at least partially awake.

Too restless to stay below deck, Val excused Mr. Adams to go to his berth in the steerage, a boon which Mr. Adams, who looked somewhat the worse for wear, accepted gratefully. Val retrieved a book from his stateroom and settled himself in Mercy's chair, beneath the starboard skid, but each time he looked down at the tome the black marks upon the page refused to organize themselves into comprehensible words. He spent the better part of an hour in this fruitless activity.

Flinging the book down in disgust—at it for refusing to divert him and at himself for his inability to be diverted— Val began to pace the deck. He moved first to the stern, gazing out at the open sea, then lethargically up the larboard side of the ship. There was little activity among the other vessels anchored in the harbor—a dory or two ferrying sailors between ship and dock, a bored or weary officer perambulating the deck as Val was doing—nothing certainly to catch the much divided attention of our poor Mr. Mayhew, reader. But as he came up behind the carpenter's bench he did see something that engaged him. A sailor whom he had not known was on board was emerging from the fo'c'sle hatch. Because of the obstruction of the tryworks, however, the sailor did not see him.

Her shoes and seabag hoisted over her shoulder, Jane climbed quietly and carefully out of the fo'c'sle. She stopped when she could see the deck and looked around cautiously. The two foremast hands on duty were sitting up on the stage by the bow, their backs to the hatch. Neither Mr. Chase nor the harpooner appeared to be on deck. She continued her ascent and made for the larboard side of the vessel. She'd left a dory there, climbing up to the boat on the wooden stepping blocks used for getting in and out of the whaleboats. A quick hop up and over the bulwarks and she would be gone. But just as she was about to scramble over the side, she heard someone call out her name.

She looked around. "Mr. Mayhew!"

"Going somewhere, Harding?" he asked quietly.

"Yes, sir, I mean, no, sir, I mean..." She had been caught trying to jump ship. And by Mr. Mayhew himself. What was he doing here? Where was Mr. Chase? She didn't know what to say, where to look, and she dared not think of her punishment. If it was as severe as a flogging, her secret would be revealed and she would be put ashore anyway. Perhaps insolence was her way out. But she could not bring herself to defy Mr. Mayhew. It was hard enough to speak to him without blurting out what was in her heart.

"I didn't think you were going anywhere," he said, his voice still very quiet. "Put your shoes on, then, if you've nowhere to go." In a louder voice, meant to carry to the hands on the bow, he said, "Are you as nimble at sums, Harding, as you are at climbing the rigging?"

Jane was quick to catch on. "I can add, yes, sir," she answered compliantly.

"Then come this way," he said, and led her sternward.

"Thank you, sir," she said when they were out of earshot of the others.

"I am not aware that you have anything to thank me for," Val said carefully. "Wait here," he added, loudly enough for the sound to filter down the booby hatch to the steerage, just in case Mr. Adams was still awake. He raced down the companionway and returned with the ship's account book and a stack of bills for supplies purchased in Honolulu. Should any officer return before the end of liberty, Val and Harding would be engaged in a legitimate enterprise. Unusual, to say the least, but explicable.

The course he was taking was a dangerous one, Val knew. He had just caught a man about to desert and he was doing nothing about it. Yet he felt himself incapable of any other course of action. Had he not fortuitously returned to the ship this afternoon, Harding would have made his escape. Sam would have been furious; Chase would have been reprimanded; another sailor would have been found; the *Meribah* would have continued her voyage. And John

Harding would have slipped out of his life. Perhaps that was as it should be, perhaps then he could get over this bizarre infatuation and return to his once-normal life. But Harding had not escaped. They would have yet many months, even years together.

"Did you enjoy your liberty?" Val asked, knowing that Harding would say nothing unless asked a direct question.

"Mostly, sir," Harding replied.

With a bit of coaxing, Harding was persuaded to give an account of his onshore activities, and Val listened with pleasure to his sharply observed, amusingly told account.

For her part, Jane could have babbled on to Mr. Mayhew for hours, sharing with him as she had with no one else her impressions of Honolulu and the people she had encountered there, leaving out of course the part about the cutthroat and the truth about herself. He was so easy to talk to, such an attentive listener that after a while she could almost pretend that it was John, not Jane, who spoke. Almost, but not quite.

The afternoon passed quickly, with more conversation than work accomplished. But soon the curfew hour approached, and Val was forced to send Harding forward before the others began to return. For a few brief hours Val's melancholy had vanished, but stealing such a time together again would be well nigh impossible. The following day the *Meribah* would put out to sea. The Pacific itself was not as wide as the gulf that must once again necessarily come between him and Harding. The familiar, unwanted heaviness descended on him yet again, and Val wondered how all this was to end. Unhappily, he supposed. Most unhappily.

Chapter Fifteen

The day after Christmas the *Meribah* sailed out of Honolulu harbor and headed due south, making for the equator. For the next year or two, until her hold was full, she would cruise the line, moving east and west along the equator, venturing north or south as the weather or whim or whales dictated. The first weeks of 1844 brought good fortune: several whales, one of them approaching eighty barrels, were caught, tried and stored in the hold. Refreshed from their revels in the Sandwich Islands, the men hunted avidly and completed their tasks quickly and smoothly.

Not so smooth, however, were relations between Mercy and Captain Starbuck. Nor between Mercy and Valentine or the captain and his mate. For Val had been placed, against his will, in the middle of the dispute. Hoping to appease both sides by keeping silent and distant from the entire affair, he succeeded only in alienating both his friends. This predicament, added to his other one, served to darken his mood further, so that his once-sunny disposition was in an almost permanent eclipse.

Valentine Mayhew, therefore, was probably the person who was most heartened when the *Meribah,* chanced to speak, while cruising in the vicinity of the Kingman Reef, the ship *Eliza Morgan*. A gam was arranged, and the sailors of the *Meribah* accompanied by their mate and his harpooner, boarded the *Eliza Morgan,* while the officers and petty officers of the *Eliza Morgan* received the hospitality of Captain Starbuck. Val thus escaped sitting at table with Mercy and Sam and was also released from the obligation to treat the *Meribah*'s guests with a graciousness and affability he did not feel. Being in command of the gam on the *Eliza Morgan* was a far more pleasant assignment, for there would be music and yarns, plenty of plum duff, perhaps even dancing and a ration of rum.

At the end of the first dogwatch, when both vessels had been prepared for the night, the exchange took place. Val, carrying his fiddle, and Big Jack, along with the foremast hands, ferried themselves in the whaleboats to the *Eliza Morgan*. Turning his ship over to Val, Captain Joseph Coffin, his mates and petty officers, rowed to the *Meribah*.

It took very little time for the festivities to begin aboard the *Eliza Morgan*. Captain Starbuck had sent a tin of tobacco, which Val presented and Jack doled out as soon as they arrived. Moments later clouds of fragrant smoke billowed above the deck. The men smoked in silence for a moment, savoring the excellent tobacco. But as soon as the first appreciative puffs had been taken, tongues began to wag merrily. Unlike the sailors of the *Meribah,* the *Eliza Morgan*'s crew had not been in a port the size of Honolulu for over a year. They were both starved for news and bursting with the tales of their own adventures in the South Seas. Tongues were further loosened by the ration of rum Captain Coffin had authorized his steward to provide for each man. There was a stew of salt pork, beans and onions, and a cheer went up for the plum duff.

The meal consumed, it was time to get down to the real business of the evening, to stop chattering and start spinning yarns. Val threw himself headlong into the revelry. His laugh rang out louder and longer, above all the others. The more profane the story, the more foul the yarn spinner's language, the harder he laughed, until the yarn spinners were competing to see who could say something strong enough to offend Mr. Mayhew.

Now this was a wrongheaded, even dangerous, business for Val to indulge in, reader. As the sole officer aboard the *Eliza Morgan,* it behooved him to comport himself with some degree of discretion and not to make himself so familiar with the men that he breached the barrier between officer and foremast hand. But Val was past caring about all that. He felt himself on the brink of ruin, and like many in his position, he responded by courting his demons, daring them to show themselves and finish him off, destruction seeming far preferable to the discomfort of teetering on the edge.

It pained Jane to see Mr. Mayhew in such a state, casting aside his gentlemanly nature, acting the fool. She had been hoping for an opportunity to speak with him this evening, but he never so much as once glanced in her direction. In fact, he seemed to be making a concerted effort to avoid looking at her. But perhaps that was as it should be, for spending time with him, as she had on Christmas afternoon, only made her long for more. Joyous as those few hours had been, had they been worth the days of aching emptiness that had followed? The answer being too difficult to calculate, Jane turned her attention to the story being told by one of the *Eliza Morgan*'s men, a thickset, muscular man who gesticulated wildly as he spoke.

The yarns spun by her fellow sailors were entertaining, she found, but not entirely credible. This one, however, was preposterous. A tale of a mutineer who'd become the chieftain of a tribe of hostile natives in the Black Islands, who preyed on whaling ships. While Jane remained skeptical, the other men drank the story in as easily as a ration of rum. At the end of the performance, the *Eliza Morgan* man sitting next to her leaned in and whispered, "When we spoke the *Morning Star,* a month or so ago, one of their fellows told me this renegade was the son of the captain. He mutinied against his own father. Can you imagine that?" Hiding a smile, Jane told the sailor that she couldn't, without adding that there were many other things she couldn't imagine, either—snow in July in New Bedford, cows that could talk or machines that could fly like birds, for example.

Curiously enough, however, a similar story was being told aboard the *Meribah,* behind the closed doors of the day cabin. Captain Joseph Coffin had been cruising in the South Seas for almost a year and had heard the story of the renegade mutineer in the Black Islands enough times, from the captains of other ships the *Eliza Morgan* chanced upon, to give some credence to it. To show Captain Starbuck the approximate location of the island to be avoided—reports varied as to its exact position—he spread the *Meribah*'s charts on the narrow table opposite the sofa.

"These reports disturb me more than I can say, Sam," Joseph Coffin said when he had finished telling Starbuck everything he'd heard about the renegade. "It is particularly difficult to speak of these things aboard the *Meribah.* To think that one of our own could have joined with savages. I cannot fathom it."

Passing through on an errand, Mercy had heard voices in the dayroom and, to her shame, had stopped to listen. Joseph Coffin's tale was a chilling one for any whaling vessel. But why, she wondered as she continued belatedly with her task, should he be particularly loathe to speak as he did on the *Meribah?*

She expected to hear more about this renegade at the meal, but the topic never arose. Since she knew about it only from eavesdropping, she could not raise it herself. But that was not her only disappointment. The gathering was not the jolly occasion she had imagined a gam to be. Conversation seemed unusually constrained, although it was conceivable that the curbed spirits of the guests were attributable to the mere fact of her presence. Even though many captains' wives did travel aboard their husbands' ships, a hen frigate was still a comparatively rare phenomenon, and a hen frigate where the "hen" was not the captain's wife was certainly an anomaly. The officers were probably unsure of how to behave with her, hence the stilted talk. Not wishing to be a further hindrance to the men, she retired to her cabin directly after the meal. No one objected.

The next morning whales were sighted, and the whaleboats of both ships were lowered. Although the oil from any whales caught would be shared equally by the two vessels, the competition between the *Meribah* and the *Eliza Morgan* was fierce and heated. Ordinarily Mercy would have watched the contest, but while Sam was engaged in directing the pursuit and the few men aboard were busy assisting him and sailing the ship, she slipped below to consult the *Meribah*'s charts.

The ambush of the *Abishai* had taken place in the Black Islands, where this renegade was reported to be operating. Perhaps he had been a party to the demise of the *Abishai*, perhaps that was why Captain Coffin had been reluctant to relate the stories he had heard, aboard the *Meribah*, so as not to cause her pain by bringing to mind the event that had cost her her husband and ultimately her father. But if that were so, why had she not heard of this blackguard before?

She unrolled the paper chart and located the coordinates Joseph Coffin had quoted to Sam. They *were* approximately the same as those of the place where it was thought the attack on the *Abishai* took place. Perhaps the news of this renegade was the thing her father and Sam were withholding from her. From the first, she had believed they were shielding her. But why should the news of this traitor be so potentially threatening to her? Unless, the anxious thought came to her, this pariah was a survivor of the *Abishai*.

Suddenly an image forced its way into her thoughts. The disdainful face of Josephine Gardner in the hotel dining room. Then a second intruder barged into her mind. The gossiping ladies in the churchyard. Perhaps the renegade was Nathaniel. Perhaps such a rumor had occasioned the cold whispers and withering glances that had been hers all over Honolulu. But that was ridiculous. Nathaniel leading a tribe of marauding savages? The thought was so ludicrous that Mercy began to laugh nervously. If alive and stranded on such an island, Nathaniel would be more likely to tame the natives—he had great powers of persuasion—and teach them music and poetry. She quickly banished the thought of Nathaniel as a renegade; it was merely a product of her own remorse for having fallen in love with Sam. She had committed a sin; let hers be balanced by one of equal magnitude on Nathaniel's part.

Mercy rolled and replaced the chart and returned to the deck, where she watched the competition and made herself useful in whatever ways she could. Three whales were caught that day, two by the *Meribah*'s men. It took four days for the beasts to be tried and stored, even with both crews working. But finally the task was finished, and the *Meribah* and the *Eliza Morgan*, both sixty barrels richer, parted company.

After the meal that evening, Mercy asked Sam if she might have a word with him. Since leaving Honolulu, they had been cautious and polite with each other, but had taken care not to be alone together. Both were bristling under this self-imposed restraint, but the impasse demanded it. They could not continue as they were, nor could they go forward until they knew the truth.

How much easier it would be for them if they could pretend that the *Meribah* was the only world that mattered. But they could not—at least not for long. Only knowledge could set them free. Sam might refuse to repeat conjecture and rumor to her, but he could not refuse her, or himself, when it came to the truth. He might resist, and strongly, but he had no defensible grounds for refusing to seek the truth about Nathaniel. She intended to argue her case, to insist as the *Meribah*'s owner, if she had to. Sam, however, did not oppose her request that they proceed to the Black Islands as soon as was feasible.

"We both must satisfy our conscience," he replied, with as much relief as resignation, she thought.

She smiled at him then, sadly, but a smile nonetheless, for the final period of her waiting was about to begin. Once they had searched the Black Islands, she would know what had happened to Nathaniel. She would know if she was a widow or the wife of a man she was no longer certain she loved. Perhaps it had been a mistake to follow her heart when she met Nathaniel. Perhaps she should have done the expected thing and married a Nantucket whaling man. Sam, even. What a match that would have been, if she and Sam had married out of duty or by default. An unexpected burble of laughter escaped her lips. Sam looked at her quizzically.

"I was just thinking," she replied, "about what might have happened if I hadn't met Nathaniel and had married you instead, to please my father or because no one else would have me."

Sam looked at her incredulously for a moment, then let out a loud guffaw. "You wouldn't be sailing with me now, that's certain. And I'd be planning the longest whaling voyages in history!"

"We are an unlikely pair, aren't we, Sam?"

"Very unlikely," he agreed solemnly. And with one lengthy look of longing, he turned on his heel and left her.

The next day Sam put the *Meribah* on a course of south by southwest, planning to cross the equator at approximately 170° west longitude and then head due west at about 7° south latitude. The island Joseph Coffin had warned him about was on that latitude, at about 175° east longitude. With good winds and no whales they would make their destination in two to three weeks. But there was a whale, and a particularly large, ornery beast it was, too.

The *Meribah* was two or three days' sail south of the equator when the majestic old monster, close on ninety barrels and swimming fast and strong, was sighted. Sam ordered the pursuit to begin immediately, but the *Meribah* chased him for half a day before getting close enough to lower the boats. The whale seemed to know that he had been sighted, for each time the ship began to close in, he changed course, a maneuver easier for a whale than a whaling vessel. By the time his sailors had been sent aloft three times to adjust the sails, Sam was getting angry. He would have that whale if it was the last thing he did, he vowed. "I'll be damned," he remarked to Val, "if I'm going to let that fat tub of blubber make a fool of me and this ship."

But finally the whale seemed to tire of the game and slowed his pace, and by midday the *Meribah* had edged close enough for the boats to be lowered. The whale skimmed along at a leisurely speed now, and the boats made easy progress toward their prey. Val and his men had not been the first to fasten a whale since before the ship stopped in Honolulu, which Val credited to his own suppressed appetite for all things, victory included. But this wily creature sparked a competitive fervor in him, and he strove to inspire his men as he had not in many long weeks.

Val's fire spread quickly throughout his boat, catching Jane in the first seat, Big Jack in the last and the four men in between. And it stayed lit, undampened by swelling waves or rivers of sweat. The mate's boat surged ahead of the others, bearing down on the huge, glistening creature. As they got closer Val could see that the whale's thick, ancient skin bore the scars of past battles. Many men had tried to capture him, but none had succeeded—yet. He signaled the men to row faster and harder. They sensed his excitement and bore down on their oars, gaining quickly on the whale, who had slowed his pace yet again and was hardly moving. He seemed almost to be beckoning them, daring them, and Val accepted the challenge.

There was no telling what the beast would do, so Val signaled the men to ship their oars and continue the approach by paddle. The whale had stopped swimming and sat bobbing and swaying in the gently rolling sea. When ordered, Big Jack readied his harpoons and prepared to attack. He stood poised, waiting for the moment when the boat was skin to skin with the whale. As soon as the boat touched, he drove his harpoon into the creature, thrusting as hard and deep as his considerable strength allowed.

The hook went in and held fast, but before Jack could recover and sit down, the whale took off like a cannonball. Jack was jolted back into his seat. The men scrambled to play out the line and dowse the smoke that rose up almost immediately around the loggerhead from the rapidly reeling rope. Val worked the steering oar with all his might, but the whale was so strong and fast that the long oar had virtually no effect. It slowed the monster down not one whit. Once played out, the rope never slackened. All Val and his men could do was hang on for the ride.

They were jolted and bounced until their insides churned and their hands bled from clinging to the wet rope. Then suddenly there was a mighty jerk on the line and it went slack for a second. The boat slowed and the men started to haul in, but almost before they could move one hand over the other on the rope, it was pulled taut again, and the whale was off once again. He had stopped only to change course, and now he was headed swiftly through the waters, this time with the *Meribah* dead ahead.

Sam saw the whale turn and head straight for the *Meribah*, but knew immediately he did not have enough time to get out of his way. He might as well have tried to halt the tides. The only thing he could do was maneuver the *Meribah* so that the whale might hit her at an angle and not broadside. He took the wheel and ordered Mercy and the others to brace themselves for the impact. The whale hit larboard aft, and with such force that he tore through the planks, leaving a gaping hole. On impact, the *Meribah* was rolled back into the water, her starboard bulwarks almost touching the sea. Had the whale hit again, she might not have been able to right herself. But the whale seemed to have done as much damage as he wanted to do, and took off again, still towing Val's boat behind him.

Sam could not spare a hand to try to keep an eye on Val's boat. He had all he could do to keep the *Meribah* afloat. He signaled the rest of the boats to return to the ship and ordered the steward to start the pumps. The carpenter and the cooper immediately gathered their tools and materials and began to prepare a rude patch for the hole. That left only Mercy, the cabin boy and the cook to bail out the hold.

Thick with slime and grease, the hold stank from a combination of rancid whale oil, brackish water and rat offal.

Mercy found it hard to keep from slipping as she bent and straightened, bent and straightened, filling her bucket and then heaving its contents away. Her face was soon streaked with dirt and covered with a film of greasy sweat. Her skirt, saturated with filthy, oily water, stuck to her legs. The water was coming in faster than she and her tiny contingent could get rid of it, and her arms quickly grew heavy and sore. Each bucketful took greater and greater effort, and soon the only way she could continue was to work mechanically, without thinking of anything except bending and straightening and filling and heaving. She was utterly exhausted by the time the first of the whaleboats returned and she was ordered out of the hold.

Her work did not stop then. A man in Mr. Hunter's boat had torn his leg when a lance slipped out of its fastening. She washed her hands and tended to him. Then she took over the cook's duties, allowing him to remain below. Throughout the afternoon there were more injuries, including a bloody gash on the head when the cooper slipped in the hold and ripped his head against a sharpened saw. At every opportunity, Mercy scanned the horizon for Val's boat, but blue faded smoothly into blue. The line between sky and sea was unbroken by the silhouette of the small whaleboat.

The boat, though lost, was still afloat, and its occupants, though dazed and weary, were very much alive. After bashing the *Meribah,* the whale had run for a full hour before slowing down and finally sounding. Val could have ordered the line cut at any time, but he was utterly determined to have the satisfaction of lancing the beast. The attack on the ship had happened so swiftly that he had not been able to assess the damage. At the very least the creature had disabled the ship; whether he had sunk her remained to be seen. More than pride was involved now: the whale could not be allowed to live if he had the blood of

Sam and Mercy and the rest of the crew—and only the Lord knows how many others—on his stubborn black head.

If the ship had sunk, and he and his crew were alone, the whale would provide sustenance—albeit greasy and unpalatable—until they found land or sighted another vessel. He did not allow himself to consider for more than a fleeting second the possibility that they might spend the rest of their shortened lives in the whaleboat.

Wanting to take no chance that the boat would be in the whale's path when he surfaced, Val positioned his craft at a cautious distance from the place where the whale had gone down. He could do no more than guess at the optimum spot to wait—too close and the boat would be broken to pieces, the men snapped in two; too far and the whale, now rested, could take them for another ride, putting even more distance between them and the *Meribah,* if she was still seaworthy.

The wait was a long one—two or three hours, he reckoned by the passage of the sun. Val doled out some water and biscuit, which the weary men ate slowly, without talking. After the abbreviated meal they remained quiet, restoring and preserving their strength. The sun was hot, and there was no shelter from it, but there was a steady, cooling breeze, which kept temperatures and tempers from boiling over.

Jane tried to rest as they waited for the whale to surface, but she was still too agitated, as much from the triumph of staying fast to the whale as from the physical exertion of rowing and tugging. Something more, though, contributed to her unease, as well. She found herself searching the horizon every few moments, looking for some sign of the *Meribah.* Losing sight of the ship had unnerved her, and her head kept filling with the most gruesome thoughts—of days of slow torture, of men going mad from thirst, of feeding on one another and then . . . She tried to banish these thoughts and regain her usual courage, but eerie notions continued to dog her.

She had often heard that faced with possible death, scenes of the past flash before one's eyes in rapid succession. But that did not happen to her. She was plagued instead by scenes of the future, of things that had not happened and now might never happen. A ship kept appearing in her mind, on which Val was the captain and she was the mate, a most unusual vessel on which captain and mate were also husband and wife. She had had fantasies like these before, but now they filled her with a profound regret, a deep sadness for having lost something very precious. How, though, could she have lost something she never had?

Lulled by the silence, the sun and the gentle rocking of the sea, Jane, although she did not sleep, drifted in and out of a strange dreamlike state—until she was jolted into full wakefulness by Big Jack's whispered warning.

"I think he's a-comin' up, Mr. Mayhew. To windward, there."

Jane and everyone else in the boat peered in the direction of Jack's pointed finger. There was nothing to see—not a ripple or a bubble, just the pure glassy surface of the sea. Was Jack already beginning to imagine things? Jane wondered. Almost before the thought was fully formed, though, the sea began to rise. Not twenty full yards from the boat, a wall of white water spurted straight up with a crashing roar, and a great black hulk appeared. This first wall of water cascaded over the side of the whale, while a second shot up from the whale's spout. The steaming jet dispersed into the atmosphere, spraying the occupants of the boat with a hot, malodorous mist.

The foul spray was the last of their worries. Preparing to battle the whale was the first. The line had been checked and was securely fastened, in case the beast should run again. If he didn't take them for another ride, they were prepared to move in on him with paddles, and Val was ready with his lances. Jack and Val had already changed places in the boat, with Jack now bringing his considerable strength to bear on the steering oar.

The whale did not run. Perhaps he had forgotten the prick of the harpoon in his side, perhaps he was old and tired from his earlier run, perhaps he was injured from bashing the *Meribah,* perhaps he was merely wily. He began to swim fast, but not so fast that he ran out the line. The men paddled madly, gaining on the monster inch by silent, sweaty inch until they were finally within striking distance of him. As they slipped alongside the still-moving whale, Val steadied himself, his knee in the clumsy-cleat notch, and raised his lance, poised to thrust.

Almost as if on cue, the whale began to dance, a frenzied flopping from side to side, his great flukes flapping the sea into a froth. The boat would have been smashed to sticks had Jack not, at the last possible moment, used the steering oar against the beast's side to push them out of danger. When the flukes did come down in the spot where the boat had been, the small craft was inundated. The men, drenched to the skin, grabbed for the piggins and started to bail. But the whale reared, his huge head reached and his giant jaws opened. He dipped his head, poised to snatch up a tasty morsel of wood garnished with human flesh.

Desperately Val yelled to the bow oarsman to grab hold of his legs. Thus anchored, the mate jumped up on the box and, just as the whale was about to bite down on the boat, thrust his lance behind the creature's ear. The split second between that thrust and the first drops of the red torrent that then poured out of the whale was the longest Jane—or any of the others in the boat—had ever experienced. They had been a hair's breadth away from being snapped in two by a whale. The monstrous jaws now went slack, and the whale shuddered and pitched over onto its side.

No cries of victory rent the air, however. For they were six exhausted men, adrift in the Pacific Ocean, with water and food enough for only a day or two, if they rationed it severely. They had killed a whale, but that whale might have sunk their ship. And night was fast approaching. If there was a ship—theirs or another—nearby to rescue them, it would not be until morning. Val ordered the lantern lit anyway. If the *Meribah* had not gone down, she was probably limping, possibly so badly that she could not search for her lost boat. But if she was still out there in the gloom, the glow of the lantern might reach her, even if she could not come to their rescue tonight.

The final task of the day was to secure the whale by cutting a hole in its fluke and attaching it to a towline. Then the men bailed the boat and settled down as best they could in the bottom of the cramped craft. Conscious that every drop and crumb were precious, Val doled out a small ration of water and biscuit. Jane was so tired she had no appetite, but she took her water and biscuit anyway, knowing she must keep up her strength in any way she could.

To dole out the rations, Val had moved aft again, and now he stretched out in the boat bottom next to Jane. No one had anything to say, even now that they could talk—a dead whale could not be gallied. Each man was lost in his own thoughts, well aware they could be among his last. Jane was all too conscious of Val's taut, tired body next to hers. She wanted desperately to reach out and comfort him and be comforted in return, for she was fearful. She felt the fear of the others in the boat, too, but knew that no man would own up to his true feelings. To admit hers would be womanish.

So she remained silent, trying to keep her body from touching Val's. But he was so close and the boat was so small. Night and exhaustion closed in around them. Jane dropped off, into a deep sleep that banished dread and worry. When she awoke in the dawn's rosy gray light, she felt curiously calm and untroubled. She was also curled up against Val, his arms encircling her securely.

Chapter Sixteen

Reluctantly Jane disengaged herself from Val's embrace, moving slowly and carefully to avoid waking him—or anyone else in the boat—and to prolong the experience for as many precious seconds as possible. In sleep, Val lost the tense, hardened look he had lately acquired. His expression softened, he seemed younger and relieved to have avoided, for a few hours, the pressing cares of waking life. Resisting the temptation to caress his cheek, stubbly now with a day's growth of beard, Jane gingerly rolled away from him. Every muscle was stiff and sore from the previous day's exertions and the cramped, uncomfortable quarters. Her bladder ached, too, and she quietly let herself over the side of the boat.

The sea was warm and soothing and cleansing, and she paddled around in it quietly, enjoying her moment of solitude—a most rare and precious commodity to those who follow the whaling life. The sky was a deep rich blue unbroken by clouds; the sea a shade deeper and richer and unbroken by waves or whitecaps. For a moment she was enchanted by its beauty, allowing herself to forget that for six stranded people, that beauty could also spell death.

She dove under the water and swam until her lungs were about to burst, stretching her aching body, letting the water soothe her. She was fifty yards or so from the boat when she surfaced. Refreshed and renewed, she wiped the salt water from her eyes. When she opened them she saw a flash of silver, a trick of the light she thought at first. But the flash grew into a triangular fin, bearing down on her at a great speed.

What had she been thinking of, she railed to herself, to stray so far from the boat with a dead whale in tow? The sharks would have had a good dinner last night while she and her fellows slept, and now this hungry hunter had picked her for his breakfast. She turned tail and swam as fast as she could, her arms paddling like a windmill in a hurricane. But the shark was faster. She shouted loudly to the others in the boat, praying that at least one of them would waken and come to her rescue. But she couldn't afford to stop swimming and look to see if help was on its way.

She was closing in on the boat, but the shark was closing in on her. Her lungs burned for lack of breath and she raised her head out of the water long enough to gasp for air. Then she heard the shout. "Oar! Grab the oar!" Her eyes stinging with salt water, she looked around desperately. Val was standing on the tiller platform, holding out the steering oar for her. Reaching deep for a final burst of energy, she raced for it, her fingers touching its tip just as she felt the movement of the shark disturbing the water at her feet.

At that crucial moment, she was hauled up out of the water. Val had raised the steering oar and she was dangling on the end of it, the shark circling just inches beneath her. "Come in, Harding!" Val was yelling to her. "Come in!" She forced her mind to focus on her predicament and assessed the situation. She would have to negotiate her way to the boat on the oar, climbing hand over hand while Val held her aloft. He could not move her and the oar without tipping the boat, nor could the others come to his aid, for the same reason. Only Sweet, the tub oarsman, had been able to reach out to anchor Val's feet and secure his position.

The shark snapping at her heels now, Jane began her perilous journey. Each time she moved, she was suspended over the water by one cramped and aching hand. The oar was wet and slippery, but somehow she held on. She progressed, inch by painful inch, until she was only a few feet from the boat. Using her last ounce of strength, she swung back and forth, gathering speed to propel herself, feet first, into the boat. Closing her eyes and muttering a quick prayer, she jumped. When she landed she was in the boat; her bottom stuck in the empty line tub.

She lay there for a moment, panting, feeling a bit like a lobster who's just escaped the cooking pot. But she wasn't entirely out of the hot water, for Val's angry voice reached her. She looked up.

"What in the blazes did you think you were doing, Harding? Are you completely daft, man?" He towered over her, waving the steering oar like a knight waving a lance.

Jane wriggled out of her ignominious position and settled herself on the nearest thwart. "Sorry, sir," she whispered. She had a terrible urge to giggle and feared that if she said anything more she would not be able to hold back her mirth. For she was mirthful. She had just escaped the jaws of death; she had been rescued by the man she loved. How she had scoffed at the silly romantic stories of such deliverances, the ones her mother liked her to read aloud in their long evenings alone. And now here she was, the main character in one of those stories. With that thought she could no longer hold back her laughter.

"I don't see what's so funny," Val sputtered at her angrily, but this only made her laugh more. The contagion caught and the others joined in. Of course she could not tell them the real reason for her merriment, but that did not matter. The release of tension was welcome to all. Finally even Val joined in.

Suddenly, however, the chorus lost its bass voice. "Sail, ho!" came a shout from Big Jack.

And surely enough there was a tiny white-and-black speck on the horizon. The vessel was too far away to know if it was the *Meribah,* but it was a ship and they were surely safe. Without being ordered, the men seated themselves, unshipped their oars and were soon pulling hard toward the vessel.

After an hour of hard rowing, Val was able to make out the vessel's flags. It was the *Meribah,* but she was listing badly to starboard and barely moving. She must have been hit very hard by the vicious beast they were towing. A red waif was flying, so he knew they had been spotted. "At least we've got the dirty dog that rammed her," he said as he spurred his crew on toward the ship. "The captain will be pleased."

Aboard the *Meribah,* Mercy watched the tiny dot that was Val's boat grow larger and larger. All through the long night she had prayed for her dear friend and the men with him, hoping against hope that they had not been lost. When the boat had finally been spotted early this morning she had been overjoyed. Sam and the rest of the men, preoccupied with staying afloat, had been too busy to share her delight, and so she had kept a solitary watch on the boat's slow progress toward them.

While Mercy stood at the rail, Sam pored over his charts, looking for a safe haven where he could put in and repair the ship. His search ended at Kanalepe, a small, outlying island in the Phoenix chain. It was the nearest place where they would find all they needed—wood, fresh water, food and friendly natives. Very friendly, as he remembered with fondness the beautiful woman who had given—and taken—so much pleasure on his last visit there. This time, with Mercy along, however, he would have to forego such enjoyment. He looked up from his charts, smiling to himself, for he was surprised by how little regret this thought engendered.

A commotion on deck filtered down to the captain, and he hurried up the companionway to find that Val's boat was drawing up alongside the *Meribah.* With relief and gratitude, he welcomed his mate and the others back aboard. "I'd like nothing more than to cut into that bastard you've got in tow and watch him melt, but he's left the ship in no condition for that." He added with a grim grin, "I'll have to forego the pleasure until we get to Kanalepe."

With the whale secured to her, the *Meribah*'s progress slowed from a crawl to a creep, but no one seemed to mind. A carnival atmosphere began to fill the air and grew more and more pronounced as the ship approached Kanalepe. Except for keeping the ship upright and moving, there was little to do—no more whales could be caught, and the one in tow could not be cut in and tried out until they landed. The captain relaxed the usual standard of discipline somewhat, a development readily accepted by the men. The *Meribah* was, more or less, on holiday.

Mercy was overjoyed by the safe return of Val and his men, but was also dismayed by the change of course their circumstances demanded. At the first opportune moment, she asked Sam to step inside the dayroom and quizzed him anxiously. "How long will it take to get to Kanalepe? How long will we have to stay there? And how long then to get to the Black Islands?" she wanted to know.

"I can't say," he told her. "We'll get there when we get there, and leave when the ship's seaworthy again."

"But you must have some idea of how long it will be."

"Not really. It depends on too many things," he said with a casual shrug. "There's no use fighting it, Mercy. You can't make the ship move any faster or get fixed any quicker."

Mercy's temper rose precipitously in the face of his equanimity. "You're glad this happened," she accused. "You don't care if I never find out about Nathaniel. That would suit you perfectly."

He turned on her angrily. "Nothing could be further from the truth. You are on the verge of hysteria, Mercy. I suggest you get a grip on yourself."

Her answering voice was low and tight. "I have been on this ship for almost a year, and I am no closer to knowing if I am widow or wife. How long am I to endure this uncertainty? How long am I to wait? How long are we going to wait, Sam?" She wanted so very much to fall into Sam's arms, but she restrained herself. Going to him would solve nothing, would only compound her difficulties, yet how hard it was to keep these few inches between them.

Sam too felt pulled across the tiny but untraversable gulf that separated them. How he missed their intimacy, how he loathed their overly polite consideration for each other. Yet he held back. Mercy had walked away from him; only at her invitation could he approach her again. "Waiting is what one does at sea, Mercy. Often it is difficult, but it must be endured. Now if you will excuse me, I have other duties." With a curt bow, he left her.

Mercy stood aside and watched him leave the room. It galled her to admit it, but Sam was altogether right. She must resign herself to the delay. No one could undo the damage to the *Meribah*. She could best help her cause by keeping out of the way and allowing Sam to attend to the business of getting the ship repaired. And she could best help herself by finding some useful work to fill the many hours that hung heavily on her hands.

The *Meribah* sailed for four days before Kanalepe was sighted by the lookouts, and the island was nothing more than a dark green dot for another day beyond that. Mercy, fretful and unable to control or conceal her impatience, paced the deck, growing hourly more annoyed—with herself, with Sam, with the whale who had rammed the ship, even with Val for catching the beast that further slowed their already painstaking progress. But when they finally drew close to the island, Mercy could not keep her eyes off it. It seemed to exude an aura of repose and tranquility, which first penetrated her defenses, then dissolved them and finally enfolded her. Her anger and restiveness melted away, and she gave herself over to the lush, rugged beauty of Kanalepe.

Beyond the sandy cove where the ship would anchor, there rose undulating hills covered with thick vegetation of a dark bluish green. The sand on the beach was pure and white and fine. Through the palms that ringed the beach she could make out—but only barely, because it was blended so skillfully with the landscape—a small village of thatched dwellings.

From inside the ring, a human figure appeared, a brawny man with honey-brown skin and straight black hair, wearing a loincloth of flowered tapa cloth. He was soon joined by others, two first, then four, then a dozen, then too many to count—men, then women and children, too. The crowd went to work, dragging a flotilla of dugout canoes onto the beach, and soon the waters of the cove were crowded with bobbing, singing natives.

When the *Meribah* finally anchored, the Kanalepeans swarmed aboard her. Their chief, the man who had first appeared in the clearing, embraced the captain, and the two began a conversation consisting of the few words each knew in the other's language and a great many gestures and smiles. Meanwhile the people roamed the decks, touching and fingering everything and everybody, as if sight alone was not sufficient to know a thing or a person. Mercy was first astounded when several Kanalepeans—men and women alike—stared at her and patted her hair, her arms, her skirts. But they explored her in such a friendly, open manner that she wasn't at all frightened. It occurred to her that perhaps they had never seen a white woman before, and this was their way of figuring out what she was. She saw Sam gesturing toward her and saying something to the chief, who then nodded to her. Mercy returned the gesture.

The formalities observed, the men of the *Meribah* then scrambled over the side of the ship, dispersing themselves into the scores of canoes in the cove. Mercy, Sam and the chief were lowered into the water in a whaleboat, which four of the chief's men then paddled to shore, the whaleboat heading up the landing party.

"I feel like arriving royalty," Mercy whispered to Sam as they approached the shore.

"You are," Sam told her. "Accept everything you're given graciously. We must ingratiate ourselves, and do nothing to offend our hosts."

"Of course," she agreed.

Upon landing, Mercy was taken by a group of women to a shaded, sheltered pool. Without the least shyness the women unwrapped their sarongs and dove into the water. Mercy tried not to show her surprise or her reticence, but sat down on a flat rock and began to unlace her boots. The women watched, giggling and pointing, as she removed her many layers of clothing—shoes, stockings, skirt, blouse, petticoat, pantalets and chemise. Modesty had been ingrained in her from the day she was born, and it was very difficult for her to undress in front of so many strangers, but she reminded herself that she was no longer in New England. She was in a place where women doffed their meager attire as a matter of course, where it was normal, acceptable behavior to appear naked in company. Still she was shivering when she stood at the edge of the pool. To hide her extreme discomfort, she dove in quickly. And came up sputtering. She had braced herself for a shock of cold water, but the pool was hot. How extraordinary, she thought. And how delightful. Then she noticed the eldest of the women, who seemed to be the leader of the group, gesturing to her hair, pulling on her free-hanging locks. She pointed at Mercy's head and pulled on her own hair again. Mercy nodded to show her understanding and began to pull the pins from her hair. The women nearest her quickly moved toward her and ran their fingers through her hair, comparing its length and texture with their own, gesturing that they found it very pretty. Mercy gestured back that she found their hair very pretty, too.

Now, reader, knowing Mercy as I do, it is hard for me to imagine her reveling naked in a pool filled with laughing South Seas women, but this is not the sort of story a well-bred lady from New England is apt to contrive. And I must confess, on evenings when I am feeling very bored and wicked, I imagine myself cavorting in that pool as Mercy did. Such an indulgence has cheered and warmed me on many a cold winter evening.

But enough of my own foibles. Once immersed in the pool, her now-loose hair wet and heavy on her shoulders, Mercy felt she could stay there forever. The younger women and girls chased and splashed each other playfully, drawing Mercy into their games. When they were all panting and tired, they climbed out of the pool and beckoned to Mercy to follow them. A fresh length of tapa cloth had been brought to the side of the pool, and Mercy was wrapped in it. Her hair was then dressed with a fragrant oil and held back from her face by a red flower placed behind each ear. Beside the beautiful sun-darkened Kanalepeans, Mercy felt as pallid and washed out as an oft-laundered sheet. The women, however, seemed pleased with their handiwork, and she was led from the pool to the center of the village.

There, a great feast was being prepared—toasted wild pig and various baked roots and tubers, all cooking in underground pits covered with palm fronds. The fragrance was strange, reminiscent of roasting pork and baking potatoes, but as unlike that as the bathing pool was to the tin bath in the kitchen on Orange Street. She was so taken by the smells and the preparations that she forgot to feel embarrassed by her attire, which would be considered no less than wanton in any "civilized" place. Only when she caught the sight of Sam, walking with the chief, did her face flame—until she realized that he, too, was dressed in the Kanalepean manner, in a tapa loincloth and nothing more.

From his animated voice and gestures, Mercy divined that the chief was inviting her to join him and Sam under the palm frond canopy, obviously the place of honor from which all the festivities might be observed. She sat down on the straw mat that covered the ground, mimicking the graceful movements of the Kanalepean women, kneeling first, then sitting back with her knees bent and to one side. A young man handed her a coconut shell filled with a frothy liquid. She glanced at Sam and drank from her shell when he did. The taste was unpleasant, like sweet soapy water, but she smiled bravely and declared it delicious.

"Take it easy with that," Sam warned, grinning as if concurring with her remarks about the beverage, "it's quite powerful."

Already Mercy could feel herself growing warm, and after a few more sips, taken when the chief also raised his shell, she began to feel light-headed. "I do believe I am intoxicated," she confided to Sam.

"I wouldn't be surprised," he answered.

The rest of the day and most of the night were filled with eating and drinking and singing and dancing. First the Kanalepeans entertained their guests with singing and dancing, and then their guests entertained them with sea chanteys and fiddling and yarnspinning. Though the islanders understood barely a word of English, they seemed to sense what the storytellers were saying, for they laughed at all the right moments, gasped when they should have, even wept when there was a tragedy. They were uncannily perceptive, which Mercy attributed to a well-developed intuition. In her own society, she had observed, this valuable aid to communication was all too often neglected, and only what could be heard or seen or touched was deemed important. As the evening progressed, her admiration for the Kanalepeans grew.

There was one aspect of their behavior, however, that she found somewhat difficult to accept. Throughout the evening, sailors from the *Meribah* and young Kanalepe women disappeared from the gathering, often returning with their arms twined about each other. She could hardly believe that these charming, beautiful young women were freely and openly offering themselves to the *Meribah*'s sailors, but they were. In her world, physical intimacy was the most private of matters, closely governed by strict, if largely unspoken, rules. But here, physical intimacy seemed to be a pleasure offered to honored guests, much as she would offer specially prepared foods and a clean, comfortable bed. She knew that many of her friends and acquaintances would be morally outraged by the Kanalepeans' behavior—the women for going with strange men, the men for

sanctioning it. Her difficulty was not so much a moral
one—she understood that Kanalepe customs were different, not wrong—but a personal one. She simply could not
imagine being intimate with a man she did not know and
love. She had to admit that the magical strangeness of the
night—the languid rhythms, the scanty attire, the balmy
atmosphere—had awakened in her an expectant inner
throbbing, but this desire was not simply for fulfillment itself, but for fulfillment coupled with communion with
Sam. She hoped then, fervently, that no Kanalepe man offered himself to her, for she would have to refuse. She
smiled to herself, thinking of Sam's admonition to accept
all she was offered. She suspected this was one instance
where he might be rather displeased if she did not refuse!

Fortunately for Mercy the problem never arose, for the
Kanalepeans made it exceedingly difficult to refuse anything they chose to offer. In fact, only one of the *Meribah*'s
sailors succeeded in meeting such a challenge. Throughout
the festivities, while enjoying them immensely, Jane held
tightly to her coconut shell full of liquor, pretending to
drink from it and managing, whenever necessary, to convey the impression that someone else had just refilled it.
There was one particular maiden who took a strong fancy
to her, but by deflecting the maiden's interest to Aaron
Cole, she was able to forestall being pulled into the palm
trees by the eager young woman.

What she seemed unable to deflect, however, was Mr.
Mayhew's scrutiny of her. While discreet, she nevertheless
was aware of his eyes on her, particularly while she was
wriggling away from the insistent maiden's embraces. Soon
after that, Mr. Mayhew himself was approached by a different young woman. He, however, allowed himself to be
enticed, and with a defiant backward glance at Jane disappeared from the festival grounds. Watching this, Jane
was struck by an ugly bolt of jealousy. She knew it was irrational. After all, Val was a man, and one who must be
entertaining some rather disturbing uncertainties about
himself. Why should he not seek to reassure himself?

After several long and extremely unpleasant moments of inward raging, Jane came to the conclusion that she was angry with him for not guessing her secret—yet another irrational position. She always had the option of revealing herself, but once she did that, her life as a sailor would be finished, and she wasn't ready for that yet. Despite the strain on her emotions, she was still enjoying her life as a man. And so she tamped down her feelings and concentrated on savoring the sights and sounds and tastes and smells of the strange new world in which she had landed. But the revelry seemed empty now; she was only a spectator, not a participant. At the first opportunity, she quietly took her leave.

For his part, Val had no trouble responding to the caresses of his Kanalepe lady. He was well acquainted with the charms of the island's women, for he had been in Kanalepe once before. Then, he had found himself in a state of almost perpetual sexual excitement, which he had alleviated in a most gratifying manner. Now the physical release left him curiously unsatisfied. It was pleasant, that he could not deny, but some important element was missing. It made no sense, but he had been more content, had felt more manly and complete, after saving John Harding from the shark.

After escorting his lady back to the festivities, Val slipped away and went to sit by himself on the moonlit beach. It was not long before he noticed another solitary figure—John Harding—wading in the midnight sea. Suddenly a dim memory surfaced, of lying somewhere hard and cramped, holding John Harding in his arms. The whaleboat. When they were stranded. Val was aghast. Had he actually touched Harding in such a way? Or had it been a dream, a way for his sleeping mind to consider what his waking mind could not? Hastily he rose and retreated, hoping he had not been seen. Being alone with John Harding on a sultry, moonlit night like this one was not wise.

Jane did notice Val's quickly retreating figure, but she did not hail him or run after him as she wished to do. Until she felt ready to reveal her secret, it was kinder, for both of them, for her to stay away from him.

The sky was beginning to lighten before the revelers had finally exhausted themselves. The men were left to their own devices as far as sleeping quarters were concerned, but for Sam and Mercy the chief had ordered the construction of two small lean-tos, ingenious arrangements of thin poles and palm fronds lashed together with vines, sitting side by side at the edge of the village.

They were lined with thick straw mats and made private by makeshift curtains of dried grass strung across the front and sides.

Sam accompanied a dreamy, languid Mercy to the door of her impromptu dwelling. "You made an excellent impression tonight," he complimented. "The chief is very taken with you."

"I hope not so taken," she replied with a soft smile, "that he comes knocking at my door. Or shaking at my grass, I should say." Mercy fingered the hanging curtain, adding its quiet rustle to the other sounds of the night—the breeze ruffling the palms, the humming swell of the sea.

A thrumming wave of desire passed through Sam as he watched Mercy's delicate fingers weaving through the strands of grass. He had told himself so often that he must wait for Mercy to approach him again, but he had not counted on having to wait while sojourning in a tropical paradise. He longed so to touch her that, before he could stop himself, he had reached out and taken her hand in his own. She started slightly but did not withdraw it. "I've explained to the chief—or at least I hope I have—that customs are different in our tribe. He thought it very odd, but seemed to accept it."

Mercy looked down at their hands, watching with a growing excitement as Sam's fingers twined with hers. "So he accepts what you and I have swept aside?" she asked. "When it suits our convenience, we invoke custom, but when it doesn't we simply defy it. That does not speak well for our integrity, does it, Sam?"

Sam cradled her troubled face between his hands. He could not bear to see her pain mar the beauty of this perfect night. "Perhaps we have defied custom, but we have been true to ourselves, Mercy. Since Honolulu you have doubted me, and although it has been damnably hard at times, I have respected your doubts. But here, tonight, I am finding that distance impossible to maintain."

"As am I," Mercy admitted quietly. "So what do we do, Sam? I feel a great love for you, yet I do not possess the freedom to share it with you."

"You are free, Mercy, as free as you allow yourself to be." He took her into his arms and held her close. "We must follow our hearts, love, and find the courage to forge our own path."

"No matter where it leads?"

"I am willing to do that. Are you?"

"I don't know," she whispered. "I don't know." But what she did know was her yearning for him, for the comfort of his body. She leaned against him, burrowing her head into his shoulder.

Gently he stroked her hair. "Let us make our time here an idyll, Mercy. If it is our last time together, so be it. But it will be ours, irrevocably, forever."

Her heart torn almost to breaking, Mercy pulled away and stared quietly into the dying night. The first time she went to Sam's bed, the decision had come almost easily, fed by an insistent hunger. Each subsequent choice had been more difficult, more complicated. Once again, she must choose. Should she cling to the past or seize the present? Should she save herself against future pain or spend herself in pleasure now? Had she not always been taught to save, to fill the root cellar against the winter? But joy was not something to be put by like potatoes. It must be seized; it does not last. If seized, it satisfies; if allowed to disperse, it leaves only emptiness. Finally she had her answer.

"So be it," she echoed Sam's words, and held aside the grass curtain, inviting him into her heart once more.

Sam left her before the village was stirring, and when she woke she abandoned her sarong and dressed once again in her black skirt and white blouse. Appearing in native garb for welcoming festivities at which she was an honored guest was one thing, but adopting such permanently was quite another. The private resolution of her differences with Sam notwithstanding, there was work to be done—a whale to be cut in, the *Meribah* to be made seaworthy again. She did not think it conducive to such work to be seen as lax, perhaps even wanton, by other men "of her tribe." The magical night was over; the day, under a hot, clear, demanding sun, had begun.

Even as the work progressed, though, Mercy continued to be seduced by Kanalepe. Life on the island was not easy. Much laborious toil was required to keep a tribe of some three hundred alive on a small, remote island. But here work was life, not something separate from the rest of life, as it was for her people. There was death and disease and suffering, but the Kanalepeans seemed not to expend too much energy fighting and railing against the dark side of life. They tried to live in harmony with nature and not to bend it, with extraordinary force if necessary, to one's own ends, as her people did. Each new day in Kanalepe, she found much food for thought.

And much beauty. Often in the late afternoons, when the day's work was finished, she walked with Sam into the hills. There they swam in crystal-clear pools fed by thundering waterfalls, listened for hours to the strange clattering, chattering music made by the inhabitants of the tropical forest. The hills were their private paradise, where they had only each other to please and to love.

But finally there came a day when Mercy noticed that the work on the *Meribah* was nearly completed. "How much longer?" she asked Sam as they sat by their favorite secluded waterfall. It was as high up in the hills as it was possible to climb, and through a natural clearing they could gaze down on the turquoise waters of the Pacific. It was utterly peaceful and perfect.

"Four or five days, a week possibly," he told her.

"Good," she answered after a time.

"You won't be sad to leave?"

"Very sad. But it's time, Sam."

"We could stay," he said. "Send the *Meribah* on with Val."

She smiled wistfully. If only that were possible. But she shook her head. "No, Kanalepe would become a prison then. We have to move on, no matter what lies ahead."

"I'll never come back here," he said, taking her tenderly in his arms. "Unless I'm with you. I can't promise you anything else—"

"Nor can I, Sam," she interrupted.

He touched a restraining finger to her lips. "But I can swear to you that this time, this place will belong to us alone. Forever."

"Forever," she agreed, abandoning herself to his caresses.

Four days later, at the start of March, 1844, the *Meribah* was once again seaworthy. She was launched from the beach and anchored for the night in the deep water of the cove. The following day she was loaded down with wood and fresh food and water, and the chief accepted Sam's gifts, given in thanks for his hospitality—tools, buckets, bolts of cloth and canvas and several pounds of tea, for which he had developed a special fondness.

After a night in which few people on the island—inhabitants or visitors—slept much, the *Meribah*'s men piled into their whaleboats and rowed out to the ship. They were accompanied by every man, woman and child who could wedge him or herself into a dugout canoe. During the short journey, the Kanalepeans, many wearing some trinket or small trophy given by a *Meribah* man, sang and played their shell horns. The water and the whaleboats were littered with flowers that the Kanalepeans had gathered and now tossed at their departing guests. The sailors sang back and shouted impassioned goodbyes to their favorite maidens, to the children to whom they had become instant, doting uncles, to the men who had worked side by side with them these past weeks.

Tears welled in Mercy's eyes as the island retreated, but she blinked them away, concentrating on fixing a final picture of Kanalepe in her mind. She understood all too well what she was leaving behind, leaving to face she knew not what. It was difficult to control her emotions, and she clutched the sarong, folded into a small, neat square, which her women friends had insisted she take with her. She might never wear it again, but it would serve to remind her of the island where she had, for a brief, lyrical time cast off the cares of her own civilization and luxuriated in the ample, comfortable bosom of a gentler, more forgiving place.

The islanders remained in their canoes while the *Meribah*'s crew hoisted the sails and prepared to weigh anchor. The singing and the shouted goodbyes continued as the work progressed. But once the wind billowed out the sails and the ship began to move, a sad quiet descended on the scene. Only the lapping of waves and the sniffling of a few youngsters could be heard. Mercy waved goodbye to the chief and the women she had bathed with every day for the past weeks, and finally the islanders, paddling their canoes slowly, turned back toward shore. The others on board continued to watch as the island retreated, but Mercy determinedly walked to the windward side of the ship and looked ahead, into the open sea.

Chapter Seventeen

For the next two weeks, the *Meribah* sailed due west, but the winds were sluggish and reluctant. Her progress was slow, and she sailed through only half as much sea as she might have with a favorable force behind her. With each passing day the winds diminished, the weather became oppressively hot and the men grew lethargic and irritable. At 180° latitude Captain Starbuck changed his course to south by southwest. A week of propitious winds would carry the *Meribah* to the vicinity of the Black Islands, where she would cruise, searching for information about Nathaniel Wright and the *Abishai*.

The winds, however, were not propitious. Occasional bursts of fair wind did interrupt the frequent periods of near calm, and the *Meribah* made some headway, but when they were one or two days' good sailing from the outermost islands in the Black chain, they hit a dead calm. There was not a breath of wind. The *Meribah* could do nothing but drift where the currents would take her and try to survive the vicious onslaught of the sun.

A calm could last twenty-four hours or twenty-four days, as Sam well knew. Sitting one out required patience and absolutely strict discipline. Every effort must be made to preserve strength and sanity. The captain gathered his officers and discussed his plans. The fresh food taken on at Kanalepe had already spoiled in the heat. The water stores were beginning to sour. Therefore, food and especially water were to be strictly rationed. Each man would be issued a half cup in the morning. The rest of the day's rations would be kept in a small water butt in the crow's nest. If any man was so thirsty he wanted more water he would have to climb to the top of the rigging to get it. Anyone climbing to the water butt would be watched by an officer to be sure he took no more than one ladleful. There was also to be a twenty-four hour watch placed on the water stores. Any man caught stealing water, either from the stores, another man or the butt aloft, would get twenty lashes, a certain death sentence in this heat.

Work details were to be scaled down to an absolute minimum. Makeshift canvas awnings were to be erected on deck to create additional shade. There was to be no talking unless it was essential to completing an ordered task. All tobacco would be confiscated. Men caught withholding tobacco or smoking earned themselves five strokes. It was five strokes as well for all caught fighting, no matter who provoked the confrontation.

For the first two or three days, the men took the restrictions in stride. The heat and short rations sapped them, and lying under the canvas awnings was all they had the will to do. But then boredom and frustration began to set in. The sun beat down relentlessly. There was no respite, day or night, from the dulling, draining heat. The ship stank of rotting food and melting pitch. The deck was covered with sticky, oozing tar and every object on deck burned when it was touched. The men's faces and hands were burned red by the sun; some bore painful blisters or sores from the punishing glare. They also suffered from dysentery and violent stomach cramps. Many could not keep down the food or the water. Mercy ministered to the sick, but she herself was unwell, constantly nauseous and unable to keep anything, even water, in her stomach. She tried to convince Sam to boil the water, but he would not chance lighting a fire in the heat. A single stray spark could turn the *Meribah* into a tinderbox.

After ten days of this torture, the *Meribah* crackled with barely suppressed rage. The inmates of the floating inferno hardly dared speak or even look at one another for fear of exploding. Even the most volatile of the sailors, Crebbs and Flubb and Hayward, kept themselves in check, knowing that five lashes, or even two, would buy them a watery grave. After the tenth day, however, the rage began to dissipate as men and officers alike sank deeper and deeper into despair. To a man—and a woman—all began to think that the end was near. They could not endure for much longer the parched throats, swollen tongues and churning bowels, the blistered skin and the blurred vision.

Then on the fourteenth day, when all had nearly given up hope, land was sighted. The captain stared at the dot on the horizon through his glass, then asked each officer in turn to do the same. One or two of them could be hallucinating, but not all of them. When the cry went up, the men clamored to starboard, to gaze at the horizon themselves, shielding their sun-blinded eyes with their hands. His mate in tow, Captain Starbuck descended to the officer's mess and spread his charts out on the table. As he had feared, the land mass just sighted was the island Joseph Coffin had warned him against. Unless the calm lifted, the currents would wash the *Meribah* up on the coral reef that surrounded the island, making her easy prey for marauders.

After a moment's thought, he instructed Val to put Mr. Jack in charge of the deck and to send the mates below. He was also to make sure Mrs. Wright was kept busy on deck for the time being. Although she had never complained, he could not help but notice how unwell she was. He did not want to alarm her any more than was necessary, he told Val.

When his officers had gathered, Sam repeated Captain Coffin's warning to them. "I'm sure some of you have heard rumors about who this renegade might be, but for obvious reasons I don't want to hear any talk of that on board this ship. You are to squelch any mention of such rumors immediately. You are also to prepare for an attack." Each man was assigned his duties and returned to the deck to carry them out.

As Harding was the best fisherman aboard, Val had been instructed to get him to catch a sunfish. He had avoided Harding assiduously since leaving Kanalepe, but now noticed how poorly the lad looked. His delicate skin was burned to a flaming red, his eyes were puffy and dull, he was even thinner than usual. But when Val asked how he was, Harding replied stoically, "As well as any of the others, sir."

"Well enough to catch a sunfish?"

"Sunfish, sir?" Jane could not imagine what use a sunfish could be to a becalmed ship. They were no good to eat. The only thing they were good for was to squeeze the oil out of the liver and sell it for tanning leather. But you had to let the liver rot first to get the oil out. It set up a horrific stench.

"That's right. Are you up to it?"

Jane shrugged. "I'll do my best, sir." At least it was something to do, something that might keep her mind off the pain in her face and the gnawing in her belly. She set off to get her line and some bait.

The others were set to work, too, gathering every sharp implement on board and taking turns running the whetstone. The ban on unnecessary talking had not been lifted. On the contrary, the officers had firmly reiterated it, adding further that all work was to be accomplished with a minimum of noise. Even though they could drift for a day or more before running aground, sound carried far in this kind of dead quiet.

By trying different baits—the ship did not lack for rotting, stinking morsels—Jane attracted and hooked a sunfish within two hours of getting her assignment. She was then ordered to remove the liver and set it on the hottest part of the deck. This distasteful task accomplished, she joined the sharpening brigade.

The burning sun worked quickly on the sunfish liver, and soon what little air there was on deck was unbreathable.

The men stopped breathing through their noses and took air in through their mouths as much as possible, but no one could keep that up for more than a few minutes at a time and the stink of the liver fairly singed the nostrils on every inhalation.

Once the liver had begun to rot, the captain personally ordered Mercy below. He told her to put the sick bay in order and then to go to her cabin and stay there. Under no circumstances was she to emerge unless she had his express permission to do so. Mercy was too tired and too ill either to chafe at these restraints or to find out exactly what Sam was planning. It was clear that he was preparing for some kind of attack, but why and against whom she had no idea. Her head was pounding too badly for her to think. Her stomach heaved, and she felt faint and weak. She quietly did as she was bid.

The captain stayed awake all night, perfecting his plans and listening for the telltale signs of the ship bottom scraping coral. At first light, he saw that it would be only a few hours before the *Meribah* ran aground. He summoned his officers and had them gather the men on deck.

"Unless the wind comes up swiftly it is almost certain we'll touch coral in the next few hours," he told the sailors. "We're likely to be attacked by hostile natives on this island, and the only element in our favor is surprise." He carefully laid out the details of his plan and then picked the stalwarts who would remain on deck with him—Mr. Hunter, Mr. Jack, Sweet and Owen Weeks. Under the command of Mr. Mayhew, the rest of the men were sent below, a group manning every hatch and companionway. The deck crew created a disorderly scene on the deck and hid the rotting liver under an overturned bucket to disguise the source of the stench.

Before he took his place on deck, Sam visited Mercy in her cabin. She looked even paler and more ill than she had the day before, but her looks were deceiving. She was feeling better than she had in weeks and protested vigorously when he informed her that she was to be locked in her cabin. "This is not Kanalepe," he warned her, removing the key from the inside of the cabin door.

"Then where is it?"

"The far reaches of the Black Islands, Mercy. Where you wanted to be. We are in grave danger, and I insist on protecting you, even if you are so foolhardy you do not wish it. I wish it, and today that is enough."

With that, he turned sharply and left her. He had no intention of losing Mercy to a savage's spear. If he was to lose her it would be to no one but Nathaniel Wright, if that blackguard still lived. Could he spare a man he'd have stationed a guard at her door, for he knew it was unlikely she would fold her hands and meekly accept her imprisonment. Still the lock was stout and would keep her occupied for some time, long enough, he hoped, for the *Meribah*'s men to prevail. Which they must, for he would not let himself consider Mercy's fate were he and the others to fail.

Mercy heard the bolt of the cabin door slide into place and stood staring angrily at the offending lock. After so long and arduous a journey, she was not about to be confined to her cabin when she had at long last arrived at her destination. She could understand Sam's concern for her safety. After all, she knew nothing about battles and fighting. But her medical skills, which he apparently had forgotten, were valuable. She could patch up the wounded and enable them to stay in the fight. By locking her in, he would deprive his men of an important weapon for the attack. From that perspective, her services were not only valuable, they were essential. Immediately she started to plan her escape.

Dismantling the lock on her cabin door provided Mercy with an absorbing occupation during the next long hours. The rest could do nothing but wait silently, without moving, doing nothing to reveal there was anything more than a rat or two alive aboard the *Meribah*. But finally, when their bodies and minds were nearly numb from the inactivity and tension, Starbuck and the others on the deck recognized the soft rhythmic splash of paddles in the water, barely audible over the ebb and flow of the sea itself.

The captain silently signaled his men, and they took their positions, facedown on the deck, nose to nose with the burning, oozing tar, the salt-stained wood, inhaling the foul odor of death. Feigned or not, it was an acrid, stomach-churning smell. Dozens of truncated breaths later, the subtle sound of the paddles receded, and then there was nothing but the creaking of timber, the slap of the tide, followed soon by the muffled thudding of bare feet against the side of the *Meribah*.

Sam waited, holding his breath in the eerie silence, until he felt the presence of the natives on the deck. Then he slammed his clenched fist into the wood. This single, sharp rap brought the crew swarming up onto the deck, brandishing their razor-sharp arms—knives, lances, harpoons, cutting spades, grappling hooks and hatchets. Every man had two weapons, one in each hand, and lost no time in using them on the startled natives.

It seemed for a moment that surprise would win the battle for the men of the *Meribah*, who succeeded in striking down many of the island warriors before they could ready their own weapons. But a fierce yell from one of their number brought two score more clambering over the bulwarks. The *Meribah*'s crew was now outnumbered more than two to one.

The natives were fearsomely outfitted—their faces and bodies smeared with stripes and whorls of garish-colored paints, their chests covered with ugly, forbidding amulets. They fought ferociously, hurling themselves into the fray with a chorus of bloodcurdling screams. The weapons they brandished had once been ordinary whaling tools, refashioned now into diabolical-looking instruments capable not only of wounding or killing a man, but also of doing it in the most painful and destructive way possible. To the men of the *Meribah*, unaccustomed to battle, it seemed they were fighting demons rather than men.

Sam found himself singled out by their leader, the most demonic of them all. The man honed in on him the way a bat attacks its prey in the dark—surely, swiftly, singularly, as if some special sense led him directly to the ship's captain. This devil was taller than most of his warriors, and thinner, but his muscles, though lacking in bulk, were as hard and unyielding as the iron in the weapon he waved. His skin, beneath the macabre patterns painted on it, was as dark as that of his fellows. But his features had none of their round fullness. He was hawk nosed and thin lipped. Most incongruous, however, were his brilliant blue eyes, shining wildly from inside the two large white circles painted around them. His hair further contributed to his fiendish appearance. It was stark white, the polar opposite of the rest of the barbarians.

Great God in heaven, Sam thought on seeing the savage stalk him. The rumors of the renegade were true. Unless he prepared himself quickly, though, he would be one more captain unable to substantiate them. He whipped out his knife from the waistband of his trousers and shouted to the nearest sailor for another weapon. Lance and knife in hand, he readied himself to meet his attacker.

At the other end of the *Meribah,* Jane Harding was battling a gigantic native as heavy and as solid as a block of stone. Believing she had a better chance of staying alive with long-handled weapons that might keep an attacker at bay, she had chosen a harpoon and a boating spade to carry into battle. When the huge savage first came at her, she tried to fend him off with a stab of her harpoon, but he reacted as if he had been stung by a fly. She fared better with the boating spade, drawing blood when she raked it across his middle, but she also raised the man's blazing fury. With two rapid-fire kicks, he knocked both weapons out of her hands.

Luckily for Jane, however, her attacker was about as nimble as the rock he resembled. By turning her size to her advantage and using her considerable agility, she was able to escape several blows of his nail-studded wooden club.

But sidestepping the sweeping swathe of the savage's weapon was not easy on boards slick with blood. She slipped several times and escaped having her head bashed in only by rolling over quickly in the slime. Still the sharp nails of the enormous club grazed her twice, gouging a trail of gashes first above her left eye and then down her right arm. Blood streamed into her eye, making it difficult for her to focus on her opponent, who continued to swipe at her wildly. She feinted and ducked and whirled, first one way, then the other, but with her dimmed sight, only fortune kept her out of the path of the lethal club.

Each time she escaped a blow she sought an opportunity to retrieve her weapons, but they were soon gone, picked up by one or another participant in the melee. No one dropped another conveniently in her path. The giant native grew more and more angry with Jane's every escape. He growled and gnarred and screamed and shouted, each blow fueled with growing hatred and frustration. With an ear-splitting yell, the loudest and angriest yet, he came at Jane again, this time not wildly but deliberately, and Jane found herself directly below his weapon, unable to move because other fighters had crowded her on three sides. To escape she would have to put herself in the middle of another battle.

In desperation, as the club began to fall, she ducked and dived between the native's parted legs. She heard the whizzing of his club as it descended and split the deck in exactly the spot where she had been standing only a second before. She pushed herself forward and leaped to her feet, looking desperately for a place to run. But there was none. The battle was raging, the deck packed with fighting men wedged together tighter than barrels in a full hold.

As Jane stood pondering her next move, her attacker turned and raised his club against her once more. Just as he was about to strike, she saw Crebbs charging through the crowd, harpoon ready to thrust, aiming straight for her attacker. She relaxed; Crebbs was coming to her rescue, in payment finally for saving his life in the Strait of Magellan. But suddenly her rescuer changed course. He was bearing down on her, not the native. For a moment she was stunned, but seeing him toss the harpoon galvanized her. She feinted and the weapon missed her chest, hitting her instead in the left shoulder.

A searing pain cut through her left arm, momentarily taking her breath away. Gasping for air, she shut her eyes against the pangs, but forced them open when she felt a pair of hands close around her throat. She was eyeball to eyeball with Crebbs, who was doing his best to choke the life out of her. She began to writhe and struggle against him, trying desperately to land her knee against the most sensitive portion of his anatomy. Finally she connected, garnering a loud, and, to her, highly gratifying, screech of pain.

She was losing blood fast and could feel the strength ebbing out of her, but if she was going to die today she was determined it would not be at the hands of a member of her own crew. Though the pain was excruciating, she yanked the harpoon out of her shoulder and turned it on the still-breathless Crebbs. Aiming for his thieving, miserable heart, she brought her weapon home. Her adversary crumpled to the deck.

Her head swimming, Jane fought to stay upright. All her senses were dimming—her vision was blurred and her ears felt as if they were stuffed with pieces of cloth. But she did hear a muffled savage yell. Looking up she saw not one but two rock-sized natives, wielding a pair of clubs at her. Then her vision cleared and she realized that she had only one attacker. How would she dodge him now? There was another garbled cry, but her adversary's mouth had not moved. She saw a black streak, then everything went blank. As if from a great distance she heard a series of thuds and thumps, and then she seemed to be floating down and down on a feather cushion.

Below, in her cabin, Mercy had put her hairpins to good use. After hours of painstakingly jiggling and fiddling, she had finally opened the lock to her door. From the sounds that had filtered down to her, she knew that there was a battle raging. The *Meribah*'s men must need medical attention. Despite Sam's desire to protect her, she could not sit by and let men die needlessly for want of treatment. The problem that remained, however, was how to get from her cabin to the sick bay where her supplies were stored. There was no direct access from the officers' quarters. She would have to go up the aft companionway, make her way through the fighting and then down the booby hatch to reach them. Dangerous it would be, but she had to try.

Cautiously she opened the door of her stateroom. The mess area was empty, eerily quiet in contrast to the terrifying clangs and bellows coming from above. She crept out, her heart pounding with fear, not so much for herself but for the carnage she might find on the deck. What if Sam or Val or any of the others she had come to care about had been badly hurt, or even killed? She steeled herself against such thoughts and proceeded up the companionway. She had just rounded the curve in the stairs and caught a glimpse of daylight at the top when the light was cut off by a bulky figure. The figure started down the stairs, and Mercy stopped her ascent, debating her course of action. Should she stand her ground or flee?

Then she recognized the figure. "Mr. Jack!" she exclaimed. He was carrying another man over his shoulder.

"Harding's hurt bad, ma'am. I figured you'd be down here and might help."

"We've got to get to the sick bay. All my supplies are there."

"I can get you there," Jack volunteered. "But I'd have to carry you the way I'm carrying Harding," he said uncertainly.

Mercy ran up the steps. "Whatever is necessary, Mr. Jack."

Within seconds she found herself being carried, like a sack of meal, through the horrifying battle. As Mr. Jack charged through the melee, she searched the chaotic scene for Sam and Val, but did not find them. Warning herself against jumping to conclusions and assuming the worst, she felt Jack begin to descend into the steerage.

Once on level ground again, Jack lowered Mercy to the ground and she unlocked the door of the sick bay. "Put Harding on the lower bunk, please, Mr. Jack," she instructed.

"Is my friend going to be all right?" he inquired, looking with worry at the inert form.

Mercy examined Harding quickly. "I'll do everything I can," she answered quietly.

"Thank you, ma'am," Jack replied.

"No, thank you, Mr. Jack."

Jack smiled wanly. "Guess I'd better be getting back. The fellows could probably use some help along about now." He left the sick bay and hurried back up through the booby hatch, muttering to himself. "No damned place for a female. No damned place at all."

Mercy's first concern was to stanch the flow of blood from Harding's left shoulder. Pulling a clean compress from a pile on the shelf, she began to rip open Harding's shirt. Suddenly Harding's eyes fluttered open. "You're in the sick bay," Mercy said gently. "I'm going to dress your wound." Then she tugged once more at Harding's shirt.

Harding's hand reached out shakily. "No," came the feeble murmur.

Mercy pushed the boy's hand away. "This is no time for modesty," she said firmly, but did not know if he'd heard her. After so much effort he had fainted again.

Mercy continued her task. The blood-soaked shirt tore easily, and she leaned over to inspect the wound. Because of the still-gushing blood she did not at first see the tight white band around Harding's chest, but once she had managed to stem the tide of blood, her attention was drawn to it. Even then, Mercy did not immediately grasp its significance. At first, she thought of it only in terms of her work. The blood-soaked band was hindering Harding's already laborious attempts at breathing. So she cut it away. And then she saw. John Harding was not a John at all, but a Mary or a Susan or an Ellen. Stunned, Mercy sank down onto the edge of the bunk.

In a moment, she regained her senses and began to chortle nervously. Her discovery explained so much—Harding's excessive modesty and gentle ways, and Mercy's tender feelings for this young person. Not hers alone, but Val's, as well. As Mercy went about her work of cleaning and dressing the young woman's wounds, she found herself laughing aloud. How odd to feel so lighthearted in the midst of a terrible battle, but Harding had fooled them all. Mercy could only admire her courage and her cleverness. She had to wonder, too, what had sent a young woman on such an adventure. But the answer to that most intriguing question would have to wait. Her patient, exhausted from her exertions, the loss of blood and the pain of her wounds, was sleeping deeply now, and it appeared quite likely that she would continue to do so for several hours.

If the scuffling and shouting going on above her head were any indication, the battle had reached a fever pitch. Some of the *Meribah*'s men must be wounded—they could not all have escaped injury. And she was the only person who could help. Sam would be livid to see her on deck, but she had a valuable service to offer the men who were fighting to save the *Meribah*. If she could patch up the wounded well enough for them to carry on, they all might survive this ordeal.

She checked her patient one last time, arranged the tatters of her shirt over her breasts and covered her with a sheet, tucking it securely around the straw-filled mattress. Then she prepared a small kit of compresses, bandages, water and whiskey and went up through the hatch.

As soon as her head cleared the top of the stairs, the stink of blood and gore immediately assailed her nostrils. The deck was covered with a slick red film and littered with bodies, some *Meribah* men, many more natives. But among those still fighting there seemed to be two islanders for every crew member. Mercy was gripped with sudden fear. Until this moment she had not seriously considered the possibility that the *Meribah* could be defeated, but now she saw clearly that the natives might prevail. They appeared well fed and well rested and were amply armed and skilled in making war. Even an untrained eye such as hers could see that. But she could also sense a determination in the men of the *Meribah* that the enemy warriors lacked. Though haggard, hungry, thirsty and wounded, they fought with an almost inhuman ferocity.

Mercy's entrance, on her hands and knees, into the chaotic scene went unmarked. She kept her head down, crawling as quickly and unobtrusively as she could among the downed men, determining which were breathing, which were not. The enemy wounded she passed by, although not without a pang of conscience. No human suffering should go unalleviated, but the survival of the *Meribah* might well hinge on the ability of a single wounded man to continue fighting.

The first *Meribah* man she came across was the Western Islander, Pedro, lying motionless on his stomach. Exerting all her strength, she turned him over, only to find a long ugly gash running from chest to abdomen. He was not breathing, and it was beyond her power to do any more than say a brief prayer over him. Grimly she moved on.

Owen Weeks she discovered trying desperately to raise himself up on a leg that was spurting blood from a wound on the inner thigh. The boy was so shocked from the rigors of battle that he seemed not at all surprised by her presence. Hastily she bound up his gash and lifted first the water then the whiskey bottle to his lips. "Drink, Owen," she ordered, holding his head as he downed the liquids. Grimacing against the pain and then burning sensation of the whiskey in his throat, he did as he was told. Then he took a deep breath, thanked her and charged into the fray again.

Mercy crawled on, moving toward the *Meribah*'s bow. Between the main hatch and the tryworks, she encountered a wounded man who did not take her presence so matter-of-factly. Val stared at her wide-eyed for a moment, then shook his head. "You're not imagining anything," Mercy told him tartly. Her eye fell on the deep gash in his arm. She uncorked the whiskey bottle and poured a liberal dollop over the wound. Val yelped in pain. "That will keep it from festering," she said as she wrapped and tied a clean bandage around the arm.

"A festering arm won't make much difference to a dead man," Val muttered. "We're doomed, Mercy."

Mercy raised the whiskey bottle to his lips. "There's courage in here, friend. Drink up. And in here." She gently touched his heart.

Val took a long draft and closed his eyes, his lips moving in silent prayer. "Be careful, Mercy. And don't let Sam see you. He'll kill you. If he's not too busy killing someone else," he added with a bleak smile.

Mercy crept on, moving around the starboard side of the tryworks. Glancing up, she saw the glint of a knife in the dazzling sun. She followed its trajectory, momentarily unable to see anything but the gleam of metal in the blinding light. But when her eyes adjusted, she saw that the knife was headed straight for Sam's throat. And that it was wielded by the most extraordinary-looking native, tall and slender with shoulder-length white-blond hair.

There was another blinding flash, this time of Sam's knife as he raised his arm to parry the native's thrust. The savage's reflexes were lightning fast, however, and he brought his knife down again. Sam jumped sideways to avoid the attack. His enemy countered the movement, and when the combatants squared off again, the native was facing Mercy.

The man's eyes were blue! A luminous blue that stood out against his sun-browned skin and sun-bleached hair. She could not stop staring, could not help thinking she had looked into those eyes before. But how...

"Nathaniel!" she cried, leaping to her feet and racing across the deck. "Nathaniel!"

Sam's brain could not work fast enough either to assimilate the sounds he was hearing or to determine their source.

He had been locked in battle with the chief since the fighting began, and he had expended nearly all his strength and resources on outsmarting his wily and seemingly indefatigable opponent. He did not understand why, but he did see that his attacker had been distracted. Taking advantage of the unexpected opportunity, he whipped his arm down and with a sharp upward motion plunged his knife into the chief's belly. The man's eyes widened in surprise, then he threw his arm back and made one final desperate attempt to kill his prey. But he moved as in slow motion, and Sam easily avoided the assault. With a gesture of supreme defiance the man pulled the knife from his belly and heaved it at Sam, again missing wide of his mark. Then he sank to the deck.

Mercy rushed to the chief, and Sam watched in astonishment as she cradled the dying man's head in her lap. And then his brain began to work. Disparate sights and sounds, pulled asunder in the heat of battle, finally converged and he realized whom he had slain. He was flooded with emotion, but exhaustion reigned over them all. He dropped to his knees opposite Mercy.

"Nathaniel, it's Mercy," she said softly to the fallen man.

The blond savage looked up at her. His eyes took on a cloudy, hooded look, and he closed them briefly. Then he answered with a wan, cruel smile. "I had hoped never to see you again."

Mercy set aside the pain of his words, set aside the task of reconciling this living, breathing Nathaniel Wright to the one who had lived in her heart. "But why?"

"Did you think I loved you?" he spat. "I loved your father's money, that's all. Continuing a life of genteel poverty with Aunt Mabel and Aunt Honoria was not what I—" He paused, as if searching for words. "My English has lapsed somewhat," he explained. "Ah, yes, aspired to. At least you were tolerable. The rest of the women I met were so silly and, er, vapid."

"Your command of words has not entirely left you, Nathaniel," Mercy commented dryly.

"But my senses have, you imply?"

"I imply nothing," she answered with dignity. "I only want to know what happened to you, why I lost you."

He smiled weakly. "And you came all this way to find out. I'm flattered. I underestimated you."

"And I you," she replied sadly.

"I haven't much time left, so I will tell you, Mercy, the sad and glorious tale of Nathaniel Wright of Boston." Grimacing against the pain, inhaling with an agonized rasp, he began. "Once we'd married I realized I'd exchanged one prison for another. Nantucket was small, provincial, and insular, and I craved adventure and freedom. So I convinced you and your father that I should sail on the *Abishai*. But I found myself in yet another prison, with the self-righteous, self-satisfied Captain Hussey as my jailer.

"So when the old buzzard succumbed to a fever, I took over the ship. I cast myself as the pirate captain. My men and I would live by raiding, not whaling, perhaps live out our days on a South Seas island. I had a few loyal men, but the rest of the scared sheep masquerading as sailors didn't have the gumption to join me." He laughed bitterly. "But they did have the spirit to try to mutiny. I knew I couldn't hold the ship forever unless I got rid of the ringleader—the ever-honest Second Mate Harris. So I anchored near the first island we happened on. This one.

"The natives—as you have seen—were somewhat indisposed to whaling ships. A man from a landing party had killed the chief's favorite daughter, you see. They came, in a most inhospitable manner, to see how much they could extract in exchange for our lives. But I befriended the chief and offered him something better—the ship's goods *and* the sailors, in exchange for my life and future services in capturing other whalers.

"Always having been a bit of a linguist, I picked up enough of the language to impress the chief with the sincerity of my intentions, and we struck a bargain. With my

help, the *Abishai*'s crew was captured. And put to good use
in the ceremonial dinner that followed,'' he added with a
wickedly contemptuous glance first at Mercy, then at Sam.

Mercy wished greatly to shudder in revulsion, but she
stemmed her response, determined to deny Nathaniel the
pleasure of seeing the effect his story and his manner was
having on her. He had betrayed her, duped her, made a fool
of her. She felt sick in her stomach, her eyes burned with
bitter tears, her throat was crowded with a lump of outrage. But she spoke coldly, betraying none of her churning
emotions. "Two men escaped. They were picked up by the
Mary Grant but died soon after. They thought everyone
from the *Abishai* had perished. The *Mary Grant*'s captain
brought the news. It killed my father, so you have another
death on your head, Nathaniel.''

To her surprise, Nathaniel did show a glimmer of remorse. "It must have been a great blow. I know how you
loved him.'' He closed his eyes for a moment, steeling
himself against the growing pain.

Mercy wiped his brow with a clean compress and wet his
lips with a few drops of water. Sam shot her a dark look.
Mercy stared him down. No matter what Nathaniel had
done, she could not withhold what little measure of physical comfort she could offer in his dying moments.

"Get on with your story, man,'' Sam growled. "Which
ships did you and your 'merry band' capture?"

"The *Star of Bethlehem* was the first. She sailed into the
cove and I lured a crew ashore. I still looked like a white
man then. They thought I was the survivor of a wreck and
sent a party to rescue me. By the time they realized their
mistake, it was too late to escape. That worked on the
Queequeg, too. But then the old chief died, and I became
the leader of the tribe. We captured the *Plymouth Maid* by
pretending to be friendly natives eager to trade. Your death
ship fooled me, though. We walked right into your trap,
Starbuck. You are the vaunted Starbuck, aren't you? How
sick I used to get of listening to Ben Randall talk about
you.''

"I am happy to know that I have caused you some distress in the past," Sam answered, "and a great deal more in the present."

Nathaniel moaned softly, and Mercy hastened to assess his condition. His pupils were dilated. Each breath was more shallow than the last, and she could barely feel his heart beating when she placed her fingertips on his chest. "I'm not sorry," the dying man whispered faintly. "I've been places and done things few white men have ever dreamed of. I found my freedom."

"But at such a cost," Mercy said faintly. "Was it worth it, Nathaniel?"

"To me it was," he answered, summoning his last scrap of breath. And then he died.

Mercy hung her head and wept.

Chapter Eighteen

When Mercy looked up again, the fighting had stopped. The natives, without their leader, had been subdued and corralled into the cramped space aft of the skylight. But for the moans of the wounded and a few speculative murmurs, the deck was silent.

Clumsily Mercy mopped away her tears with the back of her hand. "Is this what you've been hiding from me all this time? Is this—" she looked briefly at Nathaniel "—what really killed my father? How much did you know, Sam?"

"I knew that Wright had commandeered the *Abishai* after Captain Hussey died, and that Harris had tried to take it back. And that they had run into trouble with natives on one of the islands in this group. But I believed that Wright had perished with the rest of the *Abishai*'s crew. It wasn't until I began hearing the rumors of a renegade in this area that I entertained the possibility Wright could still be alive.

"The two who escaped assumed he was dead, too. When the islanders attacked they managed to save themselves by hiding under an overturned whaleboat. After the battle, when all was quiet, they found that the corpses of their fellows had been dragged away. Through the palm trees they saw the fires already burning, and soon they smelled the stench of burning flesh. They decided then to take their chances in the whaleboat. They managed to paddle themselves to a small atoll, but it was barren and had no source of fresh water. They grew weaker and weaker, and when the

Mary Grant finally picked them up, they were beyond hope. They lived only long enough to tell their story.

"Like your father, I believed Wright was dead. I was all for telling you the whole, unvarnished truth, but your father insisted on sparing you. He made me swear I would never tell you what had happened aboard the *Abishai*. I could not betray his trust, Mercy."

"But you could allow me to come halfway around the world to find out for myself?"

"If I had not, would you have had another truly peaceful day the rest of your life?" He reached across Wright's body and touched her hand. "You're free now, Mercy."

"We're free, Sam." She took a final look at her dead husband. "I can do nothing more for you, Nathaniel," she said quietly. "But I can help the living." She gathered her supplies, stood and walked away without a backward glance.

Before beginning her ministrations, however, she sought out Val. She found him among the men guarding the hostages. "Harding is in the sick bay," she told him.

"Badly hurt?" he asked with barely disguised alarm.

"A nasty gash in the shoulder. Perhaps you could look in while I tend to the rest up here," she suggested.

"It is bad then," Val concluded. "He's dying," he said miserably.

"Nothing of the sort," Mercy told him briskly. "I would simply appreciate it if you could look in on the sick bay."

Val eyed her suspiciously. "What the—"

"I don't have time to quibble, Val. Please, just humor me."

Bemused but intrigued, Val summoned Mr. Jack to take his place and went down through the booby hatch into the sick bay. There he found Harding fast asleep, looking pale, but to his relief alive and in no apparent danger. But there was something different about the young sailor, although he could not register immediately what it was. He stared at the sleeping form for several moments before it hit him. His chest. Beneath the sheet there seemed to be— No, it cannot be, he told himself. But how was he to find out if his eyes were playing tricks on him? He could not possibly draw the sheet down. If what he suspected were true, that would be a most ungentlemanly thing to do. In another moment it came to him that there are other senses than sight. An embrace would tell him if his wild hope was unfounded.

Slowly he approached the bunk, not wanting to startle or frighten Harding. He leaned over and carefully slipped his arms beneath the young sailor's shoulders. When his chest met that of the sleeping sailor he found the answer to what had puzzled him almost since the day the *Meribah* sailed. He had a woman in his arms. A beautiful, living, breathing woman. He let himself relax against her soft, curving body, laid his head over her heart and listened exultantly to its slow, steady beat. His beloved stirred, a small whimper escaping her lips. Gently Val disengaged himself and rose to a standing position. He would do nothing that even hinted he might be taking advantage of the situation in which he now found himself. Before leaving the sick bay he gazed down at her face, so serene in repose. What was her given name, he wondered? What would he be calling her as soon as she woke up? He left the room on tiptoe, barely breathing, taking the utmost care not to disturb his newfound love.

But once he reached the top of the booby hatch, a small, round chuckle escaped his lips, and grew and grew into a laugh that gained size and mass and speed, like a snow-covered rock hurtling down a mountainside. It was a wonderful toboggan of a laugh, as carefree and liberating as the rides he had taken as a child when visiting relations on the mainland. But now, like then, he reached the bottom of the hill.

"Have you gone daft?" Sam was yelling at him. "What were you doing down below? There's work enough for a dozen of you up here, man."

Val flashed a wide grin at his captain. "Yes, sir," he said crisply.

Sam had already sent men over the side to remove all the paddles from the natives' canoes. Now he directed Val to oversee the transfer of the survivors to the canoes, which were then to be towed out to sea behind the *Meribah*'s whaleboats and set adrift. Mr. Hunter was already directing a group of men in removing the fallen islanders from the deck. The *Meribah*'s own casualties—Crebbs; Pedro; the steward, Mr. Carmody; the second harpooner, Mr. Nicholson; and young Aaron Cole—were temporarily laid out in the blubber room. As the deck was cleared, the remaining men began slowly to clean the planks of the blood and gore of battle.

Making her rounds of the wounded, Mercy found only one seriously injured crewman. The others had cuts of one degree or another, and would bear large, ugly scars for the rest of their lives. But Doc, the cook, had lost two fingers to a native's knife. Mercy ordered a fire built and gathered the instruments necessary for cauterizing the stumps. Better to cause the man a few moments of excruciating pain now than to risk his losing his whole hand or even the arm later on. To prepare him for the operation, Mercy gave Doc a liberal dose of whiskey and a rag to bite on. Then Mr. Jack, Pete and the brawny harpooner, Mr. Morgan, held him down so that she could perform the necessary treatment. Like so many of the medical procedures she had done since boarding the *Meribah,* this was one she had never actually practiced. She prayed that she would complete the distressing job efficiently and without causing Doc any more pain than was necessary.

When the iron was a hot, glowing red, she grasped it firmly, took a deep breath and quickly applied the instrument to the man's bleeding stumps. He screamed and writhed, but her assistants held him still. Removing the iron, she examined the wound to see that it was thoroughly sealed. Satisfied she had done the job well, she knelt beside Doc, spoke to him soothingly and bathed his face with cool water. Then he dropped into a fitful, exhausted sleep. "We won't move him right now. There's already someone in the sick bay. I'll let you know when you can bring him down."

Thoroughly drained, Mercy retreated to the sick bay, where she was greeted with a shy, "Hello, ma'am," from the patient there, who then asked anxiously, "Is the fighting over?"

"Yes," Mercy replied wearily. "We've lost five men, but the natives are defeated?"

"Who were the five?" Jane inquired, her face pale with worry. One name was no surprise to her, but she was saddened by the loss of the others, especially her fellow green hand, Aaron Cole. "And Mr. Jack and Mr. Mayhew? What about them?"

"Both are fine, Miss Harding," Mercy answered.

Jane lowered her eyes. "Are you the only one who knows?" she asked uncertainly.

"I sent Mr. Mayhew down to check on you while I was tending to the others. I suspect he may have made the same discovery as I."

"What?" Jane said with some alarm. Val might know, possibly did know? Clutching the sheet to her, she tried to sit up. But a sharp surge of pain sent her sinking back onto the berth. "What am I do to, Mrs. Wright?"

Seeing her patient in distress, Mercy went to her and lifted the dressing to check the wound. "That is up to you," she said, then paused, finding the name John on the top of her tongue. "What is your given name?" When it was supplied, Mercy repeated, "That is up to you, Jane." Satisfied the shoulder needed no further attention, she replaced the bandage.

Having gritted her teeth against the discomfort of the examination, Jane exhaled loudly. "If I were to ask you, would you continue to keep my secret?"

"I would," Mercy replied without hesitation. "But I'm not certain I could extract a similar promise from Mr. Mayhew."

Jane considered her dilemma, but no obvious solution presented itself. Perhaps a talk with Mrs. Wright would help her determine a course of action. "You see," she began. "I have six brothers, all at sea. I'm the youngest, the only girl. The boys always did things I was told I couldn't or shouldn't do. It made life so dreary that I became determined to find out what life was really like."

"And what did you learn, living as a man?"

"That life *is* freer and more exciting if you don't have a flock of petticoats flapping at your ankles. But it's raw and coarse and dangerous, too. Not that I long for the tedium of washing and ironing fine linens—that is what my mother and I did—but I'm tired of pretending to be something I'm not. Especially now, when I've discovered I do have womanly feelings.

"You know," she added thoughtfully, "I always scoffed at other girls, mooning about and giggling over boys. But love does exist. And it doesn't have to be silly or sentimental, not unless you choose to make it that. But I'm in rather a fix now, aren't I? I want to stop this charade, but how can I go back to being a woman, now that I've lived as a man?"

This being a question never before put to her, Mercy took a moment to ponder before answering. Living as a man had never held an appeal for her, but she recalled a remark her friend Maria Mitchell had made on more than one occasion. Were I my brother, Maria had said, no one would pay the least attention to me. And yet Maria, despite being patronized, even ridiculed, continued to do the work to which she had been called. "As a woman, Jane," she began, still thinking but aloud now, "if you thirst for knowledge or adventure, or desire to take even some small part in the world beyond the confines of hearth and home, you must make your own way." She spoke about Maria and then, without having planned to, herself. "I have never thought of myself as a rebel, but I suppose in my way I have forged my own path. I have studied medicine, largely educating myself. My uncle has been glad of my help in his dispensary, and has taught me—informally and by example—and my knowledge and skill has been of some use on this vessel. But I never aspired to practice medicine. I never thought to defy convention in that way. But what if I had?'' she mused. "I'm not certain I would have had the courage. You, on the other hand, Jane, had both the desire and the bravery. You have proved your pluck and ingenuity many times over, and you will make your way again,'' she finished with a smile.

Jane thanked her for her confidence and kind assurances. "But I cannot allow you to question your bravery. Throughout this voyage I have watched you carefully, admired you for your ability to be forceful and strong and to command respect without having to pretend to be man.''

"Then you have seen more in me than I have in myself.'' Mercy bowed her head modestly, then raised it and continued in a brisk tone. "Enlightening as our conversation has been, dear Jane, I fear it must end, for the moment. Doc has lost two fingers and I need to install him here in the sick bay. You may either share my cabin or return to the fo'c'sle. As you desire, but you must decide.''

Jane raised herself up, wincing but not defeated by the pain this time. She had made her choice. "The only thing that bothers me,'' she said hotly, "is that the men will think of me differently now. They'll dismiss what I've done, call it a stroke of luck—climbing to the crow's nest without losing my breakfast that first day, unleashing the sails during that squall, hanging on and riding the back of that one-hundred barreler. Now that they know I'm a woman, they'll forget what I've done.''

"No, Jane, they won't forget. Some will admire you all the more, others will resent you mightily. But no one will forget you. Of that I am certain.''

Taking some measure of comfort in Mrs. Wright's words, Jane prepared to leave the sick bay, and the life she had known for more than a year. Moving cautiously, she swung her legs over the side of the bunk and put her feet on the floor. "I guess it will be your cabin, then,'' she said with more brightness than she felt. Saying goodbye to her friend

John Harding was not going to be easy. "And I'll need something to wear," she added with reluctance.

Mercy gave Jane an encouraging pat on her unharmed shoulder. "You may have a skirt and blouse of mine. They'll need some alterations, but I'll leave that to you. You will want an opportunity to collect yourself."

"Yes," she agreed. "Thank you." She began to rise, but Mercy restrained her.

"Stay here a moment while I go above and inform the captain that you must continue to rest in my cabin. If I don't, he'll put you on a work detail."

"I don't suppose I'll be allowed to work now."

"We're five men short, Jane. Perhaps I can persuade the captain to see reason."

Jane grinned. "If anyone can persuade the captain of anything, it's you."

Mercy returned the grin.

On deck, she found Sam was too busy to question her request closely. The exchange of patients was executed, and Mercy turned her attention to Doc. She stayed with him in the sick bay, watching him carefully. He was feverish and sleeping fitfully. There was little she could do except try to keep him cool, although this was difficult with only the tiny bit of fresh water she had at her disposal. Still she could comfort him in his waking periods and seek solace for her own loss during those stretches when her patient did not require her.

Sitting on a small stool in the corner of the sick bay, she allowed herself to take in the full significance of the day's events, and to begin to mourn the demise not only of her husband and her marriage, but also of the innocence and trust that had led her to fall in love with Nathaniel and to marry him. She had been betrayed, been made a fool of, and she fought hard against the bitterness that assailed her. Nathaniel had taken advantage of her, of her father, of Aunt Elizabeth, but she could not deny her own part in the debacle. She had seen in Nathaniel what she had wanted to see. She had wanted to marry someone who knew a different world than whaling, whaling, always whaling. She had longed for someone who esteemed knowledge and discourse for their own sakes, who knew the world of the mind. Nathaniel had answered these needs, or he had seemed to. Wanting these intangibles so badly, she had looked no further than his surface. She had not seen the destructive power simmering beneath his placid facade. The signs had been there, but she had not seen them.

And now there was Sam. A whaling man through and through. With him she would live the life her mother had—of long separations unless she sailed with him, of hardship and confinement if she did. But she was certain at least that he harbored no deep, festering secrets. He could still surprise her, but only in the way a cache of ambergris in a hundred-barrel whale surprises: good fortune made better.

Her thoughts were interrupted by her patient, who began to thrash and moan loudly. She stood up quickly to go to him, but was overcome by a wave of nausea. Clutching her stomach, she waited for it to pass. The heat, the hunger, the thirst, the stench, the hard work and emotional blows, all were conspiring against her. But the sick feeling subsided and she was able to go to her patient.

On deck, the weary, wounded men were finishing the last of the captain's tasks. The enemy warriors were gone, the *Meribah*'s dead patiently awaited their last rites, the deck had been cleaned and the ship readied for sailing. But there was no wind. The same deadly calm prevailed, leaving the *Meribah* high and dry on the coral reef.

With his mate, Sam debated the wisdom of sending a landing party for fresh water and food. The island might be safe now, with Wright dead and the warriors adrift. Or there might be an attacking party on shore, lying in wait. Even if no warriors were left on the island, surely there were women, children and elderly people there. Were they as fierce as their men? There was no way of knowing. Still, without fresh water, the *Meribah* might as well have lost its battle with the natives. In fact, it might have been preferable. Falling in battle was quicker and less painful than a slow, wracking death without water.

The captain was on the verge of chancing to send a landing party when he thought he felt the hint of a breeze on his cheek. At first he attributed the sensation to his imagination, but then he looked up at Val, whose alert, watchful visage mirrored his own nascent hopes. They spoke with a silent glance. Then another draft of air brushed past Sam, this time less elusively, less uncertainly. He and Val stood absolutely still, holding their breaths, every sense concentrated on the breeze. Was it siren or savior, he wondered.

Then suddenly the air began to move discernibly, as if a great hole had formed in the atmosphere, and the hot, stagnant haze was sucked away. Sam and Val waited several breathless seconds before breaking out in grins of glee. The wind was up *and* the tide was rising! The *Meribah* was saved!

By now the glimmers of a breeze had turned into gusts of wind. To a man, the crew stopped whatever they were doing and put their faces into the current. A cry and huzzah went up, and the captain ordered the men to set the sails. Their luck was running now. With this wind and the swiftly rising tide, the *Meribah* would be knocked off the reef without damage to her hull. She and her men had been tested sorely, but they had prevailed.

Down below, both Mercy and Jane heard the hubbub. Charging up through the booby hatch, Mercy was the first to reach the deck and feel the fresh drafts brush her face. She let out a whoop of joy, which was echoed by the men. Then Jane, unmindful of her much-altered appearance, concerned only to learn the source of the hue and cry on deck, appeared at the top of the aft companionway, and she too shouted with glee. Her cries, however, were greeted with dead silence. The men stopped their work in midmotion and stared at John Harding—who was wearing a skirt!

For a long time no one moved, no one spoke, no one breathed. Then a low bass rumble of laughter started up. It came deep from Mr. Jack's chest, more like distant thunder than anything else. As if moving closer, it gathered speed and volume, finally exploding in a startling clap of merriment. After this, the laughter poured down like a cloudburst after a long drought. All the men threw back their heads, roaring and cackling and cawing and hooting until their stomachs hurt and they were gasping for breath.

Jane's face grew redder than the sun had turned her when she'd first come to sea. She flushed hot with embarrassment but also with anger and wounded pride. But then she looked at Mr. Jack's benevolent face and saw just how funny the scene was. She began to laugh, too, then raced to the center of the deck, near the main hatch. "Ha!" she cried. "Fooled you, didn't I?" This declaration occasioned a second cloudburst of laughter, to which Jane herself contributed a hail of droplets.

Sam stalked over to Mercy. "How long have you known about this?" he hissed.

"Only a few hours," she hissed back. "Should I have interrupted you in the middle of the battle to tell you?"

Mercy's retort called for a hasty retreat, so Sam edged away from her while the rest of the drama unfolded. Jane had approached Mr. Jack. While waiting in Mrs. Wright's cabin, the details of her clash with the rock-shaped native and then Crebbs had come back to her. How had she gotten to the sick bay? she had wondered. Someone must have carried her. But who? Then she remembered the looming black figure that had crossed her path just before she'd lost consciousness. Mr. Jack must have carried her out of harm's way. But why only her? He had not done the same for any of the other wounded sailors. There was only one explanation she could think of.

"Thank you, Mr. Jack, for saving my life," she said. "I will always be grateful, but I must chide you, too, sir. You've known about me all along, haven't you?"

Jack rocked back on his heels, a twinkle in his eye. "Not the whole time. But I had some powerful suspicions from the time we were in the Western Islands."

At this point Val rushed in. "Then why didn't you tell someone?" he demanded.

"I thought it might be more fun to see what happened. Turned out I was right."

Val drew in a sharp breath and began to sputter. But then he stopped short and broke into a sheepish grin. "Oh, what the devil!" He rushed to Jane, took her into his arms and kissed her soundly, to her delight and that of the onlookers. A chorus of whistles and cheers rose into the brisk, steady wind.

"Belay, there!" the captain shouted. "We've a ship to sail!" His orders brought the newly united lovers out of their embrace and returned the men to their tasks. "Although how I am to sail this ship with six fewer men—"

"Five," Mercy interrupted quietly.

"Five dead, and one—" he hesitated "—unmasked."

"In the space of a few hours, Miss Harding is not likely to have forgotten how to climb the rigging or set a sail."

"But she's a woman!"

"As she was yesterday and last week and last month," Mercy persisted.

"I would like to see her climb the rigging in those petticoats. She'd break her fool head."

"Of course she would. She will have to change into her old outfit."

"But she's a woman!!" Sam cried vehemently.

"Valentine's behavior makes that most apparent." Mercy cast a glance at Jane and Val. He was holding her hand in his, gazing at her, speaking volumes with his eyes. Sam's stance softened. It was a preposterous situation all around, and until it was worked out, the *Meribah* would not be a normal ship. Why should he try, against all odds, to make her one? "Harding!" he shouted.

"Sir!" She broke away from Val and presented herself briskly to the captain.

"You are paid to be a foremast hand on this vessel. I expect you to continue to earn your keep."

"Yes, sir!" Jane replied eagerly.

"But, Captain," Val protested.

"My orders are not a matter for discussion, Mr. May-hew."

Val tried another tack. "But, er, Harding, er, dear," he began. "I don't even know your name!" he declared in frustration.

"It's Jane," his beloved informed him, then returned briskly to the problem at hand. "The ship must be sailed," she said, addressing not only Val but the Captain and all the crew. "Why should my skills be thrown away simply be-cause you *know* I'm a woman? You were all quite happy for me to work and fight until a few hours ago. I have not changed since then. I am still the sailor I was."

Val racked his brain for several moments but could dis-cover no argument to stand against Jane's. So he faced her and said in his most commanding tone. "Ready yourself for work, Harding. Then report back to the deck."

"Yes, sir!" Jane cried happily, and scampered off to obey her officers' orders.

By the time the sun set, the *Meribah* was well under way and stayed under sail throughout the night. Mercy re-mained on deck, breathing the cool, fresh air deep into her aching body. After a time she began to feel cleansed. The terrible heaviness, which she had carried for so long that it had come to seem a natural part of her, began to lift. She felt light and free.

In a quiet moment Sam came to her. "I realize you are only a few hours a widow, Mercy, and that we have much to discuss. But I wish to lose no time in declaring my inten-tions. I want you for my wife, Mercy. Will you do me that honor?"

"Yes, Sam, I will. In time."

He slipped an arm around her waist and held her close. "A short time, I hope."

"In good time," she promised. "But with all my heart when the time comes."

Epilogue

And so the *Meribah*, dear reader, sailed into the balmy darkness that night, its two pairs of lovers joyfully united. Mercy's mission was complete, but her new life was just beginning. It has turned out for her and Sam—as for Jane and Valentine—to be a full and happy one.

As Valentine remarked on that fateful day, certain adjustments were necessary for love, and so Mercy took Jane into her cabin. Jane worked on deck during her assigned watches, but retired to the women's stateroom during her off hours. It was a highly unusual and unconventional arrangement, but convention, I believe, is an excuse for timid people to live timid lives. And if I have shown you anything in these pages, it is, I hope, that Mercy and Jane and the men they loved were anything but timid.

Soon after the battle, Mercy realized that her physical complaints were not due solely to the deprivations of surviving a calm in the South Seas. She was expecting Sam's child. And so they made for Honolulu, where both couples were wed. The *Meribah* was turned over to the capable captainship of Valentine Mayhew, with the new Mrs. Mayhew sailing as first mate. Captain Starbuck and his bride returned to Nantucket on the first available packet, where they were united with their family and friends and awaited the birth of Miss Samantha Randall Starbuck.

In the years since, I have often plagued my friends for the details of their journey, which they have amply supplied, sometimes with relish, and sometimes merely to humor me. But I have recounted them faithfully here and produced, I hope, a testament to the bravery and perseverance of women with a mission.

"Dorcas"

* * * * *

Everyone loves a spring wedding, and this April, Harlequin cordially invites you to read the most romantic wedding book of the year.

With This Ring

ONE WEDDING—FOUR LOVE STORIES FROM OUR MOST DISTINGUISHED HARLEQUIN AUTHORS:

BETHANY CAMPBELL
BARBARA DELINSKY
BOBBY HUTCHINSON
ANN McALLISTER

The church is booked, the reception arranged and the invitations mailed. All Diane Bauer and Nick Granatelli have to do is walk down the aisle. Little do they realize that the most cherished day of their lives will spark so many romantic notions. . . .

HWED-1AR

HARLEQUIN'S WISHBOOK
SWEEPSTAKES RULES & REGULATIONS
NO PURCHASE NECESSARY TO ENTER OR RECEIVE A PRIZE

Back by Popular Demand

Janet Dailey
Americana

A romantic tour of America through fifty favorite
Harlequin Presents®, each set in a different state
researched by Janet and her husband, Bill. A journey
of a lifetime in one cherished collection.

In April, don't miss the first six states followed by two
new states each month!